# STEELED FOR MURDER

# THE JESSE DAMON SERIES

# STEELED FOR MURDER

## KM ROCKWOOD

*A Jesse Damon Crime Novel*

**WILDSIDE PRESS**

*For Bracey, Charles, Darrell, Derrik, Fred, Hosea, Ralph, Reggie, Scooter, Spig, Steve, Tom, Willie & everyone else, locked up or back on the street, who got caught up in the system.*

Published by Wildside Press LLC
www.wildsidepress.com

# CHAPTER 1

"Hey, buddy. New guy. I'm talking to you."

Pretending not to hear over the din of the plant floor, I put my lunchbox on the crude lunch table by the vending machines and hung my jacket on a hook on the wall. I walked over to the time clock and punched my timecard. My shift, midnight to eight, would start in a few minutes. The other workers on the same shift milled around, waiting for their assignments.

Keeping my back against the wall, I leaned into a corner next to the time clock, my hardhat tilted away from my face. Closing my eyes went against every instinct I had, but I willed myself to do it. I'd take any chance to avoid a confrontation that might jeopardize this job. Getting hired as a machine operator at Quality Steel Fabrications was a big break for me.

"You. Hear me?" Someone poked my shoulder. Hard.

I opened my eyes. Mitch, the forklift driver. Not the most rational of people. "I'm listening," I said.

"I asked you why you been staring at my wife." Mitch scratched a scab on the scrawny elbow beneath the rolled-up sleeve of his flannel shirt. A drop of blood trickled down his arm. He didn't seem to notice.

No idea what he was talking about. "Your wife? When?"

"Just now."

I glanced around. The factory floor vibrated with the pulse of dozens of machines. The air smelled of oil and hot steel. Sparks flew. "Your wife's here?"

"No, jerk. When she dropped me off."

I shook my head. "Didn't notice."

"Hell you didn't. You was staring when she kissed me goodbye." Mitch shifted his weight restlessly from one foot to the other.

"Woman in a nightgown kissing somebody when the gates opened? Hard to miss. Didn't know it was you. Or your wife."

"You think she's good looking?"

I shrugged. This could lead to nothing good. "I guess."

"You just keep your eyes to yourself, buddy."

"Will do."

"Or I'll make sure you're sorry." Mitch reached over and grabbed the leg of my blue jeans. He jerked it up a few inches.

I tensed, but I didn't move.

"Thought so," he said, grim satisfaction on his gaunt face as he stared at the black plastic box strapped on my ankle above the short work boot. "What are you? Some kind of sex offender?"

I hadn't spent more than half my life in prison without learning that when a bully persists in picking on someone, he can't be ignored. He wasn't going to just go away, no matter how much I wanted him to.

I narrowed my eyes and stared straight into his. They were bloodshot and bleary. "What's it to you?" I demanded.

He dropped my jeans leg like it burned his hand. He backed up a few steps, scratching his neck.

"I'll call the parole office and tell them you're stalking my wife," he said.

I felt the eyes of the other workers on us. "Be hard for me to do much stalking." I looked away and lowered my voice, trying to minimize the spectacle we were creating. If Mitch would leave me alone, I would have accomplished what I wanted. "Unless your wife's been over my place. Home detention. They can pull the records and see I been home or at work pretty much all the time."

John, our shift foreman, approached, battered clipboard clutched in his gnarled hand. He scowled at us, his bushy white eyebrows meeting over his nose.

Mitch grabbed his timecard from the rack and shoved it in the clock.

"What's the problem here?" John demanded.

"Nothing." Mitch put his timecard back into its slot.

I shrugged.

"Mitch, you go see if the lift battery needs to be changed."

With an ugly glance in my direction, Mitch moved off.

"You're pretty new here," John said, drawing himself up to his full height of well over six feet and staring down at me.

"Yeah." I didn't meet his eyes.

"You want to keep this job?"

"Sure do. Need it for parole." Not to mention the money.

"Mitch can be trouble. Stay out of his way."

"Do the best I can."

John nodded. "You've been working out well so far. But Mitch's been here for a long time."

"I know. I don't want no trouble." That was the truth.

"If he pushes too hard, talk to Victor, the union steward."

"No point. Better than seven weeks to go before I'm through the probationary period," I said. "Can't join the union till then."

"That's right. I forgot." John stroked his short gray beard. "You work the plating room tonight. Plater number two." He put a check mark on the clipboard. "Always people around in the plating room."

"Okay." A change from the wire tree baskets I'd been welding, over in a quiet corner of the shop.

"Plater operators don't have to talk to the lift driver," John said. "You just operate the plater. If anybody needs to talk to Mitch, it'll be the group leader, Hank."

"Thanks." I pulled my hardhat down over my forehead and looked toward the plating room. Steam and chemical odors seeped out into the passageway.

"Mitch gets like this sometimes. He'll get over it," John said.

"Thanks."

"And take your lunch. Ask Hank to put it in the office. Wouldn't want anything to happen to it."

I grabbed my battered lunchbox—two dollars and fifty cents at Goodwill, including thermos—and went to report to Hank.

Hank wrote my name and employee number on his clipboard. He handed me a pair of gloves. Then he took the lunchbox and tucked it under his beefy tattooed arm. "Office?" he shouted over the noise of the machinery.

I nodded and then turned to watch the operators on the shift that was about to end.

The four electro-platers, huge squat behemoths with their double lines of deep tanks full of chemicals and plating solutions, clanked and groaned as their overhead conveyors lurched in a circuit above them. Ladders led up to steel catwalks that surrounded the tanks. A control panel for each plater took up a good part of the front. Next to the control panel was a big red emergency stop button.

As the overhead conveyor approached from one side, operators standing on wooden platforms in front removed the bright, nickel-plated pieces with their shiny finish from the sets of hooks and replaced them with dull, greasy, unfinished ones. The conveyor continued on, raising them toward the first tank. Raise, lurch forward, dip, raise, lurch. Unendingly.

Down the passageway, I could hear the beep of the lift as Mitch swung it around and headed this way. With an effort, I didn't look toward it.

Plater number two was running hollow cabinets, about thirty inches square. Probably control boxes of some sort. Looked heavy. The other three platers were running light wire shelving. Figured. Of course the new guy got the worst assignment.

I put on my gloves and watched carefully as the operator heaved a finished cabinet off the plater hooks. He nestled it on a pallet among others and then leaned down and grabbed an unfinished one from another pallet. He lifted that onto the moving hooks. The overhead conveyor jerked it up and away toward the first chemical bath. Another set of hooks, with another finished piece, immediately took its place.

This guy had a practiced swing that I would have to master in mere seconds.

The whistle blew, signaling shift change. I stepped into position.

The guy who was leaving stepped back. "Make sure you get them snugged down good," he hollered over the noise of the machinery. "They like to fall off."

I nodded and reached for the piece arriving on the hooks. Even heavier than I'd expected.

I managed to get it off and onto the pallet of finished cabinets, but before I could grab a piece to put in its place, the next finished piece had arrived. Frantically, I snatched that one before it could be carried around to be plated again.

Hank was instantly by my side. He grabbed the next finished piece. "Just do the best you can for now," he shouted. "Get into the rhythm."

I struggled to attach the unfinished cabinet while Hank removed the next finished one. I finally got it on. I was reaching for another piece when I heard a screeching sound that ended in a crash.

Hank reached over and hit the emergency stop button. "Fell off," he said.

The piece had not only fallen off the hooks, it had become wedged at the top of the first tank. As we watched, it teetered on the edge and tumbled in.

"Gotta climb up and fish it out," Hank told me, reaching for a six-foot-long steel rod with a hook on the end that was leaning against the control panel and handing it to me.

I took it and scrambled up the ladder to the catwalk that surrounded the line of tanks. Steam rose from them. Caustic chemical fumes tickled my nose. I sneezed.

"Don't get that rod caught in the works overhead," Hank hollered up the ladder at me. "We don't have anybody on this shift who can fix it."

Great. I'd not only messed up badly in the first few minutes on this job, I had the potential to mess up a whole lot more. No wonder there was the three-month probationary period before anyone was made a permanent employee. Gingerly, I slid the rod into the tank and moved it around on the narrow bottom. I felt it hook onto something. I pulled it up, keeping an eye on the top end of the rod as it rose into the dimness of gears and chains above.

I could see the cabinet rising toward the surface. What was in this tank? I knew some of them contained corrosive acids that could eat right through a work glove. Every few yards, a big red sign designated an emergency station with a pull chain that activated a shower head. Not exactly comforting.

As I tried to raise the cabinet above the surface of the tank's contents, it slipped.

I grabbed for it. This job was my best hope for supporting myself and staying out of prison. If I got a chemical burn, I'd just have to deal with it.

The warm contents of the tank spilled over the top of my glove. The scar on the palm of my right hand itched.

I yanked the cabinet, and it tumbled onto the catwalk next to me. I carefully extracted the rod from the machinery above. Hank stepped up to the ladder and held out his hand. I passed the rod to him and then scurried down, lugging the cabinet behind me.

The glove didn't seem to be deteriorating noticeably. My hand tingled, but I couldn't tell whether it was my imagination or if the skin was dissolving.

I waited for Hank to tell me to go find the foreman and get him to assign someone else to this job. Would John put me on another job or just tell me to punch out and go home?

Hank put the rod back next to the control panel. He examined the cabinet. "No damage." He hung it on the plater hooks. It was a lot easier when the plater was stopped.

"Look," he said, picking up another unfinished piece. "You got to get the hang of this." He secured that piece on the next set of hooks. "Try it."

He was giving me another chance. Relieved, I took a deep breath and focused on the task. Other people managed to do this job. Had to be a way I could, too.

Hank started the plater moving again as I grabbed another cabinet. I swung it up and tried to place it in the same position he had.

"Good." He nodded. "Now give it a sharp tug to make sure it's seated right."

I yanked down on it and felt it settle into position.

He stopped the plater again and reached into his back pocket. "Dry glove," he said. "Gimme the wet one. You'll get blisters if you work in wet gloves. We always got a supply in the office."

I stripped off the wet glove. I couldn't help staring at my reddened hand. "What was in that tank?"

"Warm water," Hank said, taking the wet glove and tossing it off to the side. "Next one's detergent. Then rinse water. Some of the others are kind of nasty. They got a red label with a skull on them. Be careful if you have to go fishing in any of them."

I slipped my hand into the glove. No more tingling.

He started the plater again. "I'm gonna stay here and pull enough of these to let you get started," he said. "Just aim at hanging one on every other set of hooks; it'll be a little over an hour before they come around again, and I'm gonna have to go give breaks and do some other stuff. You'll get better at it."

Hank continued to remove all the finished pieces while I figured out how to settle the unfinished ones in place. Then he started letting every other finished one through so I could get into the rhythm. Lift, remove, swing onto the pallet, grab a new one, lift onto the hooks, tug down, repeat. By the end of an hour, my shoulder muscles were screaming, but I was able to keep up with the half load.

"I got to go start breaks." He stepped down off the platform. "Do the best you can. Try to speed up. Get everything off. If you have to, let a section go by without putting anything on it."

I didn't know how to tell him how grateful I was that he was giving me this second chance. "Thanks," I mouthed at him.

Hank shrugged. "Ain't nobody born knowing how to do this. You're doing fine. Just keep at it." He went down to plater one to relieve the operator.

I settled into the work. This job was more demanding than the ones I had started out with when I began working here a few weeks ago. First, they'd put me on a forming press, and then they'd moved me to the large root baskets, which were used by plant nurseries to move good-sized trees. The plater job was more specialized and more difficult. Might pay a little better if I ever got off the probationary period and into the union. I tried to pay attention to what I was doing. Thinking too much wouldn't help. Never had.

The job might be tedious. I might go home with sore muscles and a headache from the fumes. But this was a good job, with decent wages. Benefits after I reached the three-month point. Paroled convicts don't get many opportunities like this.

I heard the forklift rumble by once in a while, but I was too busy to pay it much mind. When the pallets at my work station needed to be moved, Hank made it his business to be standing there while Mitch moved them. I kept working, not glancing in his direction. I didn't need any trouble. Besides, I couldn't keep up with the plater if I so much as glanced away.

Hank was looking out for me. He and John were actually trying to help me succeed. A new experience for me.

Hank relieved me for my first break. My sore muscles begged me not to take them back to the plater. I ignored them.

After my four fifteen a.m. lunch, the muscles were so tired, they didn't care anymore.

One more break and then the last two-hour sprint to quitting time. I would make it.

Several people hurried through the plating room. I risked a glance. John, the foreman. Hank, the plating group leader. Victor, the union steward.

In the brief moment I looked away, the cabinet I'd just hung started to slip. I hit the emergency stop button so I could straighten it out before it fell in again.

With no noise from the plater right in my ear, I thought I heard a siren. I listened carefully. Definitely a siren. Growing louder as it approached. Seemed to pull right into the truck yard by the shipping bays beyond the plating room. What was going on? I glanced at the other plater operators. They heard it, too. They looked around but kept working.

My stomach in a knot, I started the plater up again.

The pallet where I was putting my finished pieces was piled high, yet no forklift arrived to remove it. I put the next piece on the edge of the platform where I stood. I glanced down the line. The operator next to me was out of unfinished wire shelves. He shut down his plater long enough to step into the passageway and shout for Hank. He returned to his plater, starting it up again. He removed the finished shelves and let the conveyor run empty.

Hank appeared. He looked at the pallets in front of us and then hurried up the steps to the offices perched above the production floor.

A few minutes later, a forklift rumbled up. A bigger lift than the usual one, and a woman, not Mitch, was driving it. She deposited a new load for the plater next to me and then pulled out my overloaded pallet. Putting that aside, she swung the lift around, picked up an empty pallet, and maneuvered it into place. Then she dismounted and picked up the cabinets I'd put on the edge of the platform. They were heavy, but she handled them effortlessly. She leaned over and stacked them on the empty pallet.

She glanced toward me. I nodded my thanks to her. She nodded back, smiled, and turned to climb up on the forklift. Her dark brown hair was drawn into a tight ponytail that cascaded down her back almost to her ample rear. I had trouble tearing my eyes away.

Felt good to have a woman smile at me.

No place in my life for that kind of complication. I renewed my concentration on the work.

I realized I had been able to keep up even while I looked at the woman. Granted, I was only working at half-rate, but I must've been getting better.

Hank stepped up next to me. "I'll take over," he shouted, moving into place and removing the next cabinet from the hooks. He made it look easy.

"Break time?" I asked. Seemed early, and he usually started with plater one.

"You're wanted up there," he said, nodding toward the stairs leading up to the offices that overlooked the production floor. "First door on the right."

My heart sank. Maybe they were going fire me after all. Reluctantly, I climbed the stairs.

As I stepped into the office, a uniformed police officer shut the door behind me. Another one stood to the side, his holster unsnapped and his hand resting on the butt of his gun. Panic rose in my throat. Couldn't let that show.

The thick office door muted the pounding of the heavy machinery.

A man I didn't know perched on the edge of the worn wooden desk. Not wearing the mandatory hardhat. Dressed in a rumpled suit. Smelled of cop.

He stood up. Didn't show his badge. "Jesse Damon?"

He knew who I was. He'd sent for me. But I answered, "Yes, sir."

"Take off your hardhat." He held out his pudgy hand for it. "Officer Simmons here is going to frisk you. For our safety and yours. Lace your fingers on top of your head and spread your feet."

Nothing to do with my safety. But as I well knew, no point in not complying.

Officer Simmons put one hand on top of mine and expertly frisked me with the other. He pulled out my wallet and unclipped its chain from the belt loop. Tossed it on the desk where it hit a silver clock, which fell on its face. He pulled out my key ring with its pathetic single key to my one-room basement apartment. He tossed it on the desk with my wallet.

Taking one of my wrists in his iron grip, he brought my hand behind me, turned the palm outward, and snapped on handcuffs. Tighter than necessary. He did the same to my other hand.

"Okay, Detective Belkins." He stepped back.

Detective Belkins eased off the desk and walked around me, eyeing me up and down. "Anything you want to tell us?"

I stared at the desktop. My wallet was new and shiny. I'd only had it for five weeks.

My throat was dry, but I managed to say, "No, sir."

"On parole?"

"Yes, sir." I continued to look down at the desk.

"Violated?"

"No, sir." What had I done that might violate my parole? Nothing I could think of.

"Sure?"

"Yes, sir." Don't show doubt.

"What was the charge?"

He knew. He just wanted to hear me say it. "Murder. Possession of a handgun during the commission of a felony. Conspiracy."

"And you pled guilty?"

"Alford plea." Copping to an Alford plea—not admitting guilt but agreeing that the state had enough evidence to convict me—had been a problem from the beginning. Anyone who had any say in my future, like counselors and parole board members, wanted to hear me express remorse. Much harder to do when the plea itself denies guilt in the first place.

"Refused to take responsibility, eh?" Detective Belkins said.

I couldn't think of any reasonable response to that, so I kept quiet.

"No armed robbery?"

"Those charges were dropped," I said. "Part of the plea bargain."

"Possession of controlled dangerous substance? With intent to distribute?"

"Dropped." The convictions would show up on any kind of check. But he knew all my original charges; he'd done his homework. Why had he bothered?

"Part of the plea bargain, too, I suppose?" he said.

I nodded. No point commenting on that.

"Been reporting to your parole officer?" he asked, rubbing his nose with a thick finger.

"Yes, sir."

He glanced down at my ankle, where the black box made a slight bulge in my jeans. "Following the terms of home detention?"

"Yes, sir." What did he think I was going to say?

"Like this job?"

"Yes, sir."

"Getting along with your co-workers?" He came closer. I could smell his sour breath.

"Pretty much, sir."

"How about one Mitchell Robinson?"

"The forklift driver? He thought I was looking at his wife, but I wasn't." Jeez. What had Mitch told them?

"He threaten to call your parole officer?"

"Yes, sir."

"That must have worried you. Don't want to go back to prison where you belong, do you?" Detective Belkins moved directly in front of me and stared at my face. Red veins showed on his nose.

I shifted my gaze to avoid his.

The office door opened, saving me from a reply. John, the foreman, came in. He had to duck to get through the doorway. He looked grave. "Jesse's a good worker. Be sorry to lose him."

If I could have trusted my voice, I would have thanked him.

The detective turned toward John. "They should never parole these killers." He swung back to face me. "You know your Miranda rights."

He wasn't even going to do the right thing and read them to me. He knew I wouldn't complain; I was a parolee, and no one would listen anyhow.

I nodded.

"You sure you got nothing to tell me?" Detective Belkins tapped me hard on the chest. I would have a bruise there. I ignored it.

"Yes, sir."

He smiled. A thin, mean smirk. "Jesse Damon, you're under arrest for the murder of Mitchell Robinson."

I willed my knees not to buckle.

"Simmons, put him in your car and take him downtown."

The other uniform said, "But Detective Belkins…"

Belkins leveled a bleary glare at the speaker. "But nothing. No mystery here. Killers kill. They think they can solve problems that way. Just a matter of clearing up the details."

"Whatever you say, Detective." Officer Simmons shook his head. "We just follow orders."

The two uniformed officers took me by the elbows. There had to be other entrances to the offices; I hoped they would escort me out another way. But they turned me toward the stairs I'd just come up.

I was going to be paraded right past Hank and the other plater operators. They were good enough at their jobs that they could look over to see what was going on.

I had no options. Keep my head up. Look straight ahead. Don't trip. Above all, don't cry.

"And Damon," Belkins said. I glanced toward him. "I can practically guarantee you'll never see the outside of a prison again in this lifetime."

He was grinning again. He was enjoying this.

What had I ever done to him?

# CHAPTER 2

I sat on a worn wooden bench at the local lockup, right next to the sign that read "No Weapons Beyond This Point." I'd been relieved of my belt and boots. I hoped they kept track of the boots; they were expensive. Almost new and steel-toed. I would never be able to afford another pair.

Of course, if I got locked up, I wouldn't be allowed steel-toed boots anyhow. So maybe it didn't matter.

I shifted on the hard bench. My hands were cuffed securely to a waistchain wound through an eyebolt set in the wall over my head. I couldn't find a way to hold my arms so my aching shoulder muscles didn't hurt. Leg irons bit into my ankles, shoving the ankle monitor into my calf.

I avoided looking at anyone or anything. I had to fight to keep myself from jerking my feet back under the bench every time heavy boots came within inches of my gray woolen socks. Talk about feeling vulnerable.

If I were in a holding cell, I'd be getting breakfast of some sort. Out here, I doubted I would be fed.

Leaning my head against the cinderblock wall behind me, I closed my eyes and tried to rest. No way of knowing the next chance I might get to sleep.

Last time I was arrested, I'd been sixteen. Over the years in prison, I hadn't given that night much thought. Certainly nothing I could do to change it.

Now the smells of stale food, unwashed bodies, and disinfectant brought a rush of memories flooding back to me, along with the hopeless feeling that I had no control over what had happened to me next.

That night, my brother Denny and the old man had been hanging out in the bedroom. They sat across from each other on the lower bunks, a kitchen chair between them. The fancy hookah that was Denny's pride and joy sat on the chair, and beer cans littered the floor.

Big Spanish test tomorrow. If I was going to graduate on time and go on to college, I had to pass that test.

I threw myself down on the couch with my textbook opened to the vocabulary section. I couldn't figure out what I was supposed to be doing with some of the verb tenses, but vocabulary I could memorize. Maybe that would be enough.

Ignoring the bursts of giggles and pungent smoke that curled from under the door was hard, but I tried.

I must have fallen asleep, face down.

Something whacked me in the back of my head. "Denny, old man! Wake up! We got places to go, things to do, people to see!"

Groaning, I rolled over. Will, my oldest brother, was standing over me, pillow raised for another swat.

"Oh. Jesse. Sorry. Thought you was Denny. Where is he?"

"Last I knew, he and Dad were in the bedroom."

Will inhaled deeply. "Smoking the evil weed again, were they?"

I shrugged.

Will stepped across the cramped space and opened the bedroom door. He took a step into the room, grabbed Denny by the neck of his hoodie, and dragged him out to join us. I peered past them. The old man was lying sideways on the bed, his eyes closed and his mouth open. With each snore, drool bubbled out of his mouth and down his cheek, puddling on the dirty blanket. A dark stain spread across the front of his pants.

I was glad I slept in an upper bunk.

Still clutching the neck of the hoodie, Will maneuvered Denny over a chair by the kitchen table and deposited him into it. Denny started to slip to the floor.

Will shoved him back into the chair and shook his shoulder.

"Look at me, Denny," he commanded. "You was supposed to meet me an hour ago. What's up, man?"

Denny glanced around with bleary eyes and giggled. "Got anything to eat?"

Will slapped him, but not hard. Not like he slapped me when I wouldn't do what he wanted. "We've been waiting for tonight. Big delivery. Come on, man. Get yourself together. We got plans."

"Good plans. Get bombed." Denny nodded vigorously, almost losing his balance.

Will looked from Denny to me and back again.

"We're gonna need your help, kid," he said.

"My help? Hell no. I got a big test tomorrow. I can't go out on one of your flaky adventures."

"Flaky adventures!" Denny threw himself against the back of the chair, laughing. "He's got a 'big test' tomorrow, and he says we have flaky adventures!"

Will narrowed his eyes. I knew I was going to end up doing what he wanted. So did he. But not without a protest.

"Shut up," he said to Denny, raising his hand again.

Denny winced and put his arm in front of his face, but he couldn't stop giggling. "Flaky adventures!" he said once more under his breath.

I picked up my Spanish book.

"Look," Will said, keeping his voice low and steady. "I know you got this thing for school, and I don't care if you want to get into college. Go for it. But tonight, we need your help. We're family. We stick together."

A number of possible responses came into my head, but Will would not appreciate any of them.

I said, "Denny'll help you. Just wait until he's straight again."

"I was gonna ask you even before Denny made himself next to useless. And it has to be now."

"It's two o'clock in the morning," I said.

"I know." As long as he thought he would get his way, Will could be patient. For a little while. "But I've been waiting for this. You got to help us."

"I'm not interested." I stared down at the words. They blurred together on the page.

"Jesse." Will's voice was honing its steel edge. "We got to cop some stuff for Dad. Otherwise, you know he'll go out on the street, looking for himself. Until he's off of home detention, that's asking for trouble. He'll get picked up and sent away."

"Rehab," I said. "Maybe it'd do him some good. He could start off clean again."

"More likely back to prison," Will said. "Then we'd lose the apartment. And the food stamps. And you, little man, will go back into the system."

He was worried about losing the Social Security check the old man got for me. And the Section 8 housing voucher. And the food stamps.

"I didn't do so bad in the system all those years he was locked up," I said. Tears pricked at the insides of my eyelids.

"Yeah." His eyes bored into me. I'd been little more than a baby when our mother died and I went into foster care. Will and Denny hadn't made out so well. They'd been sent to Boy's Village, a residence for neglected and delinquent youth.

No words formed in my dry mouth. I stared sightlessly down at the page in my textbook.

"You're sixteen now. You got a juvie record," Will pointed out. "Ain't no nice couple gonna take you to live in their house now."

I managed another shrug.

"We need you, Jesse," Will said. "I know where we can go cop a whole load of stuff, keep Dad happy for days."

"He'll just use it all up right away," I said miserably.

"Not if I dole it out to him a little at a time," Will said.

"What is it?" I asked. "More of that crap that makes him go all crazy?"

"No. This is diesel. Think of it like methadone maintenance, only with the real stuff. Keep him home and happy."

"One of these days, his PO is gonna piss test him and he's gonna come up positive."

"Chance we'll have to take. If he's compliant, they got no reason to test him. He don't have no record of substance abuse."

I couldn't imagine how that had happened.

"So what do you want me to do?" But I had a pretty good idea.

"Just carry. Be the mule. You're sixteen; they catch you with anything, it's a slap on the wrist."

"Like last time?" I shivered.

"Hey, so you picked up ninety days in kiddie jail. That wasn't so bad, was it?"

I'd been hungry and cold most of the time. I'd been the "celebrant" at a blanket party. The only reason I hadn't been raped was because I'd fought like a wildcat. But if Will didn't know what it had been like for me, I wasn't going to tell him.

Besides, while I was there, I'd managed to pass a few of the mandatory high school assessment tests for graduation. I was the only resident who had ever passed one. The education supervisor was so shocked, he'd asked for a review of my test scores.

Colleges didn't like to see juvenile detention facilities or alternative schools listed on applications. Especially on scholarship applications, and I would surely need financial aid.

Denny made a choking noise. Will hauled him to his feet and shoved him toward the kitchen sink.

"Splash some cold water on your face," he ordered. "And get yourself a drink of water. We got to get going."

"You ought to wait till he's at least a little straight," I said.

"Can't. Opportunity knocks. He's the only one they'll open the door for. Even if he's wasted. Especially if he's wasted. They'll figure he can't be up to much."

Didn't sound good. "What are you gonna do?"

"Don't you worry yourself," Will said. "You just got to come along, hang out where I tell you. Take what we give you. Bring it back here. Don't let Dad see it."

Will tossed me a dark gray hoodie like the ones he and Denny wore. I held it uncertainly.

"Chilly out there," he told me. He didn't add much harder to see in the dark than the white tee shirt I had on, but I knew that's why he wanted me to wear it.

I pulled it over my head.

We tumbled down the stairs and out into the night, Will keeping a firm hand on Denny's arm.

A chill drizzle cut through the air. I flipped up the hood, stuffed my hands in the kangaroo pocket, and hunched against the wind. Denny wavered, giggling under his breath. Will straightened him out and propelled him forward.

Two blocks away, our neglected neighborhood turned desolate. Trash blew along the curbs among the carcasses of stripped cars. Tall, thin row houses loomed over us, their windows boarded up. Something skittered across the street and ran down a storm drain.

Will stopped. A narrow walkway faded back between two houses. Denny plunked himself down on crumbling brick steps.

"You just wait here." Will nodded toward the narrow space.

I wrinkled my nose. The sinister puddles on the cracked concrete smelled of urine and vomit. I tried to position myself so the soles of my worn boots wouldn't get soaked.

"Denny and I will be coming through here from the alley. You take what we give you and go home."

"Where are you going to go?" I asked.

"Don't you worry about us," he said. "We'll be home by morning."

"And if anything happens…"

"Nothing's gonna happen."

"That's what you said last time."

"Yeah. What's the chances of something happening twice in a row? If you do get stopped, just keep your mouth shut. You're a kid. What are they gonna do to you?"

*Ruin the rest of my life,* I thought glumly. *Before I ever get a chance to do anything.*

Will yanked Denny to his feet. "We won't be long."

They went to the dark doorway of a house down the block, paused briefly, and disappeared inside.

I huddled back into the shelter of the walkway, shivering and watching the gloom.

Way down the block, a lone streetlamp cast a wan circle of light on the wet pavement and shimmering bits of broken glass.

A dark-colored van drove slowly down the street with its lights out. A surprisingly well-kept van. Another one passed in the alley at the other end of the walkway. No lights there, either.

The van stopped in front of the house my brothers had gone into. The doors opened quietly, and several men jumped out. They carried unwieldy cylindrical shapes. A battering ram and guns.

The dim light caught florescent letters on the backs of their vests. All I could make out from here were "PO…"

Had to be saying, "Police."

The cold of the night invaded my guts. I closed my eyes. As if not seeing them would make the cops not be there. My brothers were in that house.

A cacophony of disjointed sounds reached me. Battering ram shattering the door. A barking dog. Shouts. Gun shots.

Silence.

Then sirens.

Feet pounded down the walkway toward me. I opened my eyes. Two hooded gray figures ran at me.

Denny shoved some plastic bags into my hands. "Here. Take this."

"Run!" Will gasped. "Don't follow us!" He gave me a shove, and they were gone.

I juggled the bags. Something hot in one of the bags burned my hand. I caught an oily, smoky scent. Surely they hadn't dumped a burning blunt in there, had they?

I stumbled, almost dropping the bags into a puddle. I grabbed for them, willing myself not to think about the vile smells emanating from that particular puddle. I felt something sharp slice into my palm. Warm, sticky dampness spread across my hand and between my fingers.

The bags were slimy. They threatened to slip from my hands again.

Clutching them to my chest, I slid out of the walkway and started toward home.

A bright light swept past, paused, and returned until it held me at its center.

"Stop."

I took another step.

"You'll be tased. And there's a dog coming."

I'd seen people tased before. No desire to experience it myself. I stopped.

"Drop what you're carrying and turn to face the wall."

I had no good choices. I complied.

"Lace your fingers behind your head. Spread your feet apart."

A different voice said from beyond the edge of the light, "Watch out for the blood."

I didn't think he was talking to me.

A gloved hand grabbed one of my hands and pulled it behind my back. Cold metal clamped down my wrist. The other hand followed. Practiced hands frisked me through my clothes and then spun me around.

The piercing light shone in my eyes. I looked down. The bags lay at my feet. They were covered with dark red stains. So was the front of my hoodie.

Someone grabbed me by the hair, jerking my head up. My eyes closed against the bright light in my face.

"Huh. Younger than I thought. But definitely one of the two guys who were in the apartment. Better send the dog after the other one."

The grip on my hair released, but the hand moved to grasp my upper arm. I would have bruises where the fingers dug in.

"Mirandize him. Right away, before he says anything."

A voice droned on, reading me my rights. I didn't listen. I didn't have much to say. Besides, it wouldn't matter. Miranda rights didn't count in juvenile court.

The bags were dragged away from my feet to another circle of light. Gloved hands exposed their contents. Little taped-up packages. The old man's heroin. Tiny plastic bags with bits of white. Crack rocks. Lots of both. More than enough for a solid distribution charge.

Something long and metallic. A knife. And a gun.

"Do you understand your rights?"

I nodded.

The hand gripping my arm squeezed hard. "Answer out loud, please."

"Yeah."

"Do you want to answer any questions?"

"No."

"Do you want a lawyer?"

"Don't matter. I'm sixteen."

"It'll matter when you end up in adult court."

They were trying to scare me. No matter how much I was carrying, that wasn't likely to happen with possession charges.

"We got witnesses, including a few of the SWAT team. And I'd be willing to bet that's the weapon right there. First degree murder charges usually end up in adult court."

# CHAPTER 3

Here I was, twenty years later, shackled and detained again. Nothing to do but wait for someone else to decide what happens next. I was pretty sure it wouldn't be good.

A pair of boots stopped in front of me. I didn't open my eyes.

"Damon. Stand up."

I rose unsteadily to my feet.

"Detective Belkins wants to talk to you." The guard unlocked the waistchain and yanked it free of the eyebolt. He slapped it around my waist and snicked the lock down.

Grabbing my elbow, he escorted me up a steep staircase. I'd never gotten used to climbing stairs while wearing leg irons. I stumbled and would have fallen if he hadn't kept his grip. Down a long hallway to a dim interrogation room with a chair on either side of a battered wooden table. I sat where he indicated. Much more comfortable than the bench. But now my nose itched, and I couldn't reach it. What was it about being chained up that made my extremities itch fiercely? They never did when I could scratch them.

I would still miss breakfast. My stomach growled.

I knew the routine. Sit and wait. Possibly for hours. No doubt that dark piece of glass in the wall was a one-way window. If I got out of the chair or fell asleep, someone would be in immediately. I had no way to tell how much time passed. An unsettling feeling. That was the whole point. I waited.

Eventually, Belkins and another man came into the room. A light switched on directly over my head. I blinked in the sudden harsh glare. Belkins loomed over me, an unlit cigar clenched in his teeth. The other man, his shaved head and chiseled face the color of mahogany, eased his lanky frame onto the edge of the table. He was dressed in a well-pressed navy suit with a red striped tie. He smelled of breath mints, aftershave, and shoe polish.

"I'm Detective Montgomery," he said, his voice steady and smooth.

They were going to play good cop-bad cop. Guess which was which? Didn't take much imagination.

"Can I get you something?" Montgomery asked. "Sorry, I can't let you smoke. But how about a cup of coffee?"

That sounded really good, and I almost said yes. Then I remembered the waist chain. I would have to ask for one of my hands to be freed before I could drink it. Anytime I had to ask for something, I would feel like they had a little more control. They knew that.

"No, thanks," I said.

"Okay. Let me know if you change your mind."

I nodded.

"Now, want to tell me about what happened last night?" Montgomery checked his watch. Substantial and gold. "Or, I guess, more like early this morning."

Anything I said would be twisted and used against me. Although it hadn't been mentioned, I was sure a recording of some sort was being made. The less I said, the better. But total silence would be construed as failure to cooperate. Reported to my parole officer.

"Not much to tell." I stared at the scarred surface of the table. Was that irregular dark stain blood?

"Come on," Montgomery urged. His dark face radiated false concern. "If you tell us what happened, maybe we can clear all this up quickly."

*And move on to charging me,* I thought. I shook my head.

"You report for work. Mitch gets all up in your face. Calls you a sex offender. We know that much from talking to other people. Let's hear your side of it." He leaned his face closer to mine. I could smell his minty breath.

I had nothing to add. "You know as much as I do. More, probably."

"Must have made you mad," Montgomery suggested.

"No, sir," I replied.

"Aw, come on. Sex offender? Would have made anybody mad."

"I can't speak to that." I leaned back in the chair. Might take a long time.

Montgomery leaned back, too. "You get to work. Guy with an attitude disses you. You get put to work on a plater. He's the forklift driver; probably makes some remarks when he comes by. You get your break. What do you do? What would anybody do?"

He obviously wasn't aware of the noise level in the plating room. Or how careful Hank had been to make sure Mitch didn't get a chance to talk to me. I just sat there.

"What did you do on your break?" Montgomery repeated, examining the back of his hand. His fingers were long and elegant; his nails were neat and well trimmed.

"Took a leak and got a drink of water," I said.

"And ran into Mitch."

"Didn't run into nobody."

"How about lunch? That's longer." Montgomery smoothed the sleeves of his suit jacket over his starched cuffs. French cuffs, they were. With cufflinks.

"Ate lunch. Took a leak. Got a drink of water."

"Where did you go to eat lunch?"

Belkins reached down and grabbed the front of my flannel shirt. With his other hand, he tore the cigar out of his mouth and threw it on the table. He hauled me half out of the chair. "He's not going to tell us a damn thing, are you, Damon? Just sit there with that smug look on your face and not say anything." His sour breath was hot on my face.

Still gripping my shirt, he raised his other hand.

"Belkins." Montgomery's velvet voice was even. "This is being taped."

"So?" Belkins snarled. He slapped the side of my face. Hard. His ring caught the corner of my eye. I tasted blood. "This'll be a piece of tape we won't be able to use."

"Not in the face, Belkins. What's the matter with you?" Montgomery folded his hands and glared at Belkins.

Belkins let go of my shirt. I fell back in the chair with a thud. The side of my face stung, and my eye blinked rapidly. I licked a drop of blood off my lip. But I knew damn well he could have hit me a lot harder.

Montgomery sat still, his handsome face expressionless. Belkins turned away from me, running his pudgy fingers through his greasy hair.

"Just lock him up for now," Belkins said. "I'll talk to him later." He grabbed his cigar and stomped out of the interrogation room.

Montgomery looked at me. I stared down at the table.

He moved out of my line of vision. I felt my shoulders tense. "I don't suppose there's anything you want to tell me."

I shook my head.

"Keep in mind that you're on parole," Montgomery said. Like maybe I'd forget?

"As of now," he continued, "I can tell your PO that you've been very cooperative. Hate to have to change that report."

No doubt in my mind what he was he was getting at. "I got no complaints about how I been treated," I said.

"And what happened to your face?"

Reluctantly, I gave him the answer I knew he was looking for. "Ran into a cell door. On my own."

"Good. Nasty bruise; must have hit it hard. Let's get you into a holding cell." Montgomery opened the door and called for a guard to come get me.

I had the holding cell to myself. It was chilly, but at least the too-tight restraints had been removed. I paced, flexing my hands to get circulation going.

I was in time for lunch. A paper bag with a bologna and cheese sandwich, an apple, and a carton of milk. I scarfed it down. Maybe not gourmet dining, but I was glad to get it.

I lay on the narrow bench, cradling my head with my arms. I tried to make sense of what was happening and figure out what options I had. If any.

I was pretty sure Belkins would try to arrange for another interrogation session. Without being taped. And it might go on for hours. He'd probably wait until Montgomery was off duty. Then it would be just him and me. I wasn't exactly looking forward to that.

When did Belkins go off duty? He had to sleep sometime. If he was the detective in charge of investigating Mitch's death, he had been on duty last night. I knew detectives worked long and sporadic hours when they had a hot case, but he couldn't work completely around the clock. Could he?

Belkins seemed awfully anxious to pin this on me. I had to admit I looked like a pretty good initial suspect. But couldn't Hank and the other plater operators vouch for where I was most of the time? Just that break and the lunch. Belkins should have been working other leads, too. Maybe that's where he was now.

Was he just lazy, or did he have some other reason for wanting to see me locked up again? The way he was treating me felt like a personal vendetta. I had never seen the man before this morning.

Maybe I was getting paranoid.

I was tired. In spite of everything, I dozed off.

"Damon. Get up."

The cell door slid open. I started awake and scrambled to my feet, feeling the cold concrete through my socks.

"Come on." A guard stood outside the door, eyeing me.

I stood where I was, waiting for him to bring out the shackles.

"You don't want to stay here, do you?" he asked, shoving the door open wider.

Uncertain, I stepped forward. Had Belkins told them to leave me unshackled? Nothing sounds so bad to a police review board as hearing that a prisoner had been beaten while he was restrained. The way around that, of course, is to leave off the handcuffs and leg irons.

I fought the panic rising in my chest. "Where are you taking me?"

"I'm not taking you anywhere," he said, exasperation filling his voice. "My orders are to process you for release."

I could make no sense of that. Was I being set up so I could be charged with escape?

At the front desk, I was handed my belt and boots. I had to sign for the manila envelope that held my wallet and key ring. I tried to convince myself that no one would have had me sign any official paperwork unless I was really being released. Although, I supposed they could just tear it up.

I shoved the wallet and key into my pocket, passed the belt through the loops on my jeans, and sat down to put on the boots. I was careful not to jar the home detention monitor; the blasted thing would cost me cost several hundred dollars if it was damaged, and it had already been manhandled.

Under the bored gaze of the desk officer, I stood up and walked out the front door into the dark December day.

Prison issue jackets have the institution name stenciled across the back just below the shoulders; popular rumor is that it's a target for the tower guards to aim at if someone makes an escape attempt. I wasn't wearing any jacket, but my back itched between the shoulder blades just the same.

No shots. No one shouted for me to stop. No sirens sounded.

I realized that, despite the chill December wind and the spitting sleet, I was sweating.

Only after I had forced myself to walk several blocks and turned a corner did I allow myself to look around. No one following. Several cars passed. On the other side of the street, an elderly lady in a fur coat leaned into the wind. No one paid any attention to me. I tried to relax.

Did I still have a job? I wouldn't if the supervisors at the plant thought I had killed Mitch. Someone must have killed him.

Unless it had been determined to be an accident. I brightened. That wouldn't explain Belkins' animosity toward me, but it would explain my sudden release. Must be it.

I couldn't take too long to get back to my place so the phone could pick up the signals from my ankle monitor. The police would have records of the time I had spent in custody there. Assuming that even now, someone wasn't busy erasing all trace of it. That was a chilling thought.

Too many people had seen me hauled in, though, for that to work. John and Hank might not have any reason to go out of their way to help me anymore. Not if they thought I had killed Mitch. But they were honest men. If asked what had happened to me, they wouldn't lie.

The plant was only a block out of my way. I could stop in and pick up my jacket. Now that I wasn't sweating so badly, I was getting really cold. And definitely wet.

While I was there, I could check to see if I should report to work tonight.

I went up to the side factory gate that we used at night, but it was shut and locked. I thought about walking around to the truck yard in the rear and going through the shipping department, but I didn't want to be accused of trespassing. So I went to the front entrance by the offices. Well lit and welcoming, not dark and grated shut like it was when I usually showed up just before midnight.

Shivering, I went up to the receptionist. I hoped I wasn't dripping too badly on the nice carpet in front of her desk.

The receptionist raised her finely drawn eyebrows and looked me up and down. Her bow-shaped lips drew together in disdain. She sat up a little straighter, her right hand straying to finger the jeweled watch on her other wrist.

"May I help you?" she said, her voice nasal and disapproving.

I felt like saying, "Hey, you should have seen me going out of here last night in shackles. Now that was something to look down your nose at." But no good could come of such a stupid comment.

"I was just wondering about work tonight…" I started to say.

"Oh, you want personnel," she said, relaxing a little. "Through that door—" she pointed with her silver pen "—the window on your right."

When I was hired, the company had sent someone out to the pre-release center at the prison to take applications and do interviews, so I had actually never been in the personnel office.

Through the doorway, the floor turned from the plush carpet of reception and the executive suite to worn linoleum. In the shop, the floor was concrete.

The woman at this window was considerably less classy than the receptionist, but no more friendly. "We're not hiring right now." She eyed my wet clothes. Her gaze settled on the side of my face. A bruise was probably forming there. Was my lip still bleeding? I wiped it with my sleeve.

"You can fill out an application, and we'll keep it on file," she continued. "Let you know if anything opens up. But we expect to be closed Christmas week. We definitely won't hire until after that."

"I was already hired," I said, annoyed with myself that I hadn't planned out what I was going to say. "I left my jacket last night. I'd like to get it. And I was wondering if I should report tonight…"

"Are you still in your probationary period?" she interrupted.

"Yes, ma'am."

"Were you told not to report tonight?"

"No, ma'am."

"Did you work the whole shift last night?" She started to shuffle through paperwork on her desk.

"No, ma'am. Until maybe around six or so."

"Four to midnight?" she asked, turning to her computer and typing something on the keyboard. I couldn't see how she could do that with the long, pearl pink fingernails, but she managed.

"Midnight to eight," I said.

"Who sent you home?"

"I wasn't really sent home," I said, shifting from one foot to the other. "The police took me out."

Her eyes widened behind her oversized glasses. "Just a minute," she said. "I have to check with my supervisor."

She picked up the phone. "What did you say your name was?"

I hadn't. "Jesse Damon."

She turned away, spoke into the phone, and then waited a while, drawing circles with a pencil on a piece of paper on her desk. Finally, she said, "Okay," hung up the phone, and turned to me.

"Mr. Radman, the plant manager, will be the one to make that decision. You'll have to go up to his office and find out. Through the door beside you, down the corridor, and onto the shop floor, and then through the door right next to you and up the stairs. Look for his name on the door."

"Thank you, ma'am," I said.

"Let me buzz you in."

The door made a sound like an irritated wasp. I opened it, went down a short corridor, and opened another door onto the noise and controlled chaos of the shop floor. I was in the corner next to the time clock.

Thankfully, I saw the black and red checks of my jacket still hanging from a hook. I grabbed it, careful not to knock anyone else's to the floor. I'd worry about my lunch box later. If I still had a job. If I didn't, I probably wouldn't need it.

I climbed the stairs to the offices.

I was in an internal hallway, separated from the pounding machinery on the shop floor by the offices themselves. The office where Belkins had arrested me was at the opposite end, with the stairway down to the plating floor.

Most of the office doors were shut. Through glass windows on both sides of them, I could see people at work. I read the name plates. The old plank flooring creaked under my damp work boots.

The office of Sterling Radman, Plant Manager, was almost at the end. His door was open. I stopped at the threshold.

Mr. Radman was standing ramrod straight at the windows on the other side of his office, overlooking the production floor, his back to me, his hand pressed to the side of his head. He wore dark pants and a light yellow dress shirt. A suit jacket was hung over the back of his desk chair.

At first, I thought he was watching something going on below, but then I noticed the wire from his desk to his ear. He was on the phone. I waited.

He must have been listening to someone talk. He shook his head, running long, slender fingers through his mane of thick, silver hair.

"No, no, no," he said into the phone. "You can't return that shipment. You just can't."

He listened for a few seconds.

"I don't care what you do with the damn root baskets. Sell them to a plant nursery. Or an orchard. Give them to somebody. Dig up some trees yourself and go into the tree business. I don't care. Just don't return them."

He listened again.

"Well, consider it part of the price of the deal. Let them rust, for all I care. You're not going to return them, and that's final." He turned toward his desk and slammed the phone down.

He caught sight of me. "What do you want?"

"The lady down in personnel, she told me to come talk to you..." He hadn't invited me in, so I stood in the doorway.

"About what?"

"About my job. Whether I should come in tonight." Why hadn't I learned my lesson and figured out what to say? I should sound sure of myself, like I knew I was keeping the job. But that wasn't happening.

"Why did they think should you be asking me?" he said. "I don't handle personnel decisions."

"Well, I guess because of last night. I had to leave early. The police..."

His narrowed eyes looked me over. He leaned on his desk, his short, buffed nails splayed in front of him.

"You're the one the police took out of here last night?" he said. "After they found the body..."

"Yes, sir."

"And they've released you already?"

"Yes, sir."

He drew himself up to his full height. "Unbelievable. A convicted murderer," he turned away, muttering to himself. But I could hear him.

Without turning to face me, he asked, "Did somebody bail you out?"

"No, sir. I wasn't charged."

"So they don't think you did it?" he asked, tapping his handsome, well-maintained teeth with a silver pen.

"They didn't say, sir. They just told me to leave."

"And did they tell you to stay in the area?"

"No need to, sir. I'm on parole. I can't leave the area without permission anyhow."

"That's right." He shook his head.

I needed a more positive aspect to this conversation. "So I'll report for work at midnight, shall I, sir?"

Mr. Radman stepped back. "I don't think so." he said. "This company is dedicated to giving convicted felons a second chance…"

Also dedicated to the incentive tax breaks the state gives for that. But I didn't point that out.

He was shaking his head. "…but second chances are it. One of our long-term employees was killed—murdered in the warehouse. I think we're past giving any more chances."

"You can ask Hank. I didn't…" I started to say.

But he had picked up the phone. "Send security up here right away."

That's that, I figured. "You don't need to call security. I'll leave." My lunchbox would just have to be a casualty of this. I turned and headed back down the hallway.

I'd just about reached the stairs when I heard a voice behind me. "Wait."

I turned around.

Mr. Radman was standing at the door of his office, beckoning to me. "Come back."

Uncomfortably, I returned, careful to remain just outside the office in the hallway and to keep my hands in an unthreatening position at my sides.

Mr. Radman had retreated to his office and had the desk between us. He looked pale.

I made no attempt to go any closer.

"Yes, sir?" I said.

"I may have been hasty." He cleared his throat. His words were falling all over one another. "And we are shorthanded. I will have to check with the foreman on that shift. But if he says he wants you back, you can still have a job."

"Thank you, sir. I'll just report at the usual time? John will tell me whether I'm working or not."

"Yes, yes. You do that. Report to John tonight." He passed a hand over his unwrinkled brow.

I thought businessmen were supposed to be decision makers who stood by their decisions. It's losers like me who are never quite sure what to do. But people in Sterling Radman's position are paid to assess a situation, make an analysis, and act on it. Why was this stressing him out so much?

He looked like he was afraid I was going to enter the office and attack him or something.

"Anything else now, sir?" I asked, taking a step backwards.

"No. Go. Come back later and talk to John."

"Thank you, sir." I left before he could change his mind again. I heard the office door slam shut as I went down the hallway.

At the head of the stairs, two security guards rushed past me toward Sterling Radman's office. I stood aside and let them go.

John had said I was a good worker; I could only hope he would want me back.

# CHAPTER 4

Home was a one-room, furnished, basement apartment. A kitchenette with a mini refrigerator and stove beneath a five-foot counter that housed two burners and a sink. A tiny bathroom in the corner. One little window looking out onto the dead-end alley that ran next to the building, a gathering place for cheap hookers and desperate junkies. The phone—an essential, since it read the home detention monitor on my ankle—hung on the wall by the bathroom door. Not exactly luxurious surroundings. But I had the key to the door in my pocket. Sure beat a prison cell.

Loosening the laces on my boots, I put them under the radiator to dry. I took a shower, letting the hot water drive the chill from my bones. Felt good to wash the sweat away, but I couldn't quite rid my muscles of the ache or my body of the smell of interrogation rooms and jail cells. I tumbled into the lumpy bed and tried to get some sleep, without much success. I finally got up, shaved, showered again, and put on clean clothes. My boots were still a little damp, but I had nothing else I could wear to work. I just had to hope that two pairs of clean socks—first cotton and then wool—would keep my feet warm and dry enough to work.

I made two peanut butter sandwiches from my dwindling supply of food and stuffed them into a plastic shopping bag, which went into my pocket. I'd have to make do with water from the drinking fountain; my thermos was with my lunchbox, still at work, so I couldn't bring any coffee.

I studied my face in the cracked mirror over the bathroom sink. I brushed the dark brown curls out of my eyes. I didn't want to spend the money on a haircut, and it wasn't long enough to tie back into a ponytail yet. Didn't matter much at this job.

The cut on my lip was mostly on the inside, not really visible. The area around my eye was swelling and the bruise was darkening, but it didn't look like it would turn into a real shiner. Maybe the discoloration on my cheek would be less noticeable under the fluorescent lights in the factory.

On the way out, I locked the door. It opened onto an exterior brick staircase, which led up to the broken and worn sidewalk. The building had once housed a pizza parlor but was now divided into small apartments.

It was cheap, within walking distance of work, and the furniture was comfortable if old. Suited me fine.

I trotted up the wet steps to the sidewalk. The janitor had spread salt to melt the ice. It crunched underfoot.

The weather was even worse. I flipped up the hood of my jacket, lowered my head into the sleet, and stuffed my hands in my pockets. When I got paid, warm gloves would be high on my list of purchases— wool ones, since wool holds warmth even when it's wet—if I had enough money left when I paid everything else I owed. Good luck on that.

When I got to work, I hung my jacket on a hook and went to punch in. I hesitated in front of the timecard rack. Suppose my slot was empty? But it held a timecard.

The other workers clustered around the vending machines. Some nursed cups of the muddy concoction that passed for coffee.

Seemed like the other workers moved away as I approached. Was I imagining it? A few glanced in my direction, murmuring among themselves. Not much I could do about it, so I ignored them. Leaned against the wall in my usual place.

A short, middle-aged man I didn't recognize complained loudly to no one in particular. "Eleven years working days, and they put me on the midnight shift," he grumbled. "First, the union rep says there's nothing they can do. Tries to tell me it's like a promotion, 'cause lift driver pays a quarter an hour more than machine operator, plus the shift differential. I told him they can stuff their quarter an hour and shift differential. Put me back on days."

He stood, short and squat, staring belligerently and waiting for someone to share his indignation. He was met with general indifference. So what if he worked midnights? We all worked that shift.

Finally, someone asked, "Did the union rep ever do anything?"

The man nodded in satisfaction. "Said he'd talk to management, ask them to train someone else on the shift to drive the lift. Maybe I'll only be on for a few nights."

"Kind of thing we pay union dues for."

John approached, his bushy eyebrows raised questioningly. "A problem here, Simon?" he asked.

"Nah. Just talking about the lift driver job," the reassigned driver told him.

"What about it?"

"Union rep's gonna see if you can train somebody up on this shift," Simon said.

"Hasn't said anything to me," John said, scanning his clipboard. "We don't have a qualified instructor on this shift; somebody'd have to switch to days for the training." He looked over the assembled crew and raised his voice. "Anybody interested in the lift job, let me know. I'll tell personnel, see if that's what they're thinking about doing."

"Don't see why you don't have a back-up driver on the shift, anyhow." The mollified driver wiped his nose with the back of his hand.

"Kelly's a qualified driver," John said. "She works in shipping. We can pull her in an emergency. But mostly, she's needed back there. A lot of trucks on this shift. Drivers like to be loaded and out on the road before the rush hour traffic gets bad."

John began assigning jobs for the night. His gray eyes glanced down at me. "Jesse. Plater two again. Good to see you back."

A few people glanced in my direction. John was glad to see me. That was all that mattered right now. I still had a job.

I reported to the plating room. Hank waved me into the office, shut the door, and held out my lunchbox. "You forgot this," he said, holding it out.

I smiled. "Didn't exactly forget it. Got left behind is more like it. Not much choice." I took the squashed peanut butter sandwiches out of my pocket and crammed them into the lunch box.

Hank grinned back, his beard twitching. "Guess that's right." He took the lunchbox back and stashed it under the desk. "That Detective Belkins, you wanna watch out for him."

I agreed with the thought wholeheartedly. "I will if I can."

Hank scratched his chin through his beard and looked uncertain. Did he know something about Belkins? And would he tell me?

I could ask. "Seems like he's got it in for me. Thinks I must have killed Mitch."

Hank shook his head. "He's gone a little crazy, I think."

"Oh?" Not comforting to know that the detective who seemed to be sure of my guilt might be a little crazy.

Hank stared off through the window in the door. "Belkins had a daughter. Marie. Pretty little thing. And nice. She was the same year in school as my oldest boy. They dated for a while, went to the prom and things." He stopped talking, a faraway look in his eyes.

He was talking about Belkins' daughter in the past tense. Not promising. "What happened?" I asked.

"My boy went into the Marines. I guess they were never that serious—or they were just too young. They broke up." He wiped his nose with the back of his hand. "She met this guy. A paroled convict. He told her his so-called friends rolled over on him, let him take the rap for something he didn't do. A burglary. She believed him." Another pause.

"And…?"

"It turns out he was some kind of a pervert. His conviction was for rape and murder, not breaking and entering. Nobody else involved. Of course, this was before you had a sex offender registry to look people up in. When she tried to break up with him, he kidnapped her. Tortured her. She didn't survive."

I felt a chill.

Hank shook his massive head. "Belkins never got over it. Can't say as I blame him. His wife said it was his fault, and she left him."

That seemed like a stretch. "How come she blamed him? Wasn't his fault."

"Who knows? People aren't rational about these things. Something about if he'd been the right kind of a father, he'd've made sure the guy's parole was violated, and he would have been locked up again."

Not rational is right. "So I guess he wouldn't be particularly sympathetic to somebody like me with a murder conviction. Especially if he thought I might have killed someone else."

Hank nodded. "And especially if he thinks you've got some kind of background as a sex pervert."

That surprised me. "Not me. No sex offenses."

"But Mitch said you did. The night before he died. He said it right out in front of everybody, before the shift started. Then, anybody who'd listen, he went on about how he was worried about his wife. So now a lot of other people think so, too. Some of them are even saying that's why you killed him."

Didn't make much difference, but I said, "I didn't kill Mitch."

Hank shrugged. "Don't see how you could've. Not during the shift, anyhow. And that's when he died."

Pretty discouraging. "Don't know that there's much I can do about what people think. But I'll try to keep out of Belkins' way."

"You do that. He's definitely not wrapped real tight now. He used to be a top-notch cop."

I remembered how Montgomery had made it clear that it was in my best interest not to report Belkins for hitting me—even if no one would believe me. Cops took care of their own.

Hank looked away from me. "I just thought you should know."

"Appreciate it." I did. He didn't have to say anything.

Hank put the clipboard back on the desk and opened the door. The dull thud of the machinery increased to a heavy throb.

As the whistle blew, I stepped up to take the place of the departing worker. Plater two was still running the heavy cabinets. This time, I was able to swing into the rhythm almost right away. I wasn't able to load every set of hooks, but I was able to catch all the pieces coming off the plater, and I was up to maybe seventy-five percent of the unfinished ones.

Hank watched me for a few minutes. He leaned over and shouted, "Good job. You'll have it down by the end of the shift."

"Hope so." I put a cabinet on the pallet.

"'Course," he shouted with a grin, "we're almost done running them. Something else tomorrow."

Figured.

Hank brought me the lunchbox when he came to relieve me for lunch.

Most of the shift had lunch from four o'clock to four eighteen a.m. Workers on jobs that couldn't be shut down, like plater operators or packing line workers, got staggered breaks as the group leader—Hank, in my case—filled in. The plater operators ate at a picnic table in a back corner of the shipping department.

It was a relief to get away from the steam, noise, and the chemical odors. I stopped in the men's room, where I rinsed the old coffee residue out of the thermos and filled it with water. Better than nothing. Peanut butter sandwiches go down pretty dry.

I rounded the corner into shipping and came to a dead stop. Someone was already sitting at the table, lunchbox open. A female someone.

The woman looked up at me. She was the one who had been driving the forklift last night. Undoubtedly the Kelly person John had mentioned earlier. Lift drivers got lunch whenever their supervisor decided they weren't needed immediately.

Our midnight shift was small. Never been a secret that the company hired parolees; if everybody hadn't been aware that I was a convicted felon before Mitch's murder, they had to know now. Here this female driver was, by herself in an isolated part of the plant. She might be uncomfortable if I sat down near her. Not fair to her, and she might complain. I could do without that. I hesitated, wondering where else I could go to eat.

"Come on over and sit down," she yelled to me. "I don't bite."

I had to grin at that. "I don't, either," I said, slipping onto the bench on the other side of the table. I was careful not to let my knees touch hers.

She was just unwrapping a sandwich. I tried not to stare at it. Sliced meat and cheese spilled out from between thick slices of dark bread. She had a little plastic bag with lettuce, tomato, and onion that she added to the sandwich. She ripped open a bag of chips.

"My name's Kelly," she said.

She had a cute little gap between her upper front teeth that showed when she talked. Her long brown hair was drawn back into a ponytail.

She'd flipped it over her shoulder while she sat at the table. It made a thick, glistening rope that invited me to reach out and touch it. I kept my hands to myself.

"You're Jesse, right?"

I nodded. She did know who I was.

"What happened to your face?" she asked.

I touched the swollen eye and cheek. I remembered Montgomery's promise to tell my PO I'd been cooperative. "Ran into a cell door," I said.

She threw back her head and laughed.

What was so funny?

"And did that 'cell door' have a fist on it, by any chance?" she asked.

Once again, I had to grin. I hadn't smiled so much in years. "Maybe."

"My dad's been locked up a lot. Doing life on the installment plan. Can't count the number of times I've gone to visit him and found him with his face all messed up. Always 'ran into a cell door.'" She took a big bite of her sandwich.

I took a bite of my mangled mess that had once been a peanut butter sandwich.

She chewed for a minute and swallowed. "One of the guards or another prisoner?"

"Detective," I said, examining what was left of my lunch.

"Interrogation?" she asked.

"If you want to call it that." I tore my gaze off her sandwich.

"Did they charge you?"

I shook my head. "I wouldn't be here if they'd decided to charge me," I said. "No way I'd ever get bail set on a homicide charge. And no bail bondsman in his right mind would post it—even if by some miracle it was set and I could come up with my ten percent."

"Probably true." She pulled the top off her sandwich and rearranged the contents. It smelled delicious. "From what I hear, though, Hank says you couldn't have killed Mitch. Weren't away from the line long enough. Not at the time he must have been killed."

I was surprised at how relieved I felt to hear her say that. "Anybody on break when they said he was killed?"

She scowled. "Not that I know of. But that damn Aaron was away from the packing line half the night. Said he had the runs. John finally told him to go punch out if he couldn't stay and work."

"So what did he do?"

"He was still there at the end of the shift."

Definitely not what Belkins wanted to hear. "I was thinking maybe they'd decided it was an accident and that's why they didn't charge me."

Kelly looked at me. "I think it's pretty clear it wasn't an accident." She extracted a dill pickle from her lunch box and broke it in half. "Somebody beat the crap out of Mitch and ran over him with the forklift." She offered half to me.

I felt my gut tighten up. So Mitch had been murdered. Not good for me. "Why would anybody do that?"

Kelly still held the pickle. I shook my head. It did look good.

She took a bite. "It's not like Mitch was real popular or anything. Especially lately." She rummaged further in her lunch box. "Everybody knew he'd been getting crazy. I mean, he'd never been entirely sane, but he'd really gone off the deep end lately."

"Like how?"

"Lots of things. He's been forgetting what he's supposed to be doing. People have been complaining that he's brought them the wrong parts. And that was just at work." Kelly shoved the rest of the pickle into her mouth.

"Was he losing it other places, too?" Too bad he wasn't killed in one of the other places.

"Look at the way he treated his wife. Made her come drop him off wearing a negligee and then made her get out of the van so everybody could see her in her nightie. In this weather. I heard about that. Kissing her and feeling her up like that in front of everyone."

I nodded. That was the incident that had started all this. At least for me.

"No reason for that but to humiliate her." Kelly licked pickle juice from her fingers. "Wanted to show everybody what a hot woman he's got and how he could make her do anything he told her to. Disrespecting your woman like that makes no sense."

I hadn't given it much thought. Kelly might be right. At any rate, it wasn't entirely normal. "Treating her like that was something new?"

"Yeah. Although he's always been a little weird about her. They live in a cabin on a few acres back in the woods. You know that alley that runs next to the shipping yard?"

"Yeah."

"That turns into a gravel road a mile or two outside of town. Their house is off of that, about four miles up in the hills. It's set back off the road. Really isolated. He'd brag about how he never let her go anywhere by herself. If she did have to go somewhere, he'd drive her. She was mostly just stuck up there at home by herself with the kids. I know they—she—has a set of twins and at least one more older one."

"So why would he have her drive him into work now?" I started on my other mangled peanut butter sandwich. No improvement over the first. "Wouldn't the kids be home asleep at midnight? Somebody ought to be at home with them."

"You'd think." Kelly shook her head. "I know some of the guys had been buying drugs from him. Maybe he had some stuff in that van of his and didn't want it in the parking lot here. Every once in a while, they bring a drug dog by to sniff. And the dog zeroing in on a vehicle is probable cause, so they can search it."

"What was he dealing?"

"Rumor had it he could get you anything, but mostly weed and crystal meth."

I thought about how he'd accused me of looking at his wife. And the sores on his arm. "Meth can make you really paranoid. If he was doing that."

"Yeah. I wish they'd keep all that stuff away from the plant. Makes trouble for everyone." Kelly popped a few chips into her mouth and chewed.

"They'd have to be crazy," I said. "Why would anyone take a chance on blowing a good job like this?"

Kelly licked a drip of mustard from the side of her sandwich. "You have a point there. But some people are crazy. And they don't stop to think how tough it is to get decent jobs in this economy. They figure they can always pick up another job."

"Not that easy." I took a glum look at the remains of my sandwich and stuffed it in my mouth. I was pretty sure that if the state didn't give a tax break to the company for hiring a paroled convict, I wouldn't have this job.

"A lot of these guys don't think like that. Even the ones old enough to know better. Mitch was always bragging that he didn't need this job."

"Look at where it got Mitch. Some of the others might learn something from it." I wiped the last of the peanut butter from my fingers onto my jeans. They needed to be washed anyhow.

"You'd think. But I need this job for sure. And I got to steer clear of anything that even looks iffy."

*Doesn't sitting with me fall into that category?* I wanted to ask. Instead, I said, "Mitch was certainly in the 'old enough to know better' category." I took a drink of water from my thermos.

"True. But most of his customers are just kids." Kelly finished her pickle. I wished I'd accepted half. "Although rumor had it he was dealing to some of the office staff, too." She took a handful of chips and shoved the bag toward me. "Have some," she said.

They looked good. "That's your lunch." I kept my eyes on the table top.

"Yeah, and if you don't have some, I'll probably eat the whole bag."

"Well, they're yours," I pointed out. "You brought them."

"That's so. But do I look to you like someone who should be eating a whole bag of chips?" she asked.

I risked a brief look at her. She was solidly built. Mostly hard muscle, not fat. Except for those magnificent breasts. Didn't want to stare at them. I blushed. "You look fine to me," I said honestly.

She laughed. "How long were you locked up?"

"Over nineteen years."

She raised her eyebrows. They were the same rich brown as her hair. "Wow. You must have been just a kid," she said.

I shrugged. "Sixteen. Back then, I didn't know sixteen-year-olds could be tried as adults. But I learned quick enough."

"Well, I was going to say that after however long you'd been locked up, probably any woman might look good to you. After nineteen years, that must really be true."

"Don't see too many women in a men's prison," I agreed. "A few women who work there. But you have to be real careful around most of them."

"What was the conviction, if you don't mind my asking?" she said.

"Murder," I answered. "Only two things get a sixteen-year-old automatically assigned to adult court. Murder and rape."

She didn't mince any words. "Did you do it?"

I sighed. I didn't have to field this question often, but I dreaded it. "Depends on your definition," I said, putting my thermos on the table.

"Why's that?"

"Well, technically, I'm guilty. I mean, I was there. And anybody who's involved in a felony that results in a death can be convicted of murder. Somebody was shot. And died."

Her deep brown eyes were sympathetic. "But you weren't the killer."

"Hell, no. I wasn't even in the apartment when he was shot. Didn't matter much, though. I'm still the one who went down for it."

Kelly took two oranges out of her lunchbox. She started to peel one. "Surprised they put that in adult court, though, if you weren't the triggerman or whatever."

"Yeah. Well, I was with my brothers." I'd kind of forgotten about oranges. I hadn't had one in years. I remembered the sweet, juicy taste. My mouth watered. "The cops came. Must have been a setup. My brothers ran out the back and shoved two bags at me as they ran by. A hundred some-odd packets of heroin and a knife and the gun. Of course, I was standing there like an idiot with my mouth open and got picked up right away."

"I'd have thought they would have tested your hand to see if you'd fired a gun recently," Kelly said, sucking the juice out of a segment of orange.

"Why bother? We'd agreed that if something went wrong, I'd 'fess up, since I was a juvenile. So before I found out about the shooting, I as good as confessed. And I had the gun and the drugs in my possession. They didn't need anything more."

"What happened to your brothers?"

I shrugged. "No idea. Never heard from them again. At that point, why bring them into it? Wasn't going to help me. I copped to an Alford plea and picked up forty-five years. Public defender said that was the best he could do. Better than he'd expected."

"And you just got parole."

"Yeah. I'm lucky it's getting overcrowded in the prisons and nobody wants to spend more tax money to build more. The parole board was looking for people to let out. I was young when I was locked up, and I have a good institutional adjustment record. Nothing I did. Just good timing."

Kelly shoved the other orange toward me. "Eat that," she command-ed. "My eyes are bigger than my stomach."

Over the heavy odor of oil and diesel exhaust, I could smell the or-ange. Kelly pushed it farther across the table, closer to me.

"No thanks," I said, trying not to stare at it. It was tantalizing.

"More than I can eat," she said. "I don't want to have to cart it home. So take it."

"Okay. Thanks," I said. I picked it up and peeled it. It tasted every bit as good as I remembered.

"When you were locked up, did you know my dad?" she asked. "He's a clerk for the records room. Goes by Old Buckles."

I smiled. "Sure. Everybody knows Old Buckles. I mean, maybe not to talk to, but everybody knows him. He's been there forever."

Kelly sighed and shook her head. "Not really. He's actually been paroled more than a few times. But he's an outlaw biker at heart. Can't keep away from the club. Next thing you know, he's drinking and drug-ging and then figures they're gonna pick him up and violate his parole anyhow, so he might as well do something spectacular. And he usually does."

"Like what?"

"Like the last time. Led half the state police force on a high-speed chase. Helicopter and all. Knew he couldn't get away, so he rode his Har-ley through a store window. Then he gets violated and locked up again, not to mention the new charges. So I put his bike back in my garage and go back to visiting him twice a month."

I remembered all the years with no visitors. "He's lucky he has you."

Kelly glanced at her watch. "I got to get back. Truck's due any minute. I got to unload it." She pushed the bag of chips toward me. "Finish these," she said, tossing her trash in the wastebasket and shutting her lunchbox. "Nice talking to you."

I sat and watched her leave, flipping the ponytail over her shoulder so it trailed down her back and swayed as she walked. It was all I could do not to run after her to touch her hair. Stupid. Was that how real sex offenders felt? Only, they followed through on their impulses and got mad when the other person didn't like it.

I stuffed the rest of the chips into my lunch box, tossed my trash after hers, and went back to work.

I resolved not to think about how exhausted I was until the shift was over. I was so wound up, I didn't know whether I would be able to sleep when I got home. I wondered if it had anything to do with my nerves being pulled up so tight, my head felt like it would burst. My shoulders ached from two nights of the unaccustomed overhead motions. I wanted nothing more than to retreat to my basement apartment, take a hot shower, climb into the lumpy bed, and at least try to sleep.

The forklift rattled by, the disgruntled driver swinging so close to the loaded pallets that he winged one on the end by plater four.

"Hey," Hank shouted, moving to shove it back into place and pick up the shelves that had fallen from it. "Watch where you're going with that thing."

But the lift was long gone.

Two men wearing suits but also with the obligatory hardhats came down from the offices. Hank went over to talk to them. I recognized Sterling Radman. They huddled in a group. Although they were raising their voices so they could hear one another over the sounds of the machinery, I could not make out anything they said. Hank consulted his clipboard, flipping back through the papers it held. He shook his bullish head, mildly at first and then with increasing animation as they apparently argued. Finally, Hank handed the clipboard over to Mr. Radman and turned away. He looked annoyed.

I renewed my efforts to keep all the plater hooks filled. It was getting easier. I didn't want to give Mr. Radman, or anyone, additional reasons to consider letting me go.

When I permitted myself a minute to glance over at the men, they were looking at me. Hank was shaking his head again, frowning. I turned away, concentrating on my work.

The next time I hazarded a glance, they were gone. I tried to relax a bit, but I couldn't help but think this wasn't good.

# CHAPTER 5

Mr. Radman came hurrying up again, this time with two more men in suits. No hardhats. They stopped in the passageway. I caught a glint of the harsh overhead light reflecting off a bald head. A very dark bald head.

Montgomery. The other hatless man was Belkins. My stomach knotted. I missed getting a cabinet on the next set of hooks and let them go empty.

Belkins stepped nearer to the raised wooden platform on which we plater operators stood.

The other men stood back with Hank, who had his clipboard clutched in his hand again. He didn't look any happier.

Belkins tried to squeeze his bulk between the pallet of unfinished cabinets and the pallet of completed ones. He couldn't fit and had to go back around the end of the pallets past plater one. He stepped up on the platform and came toward me.

"If you're gonna go up by where there's machinery operating overhead, at least get a hardhat," Hank yelled to him.

"Don't need one," Belkins shouted back, taking another step toward me.

"Then I'm gonna have to shut the platers down," Hank shouted. "Safety issue. OSHA regulations."

As Belkins stepped around the plater one operator, that worker reached over and punched the big emergency stop button on his control panel.

"Don't stop production," Mr. Radman hollered. "We're already backlogged."

"Union regs," the plater operator shouted back. "Unsafe working conditions. If you want the platers running, get this guy off of here or go get the steward."

The operators of platers three and four reached for their emergency stop buttons.

I didn't have union protection. If I stopped the plater without permission, no one would step in to save me from being fired. I glanced over to where Hank stood. He shook his head slightly.

I stowed the next cabinet on the pallet and reached for another one.

Montgomery slipped between the pallets and stepped up on the platform. He had no trouble fitting. "Belkins. Get down from there."

Belkins stopped a few feet away from me. Mine was the only plater still running.

"Get the union steward," plater three's operator said. He stripped off his gloves and rocked back on his boot heels. "Somebody's gonna stand bareheaded near my plater, I ain't running it. Somebody's gonna get hurt. They ain't gonna say I wasn't following safety procedures and blame me. I'll file a grievance if I have to."

Montgomery reached over and grabbed Belkins by the arm, dragging him off the platform. "Get down here. You can talk to him after the shift ends. It's only ten minutes."

The other operators started their platers again.

Mechanically, I continued working. When I glanced over, the little knot of men still stood there. Belkins stared at me, an unlit cigar clenched in his mouth.

Day shift workers came in, pulling on gloves and straightening hardhats. They all looked curiously at the visitors. My replacement stared at them and then at me.

The whistle blew for shift change. The day shift workers stepped up and took over.

Were they going to cuff me again and march me out of there? In front of another shift? Not a damn thing I could do about it.

I stepped off the platform and peeled off my gloves.

Maybe not. If they had planned to do that, they'd have brought uniformed backup.

Hank came up to me. "Punch out and report to Radman's office. You know where it is?"

"Yeah." I tucked the gloves in my pocket. "And Hank…"

"Yeah?" he asked, his black eyes small in his beefy face.

"Just wanted you to know I appreciate what you're doing for me," I said.

"And what's that?" His eyebrows rose above his crooked nose.

"You know." I shrugged. "Giving me a chance here. Telling the cops that I was on the plater all night. Especially when Mitch was killed."

He looked at me. "Ain't nothing special. You work hard. We need good workers. And I ain't gonna tell no lies for nobody. I keep records on breaks." He tapped his clipboard. "I know where my operators are and when they're there. Includes you that night."

"Well, thanks anyhow," I said awkwardly.

I went to the time clock and waited my turn to punch out.

For a brief minute, I thought about leaving with everyone else. I could say I'd misunderstood what Hank had told me.

But that would gain me nothing except a little time and might lose me my job—or my parole. If Belkins was determined to talk to me again, sooner or later, he would make sure he did it. I fingered my still-bruised face. Better here at the plant than at the police station. And better with Montgomery around than Belkins by himself.

I climbed the stairs to the offices, walking along the hallway until I came to Radman's door. My stomach churned. Maybe I should have gone to the men's room first and seen if I could throw up.

The office door was open. Radman sat at his desk. Montgomery was in the visitor's chair, leaning back and relaxed, his charcoal-gray suit looking like it had just come back from the cleaners.

Belkins paced restlessly, his stained suit wrinkled at the knees and elbows. His shirt collar was open. He wasn't wearing a tie.

I wondered what it would be like to have a daughter. I liked kids. Had ever since I helped take care of younger ones in foster homes. Maybe I would have some one day. Unlikely, but I could hope. But to know that a daughter had been killed and before that, tortured—on purpose—by someone who had done it before…It'd have to unhinge the mind.

I stood just outside the door. They'd tell me what they wanted me to do.

"Maybe it was a mistake, putting him back to work," Mr. Radman was saying, glancing nervously at his blunt fingernails. "But we're shut all next week, and I'm short operators. No one has any solid evidence, but opinions are mixed. I've been asking around."

"We'd rather you didn't ask around," Montgomery said smoothly, turning to look toward me in the hall. "That's our job."

Belkins stopped his pacing. His gaze followed Montgomery's. "Get in here, Damon," he said.

Montgomery got to his feet. "Sit down here, Damon," he said, gesturing toward the chair.

I would rather have stayed standing. When I sat down, they would be looking down on me and I would have to look up to make eye contact. Psychological disadvantage. Not to mention making me more vulnerable physically. Part of their method, I knew. Nothing I could do about it.

I sat.

"Mr. Radman," Montgomery said with a tight grin, "I wonder if Detective Belkins and I can have this office for a little while?"

"Well…" Radman clearly didn't want to leave. I really didn't want him to leave, either. The more witnesses, the better.

"We won't be long," Montgomery assured him.

"All right." Radman straightened the pens in the holder on his desk and got to his feet. "I'll be down in the executive suite, if you should need me."

"Thank you, and shut the door on your way out." Montgomery perched himself on the edge of the desk, facing me. "Why don't you have a seat, Detective Belkins?" he said, indicating the chair behind the desk.

Sounded like a good idea to me. He would be too far away to reach over and grab me.

Belkins moved his ponderous bulk behind the desk, but he didn't sit down.

"I hope you had no unfortunate aftereffects from our encounter yesterday." Montgomery's eyes bored into my face.

"No, sir." I realized I was rubbing my swollen eye. I dropped my hand into my lap and looked at the floor.

"That's good." Montgomery rested his slim dark hand on the polished surface of Radman's desk. He wore two rings, both gold with some kind of green gemstone. They'd really tear up my face if he hit me with them. "I would hate to have to change my report to your parole officer. I told him you were cooperating fully."

I nodded.

"Now," he said. "I don't think we had an opportunity to go over your whereabouts last night as completely as we would have liked. Can we start with what time you arrived at work?"

I stared at my hands in my lap. If I could give them the information they needed, maybe Belkins wouldn't be hauling me in again. I much preferred Montgomery's methods of questioning.

But I could practically guarantee they'd distort whatever I said. Not answering questions, though, was being uncooperative.

"About eleven fifty, give or take," I said. "Shift starts at midnight."

"And what time did you leave your apartment?"

Belkins scoffed. "Call that rathole an apartment?" he muttered.

Montgomery turned and glared at him. Belkins shifted on his feet and was quiet.

"What time did you leave?" Montgomery repeated.

"Eleven thirty," I said. "I'm allowed a half hour to get to work."

"And if I check the monitoring records…"

"Eleven thirty almost exactly," I said.

"You're pretty good about sticking to the schedule your parole officer set?"

"Yes, sir. Except for yesterday."

"What happened yesterday?" Montgomery asked.

"You guys pulled me in. I couldn't go home," I said. "I was pretty late checking in."

Two hours later, Montgomery was still asking the same few questions in different ways. Belkins had hardly participated. But he finally sat down. I was still answering the questions the same way. If I'd been trying to hide something, I couldn't have kept the answers straight. Montgomery would have figured out I was lying in no time.

Montgomery finally got to his feet. Belkins stretched, yawned, and stood. I remained seated, waiting to be told what to do next.

"I think you can go," Montgomery said. "I'll call your PO—Mr. Ramirez, is it?—and tell him if you're checking in late that you were with us."

"Thank you, sir," I said.

My shoulders ached. Despite that and the storm raging in my head and gut, I was exhausted, and my eyes kept wanting to close. And I was hungry.

"I think we should take him downtown and grill him some more," Belkins said, looking at his watch. "We got time."

"We want to talk to a few more people here." Montgomery shot up the cuff of his starched shirt and consulted his watch. "I think we've gotten everything Damon has to tell us."

"You mean everything Damon's *going* to tell us," Belkins said, coming around the side of the desk and looming over me menacingly. "I think if we got him into the right situation downtown, he might have a lot more to tell us."

Montgomery smoothed the front of his jacket. The green gemstones in his rings glistened in the overhead light. "You might be able to coerce a confession from him. Although I doubt it." He gave me a calculated look. I kept my eyes focused straight ahead. "But then what would you have? A coerced confession. Probably be thrown out of court. No point undermining our credibility."

"A confession is a confession," Belkins said, leaning down so his face was close to mine. I could smell alcohol and stale cigar mingled with his aftershave. "And scum is scum. He ought to be locked up."

Montgomery moved over to the door and opened it. "We know where he works. We know where he lives. We can always pick him up again, anytime. Isn't that right, Damon?"

I moved my gaze to the floorboards just beyond the tips of my boots, avoiding eye contact with either one of them. "Yes, sir," I said.

"You can go now." Montgomery gestured toward the open door.

"Thank you, sir." I stood up.

Belkins coughed. "And stay away from women and children, you hear?" he said, "or I'll see you spend the rest of your life locked up."

I wasted no time scrambling down the hallway and the stairs. I grabbed my lunchbox from the plating room office and my jacket from its hook by the time clock. I struggled into the jacket as I pushed through the doorway to the street. Flipping up the hood and hunching my shoulders into the weather, I headed back to my tiny apartment.

Exhausted, I took a quick shower and fell into bed.

\* \* \* \*

When I got to work that night, John put me back on the plater. The heavy steel cabinets were done; my plater was running some long wire shelving. After the cabinets, they seemed weightless and easy to handle.

Hank nodded as I quickly swung into the plater's rhythm. He leaned in close and shouted, "Figured you'd make a plater operator. You may not be all that big, but you're quick and wiry."

I nodded my thanks.

As lunch approached, I was surprised to feel a cramp in my gut. But not the same kind of cramp as when I heard a cell door slam behind me. Strange, yet not an entirely unpleasant sensation.

I realized that I didn't know whether I hoped I'd see Kelly at the lunch table again or if I dreaded it.

On my budget, my lunch wasn't much different from last night's. Two peanut butter sandwiches, somewhat less squashed because they had been in the lunchbox, not my pocket. And the thermos was full of hot instant coffee, not water.

Had Kelly felt sorry for me? Did she see me as some kind of pathetic loser? My stomach, cramp and all, lurched at that thought. Whatever happened, I didn't want to look pathetic in Kelly's eyes.

I was a convicted murder, for heaven's sake. Most people thought I was a pathetic loser. What difference would it make what Kelly thought?

But I did really want to sit across the table from her, to see her long dark hair, hear her laugh. I could do that all night. A new feeling for me.

Kelly's lunch time was another one of the many things not under my control. Probably fortunate. By the time I got to the lunch table, I was so tongue-tied that I would have made a fool of myself if I'd tried to talk to her. When I arrived, the only one sitting there was a skinny kid with acne, morosely sipping from a can of grape soda. His lunch seemed to consist primarily of a cold hot dog and several candy bars.

At least my peanut butter sandwiches were meant to be eaten cold.

I plunked myself down and opened my lunchbox. The kid looked over at me and stopped with his hot dog halfway to his mouth. He stared, blinking rapidly.

"You're Jesse Damon, aren't you?" he asked. His teeth were discolored and worn.

I briefly wondered if I should have gone somewhere else to eat, and then decided, no, if this kid didn't want to eat lunch with me, he could find someplace else.

"Yeah," I said, unwrapping one of my sandwiches.

"Name's Aaron. I heard about you."

I nodded an acknowledgement and wondered what he had heard about me.

"I just want you to know, a lot of us understand that Mitch had it coming," he said, wiping his hand on the front of his greasy gray sweatshirt.

"Yeah?" I asked, taking a bite of my sandwich.

"Yeah. He'd been cheating a lot of us," the kid said.

"You don't say."

"At first, he was pretty reliable. Could get hold of all the weed you wanted. And then he started selling that crystal meth."

The kid scratched the back of his hand. Probably a user himself. None of my business.

He glanced at me and looked away. "I think he started using himself."

"Pretty common." I poured coffee into the thermos cup.

"Now we got to find a new dealer."

Didn't seem it would do any good to suggest maybe he kick the habit before it got him locked up, so I just nodded.

"You know anybody?" he asked.

That took me by surprise. "Sure don't," I said. "I don't need to be messing with nothing like that."

"But you must have contacts," he whined.

"Not that kind, for sure. And I like going home at night. Beats the hell out of a prison cell."

The kid looked at me. "People make a lot of money dealing," he said. "Most of them don't get caught."

I narrowed my eyes and stared at him. "Most do eventually. Street-level dealers don't last long. They either wise up and get out of the business, get locked up, or get killed."

"Well, Mitch'd been doing it for a while. He made a lot of money."

"Mitch got killed."

That shut him up for a few minutes. I finished my sandwiches and drained the last of my coffee.

"Did Mitch make his own meth?" the kid asked.

"Don't know."

"Must have come from somewhere. And it ain't that hard to make." The hot dog lay half eaten on the table in front of him.

I shrugged. If this kid really thought I was involved in the drug trade with Mitch, nothing I said to him was going to convince him otherwise. I just hoped he didn't feel compelled to share his thoughts about my "contacts" with Belkins or Montgomery.

"A couple of us was wondering, if Mitch made his own stuff, what happened to the lab equipment and supplies?" So much for keeping his thoughts to himself.

"Don't ask me." I screwed the top on my thermos and put it into my lunchbox.

"Well, could you pass on the word that we'd be happy to take it off of whoever's hands, if they want? I got a good place to set it up, an old barn nobody ever goes to." His hands were twitching nervously.

"Don't hold your breath." I shut my lunch box and got to my feet.

The kid sat there. He must be overstaying his eighteen-minute lunch. I wondered if his pay would be docked.

"I get it," he said, rubbing the side of his face nervously. "You don't know me, so you can't talk to me, right? Well, I was a good customer of Mitch's. And I never said a word. Anybody'll tell you that."

I thought about pointing out that, for someone who claimed to have never said a word, he'd just told me a lot. But I couldn't see that it would do any good, so I just threw away my trash.

"Somebody like you, you're more of an enforcer than a dealer, anyhow, aren't you?" He scratched the side of his face. "I can tell. You have those cold gray eyes."

Enforcer. How many of my co-workers thought that? I could just imagine Belkins questioning everyone on the shift, which I was quite sure he and Montgomery either had done or were going to do, and having several people repeat that. Belkins had already made up his mind about me. I'd just as soon, though, he not get anyone else contributing to his suspicions. And it might influence the way Montgomery looked at me.

"Look." Aaron tossed the half-eaten hot dog in the trash. "I don't care what you done. Ain't nothing to me. I'm ready to do business. If you want."

I shook my head. A common prison saying—"Don't deny, don't defend"—flashed through my mind. People like Aaron believed what they wanted to believe. Saying anything to him would just encourage him to keep badgering me. I picked up my lunchbox and headed back to the plating room to finish out my shift. Hank treated me just like he always had.

When I got out at eight, the weather was even worse, at least for walking. The sleet was changing to a driving rain, but the sidewalks were still icy underfoot. The dark, empty storefronts loomed over the cracked sidewalks. Of the few places that remained in business, only the Laundromat and the Korean convenience store were open. The gloom swallowed up the feeble light shining through their windows.

I had my weekly appointment with my parole officer in two hours. The whole municipal complex, with the courthouse, the local lockup, and the parole office, was in the opposite direction from my place. Maybe I could find someplace to hole up for an hour or so.

The library. I loved the library. Mrs. Coleman, the mother in the foster home where I had lived for most of my early teen years, had unlocked the treasures of the public library for me. She took all "her" kids there on a weekly basis and encouraged us to read.

It was prison, though, that really taught me to appreciate libraries. When I was first settled in at the institution where I would be spending the foreseeable future, I faced a mind-numbing succession of hours and days and years stretching out before me, and I put in to visit the library as soon as I could. The prison's collection was limited, and each inmate could only go once a week and only take out three books at a time. I read everything I could get my hands on. A librarian at some point had purchased a whole set of classic literature. I became quite fond of Shakespeare and Dickens.

When I was released less than two months ago, I knew home detention meant I was going to be in my apartment for hours at a time. I didn't have a TV or radio. The public library would be free, and I made it a priority to find it. I was lucky it was located in same county government complex as the parole office.

Mr. Ramirez, my parole officer, allowed me some time to run errands and become familiar with the neighborhood. I headed straight for the library.

Of course, I needed a card before I could take anything out. To get the card, I needed proof of residency and some form of picture identification. My month-to-month lease provided the proof of residency. My only form of identification was my prison ID.

The lady at the desk was a tall, sallow blonde with a name tag that read, "Mandy." She was very pretty, but otherwise looked just like I would expect a librarian to look. Reluctantly, I pulled out my prison ID and handed it to her.

She frowned. "Is this all you have?" she asked.

"With a picture? Yes." I felt the heat rising on my neck.

"I guess I can be content with that," she said, filling in the blanks on the form.

"Thank you."

She smiled. "'My crown is called content...'"

I grinned back. "'...a crown that seldom kings enjoy,'" I finished.

Her eyes opened wide. "You know Shakespeare?"

"I've read a little."

She laughed. "He also said, 'Neither a borrower nor a lender be.'"

"I don't think he was talking about libraries."

"You're probably right. Or I'd be out of a job." She punched something into her keyboard. The gray machine on the desk whirred to life and spat out a card, which she handed to me.

I always looked for her at the front desk when I went into the library. Often, she was working. She'd smile at me. I always smiled back. Pleasant interactions like that, even if they seemed pretty much insignificant to most people, meant a lot to me.

The library steps were covered with salt and melting ice. I bounded up them.

But the library didn't open until nine. I stood in the sleet, my hands jammed in my pockets and my hood up, wondering if I should just wait. The entrance offered no shelter.

The sleet cut into my face. I could feel dampness beginning to creep through the shoulders and back of my jacket. I shivered.

A twenty-four hour diner was about two blocks away. Maybe I could nurse a cup of coffee for a while. I headed in that direction.

I hesitated on the sidewalk outside the diner's door. But the wind picked up, driving an icy trickle down my neck. I shoved the door open and stepped inside.

Bacon. Coffee. Fresh bread and cinnamon. The comforting scents filled my nose. A line of people stood at the cashier's station, ordering coffee and breakfast for takeout. The diner itself wasn't crowded. Several of the booths were occupied. Only one person sat at the counter. A tall, well-dressed woman with her back to the door.

I stood aside from the line, my battered lunchbox under my arm. Pulling a handful of change from my pocket, I counted it. I looked up at the breakfast menu. The prices weren't bad, but I really couldn't afford much.

The plant would be closed all next week for Christmas. For long-term employees, it was a paid vacation week. For new hires not yet in the union, it would be an unpaid week. I hadn't even been there long enough to collect unemployment compensation for the week. It was going to put a real crimp in my already tight budget. And I'd probably have to stay home the time I'd normally be out working. Depressing.

Not realistic to think Mr. Ramirez, my parole officer, would let me wander the streets from midnight to eight. Maybe if I asked, he would extend my daytime hours out.

And maybe not. Why should he?

Definitely have to make it to the library and get out some of the biggest books they had. A week in that little room without enough to read would drive me crazy. Or crazier than I already was.

The line at the cashier's station had grown much shorter. I stepped to the end to order. If I got my coffee here, I hoped I could get away with not leaving a tip. Then what? Maybe I could go sit way at the end of the counter, up against the wall. I hated the exposed feeling of sitting in the middle of the diner.

My steaming coffee came in a thick white mug. If I'd ever noticed how good fresh-brewed coffee smelled, I'd forgotten.

Someone—a woman with a floppy red hat that shielded her face—half-stood in one of the booths. She was gesturing in my direction. I glanced behind me to see who she meant. Everyone else had left.

Surely she wasn't gesturing at me? Why would anyone be doing that?

# CHAPTER 6

The woman pushed the hat back. It was Kelly. I turned again to look behind me, see if she could mean anybody but me.

She put her hands on her hips and glared toward me. "You," she mouthed. "Jesse."

Unsure, I approached her.

"Have a seat," she said, indicating the worn vinyl bench across the table from her.

I put my coffee on the table and slid across the seat to where the back of the booth and the wall made a corner. Although I tried to be careful, my leg brushed hers as I slid in. Felt like a contact with an electric magnet. My knee tingled and wanted to go back to touch hers again. I glanced across the table at her. She leaned forward, her heavy breasts in a loose blue sweatshirt resting on the tabletop. Her hair was escaping from where it was loosely gathered at her neck. It covered her forehead and dipped toward her snapping dark eyes. She gripped a mug of hot coffee in her hands.

Gentle wisps of steam rose from my wet jacket. It smelled of wet wool. We both smelled of the factory: oil and chemicals. I'd been working in the hot plating room all night; I probably smelled of sweat, too. I didn't want to get too close and have to watch her wrinkle her nose at me.

I didn't know what to do with my hands. I began to make a star pattern around my coffee mug with the sugar packets.

"They make a good breakfast here," Kelly said. She lifted her nose and inhaled.

"Yeah," I said. I hoped it was the bacon and coffee aroma she was getting. Not me.

"You live around here?" she asked.

"Kind of," I said, embarrassed to admit to the dump I called home. *Lots better than a prison cell,* I reminded myself. "I got a meeting with my parole officer at ten. Didn't make much sense to walk all the way home and then back in this direction. Not in this weather."

She nodded. "How's the parole going?"

I sighed and lowered my head. "That arrest. It's a violation. Could lock me back up." I moved the sugar packets into a new pattern. Prison bars.

"But they didn't even charge you," Kelly said.

"Still a violation, if they want to call me on it." I rearranged the sugar packets so they formed thick bars.

The waitress arrived with two breakfast platters. Eggs. Bacon. Fried potatoes with onions. Pancakes. She put one in front of each of us.

"Freshen your coffee?" She filled both mugs without waiting for an answer and hurried off.

"I didn't order this," I protested, staring at all that food.

"I ordered it for you," Kelly said.

Miserably, I reached into my pocket. "I don't think I've got enough to pay for it."

"I wouldn't have ordered it for you if I'd expected you to pay for it." Kelly picked up her fork and broke the yolk of one of her eggs.

"I can't take this," I protested, watching the rich yellow flood toward her potatoes. The tantalizing scent of onions and bacon filled my nose. I was usually a little hungry. Now I was ravenous.

"Why not?" she asked, pouring syrup on her pancakes. "It'll just go to waste if you don't eat it."

"You can't be buying me breakfast," I said. Syrup mixed with melting butter and soaked into the pancakes on her plate.

"I just did." She cut a wedge of the pancakes and lifted it toward her mouth. "It'd be rude of you not to eat it."

I stared at the sugar packets.

"You don't want to be rude, do you?" she asked, spearing a piece of bacon.

I looked at the food. "Thank you," I said, picking up my fork to break my own egg yolks. I speared half an egg into my mouth. I'd never tasted anything so good.

"I hope the babysitter got the kids off to school all right." Kelly glanced at her watch. "I usually go right home and make sure everything's okay, but I have to go grocery shopping, and it's never good to go into the supermarket hungry."

My heart sank. Kelly had kids. Of course she had kids. She was a woman. Women had kids. And husbands. Why should I feel a pang in my gut when I thought of her being married? Wasn't like I had anything to offer her.

And what had I expected? She was just being friendly. Probably doing what she thought her old man would have liked someone to do for him under similar circumstances.

I should be grateful for that. More than anybody else did for me. More than I could do for myself right now.

Instead, I felt anger. Anger at myself being in a position where I had to let a woman buy me a meal. Anger at the system for putting so many roadblocks in my way as I tried to improve things. Anger at Belkins for being so sure I'd killed Mitch. Anger at the man who could take Kelly's warm body in his arms and kiss her.

I took a deep breath. Anger would get me nowhere. Especially irrational anger against a man I didn't know who hadn't done anything to me.

I wanted to take Kelly out to dinner, buy her something that would make her smile, talk smoothly and hear her laugh.

Instead, here I sat, eating breakfast on her dime. I couldn't ask her out; I was on home detention. And it had been so long since I'd had a social conversation with a woman, I was having trouble thinking of anything to say.

Right. So what gave me the idea I had any right to resent that she had a life and I didn't?

I got a grip on myself and asked, "How many kids you got?"

"Two. An eight-year-old boy and a six-year-old girl. They're both in school all day. I hire a college student to sleep in while I'm at work. She gets them up and off to school in the morning. It's a lot cheaper than daycare. But not a hundred percent reliable."

A big part of me didn't want to know the answer, but I asked anyhow. "How about their daddy? Can't he help out?" I tried the potatoes. They were perfectly fried, crisp on the outside and soft on the inside, with just enough onion.

Kelly snorted derisively. "My ex? He don't want to actually have to take care of them. All he wants is his 'rights.' Just like when we were married. He doesn't really want to see the kids, but he insists on as much visitation as he can get."

I was pleased to hear that. Then I was ashamed of being pleased. And I definitely didn't want to hear about those "rights" he demanded when they were married. Still, sad for Kelly and the kids. I couldn't see that, under the present circumstances, it did me any good.

Kelly swirled a bit of her pancake in the syrup on her platter. "He's got them for all of Christmas week." She put her fork down and picked up her napkin to wipe her nose. Her brown eyes looked watery.

*Please don't cry,* I begged silently. I had no idea how I could begin to handle that. I could never handle it when I cried, much less if a woman cried on me.

"Christmas is overrated anyhow." I cut a wedge of pancakes with my fork.

Kelly dabbed her eyes with the napkin. "Yeah, I guess you're right about that." She laughed.

I tried to remember Christmases from my childhood. My mother had died when I was three, and the old man had been in prison. The thought "like father, like son" flitted through my mind. I squelched it firmly.

I had lived in various foster homes until he got out when I was fourteen. Most of the early holidays were a blur. Big trees with tinsel that I wasn't allowed to touch. Noisy parties for foster children at the fire hall. We'd all gotten presents. Sometimes, the Santa got them mixed up. One year, all I'd gotten was a package with a Barbie doll and clothes for it. I gave it to a little girl who showed up on Christmas afternoon at the temporary foster home where I was staying. Her eyes had been swollen almost shut with bruises. She'd lost most of the doll clothes right away, but she'd carried that Barbie with her everywhere. Mostly by the hair. Later, I'd heard she'd died in a fire her mother set in their apartment.

Best years were my early teen years with the Colemans. They didn't make a big deal of holidays, mostly an extra-long church service in the morning and one of Mrs. Coleman's plain but hearty meals topped off with a special dessert. Practical presents like warm sweaters and school supplies.

"When will you get the kids back?" I asked Kelly.

"New Year's Eve." Kelly brushed her hair off her forehead. "Of course he don't want to be tied down on party night. Although he usually foists them off on his mother or his sister anyhow." She took a big gulp of her coffee.

I looked in dismay at the empty platter in front of me. I had gobbled it all down. In the prison chow hall, I would barely have time to grab my food, sit down, and shovel it in before we were being hustled out to make room for the next group. Deeply ingrained habits die hard.

No doubt about it, this was the best meal I had eaten in a long, long time. Least I could do was let Kelly know. Why was that so hard?

"That was wonderful," I made myself say. "Thank you."

"You're welcome." She beckoned the waitress over for a refill of the coffee mugs.

I warmed my hands on my mug and stared out the window. The icy rain was as heavy as ever.

"So," Kelly said, stirring thick creamer into her coffee. "What do you think happened to old Mitch?"

I shrugged. "I thought he was beat up and maybe run over by the forklift."

"I heard he got hit over the head. Probably from behind. They did say something about him being run over, but that might be somebody exaggerating. The forklift was next to him, though, and it was running."

"Where did they find him?" I added the luxurious creamer to my coffee, too. I hadn't realized such a thing existed.

"Back in the warehouse. And they found a lot of other stuff there, too. Some of his drugs. Kind of confirms what we all knew, huh?"

"Yeah," I agreed, thinking of Aaron, the kid who thought I knew where to get drugs. And who was away from the line when Mitch was killed.

Kelly leaned back and stretched. Her full breasts strained against her sweatshirt. I tried to keep my gaze on the table. It wasn't easy.

"What did he have?" I asked. Why would he be stupid enough to keep drugs at work? Unless he'd been taking enough meth to totally rattle his brains.

"A lot of grass," she said. "Can you believe it? Whole bales. Shrink-wrapped. Using the company equipment. Like he was going to ship it. I can't quite figure out how he managed to do that."

"Really?" Did sound a bit outrageous, but I supposed it could happen.

"Yep. He's pretty much the only one who goes back there on our shift. If the afternoon shift doesn't get everything out to shipping, he's supposed to take care of it. I'm the only other person who might go back there, and then only if he's forgotten to get something I need to load. Except the foreman, of course. But as long as Mitch's job is getting done, he's not going to hike all the way back there. That's how they found him; John went looking for him 'cause nobody was delivering parts to the work stations."

"Wouldn't somebody on the other shifts notice whole bales of grass? Or smell it?" I asked. "Even shrink-wrapped?"

"I guess he hid the stuff pretty well." Kelly shook her head. A few strands of hair worked their way loose. "All he'd have to do was move empty containers out, put the bales behind them, and then put the containers back in front. And I guess a good shrink-wrap job would keep the smell down."

I wanted to tuck the loose hair back behind her ear. Instead, I concentrated on my coffee. So much better than the instant stuff I'd been making. And so rich and smooth with the creamer in it. I put a coffee maker on my short list of things to get as soon as I could afford it. Along with the warm gloves. Goodwill hadn't had any gloves when I was there, but they'd had a whole section of small appliances.

"And I guess there was some meth, too," she said. "I thought a few of those kids on the packing line were gonna cry when someone said they'd confiscated that. They might be into it kind of heavy."

I wondered if Aaron could have been out looking in the warehouse where Mitch had some stuff stashed. Would they have been stupid enough to be dealing right there, during work hours? And could they have gotten into an argument?

Kelly stacked our platters and put the utensils on them. "It was all in little baggies, packaged for sale. And right out in the open. Kind of like he was sorting it out to fill orders or something."

I held my coffee where the comforting aroma filled my nose. "If he was selling to people at work, maybe Mitch got in a fight with one of his customers." Thank goodness I'd been in plain sight most of the night on the plater.

"I guess that could happen." Kelly brushed her hair out of her eyes.

The warm mug felt good on my hands. "Or maybe he was getting so paranoid that somebody decided to permanently take care of the problem before he did something totally stupid and got other people in trouble, too."

Kelly gave me a strange look.

Was that the kind of thought that would only occur to a killer? I shifted uncomfortably on the seat. I had to be more careful of the dumb things I blurted out.

"You know who Sterling Radman is?" Kelly drained her mug.

"Yeah. I had to go see him yesterday. See if I still had my job."

"He's been acting weird lately. Some people say he's been buying stuff from Mitch."

"The plant supervisor?" I tried to picture the man I had spoken to buying illegal street drugs. Carefully dressed. A little on the fidgety side, but being in an office alone with someone he knew had been convicted of murder might account for that. As far as I could remember, he'd been a nice pink color, cheeks well filled out, no obvious paranoia or itching. Not my image of a meth user. "Doesn't he work days?" I asked.

"Well, yeah." Kelly pushed back the sleeve of her sweatshirt. Her wrists were thick and capable. "But he's the plant manager. He likes to come into the plant at night and sneak around. See what everybody's up to. And he was in that night."

"I didn't see him."

"I didn't see him, either," Kelly said, "but I was a little late. My babysitter had car trouble. And then, when I finally got here, a semi was trying to back through the shipping gate, so I drove around behind the plant to get to the parking lot. His silver Mercedes was parked by the fence along the road back there. He usually parks in a reserved space up front."

Someday, I'd have a car—or a pickup—if I was able to stay out of prison long enough.

Kelly nodded toward the tall woman who was getting up from a stool at the counter. "That's his wife right there. I went to school with her. Only reason she'd be stopping in here to get breakfast is because hubby wasn't home to cook for."

I was surprised I recognized her. Mandy. I'd never have thought of them as an item. Shows how much I've got to learn about how people get hooked up.

We watched as she straightened her skirt, went up to the cashier to pay her bill, and left.

"Didn't anybody see Radman last night?" I asked.

"I imagine the foreman must have." She wiped her mouth with a paper napkin and put it on the stacked platters. A plump, inviting mouth. "John was mad. I heard him tell the day foreman Radman'd left a whole list of things they'd have to take care of. Stupid stuff like moving the empty pallets from the loading dock and making sure no one's smoking in the bathrooms."

"Does Radman do that a lot? Come in during the middle of the night?"

"He seems to. I think even John has finally figured out that Radman's been spying on all of us, trying to make trouble for anyone he can."

I leaned back in my seat. "Why would he want to do that?"

"Who knows? Radman's only worked here for a few years. He was hired from outside. They said they wanted fresh oversight. Maybe this is his idea of 'fresh oversight.'"

"Doesn't his wife work at the library?"

"Yeah." Kelly gathered up all the empty sugar packets and put them on top of the platters. "She quit for a while last year when she married Radman. Plenty of money. But after a while, she asked for her old job back. She told everybody she didn't like being home alone all day. Maybe she really meant being home alone all night."

"She's pretty. You'd think any man would want to stay home at night with a wife who looks like that."

Kelly grinned. "You'd think, wouldn't you? And she's nice, too. Or she was when we were in high school. A little spoiled, maybe, but shy, not stuck up. She was an only child, and her parents gave her everything. She inherited her parents' house and money, so she's okay financially, too. Even without Radman."

"You don't think Radman could have introduced her to meth, do you?" I didn't want to think of Mandy using, but she was very thin.

"Who knows? She doesn't seem like the type, but then, who does?" Kelly stared into her now empty mug. "One thing for sure. Mitch had something going with Radman."

"What makes you say that?"

"Mitch was absolutely golden. He could do no wrong. I had to pick up the slack, so I bitched to John. John was already aware of what was going on. I know John's complained about him. He even tried to get him fired or transferred to another shift where he'd get better supervision. But no go."

"Wouldn't the union step in and try to save his job?"

"If it got to that. But it's hard to keep that kind of union action quiet in the shop. So don't think it ever got that far. Somebody's protecting him. Probably somebody in management."

"Why would they do that?"

"How can you ever tell why management does anything? Although a few years ago, they planted someone on the packing line. Cops trying to figure out a fencing operation."

A chill ran down my spine. Were any of the people I was working with police informants? Like Aaron? "They get anybody?" I asked.

"Got the goods on a truck driver who was transporting stolen goods, but I heard he rolled over on his sources and wasn't charged. Turned out nobody working here was involved, although they tried hard to pin something on the packing line group leader."

Changing to another important subject that didn't unsettle my now-full stomach, I said, "Union protection pretty good?" I would be grateful for that when I got it. *If* I got it. I still had a ways to go.

"Yeah. As long as you're not a total goof-up." Kelly put her mug on the table. "I've even seen Radman talk to Mitch a few times. Radman pretty much thinks he's only required to talk directly to God. Otherwise, he leaves notes for the foremen or sends one of the office girls to carry his messages."

"Do you think Radman could have killed Mitch?" Didn't seem likely to me, but then, I'd known a lot of unlikely seeming criminals over the years.

"Who knows?" Kelly said again. "Although, it's not like Radman to get his hands dirty. So even if he was involved, he'd get somebody else to do it for him. And he would have made sure he was far away when it happened. He wouldn't be roaming around the plant."

Being far away when it happened made sense to me, but leaving someone else around who could snitch him out didn't.

She tossed money on the table. Enough for the check and a generous tip for the hardworking waitress. "You want me to wait for you to get done with your PO so I can give you a ride home?"

I was surprised. Why would she do that? "No. You done more than enough."

"If you have to walk, you'll get soaked," she said.

I shrugged. Big deal. "Got no idea how long I'll be. Sometimes they like to keep you waiting. It's a game, like. Could be hours."

"I can swing by after I get my shopping done."

"Besides, if they decide to violate me, they'll hold me for a hearing and lock me up right from there. I'd have no way of letting you know." I wanted to add, *If they do that, I may never see you again. And I want to see you again.* But that sounded stupid, even in my mind.

She looked uncertain.

"You got to get some sleep," I said. "Especially if your kids are coming home after school. They don't need a mom who's exhausted."

"You're right." Kelly stood up and grabbed her jacket from the seat beside her. "I do need to get up when they get home. I'll just drop you off."

"My appointment's not until ten. Why don't you drop me off at the library? It's right down the block, and I can read the newspapers or something." Newspapers were a luxury too expensive for my budget.

"Sounds like a plan to me." Kelly led the way to the door and began to struggle into her jacket.

I had enough sense to hold it so she could slip it on. My hand tingled where it brushed her hair. When she had it on, she smiled and tilted her face up at me. I was very tempted to put my arm around her shoulders and give those lips a quick kiss, but I thought much better of it.

Walking behind her out of the diner and to her car, I felt a whole new set of feelings raging inside me. It was all I could do to keep them from surfacing, much less try to sort them out. Alone at night, lying in my bed, would be the time to deal with them. Not here. And certainly not at the parole office.

I rode silently in the passenger seat of her car. The last time I'd been in a car without being handcuffed was years ago, when my brothers had stolen one and taken me joyriding with them. They had gotten so drunk, I'd had to drive, even though I was only fifteen and had never driven before. They'd had to tell me what to do. They'd thought it was hysterically funny.

The streets were slick. Drops of frozen rain lashed the windshield and melted, only to be swept away by the wipers. Kelly concentrated on her driving.

She pulled up in front of the library. Long, wide steps reached up to the heavy double front doors set between concrete pillars. I climbed out and thanked her.

"See you at work tonight," she said.

I watched her drive away. I hoped I would see her, too.

I bounded up the steps and pulled open the door. The welcoming scent of paper and ink greeted me. A harried woman with several children stood at the front desk. Mandy was explaining how to fill out the forms to get library cards. She wore a green vest with sequined snowmen over a turtleneck shirt. Her hair, usually done up, swirled around her trim shoulders. I smiled at her, but she was too busy to notice.

The newspapers were laid out on a table by a few worn easy chairs. Only one of the chairs was occupied, by a gaunt man who sat staring blankly across the room. I'd seen him at the library before; he must've hung around a lot.

The headline of the local paper blared, "Holiday Parade a Success."

I reached for it. I wanted to see what the paper had to say about Mitch's death. Surely they'd have something, even if it was on an inside page.

The other man's hand darted out and snagged the paper before I could pick it up. Surprised, I looked at him. He glared back at me, clutching the paper to his chest.

Okay. No big deal. I picked up the Washington Post. Regional and national news. Probably the paper I would get if I were buying. For one thing, it had great comics. Two pages of them.

I settled into a chair against the wall and flipped to the comic pages. I kept an eye on the other man. He wasn't looking at the paper he had so rudely snatched away from me.

One of the scariest prospects for someone who's been locked up for years is being released with no job and nowhere to go. Public libraries were known to be usually pretty tolerant of homeless people who wanted a warm, dry place out of the elements for a few hours. This guy looked like he fit the bill.

When the clock read half past nine, I folded the paper neatly and put it back. The strange man was still sitting there, still holding the local paper. Still not reading it. I wondered whether he ever gave the staff grief. I didn't like the thought of Mandy having to deal with him.

Mandy was alone at the desk when I went by. I paused to say hello. She stopped her filing and smiled at me.

"Is that guy over there okay?" I kept my voice low and nodded toward the man.

Mandy looked over. "Yes. That's Gustavus. He's a little strange, but he's okay. Been around for years. I think he stays at the homeless shelter. He does odd chores around the neighborhood. Sometimes my husband hires him to rake leaves or something."

I wasn't particularly reassured, but if Mandy was comfortable with him, it really wasn't any of my business what he was up to. I shrugged.

"Not checking out any books?" Mandy asked.

"I got an appointment. Might stop on the way home if I have time." I didn't want to have to worry about library books in the parole office. Not a good place to leave stuff lying around.

"Take care now," Mandy said. She shook her hair back.

Dusky round marks on her neck, partially hidden by her hair and the turtleneck. Bruises made by fingers? I tried to see without staring.

Mandy turned away and picked up a stack of books.

"You take care, too," I said.

She nodded.

Nothing I could do. I zipped up my jacket and headed out the door.

# CHAPTER 7

The basement waiting room for the parole office was hot and stuffy. The radiators up against the scarred paneled walls hissed and groaned. Moisture condensed in droplets on the windows set high in the wall.

The receptionist's frosted glass window was closed, but a clipboard lay on the ledge. I took it and printed my name and time of arrival on the otherwise empty sheet of paper. Taking off my damp jacket, I bundled it up and tried to wipe a spot dry on the seat of a worn bench. I was early. No one else was there yet. I leaned back and waited, my jacket and lunchbox next to me.

The inner door opened, releasing a blast of dry, cooler air. A shapely woman I had never seen before took the clipboard in her well-groomed hand. Her name tag read, "Miss Haverford."

I watched her through half-closed eyes.

She studied the clipboard, reaching through the helmet of her hair to scratch her head with a long scarlet fingernail. Snapping her gum, she looked around the room. I was still the only one there. Her gaze skimmed over me. She replaced the clipboard, turned on her spiked heel, and retreated, shutting the door and with it, the relief of the cooler air.

Not much for me to do but wait. Was Mr. Ramirez, my parole officer, even now calling for a police escort to take me upstairs to the local lockup pending a violation hearing? I'd seen people hauled off when they showed up for an appointment with their PO. Much easier than having the police go out and actually look for someone.

If Mr. Ramirez decided to hold a violation hearing, I had no illusions what the outcome would be. I would be violated and sent back to prison to serve out my sentence.

I couldn't sit still. I got to my feet and paced.

"Jesse Damon?" Miss Haverford was holding the door open.

"Yes, ma'am?"

"Please come back to my desk."

At least they hadn't just called to have me hauled in. I grabbed my things and followed her swaying hips. Her cloying perfume wafted back to me. I hoped it was strong enough to overpower my sweaty, oily smell.

She eased her rounded derriere into her desk chair and began to sort through some of the paperwork on her desk. Nothing for me to do but stand there patiently. She snapped her gum several more times.

Finally, she pulled a file folder up from one of the piles on her desk. She opened it and studied its contents.

"You're on home detention," she said.

"Yes, ma'am."

"Do you have the weekly monitoring fee?"

I reached into my pocket and pulled out my wallet with its meager supply of cash. I extracted two twenties and handed them to her. Pretty much the end of my folding money.

"Now." She scrutinized the papers in the file more closely. "Thirty-five dollars' weekly fee for urinalysis. Whether a sample is actually taken or not."

"I don't think I need one, ma'am." I hoped not. I didn't have another thirty-five dollars.

"Really?" she said. "Most people do."

"Yes, ma'am, but I have no recorded history of drug abuse."

Not quite sure how I had lucked out on that. When I was originally arrested, I was carrying enough heroin to supply half the state for a month. That got buried in the plea bargain to the more serious murder charge. And since the only drug use I actually had was breathing secondhand marijuana smoke from my father and brothers in the apartment when I was a kid, I'd been honest when I told the prison intake counselors I didn't use. That second-hand smoke hadn't been enough to show up on the tests.

She frowned, scanning her computer screen. "So I see. How about restitution?" She continued scrolling down.

"No restitution ordered, ma'am." The victim had been a drug dealer in his early twenties with several convictions under his belt and no relatives clamoring for a financial settlement. No one would claim him. Miraculously, no known offspring. Again, I had lucked out.

Miss Haverford peered at her screen and then at her keyboard. I wondered how her elegant fingers with those long nails could type anything, but they did. She waited for it to print and then handed the paper to me. "Your receipt," she said.

"Thank you." I folded it and put it in my pocket.

She turned away from the computer and shuffled papers for a few more minutes. "Mr. Ramirez is not in," she said. "Didn't you get a phone call this morning before you came in?"

I winced. "I work nights, ma'am. I came straight from work." Would I have to make a new appointment?

"Well, he called in sick. Then he's on vacation until after the new year." She lifted a sheet of paper from another pile on her desk and studied it. "He's left instructions for his caseload." She ran a scarlet fingernail down a list. "Some parolees have been given permission to go out of town for the holidays. Usually to visit relatives."

That wouldn't be me. I didn't know where any of my relatives were, and I wouldn't want to visit them if I did.

She put that list down and picked up another piece of paper. "You're on the list to be off monitoring from now until January second." She put a check mark on the list next to an entry.

I stood there stunned. "Are you sure?" I asked. "I mean, I don't have anyone to visit or anything. And I was picked up..." I let my voice trail off. I'd been about to volunteer that I'd been arrested. How stupid could I be?

If I'd seen Mr. Ramirez, I would have said something. Even if I'd seen a substitute parole officer. This lady hadn't introduced herself at all, much less as a parole officer. She seemed to be pushing paperwork, not making decisions. She didn't seem to care.

He should have gotten a routine notice when I was arrested. It usually didn't take long. Unless he'd been out sick for a few days and it was sitting in his mailbox right now. Probably he'd made up the list before that. Would he be mad that I didn't say anything?

"Well, I'm sure I don't know anything about that." Miss Haverford looked annoyed, reinforcing the idea that she didn't want to be bothered with troublesome details. "All I know is that's the list you're on. Don't take the box off. If you cut the strap, it'll cost you $350. It's just the monitoring that's suspended until then. And don't leave the state." She looked up at me sternly. "You do have to bring in the weekly monitoring fee anyhow."

"Yes, ma'am. I get paid tomorrow. I'll bring in the fee after I cash the check."

"Doesn't have to be so soon," she said. "You can pay two weeks' fees when you come in the next time."

What with the unpaid week off from work, that was going to leave me very short of cash. But it was non-negotiable.

A whole week and a half when I didn't have to watch the clock and be home by a certain time. That giddy concept was just beginning to sink in. Especially welcome when the plant was closed and I would have been stuck in my tiny apartment so much of the time.

"When does the monitoring start being suspended?"

"As of right now. Until your appointment the Thursday after New Year's." Miss Haverford was looking at me, her eyes cautious.

I made an effort to clear my face of emotion. Didn't want to set off alarm bells and have her decide she should get someone in to review the situation. "Yes, ma'am. Thank you, ma'am."

She turned to her computer again and started typing. I waited to see what else she had to say, but she didn't bother to look at me again. "That's all. You can go."

I walked out through the still-empty superheated waiting room, up the stairs, and onto the slushy sidewalk. The rain was turning back into sleet. A strange feeling of elation filled me. I didn't have to go straight home. I could stop at the library without worrying that I was spending too long picking out my books. I could go to the Laundromat. I could go for a walk. If I had any money, I could go shopping. And all whenever I wanted.

What I did was go straight home. I'd worked all night, and I hadn't gotten all that much sleep the day before. I had to work tonight. I was comfortably full from breakfast. A shower and bed beckoned. Tonight was the last night of work for a while. I would have an entire week to do other things.

Back in the apartment, I hung my wet jacket on the back of the wooden chair, draped the damp woolen socks on the radiator, and pulled the tongue of the work boots out so the inside could air out and dry. Maybe someday I could buy a second pair of boots. Then I took a quick shower and tumbled into the lumpy bed, and for a change, slept soundly until the alarm got me up for work.

An easy night. I ran light shelving on the plater the entire time. I was hoping to see Kelly again, but plater four broke down, making Hank late to relieve us for our breaks. I ate my peanut butter sandwiches at the table by myself.

Friday. Payday. When the shift broke, I hung around for my paycheck. Most people had direct deposit. When I had enough extra money so I could open a checking account, I would get direct deposit, too. Then I wouldn't have to wait around for the lady from payroll to bring the checks out to John.

Aaron was waiting for his paycheck, too. He approached me as if to say something, but seemed to think better of it and went to put a few coins in one of the vending machines. He got a candy bar, ripped it open, took a bite, and looked at it like it was made of sawdust. Swallowing what he was already chewing, he tossed the rest in the trash. He slid onto a bench at one of the tables and scratched his cheek so fiercely that he drew blood. Although any sound was lost in the din of the machinery, his fingers beat an unholy rhythm on the table. His leg trembled.

Hank came by; his oversized fur-trimmed anorak zipped against the cold outside. He handed John his clipboard and pointed to an entry. "Problem with plater four," he said. "But we got it going again. Might have somebody take a look at it."

"Thanks." John rifled through the sheets of paper on the clipboard.

Hank walked by me on his way out. He stopped and clasped my shoulder with his ham hock of a hand. "See you a week from Monday, okay?"

He'd caught me by surprise, but I didn't flinch. "Sure. Hope you have a good holiday with your family."

Hank nodded and left.

The lady from human resources finally arrived with the checks. She looked suspiciously at the small handful of us waiting, gave the checks to John, and retreated.

John handed me my check. He raised his bushy eyebrows. "You stay out of trouble, you hear?"

"Yes, sir," I said.

As I left, I mulled the fact that both Hank and John had gone out of their way to encourage me. Made me feel warmer than a jacket ever could. I would do my best to show them that their support was not misplaced.

Under the usual schedule, I would have to go home and stay there until Saturday morning, when Mr. Ramirez had designated six hours "errand time." I'd still go home to take a shower and change into a clean pair of jeans and a warm sweater—thank you, Goodwill thrift shop—but with the monitoring suspended, I didn't have to stay there.

I could go cash my check right now. The bank that handled the payroll opened at eight on Fridays so the night shift workers could stop in before their weekend started.

Without a bank account of my own, the best option I had for cashing my check was the bank on which it was drawn. The check cashing and payroll loan places charged a hefty fee for their services.

I walked the few blocks over, through the nearly deserted streets, stopping for an ambulance screaming up the ramp to the emergency entrance at the hospital. Seemed like while the rest of the jobs in town were drying up, the health industry was booming.

The bank building was old and elegant, dating back to the times when Rothsburg had been reasonably prosperous. As the teller counted out the money, I thanked Quality Steel for issuing picture ID cards to its staff. Otherwise, I would have been stuck with my old prison ID, like I had been for the library card. Maybe someday I could get a driver's license and use that for ID. Maybe someday I could even get a car. Seemed impossible, but not that long ago I would have laughed if someone had suggested that I would be standing in a bank, cashing a paycheck that I had earned myself.

When I got the money and moved away from the window, I peeled off four twenties to pay for two weeks of home detention monitoring and tucked them into the back of my wallet. Next Friday, I'd get a check to cover this week's work. The pay would be a few hours short since Belkins had me dragged out of there early that one morning.

*At least it was only a few hours,* I reminded myself. Things could have worked out a lot worse. Still might.

Then I'd go a week without a check for the holiday layoff. Next week's check would just about cover the January rent. I'd have to stretch what was left of this one for three weeks' worth of living expenses. More peanut butter and instant coffee.

*Peanut butter and instant coffee on my own terms, though,* I told myself firmly.

The wind had let up, and while the winter air was brisk, the sky was clear. I tossed back my hood to let the crisp morning air blow freely through my hair. I walked back toward my apartment. I'd catch a nap and then hit the library and get a few books.

Marvelous creations, public libraries. Aside from proof of identification and residency, they asked nothing from their users except respect for the library and its materials.

Torn newspaper and cigarette butts swirled in a sudden gust as I approached the faded brick façade of my building. Clouds scuttled in front of the sun. I flipped up the hood and pulled the jacket a bit tighter, quickening my pace.

Then I stopped short. A marked patrol car sat at the curb, right next to the stairwell that led from the sidewalk to my room. Probably not there by coincidence.

Slipping into a recessed entryway to a defunct grocery store down the block, I watched. I started to feel dizzy and realized I wasn't breathing. I made myself inhale.

A man in a wrinkled overcoat and crumpled hat emerged from the stairwell and approached the idling car. He removed the hat and leaned down to talk through the driver's window. As I watched, he straightened up and looked around.

Belkins. Only one reason to be there. Wanted to talk to me. Probably take me in for more questioning.

Montgomery was nowhere in sight. Not good.

The patrol car swung around and backed into the alley. If I'd been in my apartment, I could have looked out the window and seen its tires. But if I'd been in my apartment, I would probably be in the back seat of the car, hands cuffed behind my back.

No other outlet for that alley. The car had backed in far enough that it wasn't visible from the street.

Belkins turned away from where the car had stood and hunkered down in his baggy overcoat, mashing the hat back on his disheveled hair. He flipped his coat collar up and stepped into an entryway very similar to the one in which I stood. It, too, belonged to a defunct storefront—that one advertising video games, CDs, and DVDs. From it, he could keep an eye on the stairs leading down to my room.

Trash eddied on the sidewalk. A city bus swished through the half-frozen puddles at the bus stop. No one was waiting, so it didn't stop. A siren in the distance sounded, heading in the other direction.

I didn't have to go home. Belkins probably didn't realize that. He thought if I wasn't home already, I'd be there soon. If I didn't show up, he would be calling it in to Mr. Ramirez, who would not be back until after the holidays.

I rubbed the side of my face. Still a little tender, but the swelling was mostly gone.

With sudden resolve, I jerked up the hood of my jacket, stepped out onto the sidewalk, and walked back toward the plant. I kept my back to my apartment, Belkins, and the waiting patrol car. I wasn't sure where I was going, just away from Belkins and his handcuffs and interrogation rooms. I forced myself not to rush, to hold my head up, not to turn around and look back. I wished my jacket wasn't in such a visible black and red check pattern. It was the warmest one Goodwill had had for sale in my size. A hunter's jacket, with big patch pockets. At least a lot of people around here wore ones like it.

Belkins thought I had killed Mitch. Even if Hank continued to insist that he had seen me working the entire time, Belkins would be just as sure that I had been able to slip away for a few minutes or that Hank's records on when he gave breaks were wrong. People made mistakes about little details like that all the time. And the more they were asked about it, the more they convinced themselves they were right.

He thought if he kept at it, he would find the cracks in my alibi.

Belkins would not give up until he saw me off the street. In his mind, I was a danger to the public. Especially if he believed that garbage about me being some kind of sex pervert. Why didn't he check the sex offender's registry? I wasn't on it.

Was there anything I could do to convince him I wasn't the one he was looking for? At this point, he probably wasn't even listening to any alternative ideas, much less following up on them.

But Montgomery might listen.

Belkins was probably just hanging on until he could retire. Montgomery had Seeking Promotion written all over him.

So Montgomery was concerned about his career. Solving a difficult murder case would be a feather in his cap. And he wouldn't sacrifice his credibility in the courtroom; he wanted a case that would result in a conviction that would stand up if it was appealed.

Like any cop, he would shield a fellow officer from misconduct charges. Had to be frustrating, though, for him to watch Belkins push boundaries that might get them both in trouble.

I had one major advantage over Belkins and Montgomery in the investigation. I knew I wasn't involved in either Mitch's death or his drug dealings. Nobody else could be sure of that.

If anybody gave Montgomery some real lead, I couldn't see him ignoring it. He'd follow up on it, even if just so it couldn't be raised in court.

Maybe I was the one who had to give the lead to him. Maybe nobody else would.

Of course, first I'd have to find a lead.

Up until now, all the important decisions in my life had been completely out of my control. Only thing I could ever do was to live with the results as best I could. Thinking about things just made it worse.

The time had come to change that. If Belkins wasn't going to find out who killed Mitch, and if I didn't want to go down for the charge, I'd have to get to work.

# CHAPTER 8

As I walked back toward the plant, I tried to think this out. Made sense that Mitch's murder had something to do with his drug trade. Crystal meth didn't have to be imported and processed through major pipelines like heroin or cocaine, or even grown in basements with grow lights. It could be manufactured in small batches by anyone who figured out how to get ahold of the ingredients and had someplace secluded to cook it. Some people did it in mobile labs in vans, or even the trunks of cars.

Kelly said Mitch lived in an isolated house about four miles up the dirt road that ran behind the plant. Aaron had asked whether Mitch had his own lab. Maybe he was on to something.

Four miles wasn't that far to walk. Not when I had all day. All week, in fact. The wind was cold when it gusted occasionally, but the sun was peeking through the clouds. I pulled my jacket sleeves down a little to cover my hands. The sweater added a welcome layer of warmth.

Belkins wouldn't be happy if he discovered I was trying to find out what had happened. He'd call Mr. Ramirez and ask to have me locked up for interfering with his investigation. I really didn't want to spend the rest of my life in prison.

But that's what Belkins wanted to happen anyhow. Was he even looking into any other possibilities? I felt a flash of anger when I thought about his assumption that I must have killed Mitch. Even if he thought I'd killed that drug dealer years ago—which I was sure he did—couldn't people change?

If I got locked up again, I'd never forgive myself for not taking this chance to see if I could find out what had really happened.

I circled the chain link fence surrounding Quality Steel's shipping yard, waited for two semis to pull through the open gate, and then headed up the muddy road into the hills.

For the first hour and a half or so, I enjoyed the walk. As I climbed higher, the scent of pine trees filled the air. Patches of slushy snow dropped from branches. Small animals scurried in the underbrush. Except for the road and the overhead utility lines, I saw no evidence of human existence. Felt good to be alive and free. Maybe this was why some folks raved about hiking. Maybe I'd have to look into it. After I was off home detention, of course.

Then the sky began to grow darker. The wind picked up, and I noticed that the mud in the road was beginning to freeze. A few sharp needles of frozen rain slashed against my face. More followed.

I ducked my head, but the cold wind hit my face. This wasn't as much fun as when I'd started out. What had I expected in December, though? A spring thaw? The freezing rain got heavier. I kept going, assuring myself that the return trip would be easier, since it would be downhill and I'd have the wind at my back.

I had to be pretty close to Mitch's house. Unless I had already passed it. I didn't remember any driveways or roads branching off for the last few miles. Wouldn't I have noticed? And wouldn't there be a mailbox on the road? I decided to keep going a little longer and see if I couldn't locate the house. I had to be getting close.

What would I do when I got there? I had some vague notion of poking around, looking for a meth lab in a shed or something. Even if I found one, then what? Trudge back to town and call Montgomery?

If Mitch's wife and kids were there, trespassing would not be a good idea. Any sensible woman seeing someone she didn't know on her property would call 9-1-1. I was sure those weren't circumstances under which I wanted to encounter the police.

Should have thought this through better. I could have just gone to the library and stayed there for a few hours to see if Belkins got tired of waiting.

Maybe Mitch's wife and the kids would be somewhere else, staying with relatives. Mitch had only been dead three days. The coroner probably hadn't released the body yet, so there may not have been a funeral. And it was just before the holidays. Terrible time for a family to lose a husband and father. For sure, her family wouldn't leave her and her kids in an isolated house at a time like this, would they?

I could at least find the house. If anyone was home, I would leave immediately. If it appeared to be unoccupied, I would have a look around outside. Active meth labs had a distinctive ammonia smell. That would be hard to get rid of. It might linger for a while even after production was stopped.

A mailbox came into sight as I rounded a curve. The name and number were too worn to read. A feeder line left the utility pole and snaked back along a narrow dirt track scarred with tire ruts. I followed it.

The track rose. As I climbed along it, another unhappy thought entered my head. Certainly the police had been here, at least to tell the widow of Mitch's death and ask her some questions. I hoped it had been someone more sensitive than Belkins who carried the news. They'd almost surely searched for evidence that might shed any light on his murder. If there had been a meth lab, they would have discovered it and dismantled it. Those things could be dangerous; they'd been known to explode.

I rounded a final turn in the rutted track and came upon the single-story house. Its dull yellow paint was dirty and worn. I could see a battered van parked under a lean-to attached to the small barn on the side of the clearing. The intensifying sleet and wind drove forlorn leaves and debris across the crooked front porch. The windows were small and heavily curtained. A brave Christmas wreath with a tattered red bow hung on the front door.

Dim light showed at two of the windows. The place looked occupied. I shivered in my jacket. The clearing was small. I stood uncomfortably close to the house. I should go.

The front door swung open. I backed up a step.

A boy of about seven stepped out. He was dressed in an oversized flannel shirt that nearly reached the ground.

The boy stared at me. "Uncle Carl?"

I shook my head. "Not me. I think I'm at the wrong house." I backed up faster.

"Please, mister," the kid said. "We need some help."

"Sorry," I said. "I gotta go." I couldn't imagine what kind of help I could give him.

The boy ran down from the porch and grabbed my sleeve. He was barefoot.

"Please, mister," he said again. "We been waiting all yesterday and today for Uncle Carl to come. Mom said he'd be here soon."

"Where's your mother?" I asked, trying to gently disengage my sleeve.

A tear rolled down his cheek. "She's on the sofa," he said. "She's awful sick. She don't talk to us no more."

A chill that had nothing to do with the winter weather touched my neck. "You should call 9-1-1," I said. "They'll send somebody out to check on your mother."

"Mitch got mad and pulled out the wires," the child said. "The phone don't work no more."

I glanced longingly over my shoulder at the driveway. I never should have come.

"Anybody else home but you and your mother?" I asked.

"Just the twins and Beth," he said.

"Did you ask them what to do?"

The child looked at me like I was demented. "The twins are three. And Beth's a baby."

"Oh." They wouldn't be much help.

The child stood expectantly. Somebody had to do something. Looked like I was that somebody.

"What's your name?" I asked him as I let him pull me toward the porch.

"Sam," he said. "Sam Miller. Not Robinson. Mitch ain't my real Dad." He seemed anxious to get that straight.

I let him pull me inside the front door. I was met by an odor of dirty diapers and old food. A single room opened before me. A cluttered counter separated the kitchen area from the rest of it. As my eyes adjusted to the dimness, I saw that several doors opened off the room—three against the back wall and two off the kitchen area. The house felt chilly.

"Where's your mother?" I asked, looking around.

Sam pointed to a mound of blankets on the sofa. "She said she was cold, so I tried to cover her up."

Alarmed, I hurried over and put my hand on her cheek. She wasn't cold now. She was burning up. Her face was red and dry. Her breath came in shallow gasps. I reached down and shook her shoulder gently. She moaned softly but didn't wake up.

"She needs to get to the hospital," I told Sam. "How far away are your neighbors?"

"Far," he said. "Mitch said he didn't want no nosy neighbors around his house."

As I stood indecisively, a baby wailed from the back of the house. Two grimy toddlers with tousled dark curls appeared in the hallway. One had a finger firmly up his nose. Undoubtedly the twins.

"Uncle Carl?" one of the twins asked.

Sam ignored them. "You got a car, mister? You could drive her to the hospital."

"No," I said. "I walked here."

"You could use our van," he said. "I know where Mom keeps the keys. In her purse."

Right. Like I should be driving a car. "I don't have a license," I told Sam. "Isn't there anybody else who could drive her in?"

A big tear rolled down Sam's face. "I been trying to think of somebody. But ain't nobody. Just Uncle Carl, but he ain't come yet. And you."

"Where's Uncle Carl supposed to be coming from?" I asked. Maybe I could somehow get word to him.

"Iraq," Sam said.

Big help that was.

"Mom says he's gonna be back and get leave in time to come for Christmas." Sam rubbed his eye with his fist. "But she don't know exactly when."

The woman could not wait indefinitely for medical care. She probably shouldn't wait at all. Even to my inexperienced hand, her fever felt dangerously high.

I could probably drive the van. If it had an automatic transmission. And I didn't meet much traffic. But it would be crazy to drive somebody else's van, without a license, to the hospital, where there would definitely be all kinds of emergency personnel around. Probably including cops.

The woman moaned again softly. Sam looked up at me, his eyes bright with panic. One of the twins stuck his fingers in his mouth. The one with his finger up his nose looked at me and said, "Uncle Carl?" again.

There was no one else. I'd have to do it.

"Look," I said to Sam. "We can't leave the little kids here alone." I didn't tell him they were probably headed to emergency foster care. Where else would they go? Unless the real Uncle Carl put in an appearance very soon.

The baby was crying steadily now. "Does the baby drink from a bottle?" I asked. "Or does your Mom, you know, feed it?"

Sam looked scornful. "Mitch said the babies had to have a bottle. He said Mom's boobies were his."

More than I wanted to know. "Are there any bottles we could take with us?" I asked.

Sam nodded. "In the refrigerator. And diapers, too. I can get the diaper bag."

"Do we need to give the baby a bottle now?"

"I can see if she'll be happy with her pacifier."

"Good. Then see if you can get something warm for the twins." I thought back to my childhood. "Snowsuits? Or at least some blankets to wrap them in. And you find some pants to go with that shirt. And shoes."

"What are you going to do?" Sam asked.

"If you get me the keys, I'll see if I can get the van started and pull it out front. Then I'll try to carry your Mom out to it."

With a satisfied nod, Sam went to get the purse with the keys.

I hefted the woman up slightly to see how heavy she was. She weighed almost nothing. I wrapped the blankets around her more tightly. My hand encountered a wet spot underneath her. I wondered how long she had been lying there.

Sam came back and handed me the purse and the keys. I went out to see about the van.

The ignition coughed a few times and caught. I was relieved to see the automatic transmission. I hadn't driven in years, but how different could it be? I turned on the lights and the windshield wipers. Putting my foot on the brake, I moved the gearshift into drive. Letting up gently, I eased the van out of the lean-to and toward the front of the house. It obediently went where I steered. When I got near the front door, I stepped on the brake. The van shuddered and veered to the left, but it stopped. I moved the gear shift to park. Despite the sleet, which was turning to snow, I rolled down the driver's side window. I didn't want to turn it off again, but I also didn't want to accidentally lock the keys inside.

The front door opened. Sam came out, carrying a lumpy bundle that turned out to be the baby. Behind him trailed the twins, hats on their heads and boots on their feet, but their coats unzipped.

I opened the passenger side door and reclined the seat as far back as it would go. Leaving Sam to the details of strapping the younger children into their car seats, I went in and gathered up the woman with all her blankets. She was still awfully hot, and her breathing seemed even shallower. Walking carefully down the porch steps, I carried her out and laid her in the passenger seat. I fiddled with the belt until I got it around her.

"I got to get the diaper bag," Sam said, heading back into the house.

I looked at the purse. I hoped it had some ID and a medical insurance card. The hospital would want that information for sure.

Sam came out with the diaper bag. He still wore the oversized shirt, but it was tucked into a pair of pants. Unzipped boots flopped on his feet.

I got into the driver's seat and did up my seatbelt. I glanced back at all my passengers. They seemed to be secure. The baby whimpered. One of the twins said, "Uncle Carl?"

Was this technically kidnapping?

I eased the gearshift into drive.

The van lurched down the rutted driveway. I hoped the roads weren't too icy. I could just hear Mr. Ramirez if I crashed this thing with all these kids in it.

This was crazy. I couldn't begin to count the number of parole regulations I was violating. But I saw no alternative. If I got locked up again for this, at least it would be for something I'd actually done.

Snow was beginning to blanket the road. I concentrated on keeping the van away from the ditches on either side. Huge flakes slammed into the windshield. I could barely see.

"Can't you go any faster?" Sam asked from the back seat.

Without taking my eyes off the road, I said, "No."

"But—" Sam started to whine.

"No!"

He shut up. I felt kind of bad, snapping at him like that. He was just worried about his mom. But I had to keep all my attention on driving. I tried not to listen to the rasping breath of the woman beside me.

As we came into town, traffic picked up. I inched the van over close to my side of the street. At least I knew where the hospital was, over near the courthouse and the library.

Given the road conditions, everybody had to be driving slowly, but other vehicles seemed to be whizzing by us at an alarming speed.

Took an eternity before I saw the bright red sign that said "Emergency Entrance" shining through the gloom. I turned up the ramp. The van slipped going up the slick surface, but I was going slow enough so it didn't cause a problem. Other than to my already taut nerves.

Two ambulances and a patrol car were parked by the big double doors. I thought about going directly into the parking lot instead of stopping in the driveway. I wasn't anxious for police to notice the van or my unpracticed driving. I glanced at the woman in the passenger seat. I couldn't detect even the shallow breaths anymore. Pulling the van over, I hit the curb. I was only two thirds the way up the ramp, still a fair distance behind the patrol car. I put the van in park.

"Keep an eye on the kids," I said to Sam. "I'm gonna bring your Mom inside. I'll be right back."

The double doors opened automatically as I carried her through. An alert attendant took a quick look at me and my burden, grabbed a gurney, and hurried over.

I laid her down. The attendant tossed the blankets aside, scanning the woman, feeling the heat radiating from her body. "Go to the front desk," she ordered briskly. "I'm taking her right back." She and the gurney disappeared through another set of double doors.

I went up to the desk. At least three people were ahead of me. The kids were still in the van. So was the purse. I didn't even know this woman's name.

The van was going to attract attention if I left it there. Especially with four kids in it. The last thing I wanted was for someone to ask the cops who went with the patrol car to check into it. I could do without them investigating what was going on.

I doubted a child could give permission for someone to use the family vehicle. Grand theft charges. Add in child neglect for leaving the kids in the van. In addition, of course, to the kidnapping.

I went back outside and got into the van.

"Where's Mom?" Sam demanded.

"They took her back to see a doctor," I said. "We can't leave the van here; it's in the way if an ambulance comes in. We'll park it and then go see what we can find out."

I guided the van to a space toward the rear of the parking lot. I fumbled with the buckles on the car seat holding one of the twins. Some mad genius had obviously designed them so no child could escape and few adults could figure them out.

Sam undid the twins in seconds flat. Then he did something to the baby's car seat and lifted the whole thing out. I took the baby in her car seat, now a carrier, and grabbed the purse and the diaper bag. Sam took a twin's hand in each of his, and we straggled across the slushy parking lot to the pedestrian entrance.

The waiting room was almost deserted. I put the baby, carrier and all, down in a corner by some worn plastic chairs, a TV droning overhead. Sam yanked the jackets off the twins and told them to sit and watch the TV.

I opened the purse. Probably a good idea if I had a name to give them before I talked to the people who filled out all the paperwork. How could I begin to answer all their questions?

Maybe I should just give Sam the keys and tell the lady behind the desk to call Social Services. Wasn't there some kind of law that protected people who took children to hospitals and left them? Couldn't be charged with neglect or abandonment just for that. Or did that only apply to babies?

"Is Mom gonna be all right?" Sam asked me, his brown eyes big and trusting.

One of the twins—they had to have names, and I'd have to find out what they were soon—clutched my leg and wiped his nose on my pants. "Uncle Carl?" he asked, looking up at me with another set of big brown eyes.

They were scared. They trusted me. Good thing they didn't know how useless I was. And I knew how much more scary it would be to have the lady from Social Services show up, annoyed at being called in, and have to hustle the kids off to placements with people they didn't know. Four of them—very doubtful they could keep them together. Might not even try. I'd stick with them, at least for a little while.

"The doctors will know what to do for your mom." I ruffled Sam's wild curls. "But remember, she's pretty sick. They'll probably give her some medicine, but she'll need lots of sleep. So they may not want us to bother her for a while."

I opened the purse to look for a wallet or something. The purse was stuffed with things. What could a woman possibly do with all these tubes and little plastic packets and zippered thingies? The comb, I recognized. Likewise, the wad of tissues. They'd come in handy with the twins' noses.

At the bottom, I finally found a wallet. Opening it, I saw a few twenty-dollar bills, two credit cards, and a driver's license. Tiffany Robinson. I turned to Sam. "Your mom named Tiffany?"

"Yeah," he said.

I also found a medical card with Quality Steel Products listed as the group. Would she still be covered if Mitch, who had worked for the company, was dead?

Didn't matter. She needed medical care. I took the wallet and went up to the window, where the last person in line was now leaving.

"Yes?" the lady sitting at the desk asked, shuffling papers and picking up a pen. Her fingernails were gnawed short.

"I, uh, just brought someone in…" I said. I was uncertain how to proceed. The only other time I'd ever been in an emergency room, I had been the patient. Years ago, after my original arrest. I had been shackled down completely, my sliced hand dripping blood down the back of my pants while the clerk filled out the paperwork. Even when they'd uncuffed my hand and the medical staff had worked on it, they'd dealt entirely with the police escort. No one talked to me at all. I'd felt like a dog with a questionable disposition at the vet's.

"Where is he?" the intake clerk asked, snapping a piece of paper onto a clipboard and shoving it toward me.

"She." I shifted uneasily from one foot to the other. "Somebody already took her back." I indicated the interior set of double doors.

"I see," the lady said, tapping her pen on the desk. She picked up her phone and turned away from me, shielding her mouth with her hand. She talked for a few seconds, nodded her head, and hung up.

"What is the patient's name?" she asked.

"Tiffany Robinson."

She typed away on her keyboard. "Ah, here she is. We have her records. Any change of address?"

"No, ma'am."

"Any change of medical service provider?"

"No, ma'am."

"And you're her husband?"

I blushed. "No, ma'am."

I felt a tugging at my leg. Looking down, I saw a twin, nose running and snot all over his face. He looked up at me. "Uncle Carl?" he said.

"Carl Miller? Listed on her emergency contacts? Brother?" the lady asked, tapping away at the keyboard.

The interior double doors opened, and two uniformed police officers strode out. One of them was Officer Simmons, who had arrested me just three days ago.

I turned to face the window. I didn't say anything. Contradicting her would just call attention to me. I really had no good answer to give her anyhow.

"Just have a seat over there—" she waved toward the plastic chairs "—and someone will be with you in a few minutes."

"Thank you, ma'am," I said, reaching down and picking up the little guy.

He wiped his nose with his shirt sleeve. How could one little kid produce all this snot? I tried to hold him so he shielded my face from Simmons' view. He smeared the side of my face with mucus.

The other twin was lying on the blanket on the floor, thumb in his mouth, staring at the TV screen. Sam sat on the floor next to the baby in her carrier. She was starting to whimper.

I glanced over at the two cops. Of course they had stopped and were talking to the receptionist. Each had a cardboard cup of coffee in his hand. A big cup of coffee. They were in no hurry to go out into that weather. I felt the hairs on the back of my neck bristle.

What kind of duty rotation had Simmons working the early morning hours so recently and the day shift now? At least it wasn't the same partner as last time, so the other guy wouldn't be likely to recognize me.

"What's the matter with the baby?" I asked Sam. She was attracting attention.

"Hungry," Sam said knowingly.

"Do you know to feed her?" I asked. I'd helped Mrs. Coleman take care of plenty of kids, but she always handled the babies herself.

"Yeah," Sam said. "I feed her all the time. Can you get a bottle out of the bag?"

I put the twin I was carrying down next to the other one and stepped over to the bag. Underneath the clean, folded diapers, I found a bottle. I handed it to Sam. Expertly, he pried the cover off the nipple and stuck it in the baby's mouth. She stopped her whimpering and sucked eagerly.

Maybe I should go back to the receptionist and tell her I wasn't the kids' uncle and she should see who else on that emergency contact list could come get them. When the cops left. If the mysterious Uncle Carl showed up, he could figure the whole thing out and let me off the hook. Assuming he knew how to take care of them and wanted to undertake the responsibility of four little kids until Tiffany got out of the hospital.

I refused to entertain the possibility that Tiffany wouldn't get out of the hospital to take care of them. These kids had just lost their dad; it would just be too unfair for them to lose their mom, too.

And just what evidence did I ever have of any of that type of cosmic fairness?

I was thinking too much. Therein lay insanity.

"Mister," Sam said, looking up from feeding the baby.

"Yeah?"

"That pig, he's looking at you. Real funny." He nodded toward the cops.

"What did you call him?" I said.

Sam looked down at the baby. "Pig," he said quietly.

"Police officers are your friends." I ran my fingers through my hair. "They're here to help you. They have a difficult, dangerous job, and I don't want to hear you using a disrespectful term like that when you talk about them." Jeez, where did that come from?

Mrs. Coleman, of course. Foster mother. I'd been with the Colemans longer than I'd been in any other home. I could almost see her standing there, her hands clenched in fists, resting on her sturdy hips, glaring at me through the thick lenses of her black plastic-framed glasses. She'd add, "And don't you forget it."

"That's what Mitch called them," Sam said to me in a small voice.

I wouldn't wish my relationship with law enforcement personnel on anybody, much less an unhappy little kid like Sam. He might very well need their help. I toned my voice down. "I don't care what Mitch called them; that's disrespectful."

Sam looked miserable. "He said they were stuck-up pigs and just liked to cause trouble wherever they went."

"Maybe sometimes that's true." I thought about Belkins. "There are good police officers and bad police officers, just like anything else. As long as you're not doing anything wrong, most of the time, you can count on a police officer to help you when you need help."

I wished.

I heard boot steps cross the waiting room toward us. A metallic rattle that might be keys and handcuffs from somewhere behind me. Now would be time for Simmons to prove to us all that police officers are not my friends. Right in front of the kids. I closed my eyes and waited for the command to interlace my fingers on top of my head.

Across the room, someone said, "Simmons. We got a call."

I heard radio static. The boot steps retreated.

"He's gone back over by the other police officer," Sam said. "But he's still looking at you funny."

With an effort, I didn't turn to look. "People can look wherever they want."

Could I get up and just leave? Maybe tell Sam I was going to the restroom and find another way out of the hospital? Or say I was going to get something out of the van? I could just walk home and pretend I'd had no part in this whole thing.

Like that would really work.

I looked at the kids. The feelings of anguish and despair that I'd felt when I realized I had been abandoned yet again came flooding back. My gut cramped up. Yet, when I was a kid, every time someone else showed any interest, seemed like they might care, I was ready to trust again. Even when the old man got out of prison and took me back again. I'd been ready to believe he really wanted me, not just the monthly check that came with me. Kids' basic nature, I guess. Raise up hopes just to be crushed again.

Could I do that to these kids?

Of course, if Simmons were to follow up on his well-founded suspicions, I wouldn't be the one making the decisions about where any of us went. Emergency foster care for the kids, a jail cell for me. I resolutely didn't glance around to see what the cops were doing.

A short, plump man dressed in green scrubs came through the interior doors, glanced around, and headed over to us.

He scowled as he consulted a clipboard.

"Are you with Tiffany Robinson?" he asked.

"Yes, sir," I said.

Sam stood the bottle on the blanket next to the twins and scrambled to his feet to stand next to me.

"She's one very sick lady," the man in scrubs said. "You should have brought her in sooner. Much sooner."

"We couldn't," Sam said, a catch in his voice.

I looked down at him. Tears streaked his grimy face. I put a hand on his shoulder. He moved close to me, snugging up against my leg.

"Yes, sir," I said. "I realize that. How's she doing now?"

"Well, we're going to admit her as soon as we can find a bed," he said. He reviewed the information on the clipboard. "You're not her husband?" he asked.

"No, sir." I was trying hard not to say who I was.

"I'm afraid HIPAA regulations won't allow me to disclose much information about her condition without her consent," he said. "Is her husband going to be coming in soon?"

"He's…" Sam started to say. I squeezed his shoulder. To my relief, he didn't finish the sentence.

"No. There must be some way to find out how she's doing. These are her kids. They're really worried."

The man shook his head sadly. "I know. Our hands are tied. I can tell you that she's in serious but stable condition and resting comfortably. We are actively treating her. But that's about it. When she wakes up, she can give us permission to share information with someone else."

At least he expected her to wake up. "Like a brother?" I asked, thinking of Uncle Carl when he showed up. If he showed up.

"A brother would be fine, if she agrees. You can come in tomorrow during visiting hours to see her. If she's awake, she can tell anybody anything she wants to."

"Could we see her now?" I asked.

He frowned. "You could go back. But the children can't. And she hasn't regained consciousness—she won't for a while—so I don't know how much good it would do." He glanced over his shoulder at the double doors. More people were standing in line at the desk, including a woman holding a child with a blood-soaked towel wrapped around his arm.

"Thank you. Is there anything else we should know?" I asked.

He shook his head. "That's about what I can tell you. You can always call to check on her condition." He nodded and hurried away.

I turned to the kids. "No point in staying here," I said.

"What does 'serious but stable condition' mean?" Sam asked.

"It means she's real sick, but not likely to die," I said, hoping that was what it meant. "It'll take her a little while before she can come home, but she will be coming home."

"Uncle Carl?" the snotty-nosed twin said. "McDonald's?"

"Mom said Uncle Carl would take us to McDonald's when he came." Sam glanced at the twin. "He still thinks you're Uncle Carl."

I stole a quick look over my shoulder at Officer Simmons, who was fiddling with his radio. Didn't they have to go somewhere on that call?

Getting us any place away from here sounded good. McDonald's would do. There was one right on the corner by the library. And Tiffany's wallet had some money in it. I hoped she wouldn't mind if I spent some on the kids.

"Let's go get some Happy Meals," I said, starting to gather up all the jackets and stuff.

We straggled out into the parking lot. The snow had changed to small, driving flakes, and the air felt distinctly colder. If I was going to drive back to the house—and it looked like that was what I was going to do—I wanted to make it before darkness set in.

"You could go through the drive-in," Sam suggested as I pulled into a parking space in McDonald's parking lot.

I shook my head. "I'm not used to driving, and this van is pretty big. Why don't you tell me what to get? You can stay with the kids, and I'll go in and get it."

I emerged with three Happy Meals, a bag full of pies—they were two for a dollar—and a Big Mac for me. I'd struggled with buying the Big Mac, but I was hungry.

I wolfed down the Big Mac before I started the van. Every bit as tasty as I remembered from almost twenty years ago.

The kids ate their Happy Meals. They were probably making a mess, but I wasn't too concerned about that right now. I kept glancing in my rearview mirror, expecting to see a flashing light bar following us.

Even though the road conditions were worse, the van felt steadier than it had on my way into town. Maybe I was more at ease driving. We crept up the hill and then turned into the narrow driveway and lurched up to the front of the porch.

# CHAPTER 9

The house was even colder when we got back. I looked around the big main room in dismay. I hadn't really taken in the mess before. The floor was strewn with clothes and toys. The sink in the kitchen beyond the counter overflowed with dishes.

Stuff everywhere.

Prison inmates have very few possessions. What they're allowed is spelled out by institution regulations, down to the amount of space paperwork and books can occupy. It all has to fit in a small locker. And foster children can only have what they can carry in a black plastic garbage bag. More than half of mine had been occupied by a large, ragged stuffed dog I had received for Christmas one year. Of course, he hadn't been ragged when I got him. His name was Delfie, and he was my only reliable companion for years. When I first got locked up, he'd been waiting for me on my top bunk in the apartment I shared with the old man and my brothers. I wondered if he existed any more. Probably out in the trash long ago.

I reminded myself firmly that it, not him, had been a lifeless stuffed toy without feelings. How could I care about something so stupid?

Since I'd been released, I hadn't accumulated a whole lot. Dealing with this ocean of stuff boggled my mind. Plastic bags. Broken toys. Empty food containers. Beer cans.

I put the baby in a playpen by the window. Sam turned on the TV, and the twins drifted over to the sofa to watch.

"It's cold in here," I said, looking at the wood stove. "Is that what you use for heat?"

"Yeah," Sam said. "I'm not supposed to fool with the stove, but I been shoving wood in there to keep it going. You know how to feed a stove?"

"Not really." I had no idea. "Where's the firewood?"

"On the back porch, under the tarp," Sam said. "Want me to get some?"

"Yeah." I felt the stove. It was still hot to the touch, at least. Building up this fire would be a whole lot easier than starting a new one from scratch. If the firebox wasn't completely choked with ashes. I took a pot holder and opened the door. A faint glow showed deep inside.

"Got any newspaper to get this thing going better?" I asked Sam, who was carrying in an armful of stove length split logs.

"Mitch stopped the paper. He said he could tell Mom everything she needed to know."

I kept my thoughts to myself. I hadn't much cared for Mitch, and so far, nothing I was hearing changed my mind about that. Even if he was dead.

I pulled some bark off the firewood and dredged a few paper towels out of the overflowing trash bin. When I shoved them into the ashes with a heavy metal poker, they started to blaze. I added a few lengths of wood, careful not to pack them too densely. I closed the door and hoped for the best.

"Okay," I said, looking around at the mess. "Time to get organized. First, Sam, what are the twins' names and how do you tell them apart?"

"Larry and Peter." Sam looked doubtfully at the twins. "Larry's nose is running worse than Peter's right now." As Sam said that, Larry wiped his nose again with his sleeve. "And the baby's Beth. She's the only girl."

He didn't ask my name. Might be best if the kids didn't know it. "Mister" seemed to be working just fine.

"The twins seem awful quiet for three-year-olds," I said. "Don't they run around and play and stuff?"

"They do when they can go outside." Sam scratched his head.

Had all the kids been scratching their heads? The horrible thought that they might all have lice flitted through my mind.

"But you sure don't want to make noise inside and wake Mitch up in the middle of the day when he's sleeping," Sam continued. "So we're pretty quiet in the house."

I could relate to not wanting to wake Mitch up.

I surveyed the mounds of clothes lying around. Also the blankets on the sofa where Tiffany had been lying. A sour smell, or worse, rose from them. "Is there a washer and dryer?" I asked.

"Mitch got Mom a washing machine so she didn't have to go to the Laundromat." Sam nodded toward the back of the house. "But no dryer."

"Where does she hang clothes to dry?"

"Mostly outside, but she's got two drying racks she puts next to the stove when it's too wet, like now."

I started to gather up some of the clothes strewn on the floor. "Where's the washer?"

"In the bathroom," Sam said, gesturing toward the middle of the three doors set in the back wall.

I dumped the collection of clothes in the washer, added detergent, and scrutinized the directions on the lid. Why was using washing machines so complicated? Seemed like they should all work pretty much the same way. Following them as best I could, I started the load.

Beth, the baby, was starting to fuss. "Is she hungry again?"

Sam shrugged. "Probably needs a clean diaper."

An unfortunate thought. "Where are the diapers?" I asked.

"In our bedroom." He pointed the three doors to the left of the bathroom.

If I'd thought the living room was a mess, this topped it. Two sets of bunk beds lined the side walls. A crib was pushed up against the window. Bedding lay in mounds on the floor. The mattress from one of the bottom bunks was half off. I spotted a few folded diapers on top of the dresser. A foul odor wafted from a tall covered plastic container by the crib. A diaper pail. Undoubtedly full of dirty diapers.

They might end up clogging up our landfills, but didn't everybody use disposable diapers these days?

Evidently not.

Diapers would definitely have to be the next load in the washer.

I took a folded diaper and carried it out to the main room. I handed it to Sam. "You're gonna have to show me how to do this."

He took the diaper from me, lifted Beth out of the playpen, expertly removed the wet diaper, and replaced it with a clean one. All without stabbing the baby or himself with the wicked-looking diaper pins.

I had no confidence I could repeat the maneuver myself.

He carried the wet diaper back to the bedroom. "We're almost out of clean diapers. There's a few more in the diaper bag, but…" He shook his head ominously.

I didn't care to contemplate life without clean diapers.

"Your well ever run dry?" I asked, thinking we had quite a few loads of laundry ahead of us. Not to mention dishes to wash and baths to take.

Sam shrugged. "Not that I ever remember."

I hoped we didn't find out the well's capacity the hard way.

I moved on to the kitchen area, filling the sink and putting some of the crusted-over dishes in to soak. I looked around. Sam had gone out one door to get the wood. The other led to a well-stocked pantry with a big freezer and shelves of food, including several large cans of powdered baby formula.

If Mitch had isolated his family, he hadn't intended them to starve.

We would have to eat supper. Most of the flat white packages in the freezer were labeled in black marker. "Venison" with a date. Venison it would be. I set out a package to thaw while I cleaned up the kitchen area.

The room was heating up nicely.

Looked like I was going to be here for a while. Thank goodness I wasn't being monitored, and with any luck, I wouldn't have to try to explain all this to Mr. Ramirez. Of course, if I hadn't gotten the time off, I would never have come up here in the first place.

What would have happened to Tiffany? Or the kids?

Sam found two wooden drying racks and set them up by the stove. When the washer finished, we hung the clothes on the dowels. I got the container of stinking diapers and dumped them into the washer, adding a good dash of bleach to the detergent.

I spied a crock pot on a shelf in the pantry and brought it out. Cutting the half-thawed venison into cubes and an onion into pieces, I put it all in the crock pot, along with some canned tomato sauce. Venison could be tough. Slow cooking might help.

Gradually, the room was becoming livable. Sam corralled the twins to help put the toys in the toy box. I straightened up everything else as best I could and swept the bare wood floor. The kids' room could wait until tomorrow. That would be a chore.

The tantalizing aroma of cooking meat and onions began to fill the air. I found potatoes and carrots and cut some up to add to the crock pot. The younger kids dozed. Outside, I could hear the wind roar and sharp ice particles hit the windows. We were warm and safe. A nice feeling. For now.

Following the directions on the can, I mixed up some baby formula. Sam gathered the baby bottles. Weren't they supposed to be sterilized or something? I put a big pot of water on the cooktop and loaded the newly scrubbed bottles, nipples, and assorted plastic parts in the pot. The bottles were glass, so they should be all right, but I kept an eye on everything to see if the rubber nipples or the plastic parts started to dissolve. If they did, I didn't know what I could do but watch them melt. I fished a few out before the water boiled, just in case.

Everything survived. I filled the bottles and put them in the refrigerator.

When the baby woke up, Sam changed her diaper again, and I tried to feed her. Sam showed me how to cradle her in my arms and hold her so she could drink from the bottle. She was soft and warm and fit right into the crook of my elbow. She put her tiny hands over mine and grasped the bottle as she sucked eagerly. She looked up at me and smiled around the nipple. I laughed and grinned back at her. What a goof.

When she had finished most of it, she lost interest.

"Now you have to burp her," Sam said, taking the nearly empty bottle.

"How do I do that?"

"You put her up on your shoulder and pat her back."

I did so.

"Only you should—" Sam started to say.

"Burrrrrrp."

I felt something wet on the back of my sweater. It smelled awful.

"—put a diaper over your shoulder, because she'll probably spit up," Sam finished.

She had done exactly that. All over my sweater. I felt it soak through the shirt underneath, too.

I put the baby back in her playpen and took off my sweater and shirt. Removing the diapers from the washer, I put my things in with a few towels from the bathroom floor.

The room was not warm enough to go around unclothed. I shivered. I needed something to wear.

I opened the last door in the back wall. Had to be the adults' bedroom. It was. Less of a mess than the other rooms, but not exactly neat.

The shades were drawn. A huge brick fireplace took up most of one wall, and the dank smell of damp ashes filled the dim air.

I switched on a light and opened the closet door. It contained a few pieces of clothing. Mostly men's stuff. Tiffany must keep her clothes somewhere else. The ones Mitch had let her keep. A hooded sweatshirt hung from a hook on the back of the door. I held it to my nose and gave it the sniff test. It smelled clean enough. A little big for me, but this was no time to be fussy. I carried it out into the main room. It was blue with black lettering across the back that said "Mitch."

Couldn't be helped.

I slipped it on.

Sam was rearranging the clothes on the drying racks to make room for some of the diapers. The twins were sitting up, looking toward me.

"Supper in a few minutes."

I opened a jar of peaches from the pantry and emptied it into a bowl. I put some now-clean plates and forks on the table. Sam got a half-empty gallon of milk from the refrigerator and poured some into cups.

"There's beer in the refrigerator," he told me.

I started to say drinking alcohol would violate my parole. But just about everything I'd done since I'd set foot on this property had violated my parole. Could drinking a beer really hurt? I grabbed one and popped the top.

Sam ushered the twins to the table. I wondered if there was enough hot water to give them a bath tonight. They needed it.

I dished the stew onto the plates, wondering if the kids would eat it or not. Baseless worry. They dove right in, as if venison stew was a mainstay of their diet. Maybe it was. Other than the Happy Meals, I had no idea when they had eaten last. Or what.

I took a gulp of the beer and a forkful of the stew. It tasted as good as it smelled. I took another sip of the beer. Felt good to settle down to a home-cooked meal that I'd actually fixed myself.

Someone knocked at the door.

# CHAPTER 10

My first thought was to ignore the knock. Whoever it was might go away.

I quickly recognized that as ridiculous. Lights were on in the house.

My second thought was that maybe it was Uncle Carl. If so, I could turn responsibility for the kids over to him and then go home in the morning.

Or it could be the police. If Officer Simmons reported seeing me to Belkins, he would start asking questions and wouldn't stop until he had some answers. If I didn't open the door, they might break the door down and come in anyway.

They wouldn't even have to break it down. I hadn't locked it. The wind had died down a little, but the snow was still coming down heavily. Someone had made a real effort to get to this isolated house. I needed to let them in right away.

I got up and stashed my beer can on a shelf in the kitchen, behind a can of baking powder. I went over to the door and opened it.

A hairy, snow-covered dog burst through the door, shaking himself and making a beeline for Sam, who was finishing up his supper. The dog was followed by an equally hairy, snow-covered man.

He stood uncertainly just inside the door, looked around at the now tidy room, and inhaled deeply. He overbalanced, caught himself, laughed, and said, "Smells good. Any possibility of getting some supper?"

"Sure," I said, shutting the door behind him. Unsteadily, he took off his jacket, and on the third try, managed to hang it on a hook.

The dog shook again, sending a spray of melting snow over everything. He sniffed at Sam's hand and then went over to the twins. They laughed and held out their hands for him to lick.

Sam looked at the man and frowned. He slipped out of his seat at the table. Carrying his dishes to the sink, he said to the twins, "It's bedtime. Come on."

The twins looked like they might protest, but they, too, slipped out of their chairs and straggled off toward the bedroom.

"Who're you?" the man asked me. He slurred his words.

I looked him over. He was either high or pretty drunk. "I was just about to ask you the same thing."

He grinned, his stained teeth showing through his ice-encrusted beard. "I'm Reggie. Prob'ly your nearest neighbor. I promised Tiffany I'd bring over a Christmas tree for the kids. Left it out on the porch." He put out a hand and steadied himself on the wall.

At first, all I could smell was unwashed body, but then I caught a strong whiff of alcohol on his breath. Drunk. "I hope you didn't drive too far in that condition," I said.

He ignored me. "Hey, kids," he said, raising his voice. "I brought that Christmas tree I promised your mama."

Sam had been marshaling the twins toward the bedroom, but he stopped and looked back toward us. "Christmas tree," he said, his eyes wide.

"We can set it up tomorrow," I told him. Getting the kids out of the way seemed like a very good idea right now.

"Where the hell is Tiffany?" Reggie looked around the room.

"She's sick. In the hospital."

"Really. I told her that cough was going to turn into pneumonia. Is that what she's got?"

I shrugged. "I guess. Bad fever, and she wasn't what you'd call totally with it."

Reggie looked worried. "You're sure it wasn't an overdose?"

"Not an overdose," I assured him. I hoped I was right; that possibility hadn't occurred to me. Couldn't see an overdose causing a high fever.

"So who are you?" Reggie pulled a package of rolling papers and a pouch of tobacco from his pocket and started to roll a cigarette. Tobacco scattered all over the floor. At least, it looked like tobacco. "Tiffany's fancy man?"

"Just happened by," I said. "I worked with Mitch. Before he died."

"You mean before someone killed him." Reggie tried to close the pouch. The strings tangled around his fingers.

"Yeah."

Reggie leered at me. "Mitch always figured Tiff had somebody on the side. Came in while he worked nights. She swore it weren't so. Guess he wasn't so far wrong, huh?"

Last thing I needed was somebody going around reinforcing the notion that Mitch had any reason to be jealous of me. "I worked the same shift as Mitch." I watched as the pouch strings closed tighter on his fingers the more he tried to remove them. "Couldn't have come around when he was at work. I'd be at work, too."

"Riiiiight…" Reggie yanked the pouch. One of the strings broke, but his fingers were free. He shoved the pouch back in his pocket and tucked the cigarette behind his ear.

No point in responding to his taunting.

"And to think that cute little vixen wouldn't let ol' Reggie come by and keep her warm at night."

No surprise there, given the way he smelled.

He laughed and brushed the shaggy gray hair out of his eyes. "A shame, really. The only time I even had a go at her was when Mitch set it up. And he insisted on videotaping it."

I really didn't want to hear this. I changed the subject. "You want some of the stew?" I waved toward the crock pot, still half full.

"Sure thing. And a beer." He belched and headed to the refrigerator. "I know there's got to be beer."

He sure didn't need any more to drink, but I figured that wasn't my problem. Unless he passed out here. I got a bowl and a spoon—I didn't think he could handle a plate or fork—and gave it to Reggie. "How're the roads?" I asked.

Reggie ignored my question. He spooned stew into his bowl and held it under his nose. "Ah. Here's betting it wasn't Tiffany who made that. Bitch couldn't cook worth a damn."

"No." I hoped the kids weren't listening. They didn't need to hear their mother referred to as a bitch. But kids usually hear everything. "Did you have much trouble driving here?"

"Didn't drive," Reggie said, taking a can of beer from the refrigerator. "Snow shoes. They're on the porch, next to the Christmas tree."

"Snow shoes." I tossed that thought around in my mind.

"Yeah. You just gonna stay here until Tiffany gets well enough to come home?" He belched again and popped the top on the beer.

I shrugged.

"She is gonna get well enough to come home, isn't she?" Reggie paused with the spoon halfway to his mouth.

I looked toward the kids. Sam was shuttling the twins between the bathroom and their bedroom. He didn't look toward us, but I was sure he was listening. "Of course she is. A coupla days in the hospital where the doctors can take good care of her, and she'll be good as new."

Reggie nodded. His bleary gaze followed mine to the kids. "Prob'ly before Christmas," he said.

I wouldn't have bet on that.

He belched, shook his head, almost falling off the chair, and then tried to sit up straighter.

Sam glanced at us in alarm.

"You guys got clean pajamas?" I asked. Doubtful.

"Pajamas?" Sam looked puzzled.

"You know. To sleep in."

"We usually just sleep in our clothes."

Not good. Mrs. Coleman maintained that one of the benchmarks of neglected children is that they sleep in their clothes. They were almost always neglected in other ways, too. "Okay. We'll take baths in the morning."

Sam just shrugged. "Okay. Can Chief come in with us?" he asked.

"Chief?" I looked at Reggie.

"The dog," he said. "Sure. He can go lie down with you guys. He likes you."

"Come on," Sam said, grabbing the twins by the hand. "Chief's gonna come to bed with us."

I turned back to Reggie. I didn't need years of prison living to tell me I was dealing with someone who was less than an upstanding citizen here. Reggie could probably figure me out, too. Unless he was too drunk.

"Do you know anything about the Uncle Carl who's supposed to be coming?" I asked Reggie. "A soldier or something. Sam says he's gonna get leave for the holidays."

Reggie bent down and loosened his boots. He leaned forward so far, I poised myself to grab him if he fell off the chair. He didn't.

"I know Tiffany's got a brother who's a Marine." He straightened up and rubbed his nose. "Just got back from Iraq. I heard he was in town a few days ago. Then he left again."

"So he didn't stay here?"

"Nah. He and his sister don't always get along real well." Reggie took a slug of his beer.

"Why's that?" Although I had to admit I hadn't exactly gotten along with my brothers, either.

"Carl didn't much like how Mitch treated Tiff. Or the kids." Reggie slid his feet out of the boots and flexed his toes. The smell of unwashed feet in unwashed wool socks wafted toward me. "And Mitch didn't much like Carl. Mitch and Tiff fought about it some. Guess Carl figured Tiffany was an adult. She could make up her own mind."

"So Carl did come to see her?"

"I'd guess he did. Probably at night, when Mitch was at work, so there wouldn't be any fights." Reggie grinned. "I'd expect you'd have a much better idea of whether he came by while Mitch was at work than I ever would."

No point revisiting that issue. Reggie was gonna think what he was gonna think. "You know some way to get hold of Carl?" I asked. "The kids expect him. They thought I might be him. And somebody's got to see these kids are taken care of."

"You seem to be doing a bang up job of that. I'm sure Tiffany will show you how grateful she is, if you know what I mean." A smirk crossed Reggie's face. "The kids got a good supper. The place is cleaner than I've ever seen it. And Mitch ain't gonna show up to ruin things. You might have yourself a permanent gig."

I gathered the other supper dishes and put them in the sink. "I can't stay forever," I said.

"Those kids'd be better off with you, looks like, anyhow." Reggie stared at the cigarette he'd rolled, tucked it behind his ear, and went to the refrigerator to get another beer.

"Why would you think that?"

"At his best, Mitch wasn't a real patient dad. Especially with Sam, who isn't his kid. And lately, I wouldn't say he was at his best."

"Why is that?" I repeated. Although I had a pretty good idea.

Reggie sat down at the table, looking away from me. He rested his chin on his grimy hand and thought for a few minutes. "Lately, he hasn't been exactly exercising good self-control," he finally said.

"As in smoking the evil weed and worse?" I ventured, turning on the water and adding a squirt of detergent to the water in the sink.

"Maybe," Reggie said. He laughed loudly.

"Not my concern. As long as there's nothing here that could get me in trouble for possession or something." A worrisome thought came into my head. "You think he's got anything stashed in the van?" I'd been driving that van.

"Why are you getting your shorts all in a knot? You just say it ain't yours and you didn't know it was there," Reggie said. "Perfectly reasonable."

"Just don't need the hassle." I wasn't about to mention my precarious parole status if I didn't have to.

"Don't you think they would have found anything Mitch had stashed when they searched the house?" Reggie stretched his sock-clad feet out in front of him. "And the van? It was up here."

"I'd think so. If they did any kind of thorough search."

"That they did." Reggie looked around the surface of the table. He patted his pockets. Finally, he brought out the rolling papers and the tobacco pouch again. "They brought in a drug dog and everything."

"So did they find anything?" I wondered if I should say something about the cigarette behind his ear as he started to shake tobacco from the pouch onto a new paper.

"If they did, it wasn't much." Reggie evened out the tobacco with a pudgy finger, raised the cigarette to his mouth to lick the edge of the paper and rolled it.

"Because he didn't have much?"

"Because only a total fool would keep much in their own house, with a wife and kids living there. You risk losing the house if they find anything. Mitch might have been an idiot in some ways, but he wasn't a total fool. Besides, he had other places to keep it."

"Like at work?"

Reggie laughed again. "Like at work."

"I don't see how he got all that stuff in there." I rinsed the bowls and put them in the drainer. "Security cameras on all the doors and the truck bays. I heard they found, like, a lot of pot."

"Some of that came in on trucks," Reggie let loose another belch and patted his protruding stomach. "And a lot of it left that way, too. Mitch tucked it right in there with the products they were shipping. Shipments of something called root baskets, whatever they are."

I knew exactly what root baskets were. They were stacked and tied down on a pallet for shipping. A lot of room in the center if someone wanted to pack something else in with them.

"But the other stuff—the crystal meth—Mitch brought it in himself. There's a gate along the side of the shipping yard, over by the road out here." He nodded toward the front door. "And it looks like it's never been opened, at least in years. Rusted padlock and all overgrown-looking. But you know what?" Reggie leaned forward conspiratorially.

"What?"

"Mitch had it rigged so you could swing the whole section of the fence, gate and all, open. So he could get anything he wanted into the plant. Or out. No security cameras over there."

Interesting. I wondered if that was over where Kelly saw Radman's Mercedes parked next to the road. "A lot of people know about that?"

Reggie looked around in an exaggerated way, as if he expected to find someone else listening. "Not too many people. Don't really know who Mitch dealt with at the plant. He bragged it was somebody impor-tant." A sly look stole over Reggie's face. He shook his head. "You ain't gonna go blabbing all this, are you?"

"'Course not." Alcohol does strange things to a person's thought process. If Reggie was drunk enough to be telling me all this, he was probably drunk enough to believe he could trust me.

I wondered how much of this was true. And I wondered if any of this would make Montgomery start really investigating.

Reggie licked the cigarette and put it on the table next to his can of beer.

"So the cops didn't haul a meth lab out of here when they came searching." I let the water out of the sink.

Reggie narrowed his eyes and looked at me. "I can guarantee you that they didn't find a meth lab here. You have to be real careful around those things. They can blow up. Mitch had a tendency to be careless."

"So someone else was cooking the meth and delivering it to Mitch."

"You could say that." Reggie wiggled his toes in the grungy socks.

"And that someone else is busy disassembling it and making sure it's not going to be found." I looked around for a clean towel to dry the dishes with and decided it was better to let them air dry.

"A smart person would probably do that. Even if it was the best little money-maker on the face of the Earth." Moisture glistened in Reggie's eyes, and he sniffed loudly. "In fact, a smart person would probably be planning to move away and make a new start somewhere. As soon as the roads got plowed in the morning."

"And he'd probably take his dog along," I said. "Be a great opportunity to make a fresh start." I added silently, *Don't turn into a maudlin drunk on me.*

Too late. Tears were cascading down Reggie's cheeks and into his beard. "They're gonna think it was me killed him," he wailed. "You got no idea what it's like to know they're gonna come looking for you to pin a murder on you that you never had nothing to do with."

I did have some idea, but I wasn't about to say that to Reggie. "Why will they think you killed Mitch?"

"I been supplying the meth," he said, taking another gulp of his beer. "They'll figure that out sooner or later. It should have worked out okay, at least for a lot longer than this. Let me—both of us—build up a real stash. Enough to retire."

"What happened?"

"Mitch started using. Bad move. I tried to tell him—it's like being a bartender. Maybe you can have one drink at the end of the shift. But you best not be hitting the bottle all night long. It'll get away from you. And it did."

"How so?"

"Look at the crap he pulled." Reggie wiped his eyes with his sleeve. "Got all paranoid. Thought Tiff was having men in here at night when he was at work. And going out to meet them during the day." He looked up at me. "Course, maybe she was. You'd know better than me."

"I wasn't seeing Tiffany." But I'd never convince Reggie.

"So he did all kinds of weird shit." He sniffled and rubbed his nose with his sleeve. "Sold his truck so he had to drive the van to work. Pulled out the phone wires. Kept the cell phone with him all the time. Even slept with it. Burned most of her clothes so she couldn't go out."

"He burned her clothes?" Maybe that explained the negligee.

"Yeah. All she had left was some nightgowns. Not enough to keep anybody warm in this weather."

I pictured Tiffany getting out of the passenger seat of the van, dressed in the flimsy nightgown. Not what you'd expect someone to be wearing outside in December. "Then why did he have her drive him to work?" I asked.

"Stupid." Shook his massive head and drained the last bit of beer from the can. "He had some stuff in the van he was worried about leaving in the parking lot. I don't even know what it was. And he said he was gonna have her drive him down there and then make her get out and suck him off in front of everybody, so they'd be able to see she had to do anything he told her to. Made him feel like a big man."

Big jerk was more like it. "How'd you know he was going to do that?"

"I was here when he told her."

From what I had seen, they hadn't gone that far. But he had been kissing and groping her where everyone could see. Kelly might be onto something there. He got his jollies humiliating her.

Kelly. I wondered what she was doing right now.

"I came to get some stuff," Reggie said, staggering to his feet. "Mitch was gonna get it for me. I really need it. I came to see if he left it here."

"You don't think the police took it?"

"They would if they found it." Reggie straightened up and ran his fingers through his hair. "Mitch had a good hidey hole. And even a dog wouldn't sniff this out."

"You know where to go look for it?" I asked.

"Yeah. I helped him build it." Reggie wavered for a minute, holding onto the edge of the table. He let go and went into the adults' bedroom. I followed.

He switched on the light and looked into the fireplace with its damp ashes. "The bastard," he muttered. "He better not have burned my stuff."

Moving to the side of the fireplace, Reggie began poking at the corner bricks. He gave one a shove and it pivoted out. Reaching behind the neighboring bricks, he maneuvered several of them out of place.

I didn't like the way this was looking. "That's not gonna collapse the bricks above?"

"Nah. We put a lintel in there, just like for a window opening." He continued removing bricks until he had an opening about a foot square. "Course, Mitch was a lot more coherent back then."

I imagined that Reggie hadn't been quite so drunk, either.

He reached into the hole behind the bricks and drew out a large manila envelope. Carrying it over to the unmade bed, he dumped the contents.

A dark blue passport. Several small cards. One a California driver's license with Reggie's picture on it. And the name Elmer Comings. Several credit cards, a social security card, and a Teamsters' Union ID.

Reggie opened the passport. His picture was on it, too. So was the name Elmer Comings.

He frowned. "Elmer Comings? What kind of a name is that?"

I laughed.

"Sounds like some kind of a nerd who likes to get his own rocks off," Reggie said, flipping through the passport. Several pages had stamps from border crossings. "I can't fool around being called Elmer."

I could hardly stop laughing enough to say, "You'll have to figure out some kind of street name."

"Damn straight." Reggie examined the passport and driver's license. "But this stuff is good."

"Where'd Mitch get these?" I took the driver's license. He was right. It was good.

I wondered if I should think about someday getting a driver's license in a name that wouldn't return an "armed and dangerous" designation as soon as it was called in. Assuming I got a license and started driving sometime, if I was ever pulled over for anything, it would be likely to end in a full-fledged felony traffic stop. Complete with drawn guns and me face down on the shoulder of the road.

On the other hand, getting caught with a fake driver's license would cause its own problems. And the consequences for that would be long-term and a lot more serious than an uncomfortable hour or so lying in the dirt while my car was searched.

Reggie was opening his wallet. "Don't know where he got them," he said. "And I really don't want to know. I know he was into this before he started with the weed. Way before the crystal meth. Some kind of a scam going with one of the supervisors at work."

I couldn't imagine John being involved. Or Hank, although he wasn't really a supervisor. I didn't know any of the other foremen. Could it be Radman? He didn't strike me as a particularly honest guy. But he'd been nervous just with me in the office with him. Kelly had said he was into something with Mitch.

"Do the credit cards work?" I asked.

Reggie shrugged. "Who knows? But it'd be stupid to use them. If they got turned down, it'd draw attention to you. And if they did go through, sooner or later, they'd cause problems and they'd try to trace it to you. Best not to even try. Just leave 'em in the wallet. They'll make it look more normal."

He took his own driver's license out along with a few other cards. He put the Elmer Comings one in along with those cards. He put the passport in his pocket.

Reggie tried to replace the bricks. His fingers fumbled.

"I'll take care of that, dude," I said.

"You're a good man." He slapped me on the shoulder. Probably harder than he'd intended. "Not too many good men in this world. And no good women." Reggie was beginning to tear up again. He gathered up the things he'd removed from the wallet. He carried them out to the main room, opened the stove door, and chucked them in.

"Goodbye, Reggie," he said. "Hello, Elmer. You dirty bastard."

I couldn't help laughing again. "When were you born, Elmer?"

Reggie looked up at me, his eyes bleary. "Good question. I better get that memorized. And the social security number. And all that other shit."

"You better get used to answering to Elmer Comings," I said.

Reggie nodded his head. Mistake. He caught himself just before he fell. "Soon as they plow the roads, I'm gone," he said. Belatedly, a crafty look came into his eyes. "'Preciate it if this stays between us."

"How do you know I'm not an undercover cop planted here to see who turns up and does what?" I asked.

Reggie's eyes opened wide in alarm. Then he grinned through his beard. "Not to worry. No undercover cop would be caught dead changing diapers and babysitting for four kids. And even if some fool cop was willing to do it, he'd be breaking every regulation in the books. Suppose one of the kids got hurt?"

"True. An undercover cop would have called Social Services right away to get the kids." Which is probably what I should have done.

"Yeah. And he wouldn't be here all by himself. There'd be backup."

"True again." Although I could see Belkins deciding to do it. Alone, because he didn't want anyone to interfere with what he wanted to do.

"Besides…" Reggie grinned apologetically. "Cops got a certain smell. You smell more like jailbird than cop. Can't put my finger on it, but there you are."

Smiling ruefully, I didn't answer that.

Reggie had trouble doing it, but he put on his boots again. He gave up trying to tie the laces. He gathered his jacket, hat, and gloves. He stuffed two more cans of beer in his big pockets. He whistled, and Chief came bounding out of the kids' bedroom. "He's gonna miss those kids," Reggie said. "Likes 'em a lot."

"Good luck," I said. I meant it.

"Yeah. Gonna need it. Thanks for the supper."

I watched him leave, wondering if Belkins and Montgomery knew about Reggie. Had I just been talking to the person responsible for Mitch's death? No way of knowing for sure, but as drunk as he'd been, he probably would have let something slip.

One thing for sure. I had to find out a lot more about this before I fed any information about Reggie to Montgomery.

# CHAPTER 11

My foster mother, Mrs. Coleman, used to say that one of the reasons God gave us babies was to remind us not to be a-wasting the daylight hours the Good Lord gave us. Beth was no exception. Dawning fingers of gold and pink were beginning to find their way through the smudged windows and the cracks in the curtains when she started whimpering.

A deep chill had settled into the room. I shivered in the makeshift bed I'd assembled on the floor between the playpen where Beth lay and the stove. Beth began to cry in earnest. I shook my hair out of my eyes and struggled to my feet. A bottle from the refrigerator and a clean if inexpertly applied diaper settled her down again. The fire had died back during the night. I took some kindling from the wood box and coaxed it back to life. Slipping on my boots, I stepped onto the back porch in search of more wood.

The air smelled of pine and new snow. Sunlight glittered on branches covered with pristine white ice. A bird flitted from the top of a tree and lit on a clothesline pole. I breathed deeply, letting the sharp, fresh cold fill my lungs. The only sounds I could hear were the wind in the trees and the chattering of squirrels.

If I got sent back to prison, could I stand it? Trade this for life on a crowded cell block, filled with the choking smell of unwashed bodies and disinfectant, bombarded by chaotic noise resounding off concrete floors and steel walls?

No point worrying about it. Not like I had much control over that.

I gathered an armful of firewood and carried it inside. I put a few lengths in the stove and shut the door.

The heavy towels along with my sweater and shirt I'd washed last night were still damp, but the other clothes were dry. I folded them and opened the door to the kids' room to put them away.

The twins were sitting on the floor, pushing a bent plastic truck back and forth between them. Sam was holding a book.

"Hey, guys," I said. "I didn't know you were up. You were so quiet."

"We don't make no noise until Mom tells us it's okay to get up." Sam turned a page of his book. "Sometimes it's hard. We sneak out to go pee, but otherwise, we stay in here until it's time to get up."

"Well, I think it's time. I'll see what I can find for breakfast."

I gathered dirty clothes from the floor and started the washing machine. Then I went in search of breakfast.

A big pot of instant oatmeal with brown sugar. The milk jug was almost empty, but I found a box of powdered milk and mixed up a gallon. Not a fancy breakfast, but the kids eagerly spooned it into their mouths.

"How about the Christmas tree?" Sam scraped the last of the oatmeal from his bowl. "You said we could put it up today. We could have it ready for when Mom gets home. She'd like that."

"Yep. You know if you got anything to put on it? Lights or something?"

"I think there's a box of stuff in the back of the pantry," Sam said. "I can look for it if you want."

"After your bath," I said.

"Ah, gee. Can't we set up the tree first? Please?"

I looked at the grimy faces in front of me. "Everybody needs a bath."

"Can I at least go out and see the Christmas tree now?" Sam begged.

"Yeah. See how big it is. But we'll leave it there until after the baths."

Sam opened the front door and went out on the porch. I started clearing the dishes to the sink.

Sam's face was glowing when he came back in. "It's not tall. But it's fat. It's gonna make a great Christmas tree."

"Okay. Let's get those baths going and put on clean clothes."

While I did the breakfast dishes, Sam ran water in the tub and undressed the twins. They climbed in and splashed around. I finished the dishes and went in to see about washing hair.

The bathwater was filthy. "When did they last have baths?" I asked Sam.

He shrugged. "A while ago, I guess."

I let out the water and ran a bit more to rinse the kids off. Then I took a bottle of shampoo and poured a little into my hand.

"Okay, guys. Chins up and shut your eyes really tight," I said, remembering the sting of getting shampoo in my eyes when I was a kid. I rubbed it into their short brown curls, and then rinsed their heads by pouring water from a pot. They kept their eyes closed tightly and laughed as the water cascaded over their heads and down their backs.

"Okay, Sam, your turn," I said. "You need help?"

"I can take a bath by myself," he said indignantly.

I lifted the toddlers from the tub and shooed them into the living room. We had no clean, dry towels and the room was still chilly, but they didn't seem to mind. The twins ran around naked and giggling until they were dry. I helped them into some of the clothes I'd washed last night.

Sam emerged from the bathroom and found himself some clean clothes. We gathered up the filthy ones the kids had been wearing and piled them next to the washing machine.

Beth needed a bath, too—I thought she'd fit nicely in the kitchen sink—but she was sleeping, and another thing I'd learned from Mrs. Coleman was never to wake a sleeping baby unless absolutely necessary.

Sam dragged a big box out of the pantry. To the twins' delight, he began removing Christmas ornaments, strands of lights, and a tree stand.

I went out on the front porch to get the tree. Sam was right. It was short and fat—only about five foot tall and almost as big around. Reggie must have cut it yesterday. The stump oozed sap.

From the direction of the road, I heard a distant rumble. A snow plow? I looked at the driveway where it disappeared between the trees. The van wasn't going anywhere until some of the snow was either cleared or packed way down. I wondered if Reggie were getting ready to leave and start his new life as Elmer Comings. I wondered if he'd even made it home last night, drunk as he was.

At least no one would be checking up on me and wondering where I was. I had no idea how long it would be before I could get out of here. So I might as well just kick back and make the best of it.

I shook the snow off the tree and carried it inside. Sam helped me steady it in the tree stand. We pushed it back against the wall, next to an electrical outlet and away from the stove. I draped the lights through the branches and then let the kids put the ornaments wherever they wanted. The result was a tree with decorations at waist level and below, but mostly bare above.

Sam stood back to take a look at their handiwork. "We need more stuff," he said. "There's empty spots."

I thought quickly back to Christmases with the frugal Colemans. Seemed to me we made a lot of the decorations. Chains of popcorn and paper loops and foil stars and Christmas cookies. "Maybe we could make some more stuff. It is a pretty fat tree. It could use a couple more things."

Sam looked interested. "What could we make?"

"There's popcorn in the pantry. We can pop that. If your Mom has a sewing box with needles and thread, we could make strings of popcorn. If you cut stars out of cardboard, you can cover them with aluminum foil. They make great shiny stars. And I could look in your Mom's cookbook. Maybe we have the stuff to make Christmas cookies. You can punch holes in them before you bake them, then put string through the holes and hang them on the tree."

"Christmas cookies!" Sam liked that idea.

"Santa Claus," one of the twins—Peter, I think—said.

Sam's face fell. "I know all about Santa Claus." He looked at me. "There's no presents to put under the tree."

That I couldn't help them with.

When Beth woke up, I washed her in the kitchen sink and then sat at the table, balancing the baby and her bottle on my lap as I tried to make sense of the directions in a cookbook I'd found on the pantry shelf.

"Cream" the butter and sugar? What the hell did that mean? Could I use margarine instead of butter? "Roll the dough a quarter inch thick on a floured board. Cut out." Hadn't seemed like it would be too hard to make Christmas cookies. But I'd have to figure out what the directions meant. They were in English. I didn't find that to be much help.

The twins had brought their toy cars out into the main room and were driving them along the edge of Beth's playpen. Sam was curled up on the sofa reading his book. Seemed like a much better idea than turning on the TV.

Someone knocked on the door.

Reggie back again? The police? At least I didn't have a can of beer this time. I shifted Beth to one arm and went to open it.

In front of me stood a short teenager with a hint of red hair peeking from below his hat and a million freckles plastered all over his face. He was dressed in camouflage fatigues and combat boots. Next to him were two black plastic garbage bags. A jeep stood in front of the snowed-over van. It had made two deep ruts in the snow.

We stared at each other for a minute, surprised. He blinked first.

"Where's Tiffany?" he asked.

"She's sick," I said cautiously.

"You're not Mitch." He was certainly observant.

"True, that."

"I need to see Tiffany."

"I'm afraid she's not here. She's real sick. She's in the hospital."

"Well, who in God's name are you?" he asked.

"A friend." Not completely accurate, but better than saying I was a convicted murderer on parole and now suspected of killing Tiffany's husband. "Somebody had to stay with the kids. Who are you?"

"Carl Miller. Tiffany's brother." He looked past me, into the room. "I told her I'd bring some stuff for the kids for Christmas."

Sam leaped up from the sofa. "Uncle Carl!" he cried. "You came. Mom said you would."

Carl looked down at Sam and smiled. "Been a while, Trooper." He rubbed Sam's head. "You look a lot like my nephew Sam. Only bigger."

Sam grinned. "I am Sam."

The infamous Uncle Carl. Was this my release at hand? He didn't look old enough to take care of four kids. But then, he didn't look old enough to be a Marine, either. "You best come in so we can close that door," I said. "Don't want the baby to get cold."

Carl turned and picked up his two bags. He stepped inside and saw the tree. "I think these go over there." He handed Sam the bags.

Sam opened one. It was full of brightly wrapped packages.

Delighted, Sam dragged it over to the tree and started removing packages. "Look what Uncle Carl brought," he called to the twins. He peered at the label of one before he placed it under the tree and took another one. The younger boys hurried over to join him.

"Now," Carl said, squaring himself and looking up at me. "You want to go over this again about Tiffany being sick? And where's Mitch?"

He didn't know about Mitch? Yikes. "I'm not sure I'm the person who should be telling you this," I said, "but Mitch is dead. Didn't Tiffany tell you?"

"Dead?" His face paled. "Dead? I haven't talked to Tiffany in over a week. But dead? What happened?"

To me, Carl sounded genuinely shocked, but what did I know? Montgomery would be able to tell whether he was telling the truth just by looking at him.

What would I do if I had a sister and I didn't like the way her husband was treating her and the kids? Hard to tell, since I'd never had a sister. I think I would try to talk her into leaving him, but if she wouldn't, would I feel like I should do something to get rid of him? Like killing him?

I found it a bit alarming how easily that "solution" came to mind. I didn't think it would have occurred to me before I'd spent all that time in prison. Maybe Belkins had a point.

Carl had military training. He was just back from a war zone in Iraq. No way of knowing what he'd seen. Or done. Killing an abusive brother-in-law might not seem like such a big deal to him at this point.

I found it hard to know what to tell him. "He died at work," I said.

"Some kind of industrial accident?"

I shrugged. "I'm not clear on the details. They think maybe somebody killed him."

Carl took off his camouflage jacket and stuffed his hat in the pocket. He ran his thin hand over the reddish stubble on his head. The old boot camp joke came to mind: You get a haircut? No, but I'm hoping it will grow into one.

He sat in one of the kitchen chairs, shaking his head. "Dead. Who'd have thought it?"

I finished feeding Beth her bottle and laid her in her playpen. The boys were all gathered around the Christmas tree, picking up packages and shaking them.

"Tomorrow," Sam was telling the twins. "Christmas morning. Then we can open them."

Carl stared at the boys. "When did this happen?" he asked.

"Tuesday night. I'm surprised you didn't hear about it. It was in the paper and on the news."

"My mom's kind of depressed. She was afraid she was going to spend Christmas alone. Even though she has two kids and four grandkids." Carl looked at his gnawed fingernails. "I took her on a little vacation. To Ocean City."

His mother? Tiffany's mother, too? A grandmother. These kids could use a grandmother.

I hoped she was the kind of grandmother who couldn't get enough of her grandbabies. Not the crabby kind who thought they should always be sitting quietly or sleeping.

"Ocean City?" I asked. "This time of year?"

"Yeah, I know." Carl shifted in his chair. "But she loves the ocean. It's kind of neat to walk along the shore in the winter. The waves churning up on the beach. The boardwalk's deserted. And I got a deal on the hotel rooms."

"I imagine you did."

"Mom deserves a break. She worried about me all the time I was overseas. And she worries about Tiffany and the kids all the time. But if she tries to say something, Tiff gets mad and says leave her alone, Mitch'll take care of them. So Mom doesn't call much. And Tiff doesn't call at all." He sat quietly for a minute.

Nothing for me to say.

"But come Christmas time," Carl continued, "she gets all choked up. About the grandkids, especially." He gestured toward the presents. "She bought most of that stuff. Been picking it up a little at a time, all year. And she wrapped all of it up, so the kids could have something."

"Maybe she could come for Christmas," I suggested. Then I wouldn't have to stay.

Carl looked thoughtful. "I bet she'd love that," he said. "She'd cook dinner and clean up." He looked around the room. "The place looks better than it did when I was here last."

"We been working on it."

Carl nodded. "I came to see Tiffany Monday, while Mitch was at work. We've never been real thrilled with Mitch, Mom and me." He looked from the kids to me. "I mean, I know it's up to Tiffany who she marries. And I know she had Sam. She was worried that with one kid already and no child support, she'd never find a husband. Then she started seeing Mitch and got pregnant with the twins. You'd think she'd be more careful the second time…" Carl's voice trailed off.

I closed the cookbook and put it away. Looked like maybe I could skip the cookie making. Grandmothers should be better equipped to make cookies than I ever would be.

Carl stirred himself. "Tiff's at the hospital in town? Let me call and see how she's doing. Then I'll call Mom and tell her." He shook his head in disbelief. "Mitch is dead. Tiffany is in the hospital."

"The phone isn't working," I pointed out.

"I know. Tiff told me. Mitch pulled out the wires. I have my cell phone."

Oh, yeah. Just because I didn't have a cell phone didn't mean that everybody else didn't. I didn't have anybody to call anyhow.

"Do you know the hospital's number?" he asked, flipping open his phone. "Is there a phone book around here?"

I went into the pantry and found the phone book. I looked up "hospitals" in the yellow pages. By the time I found it, he was talking into his cell phone.

"Mom?" Carl said into the phone. "Listen, Tiffany's in the hospital. And this guy—what did you say your name was?" He glanced at me.

"Just a friend." Probably do no good to keep my name out of it, but I wouldn't tell him if I could manage not to. Less he knew about me, the less he could tell the cops, who were sure to be asking.

"A friend, I guess, he's here taking care of the kids. And he says Mitch is dead." He listened for a few minutes. Beneath his freckles, his pale face went paler still. He turned to me. "Did Tiffany kill Mitch?"

Now that one hadn't occurred to me. Had Tiffany finally gotten her fill of the abuse and snuck into the plant? And killed him? In her negligee?

But I replied, "I don't think so. It happened at work."

"Did Mitch do something to Tiffany? Is that why she's in the hospital?" Carl asked.

"Not that I know of," I said. "She was real sick when I got here. Fever. I didn't see any bruises or anything like that."

"Okay." Carl turned back to the phone. "Mom, I don't know what happened. To Mitch, either. Maybe Tiffany can tell us when we see her."

He listened for a little while.

"Yeah. Huh. Okay. Yeah." He hung up.

"Mom's gonna meet me at the hospital," he said. "Can you stay awhile longer with the kids?"

"Look." I wasn't going to let this opportunity to get out of the baby-sitting detail evaporate. "I stayed with them 'cause there was nobody else. But I got to get home myself. You think your mom can take care of them? Or can you?"

"Mom says she'll do it," Carl said. "She sounded thrilled. I don't think she's even seen the baby yet. I can drive her back here after we see Tiffany."

"I got to get back to town," I insisted. "How about we pack up the kids and take them to the hospital? You and your mom can go see Tiffany and then bring the kids back here."

I could see Carl wavering.

"Tiffany told them you'd take them to McDonald's." I didn't tell him that I'd already done that. "They're really looking forward to it. I can just go home from the hospital."

Carl shrugged. "Sounds like a plan to me," he said. "But I can't fit everybody into the Jeep."

I wasn't about to let my chance to get a ride to town evaporate. "We can shovel a path for the van over to the tracks the jeep made," I urged. "It's downhill to the road. I heard a snowplow go by. You made it up here. The roads can't be that bad."

Carl looked doubtful. "I suppose."

I reached for my jacket. "Let's see if we can move the van," I said. "Sam'll keep an eye on the little ones until we get done." I eyed a pair of thick gloves and a scarf draped over the hook under where my jacket had been. Probably Mitch's. He wouldn't be needing them. I grabbed them.

Between the trees, the snow wasn't so deep. Carl found some snow shovels, and we set to work. We soon had the van sitting in the tracks the Jeep had made, the engine running. We should be able to make it down to the road. Getting it back up the driveway might be more of a problem, but it wouldn't be mine. Besides, they could leave the van parked down by the road and walk up.

Back in the house, Sam gathered up jackets and hats for the twins while I packed the diaper bag. Carl studied the squat Christmas tree with most of its ornaments on the bottom third and frowned. At least it had presents underneath it now. The kids were thrilled. That was the important thing.

I snatched my sweater and shirt from the drying rack. I'd given them low priority; the diapers and the kids' clothes were closer to the heat. They were still damp. I rolled them up and stuffed them into a plastic grocery bag from the pantry.

I grabbed Tiffany's purse. "You might need this," I said. "It has her medical card and stuff."

Carl took it and looked at me suspiciously. He rummaged inside. Narrowing his eyes, he pulled out the wallet and jerked it open. The small bunch of twenties fell out to the floor. He picked them up and looked at me, relief evident on his face. "How long you been babysitting?" he asked.

I shrugged. "A little over a day, I guess," I said.

"You think sixty dollars'll do?" he asked, holding out three twenties. "It's not a lot, but…"

Sixty dollars. Maybe not a lot of money, but it would make a big difference to me. Might mean I could actually eat the first week back to work, before I got a paycheck. In a way, I hated to take Tiffany's money; she and the kids probably needed it. But with Uncle Carl and Grandma on the scene, maybe things wouldn't be so tight.

"Sixty dollars is fine," I said, pocketing the money.

I was happy to let Carl drive the van. Presumably he had a license. And since it was his sister's vehicle, the question of unauthorized use was much less likely to come up if we were stopped.

We parked in the visitor's lot at the hospital this time. Herding the boys and carrying the baby and diaper bag, we went in the front entrance instead of the emergency room.

"I got to get going." I looked around the waiting room, half expecting to see a cop approaching, handcuffs in one hand and the other resting on the butt of his service gun.

"My mom should be here in a few minutes," Carl said. "Can't you stay with the kids for a few minutes until she gets here?"

He had just paid me a fair amount for babysitting. I didn't see so much as a security guard. And I had to get a grip. "I guess," I said.

Carl went over to the reception desk and got in the short line.

In the comfortable main waiting room, I settled down with the kids on an overstuffed couch in a corner where they could see the TV and where I could sit sideways, shielded by a big plant but still keep an eye on the room. The whole area was a lot calmer than the emergency waiting room. No big double doors constantly swinging open, no ambulances or police cars screaming up to the curb.

The room was hot. I took off my jacket and tucked the gloves carefully in the pockets. I draped it over the back of a chair with the scarf and put the bag holding still-damp sweater and shirt on the seat. Then I helped the kids get their jackets off.

When Carl's turn came, he spoke to the lady, nodded, waved over at us, and went to the elevators.

Beth started fussing. I took a bottle from the diaper bag and popped off the plastic top. Leaning back on the couch, I lay her in my lap and propped her head in my elbow. She reached eagerly for the bottle. I smiled. I was getting pretty good at this. The older kids sat mesmerized by the TV.

Two men walked up to the information desk, pushing to the head of the short line. Rude, I thought, watching idly.

Something familiar about the men. I sat up and looked more closely.

Belkins was leaning over the information desk intently. He nodded at something the receptionist said, straightened up, and strode over to the elevator bank. The doors of one yawned open. He got in, and the door closed.

Montgomery stepped away from the information desk, his gaze sweeping the room.

I turned my back and bent my head over Beth, trying to shield my face without appearing to be hiding. When I glanced back, Montgomery faced the elevators. He watched the door of another one close.

"Sam," I hissed. "I got to go. Think you can finish giving Beth her bottle and keep an eye on the twins till your grandma gets here?"

Sam's eyes grew wide. "Yeah, I guess," he said. "Aren't you gonna stay and find out when Mom's coming home?"

"Can't. I got to get going. Say 'bye to Uncle Carl for me. Your grandma should be here any minute." I hoped that was the case.

Keeping my back to the elevators and resolutely not looking in that direction, I stood up and handed Beth over to Sam. Then I grabbed my jacket and the plastic bag.

I risked a glance behind me. Montgomery stood by the elevators, watching as a door opened. Once again, the door closed without him stepping in. Another elevator arrived.

I had to get out of there before he looked around the waiting room too closely. I stepped close to the wall, skirting the perimeter of the room. Resisting the urge to look over toward Montgomery again, I made an effort to straighten my shoulders and hold my head high, facing away from him. I stepped through the double doors leading from the waiting room.

Breathing a little more easily, I hurried through the short hallway, past the gift shop, and out the front door.

Looked like I'd made it. I gulped a grateful breath of cold, free air.

Too soon.

"Damon." A rich, cultivated, commanding voice came from behind me. Montgomery. "Stop."

I stopped.

# CHAPTER 12

"Drop your things."

I tossed the jacket and the plastic bag a few feet away from me, spread my feet apart, and put my hands behind my head.

Montgomery stepped up and picked up the jacket and the bag. He peered into the bag.

"Put your hands down," he said. "Keep them where I can see them, but put them down. People going into hospitals tend to be upset already. No need to make a spectacle of ourselves."

I lowered my hands, careful to keep my arms at my sides.

"Come sit down." He indicated a bench outside the front door, under the entry canopy and out of the wind. Pale sunlight glinted off the metal slats of the seat without warming it.

I sat, resting my hands on my knees, hoping that was sufficiently in plain sight. I stared straight ahead.

Montgomery put my things on the other end of the bench. He stood in front of me, waiting. I could wait, too, even though my jeans and boxers were no match for the cold of the metal seat.

Finally, he said, "We got a weird report about somebody who looked a lot like you coming to the emergency room yesterday with Mitch Robinson's widow. Maybe posing as her brother. Seemed pretty incredible, but the source was reliable. Belkins insisted we check it out right away. Of course, he's right; we should check out everything, no matter how unlikely it seems. So he asked the hospital to call it in if anybody checked in to visit her. Especially the brother."

I had no idea how I could possibly respond to him reasonably. Anything I said was going to dig this hole deeper.

Montgomery rocked back on his well-shod heels. "So we get the call, and when we get here, we find out that the brother has already gone upstairs to see Mrs. Robinson. Belkins figures if you were saying you were her brother yesterday, maybe it's you again. Follow so far?"

I avoided eye contact. "Yes, sir."

The hem of Montgomery's heavy overcoat fluttered in a gust of wind. "So Belkins goes up to see who's visiting her, and I wait in case you—or whoever—comes down before he gets up there."

He paused again. I wondered what he would say if I asked to put my jacket on. Better not chance it.

"And who do I see in the waiting room?" Montgomery checked the buttons on the coat. "You. Jesse Damon. Over with a bunch of kids. You get up and leave the kids by themselves. Are they the Robinson kids?"

I shrugged.

"You may as well tell me. Not like I'll have any problem finding out."

I shifted uncomfortably on the bench. "They're the Robinson kids. Tiffany's mom is coming to take care of them. Should be here any minute."

"Tiffany, eh? I thought you didn't know Mitch's wife."

I shook my head. Better keep my mouth shut as much as I could.

"And what are you wearing?" Montgomery put his hand on the brick wall above my head and leaned over me. I could smell his minty breath and aftershave. "A hoodie that maybe belonged to Mitch Robinson. In fact, almost definitely belonged to Mitch Robinson."

I started. The hoodie. I'd forgotten. It said "Mitch" across the back. How stupid could I be?

"And when you notice me, you decide to leave. Right?"

Direct question. Better start answering some of these or risk being "uncooperative." "Yes, sir."

"I'm wondering why you were sitting with those kids."

I tried to find a more comfortable position on the cold bench. Not likely. "Just keeping an eye on them."

"Uh huh. Funny that when we ask if you know Mitch's wife, you say no. Then here you are, 'keeping an eye on' her kids."

"Well, yeah."

"Seems pretty strange to me. Seem pretty strange to you?" Montgomery folded his arms and glared at me.

I nodded again. Pretty strange was understating it.

"So who is Belkins going to find visiting Mrs. Robinson upstairs?"

That one at least I could answer. "Like the lady at the desk said. Her brother."

"His name?"

"Carl Miller."

"That the brother you were impersonating yesterday?" Montgomery took a step closer to me.

My wrists itched.

"I wasn't trying to impersonate him." I hadn't really implied I was him; I just hadn't corrected the receptionist's misconception. "They just assumed I was him."

"So it was you yesterday, was it?"

He was tripping me up already. Better stop saying anything. I pressed my lips firmly together. I looked down at the dirty water puddling on the sidewalk. If the hospital staff didn't do something, put salt on it or sweep it away, it would freeze and someone might slip on it.

Montgomery looked at me for a few long minutes. "You're not going to tell me much more than that, are you?"

Got to give him credit for being able to read his suspects. "No, sir."

"And even if I did, by some miracle, get some information out of you, I would have no way of knowing if any of it was the truth. Isn't that right?"

"I guess so," I agreed reluctantly.

"You know Belkins has been looking for you?" Montgomery smoothed the front of his tweed overcoat.

"Not really, sir." I was sure Montgomery knew I was skirting the truth.

"He thinks you have a lot more to tell us."

I continued staring at the ice forming on the puddle.

"So do I." Montgomery stood back and folded his arms.

I sat in bleak silence.

"Belkins thought he could pick you up at your apartment." Montgomery leaned close again, looming over me. "But you know what?" he said.

"I wasn't there." I looked longingly toward the sidewalk leading away from the hospital.

"So right. You weren't there. For hours. Funny, for someone supposed to be paroled on home detention."

"Mr. Ramirez eased up the monitoring for the holidays." They could check that out easily enough.

"I know. Belkins wanted to have you picked up right away and thrown in jail to wait for a violation hearing. But I decided to call the parole office."

"Thank you, sir."

"Only to discover," Montgomery said as he straightened up, "that you weren't being monitored until after the new year. So you could be anywhere. And as long as you hadn't left the state and you weren't associating with known felons, it wouldn't be a violation."

"Yes, sir."

"But I must admit I wouldn't have thought to look for Mitch Robinson's widow to see if you were with her. Or with her kids. After all, you don't know Mrs. Robinson, do you?"

I didn't answer that.

"Belkins will want to pull you in for more interrogation. You know that?"

"Yes, sir." My hand wandered up to where the traces of bruising remained on my check bone. I snatched it down and forced it to lie still on my knee.

"But you know what?"

"No, sir."

"I don't think he'll get much more out of you than I'm getting now. You think I'm right?" He tugged his collar a little closer to his neck.

"Yes, sir."

He leaned in closer, his bulk hovering inches over me. "So I'm going to let you go. For now."

"Thank you, sir." I glanced up at him.

"I want to spend Christmas Eve home with my family, not in a grungy interrogation room playing word games with some paroled convict who isn't going to tell me what I want to know anyhow."

I tried not to shiver. Not entirely from the cold.

"But Belkins, now…He hasn't got much of a family, you know. Not since some pervert killed his daughter. I imagine he'd be happy to spend Christmas Eve trying to get something useful out of you. Probably keep at it all Christmas Day, too."

Not an appealing thought.

Montgomery straightened up. "Don't misunderstand me, boy." He put emphasis on the "boy." He turned away and looked out over the parking lot in front of the hospital. "It's not that I don't think Belkins might be right. You probably did have something to do with Mitch Robinson's death. If I had any doubts about that before, they're pretty much gone now that I find you with his family. But I want a clean conviction. So I'm going to keep at this until I find out what happened. If I have anything to say about it—and I will—when we take this to trial, there will be no procedural errors. No confession that can be challenged as coerced. No conviction that can be overturned on appeal. Do you understand me?"

A long speech and not particularly comforting. But not much I could do about it.

He turned back to face me. "Get yourself out of here before Belkins sees you. And make sure you stay where we can find you."

"Yes, sir." I got up, grabbed my things, and walked away, struggling into the jacket as I went.

As I turned the corner, wind kicked up and a cloud scuttled over the sun. I shivered and flipped up my jacket hood. I didn't have the scarf anymore; I must have left it at the hospital. I patted the pocket of my jacket. I did still have the gloves. I pulled them out and slipped them on.

They were thick leather gloves with a fleece lining. I shoved the plastic bag with my sweater and shirt as far into the pocket as it would go.

Sixty dollars and a pair of warm gloves. And a hoodie that said "Mitch" across the back. I'd have to get rid of that soon. Not bad, though, for taking care of a few kids for a day or so.

Tomorrow would be Christmas. Most businesses would be closed. In fact, they might be closing early today. I should stop at the library. Get a few books to read and then pick up something to eat. With the money Carl had given me, I could afford something more festive than just peanut butter sandwiches and instant coffee.

The thought hit me that I was disappointed I wasn't going to be with those kids for Christmas. Made no sense. Not like I'd spent a whole lot of time with them or knew them well. They'd be much better off with Grandma and Uncle Carl. Now they had the presents Uncle Carl had brought. Grandma would fix a real Christmas dinner.

I had to keep in mind how I'd spent the last nineteen Christmases. A "special" turkey loaf meal in a noisy, crowded chow hall. Most of the day locked in with a cellmate I didn't choose and probably didn't like. Because they tried to give the day off to as much staff as possible, there'd be no classes, no library, no yard, no visiting hours. Not that visiting hours affected me at all. I wasn't enough of a hypocrite to go to church services just to get out of my cell.

A day reading in my own room would certainly beat that. I could go for a walk any time I wanted to. So I should stop feeling sorry for myself and appreciate what I had, for now, at least.

Cutting through an alley and across the corner of a vacant lot, I saw two men taking down strings of Christmas lights and rolling twine into a ball. They had been selling Christmas trees, but they had only three or four straggly ones left and they were closing up shop. For a brief moment, I wondered if I should offer them a few bucks for one of the remaining trees.

But what would I do with it? I didn't have any decorations at all, and I really had no place to put it in my one-room apartment. Unless I jammed it between my bed and the wall, where it would block my only window.

Not a good way to spend any of my unanticipated financial windfall. I kept going.

I took the front steps up to the library two at a time. As I came through the door, I saw Mandy at the circulation desk. She frowned at me.

My heart sank. Usually she smiled when I came in.

She was Mandy Radman, I knew now. Came back to work here despite her husband's undoubtedly substantial income. I wondered if sometimes being married could be even more lonesome than being single. She didn't look happy.

"We're closing early for Christmas Eve." She straightened up a pile of books on the counter. "You only have about ten minutes."

"Okay." I could see through the doorway that the lights in the book stacks had already been turned off. I went to the new book display. I could find something there. Looking over the selection, I grabbed a slim volume and flipped it over to read the back.

Historical romance. Not what I was looking for. I took another.

Murder mystery. That hit too close to home.

Fantasy. Maybe. I held onto that one.

Espionage. A fat book. I kept that one, too.

A nonfiction on the Civil War. Sounded good.

I took my three selections to the desk and dug out my library card.

Mandy wore a bright red fleece top with reindeer leaping across her trim but shapely bosom. I tried not to stare at it. She performed the computer magic that made the books mine for the next month. Computers had really taken over the world while I'd been locked up. One of these days, I'd have to come into the library and sign up for the one of the computers they had for public use. See what everybody else took for granted.

I thanked Mandy and started to scoop them up.

Her frown softened. "Would you like a plastic bag for them?" she asked. "Looks like we may get more snow. Or sleet."

"Yes, thank you," I said, watching as she slipped them into a grocery bag from a supply under the counter. "You have a good holiday, now." I grinned tentatively.

She smiled back. "And a very merry Christmas to you, too."

I was pleased to see her smile. But her smile looked brittle, as if the wrong words might break it.

She followed me to the front door and locked it behind me as I stepped out. Mandy was right about the weather; a spitting of sleet stung my face as I went down the steps.

I ducked my head into the wind and cut across the now-deserted Christmas tree lot. On to the grocery store. Maybe I would get a can of tomato soup and some bread and cheese. And margarine for the grilling. On freezing wet days like this, Mrs. Coleman used to make tomato soup and grilled cheese sandwiches. The thought made my mouth water.

I thought about the warm buttery scent of the sandwiches in the frying pan, the creamy smoothness of the tomato soup as it slid down my throat. An always-changing array of foster children seated around the oilcloth covering the worn kitchen table. Maybe not really loved, but safe and warm and well cared for. As good a substitute as anyone could ask for.

Mrs. Coleman had been so disappointed in me. I'd sent her a letter from prison, but Mr. Coleman had written back. "Please don't contact my wife," he'd said. "She had such hopes for you; she cried after she read about your crimes in the newspaper."

*Really, I didn't kill anybody, Mrs. Coleman,* I'd wanted to shout. *Please don't believe I'm such a total failure. If I could just explain.* But I'd had to respect the request not to contact her.

*No point thinking like that,* I told myself. *What's done is done. Be grateful for the good parts. Get the stuff to make the soup and sandwiches.*

Wrapped up in my thoughts but still paying attention to my surroundings—a prison survival technique—I noticed something big on the sidewalk a little way up in front of me, partially blocking my way. I looked more closely.

A Christmas tree. Bundled up and tied in twine. A car was parked by the curb next to it. A woman was bent over, struggling to lift the Christmas tree.

I slipped my hand through the handle of the plastic bag that held the books and reached down for the trunk of the tree. Giving it a heave, I lifted the bottom half up on the roof. The woman managed to get the top part of the tree up, too.

"Got something to tie it on with?" I asked. "I'll hold it while you tie it."

"Thanks, Jesse," the woman said.

Surprised, I turned my head to see a familiar face.

Hiding surprise was another prison survival technique. "Anytime, Kelly."

She snorted. "Christmas Eve is a rotten enough time to be out trying to get a Christmas tree. Without having it fall off."

I laughed. "Got some twine or something to tie this with?"

"Yeah. I tried that. But that's where I ran into trouble. If I tie it through the windows, I can't get the door open. So I tied it on with the door open, but the twine must have broken when I shut the door. The tree slid off after I'd driven two blocks."

"Can't you tie it on and then climb in a window?" I asked. "Then you can just leave the windows a little open."

"Fat chance," she said. "Look at me. I'm not exactly a featherweight. Or hugely agile. You think I'm going to manage to climb in the window? And get myself into a sitting position with my feet actually down by the pedals?"

I couldn't help grinning at the mental image of her substantial rear disappearing through the window into the interior of the car. "I bet if you took off that bulky jacket, you'd do fine," I told her. "But you get in and close the doors. I'll tie it on through the open windows."

"How will I get out?"

"You cut the twine. Or I can tie it so you can reach the knots from the driver's seat."

She got into the car and opened the front windows. I took the twine and tied the tree firmly to the roof. Then I tied a piece to the top of the tree and the front bumper. Same thing with the trunk and the rear bumper.

I stood back and looked at it. "That ought to hold till you get home," I said. "'Course, it might be a little chilly driving with the windows open like that. Not to mention wet." The sleet was turning to snow.

"Why don't you come and help me set it up?" she asked.

My stomach lurched. "What?"

"Come help me set it up. And have dinner."

A very appealing idea.

"What else have you got to do?" she asked.

"True, that," I said.

"What time do you have to be home for the monitor to be read?" She brushed her hair back.

"Off monitoring for the holiday," I said.

"Then get in."

"The doors are tied shut."

"So climb through the window." She rolled the passenger window all the way down. "Like you told me to do. You're not nearly as fat as I am."

I stripped off my jacket and gloves and tossed them with the bag of books into the back seat. Hoisting myself up on the edge of the roof, I swung my feet through the window and dropped into the passenger seat of the car.

Kelly stared at me. "Where did you get Mitch's sweatshirt?" she asked. "He leave it at work?"

"Long story," I said, settling into the seat and closing the window most of the way. I wasn't sure how much I wanted to tell her.

Kelly eased the car into gear and pulled away from the curb. "I wasn't going to get a Christmas tree at all this year. I think I told you… The kids are supposed to be with their dad all this week." She shivered. "Can you see if you can get that heat kicked up?"

I fiddled with the buttons on the heater, turning it to high. "Yeah, you said something like that."

"Well, I got a call from Fred's sister this morning. Seems he's been out drinking—surprise—and left the kids with his mother, who's almost eighty and really can't handle them. So the sister's gonna bring the kids to my place tonight."

"Really?"

"Yep." Kelly hunched forward and stared through the windshield. "They're Polish; they do their holiday thing on Christmas Eve, not Christmas Day. So after they have this big dinner and open the presents, she's gonna drop them off."

"At least you get to see them on Christmas." Seemed like a good thing; she'd been morose about not seeing them on the holiday.

"Yeah. I was kind of all broken up over that. But then I got used to the idea. Got me a fifth of Southern Comfort. Figured I'd have a few drinks tonight, get up tomorrow and finish off the bottle. Watch *It's a Wonderful Life* or something else stupid."

Watching a movie, especially that one, didn't seem stupid to me. The drinking did. But who was I to judge how other people chose to cope with what life dealt them? Not like I had a good handle on my life or anything.

"And now I haven't gotten anything ready for Christmas at all," she continued glumly.

"You got a tree now."

"I do have a tree now. And I have some of the presents I was gonna give the kids when they came home. I can wrap them up tonight."

"So you can have a good Christmas with them," I said, remembering Sam and the twins with their tree and presents.

"I guess. But I didn't do much grocery shopping."

"They're kids; fix something they like for dinner. Anything. Doesn't have to be a big, fancy meal."

"I know you're right." Kelly sighed. "Just hard to change plans so fast."

I glanced over at her. Tears were forming in her eyes. I'm no good with people who cry. Not Reggie. Definitely not Kelly. I looked away, at the brave Christmas lights shining through the gloom from the few stores that were still open.

"I just didn't think I'd ever be in this position is all, I guess," she said.

"What position is that?"

"Divorced. Single mother. I used to feel sorry for women who were trying to take care of a family on their own. Like my mother. She always seemed so lonesome after my dad left."

"Don't see nothing to feel sorry for," I said. "Lots of women raise kids by themselves. Lots of happy families like that."

Not that I knew any.

We left Rothsburg's ragged commercial area and headed into a residential neighborhood. Big, old houses, some of them divided into two apartments, lined either side of the broad road. Snow was beginning to cover the ice. I shivered and wished I hadn't taken off my jacket.

Kelly's house was impressive. Big, two-story brick structure with an attic, probably built in the 1920s. An expansive front porch and a driveway next to the house leading back to an equally impressive brick garage with a yawning door.

Kelly stopped the car by the back porch and started tugging on the twine. I unrolled the passenger side window the rest of the way, climbed out and went around to untie it. I lifted the tree from the roof and stood it next to the steps.

"I'm gonna put the car in the garage," she said, rolling up the windows and pulling forward.

I tried to shake the snow and ice off the tree, but it was frozen on pretty good. Kelly came out of the garage carrying my jacket and plastic bag. She unlocked the back door and held it open wide.

"Gonna drip all over," I said.

"Can you get it into the shower in the bathroom here?" Kelly opened a door just inside. "It can defrost for a while."

I carted the tree in and stood it in a corner of the shower. Coming into the kitchen, I looked around the huge, chilly room. An ancient kitchen range took up most of one wall. The sink under the windows was an old, white porcelain one, with a drain board attached to either side. The refrigerator was much newer. A sturdy kitchen table with four chairs stood to one side, barely taking up any room. Worn linoleum covered the floor.

"Big kitchen," I said, looking around.

"Yeah," Kelly said. "The whole house is big. And old. I'm probably out of my mind, trying to hang onto it since the divorce. But I love it, and it's in the best school district in the area. And the kids are used to it."

"If you like it, it's worth hanging onto if you can."

"I hope so. Between the mortgage payments and upkeep, it takes the best part of my paycheck. And now it's worth even less than we paid for it." She stripped off her jacket and hung it on a hook next to the back door.

I put my jacket and the plastic bag on the hook next to it.

"What time do you expect the kids?" I asked.

"Not until nine or so," she said. "The stuff for the tree is in the attic. Want to help me get it?"

We went upstairs. Four good-sized bedrooms and a bathroom. The door to the attic was stuck; she had to pull hard to get it to budge.

Kelly passed several boxes to me, and I carried them downstairs.

"Tomato soup and grilled cheese sandwiches okay for supper?" Kelly asked.

I grinned. "Sounds good." Could she have read my mind?

She went into the kitchen to fix it while I started to unpack the boxes of lights and ornaments.

"You want a beer? Or a drink?" she called.

"Nah. No sense violating parole for something like that." The scare with the beer at Tiffany's had cured me of taking that chance.

I attached the legs to the tree stand and tested a few strings of lights. Nineteen years of no Christmas trees and then two this year.

"Supper's almost ready."

I went into the kitchen and washed my hands at the kitchen sink. Warm smells of soup and grilling sandwiches had chased the chill from the air.

Kelly put a can of soda on the table for me. She took her empty glass, sloshed a healthy dose of Southern Comfort into it, and set the nearly full bottle on the drain board. She filled two bowls with soup. I carried them to the table while she put the hot sandwiches on plates. She'd gotten them golden brown with the melted cheese oozing out the sides. Perfect.

I bit into my sandwich. Even better than I'd remembered. I spooned some hot soup into my mouth. It was creamy and warmed my throat. She'd mixed the condensed soup with milk, not the water I would have used.

Kelly took a major swig from her glass. "The tree ought to be pretty much thawed out by the time we finish eating," she said. "We can set it up then."

I washed up the dishes while Kelly looked over the decorations. Then I went and fetched the tree from the bathroom. The ice had melted, but it was still pretty wet. I spent a few minutes shaking the water off it as best I could.

When I carried it into the living room, Kelly was sitting on the couch, the almost-empty glass in her hand. The bottle was now on the coffee table and the level was much lower. I frowned. How much was she drinking?

Not my business. I set the tree in the stand. "Can you hold this while I get down underneath and tighten the screws?" I asked.

Kelly heaved herself off the couch and stood a bit uncertainly. She stepped carefully over to the tree and held it straight. I lay on the floor on my stomach and adjusted the screws until the tree stood firm.

"Lights next." I scrambled to my feet and grabbed a string of lights.

Kelly let go of the tree. "How about you put the decorations on while I go and wrap the presents?" She slurred her words slightly.

"Okay," I said, untangling the lights.

She took her glass and headed for the stairs. Looking at how little was left in the glass, she came back and grabbed the bottle. I heard her heavy footsteps on the stairs.

I finished putting everything on the tree. I covered the whole tree, not just the bottom third. I plugged the lights in and stepped back to admire my handiwork. Not bad.

Kelly hadn't reappeared. I turned off room lights so the tree glowed in the darkness.

Should I just leave? I'd pretty much finished what I'd come to do. Kelly'd fed me well. I wasn't at all sure it would be a good idea for me to be here when the kids arrived. What would Kelly's former sister-in-law have to say about a strange man in the house? It seemed rude, though, to just leave. The sleet had stopped, but I was in no hurry to tackle the long, cold walk home.

# CHAPTER 13

I was sitting on the couch, doing nothing but gazing at the Christmas tree, when I heard a car door slam outside.

"Kelly?" I went over to the stairs and called up to her. "I think they're here."

The doorbell rang.

No response from Kelly. Hesitantly, I opened the door.

A boy and a slightly younger girl tumbled into the room. A short, burly, middle-aged woman followed them, carrying several shopping bags. She put the bags down and looked around.

"Where's Kelly?" she asked.

"She'll be down in a minute," I said.

"Not drinking again, I hope," the woman said, sniffing suspiciously.

I didn't say anything.

She held out her hand. "Louise," she said. "I'm the children's aunt."

I shook her hand. She had a firm, confident grip. "Jesse." I was glad to see I remembered how this little social ritual went. "Pleased to meet you."

The kids had gravitated to the Christmas tree. "It's beautiful," the girl whispered. She fingered a slightly crooked snowman. "Remember when we got this?"

"They've had a good dinner. And a bath. I made sure of that, at least." She shook her head disapprovingly. "Their clothes should all be clean; I washed and ironed them this afternoon." Louise straightened the collar of her heavy tweed coat. "Can you help me get the children's things from the car?"

"Of course." I didn't know people still ironed clothes.

I accompanied her back to the aging sedan parked in front of the house. Louise took the backpacks, and I grabbed the suitcases. We carried them inside.

"Kiss your auntie good night," Louise commanded.

Obediently, the kids tore themselves away from the tree and stood on tiptoe to kiss her cheek. Then they went right back to the tree.

"I feel for those kids. Fred and Kelly are both a little too fond of the bottle. I think they met in a bar." She looked sharply at me. "Do you drink?"

"No, ma'am," I said. "I've had one beer in the last couple of years, and I didn't finish that."

Louise shook her head sadly. "I try with those children, but I'm only their aunt. I have to take care of my mother. And I'm not getting any younger."

The little girl turned around and asked, "Where's Mom?"

I glanced toward the stairs. "Upstairs wrapping presents. She said she'd be down in a few minutes."

Louise took a last look at the kids.

I walked her to the door and said, "Thank you," although I wasn't sure for what. I shut it behind her.

I turned to the kids. "What are your names?"

"My name is Brianna," the younger child said. She took off her jacket and flung it on a chair. "That's a nice Christmas tree."

"Mom said she might not have a tree this year." Her brother took his jacket off, too, and put it on the chair. "I'm Chris. Are you Mom's new boyfriend? What's your name?"

Kelly certainly knew my name. No point trying to keep it from these kids. "Jesse," I said. "And no, I'm not your Mom's new boyfriend. Just someone from work."

"Mom needs a boyfriend," Brianna said.

"Oh?"

"Dad's got a girlfriend," Chris said. "He says only losers don't have girlfriends. Or boyfriends."

"I guess that makes me a loser," I said. Not really news to me.

"Did you get the Christmas tree?" Brianna asked.

"Your mom got it. I helped her bring it in and decorate it."

"Why aren't you Mom's boyfriend? Don't you like her?"

This interrogation was getting a little uncomfortable. Even if the interrogators were only in elementary school.

"Don't you kids need to get ready for bed?" I asked. "It's Christmas Eve."

"Could we fix hot chocolate?" Chris asked. "We used to do that on Christmas Eve. Back when Dad lived here."

"And could you read us 'The Night Before Christmas'? Dad used to do that, too," Brianna added.

"I suppose. If you know where everything is. But you need to bring your stuff upstairs and put on your pajamas first." I was willing to bet that these kids had pajamas. Undoubtedly clean. Possibly ironed.

Odd. I'd stepped out of one situation taking care of kids and right into another. And at Christmas, the most family-oriented time of the year. Felt good. Conjured up memories of cold winter evenings spent helping the ever-changing array of kids in the Coleman household. Foster care might not be like living with real family, but a good foster home could go a long way toward comforting a scared kid.

I don't think I'd felt this content since the last Christmas with the Colemans. Over twenty years ago. Made me feel like a regular person.

I went into the kitchen and found hot chocolate mix. I put two mugs of water in the microwave. After a few seconds, I added another mug for me, too.

The kids came downstairs. Just as I suspected, they had on spotless, warm pajamas. Bright red with candy canes embroidered on them. They looked like they'd stepped right out of a Christmas card. Probably exactly what Aunt Louise had intended.

"Mom's asleep," Brianna said. "She's snoring real loud."

"Don't tell him that," Chris said. "He might not want a girlfriend who snores." He held up a book he was carrying. "The Night Before Christmas." "We sit in the living room where we can see the tree," he said solemnly.

"You need to put marshmallows in the hot chocolate." Brianna pointed to a cabinet. "They're up on the high shelf there."

I got the marshmallows and plopped one in each mug. I carried them into the living room and put them on the coffee table.

When I sat on the couch, one kid snuggled up on either side of me. Chris opened the book.

We finished the book and sat drinking our hot chocolate, looking at the tree.

I thought how kids were so predisposed to trust. I'd probably been like that, once. How could adults do the horrible things they did to destroy that trust? Left a big empty hole in the gut.

"Do you suppose Santa Claus will come?" Brianna asked.

"Maybe not," Chris answered doubtfully. "We got most of our stuff already at Grandma's. You know there's not really any such thing as Santa Claus."

And the world is a sadder place for that.

Where were all these introspective, maudlin thoughts coming from? What was the matter with me? I stood up and gathered the empty mugs. Here I could barely handle my own life, and I was waxing philosophic about the state of the world. Nothing like overextending myself.

Plus, I was getting way too involved in other people's lives. Yeah, it felt good after so many years of isolation, but I just had to deal with the lonesome reality of my own life. Not to mention it was wrong to be messing with kids' heads. Two sets of kids, in fact.

"Bedtime," I said. Once they were in bed, I should go, cold walk and all.

"You gonna come up and tuck us in?" Chris asked.

"And kiss us goodnight?" Brianna added.

We trooped upstairs. The kids had bedrooms at the top of the stairs. Down the hallway, light spilled out from an open door. I took a few steps and looked in.

Kelly was sprawled out on the bed, half undressed, with a flowered blue flannel nightgown clutched in her hand. Pillows were spread across the foot of the bed. The glass and the empty bottle lay on their sides next to the bed, along with her discarded work boots. Like Brianna had said, she was snoring.

I tore my eyes away from the smooth pale skin of her inner thigh.

Strewn all over the foot of the bed and the floor were the presents she'd been wrapping. Seemed like she'd pretty much finished; they were all wrapped and festooned with tags and bows, although the writing on the tags was pretty sloppy and some of the bows were crooked.

I went back to the kids' rooms.

Clutching a pink teddy bear, Brianna climbed into her pink and white bed and snuggled down under the ruffled comforter. "Now you tuck in the sides so the covers don't come off."

I did so.

"Now you kiss me good night."

Hesitantly, I leaned down and gave her a peck on the cheek.

She giggled. "Your whiskers scratch."

Probably right about that. I needed a shave.

"Now kiss me on the other side." She pointed to her other cheek.

Once again, a quick peck on the cheek.

"Now here." She pointed to her forehead.

Quick peck on the forehead.

"Now you say, "Night, 'night, sleep tight. Don't let the bedbugs bite.'"

I laughed and repeated the phrase, adding, "Good night."

She hugged the teddy, turned on her side, and closed her eyes. "Now you can turn out the light. But leave the door a little open and leave the hall light on."

Next I went into Chris's room and repeated a similar ritual, without the extra kisses. He clutched a soft, floppy, stuffed tiger.

What about Kelly? The house was chilly and would get chillier as the night wore on. Uncovered, she'd be awfully cold. I went into her bedroom.

Still clutching the nightgown, she had rolled over on her back. Her bra was unhooked and had ridden up. Her breasts were covered only by a transparent sweep of her hair. Her sensible cotton panties were half off her butt. For a moment, I stared at her like a teenage boy who'd just gotten hold of his first Playboy.

*This is someone I work with,* I reminded myself. *Someone who has been kind to me when she didn't have to be. What would she want me to do?*

First, I gathered all the wrapped gifts together. They could go under the tree. Then I rolled Kelly over and pulled the blankets out from under her. Grabbing her feet—one bare and one still wearing a warm thermal sock—I tried to swing her around so she'd be lying lengthwise on the bed. She shouldn't be left on her back. Drunks sometimes threw up; she could choke on the vomit. Or swallow some and drown in it.

She had to be really drunk. She hardly stirred when I moved her.

I maneuvered her onto her side and shoved a pillow under her head. I took the extra pillows and stuffed them down along her back. Maybe they would keep her on her side. My hand burned where it brushed against her skin. It seemed to have developed a mind of its own and wanted to pull her panties down farther. They were already partway down. Fighting the urge, I snatched my rebellious hand away and covered her with the blankets.

I made a few trips downstairs with the packages, piling them under the tree. I was pleased with how festive it looked. I hoped it would look magical to the kids in the morning.

I went back upstairs to check on Kelly one more time. She was sleeping soundly, still snoring. I made sure the covers were tucked around her. I was tempted to give her a good night kiss, too, but I didn't. Turning off the light, I pulled the door almost closed.

I went downstairs and unplugged the tree lights. I should leave. I knew I should leave. I looked out the front window. A soft snow was drifting down, covering the ice and frozen slush.

I always found snow falling in the night to be mesmerizing. For my last few years in prison, I'd had a cell at the far end of the honor tier, overlooking the perimeter fences and service road, past the coils of razor wire and the guard tower, into the woods. When it snowed, I'd stand at my cell window for hours and watch it drift down. Buried a multitude of ugliness. This snow wasn't even covering razor wire. And it wasn't criss-crossed by roving security spotlights.

The long walk home might be treacherous. Sidewalks and roads would be slippery.

Would the kids be able to cope in the morning if Kelly were really hung over?

I was making excuses to stay. Wasn't like the kids were babies.

I had never made it to the grocery store. I went to the kitchen. I didn't think Kelly would mind if I made a couple of sandwiches to take with me. Her refrigerator and cabinets were loaded with food. I took a few pickles from a big jar, too. And two cans of soda.

Shoving them all in a plastic bag, I grabbed my jacket and the library books. The bag with the damp sweater and shirts was still in the pocket. I fastened the jacket, snugged up the hood, and pulled out the gloves.

Thank you, Mitch, for the gloves. And the sweatshirt. Although I was going to ditch the sweatshirt as soon as I had something else to put on.

Stepping out into the quiet night, I inhaled fresh, frigid air. Some of the houses had Christmas lights twinkling through the snow. Walking wasn't so bad. In fact, I kind of enjoyed it.

After all this, I knew I was going to feel very alone in my room. But I had my books and the sandwiches. And I didn't have to follow the numbing prison routine. That should be enough.

Maybe I'd managed to make the holiday better for two sets of kids. I'd tried. That was a big deal for me. Mrs. Coleman always tried to make Christmas special for the little kids who came into her home at Christmas time, almost always on an emergency basis. *Mrs. Coleman, you'd be proud of me.*

\* \* \* \*

I relished my ten days of unaccustomed freedom. I took long walks around town, looking at Christmas decorations in the store windows. I read my library books. Twice, when the sun shone weakly in the morning, I hiked the roads into the hills.

On Thursday after New Year's, I headed out to the parole office. Even if Mr. Ramirez weren't there, I had to report and pay the monitoring fee for two weeks.

I left enough time to stop by the library to drop off the books I'd read.

Mandy was working at the front desk. She was wearing the brave red reindeer top again. But she looked pretty glum. I looked more closely. She had a white turtleneck under the red fleece. More dark marks on her neck peeked above the shirt collar.

I piled my books on the desk and grinned. "Have a good holiday?" I asked.

She tried to smile. "I guess," she said. "Every holiday can't be the best one ever."

"I spent Christmas by myself in my room, mostly reading. I had a day-old, slightly squashed ham and cheese sandwich for dinner."

She did smile at that. "Watch all the Christmas TV specials?" she asked. "I did."

"Don't have a TV. Otherwise, I might have."

She laughed at that. "No TV! I thought everybody had a TV."

"Guess I'm not 'everybody.'"

"I fixed a turkey for dinner. All the trimmings."

"Invite a bunch of people over?" I leaned on the counter.

"Nope. Was just supposed to be my husband and me. He doesn't like a lot of company."

Her husband was Sterling Radman. I can't imagine that too many people would want to come over. But then, maybe he was perfectly charming to people of his own social class. "Just the two of you, huh. He like the dinner?"

"He was…busy. He didn't get home until late. Then he wasn't hungry. Just as well. The turkey was dried out." She adjusted her glasses.

What could he be doing on Christmas Day? Surely he wouldn't be needed at Quality Steel. But what did I know about how to run a business?

I smiled at her. "And we survived."

"That's so. But sometimes I think that's all I do. Just barely survive," she said.

"Sometimes that's enough." I thought of the years in prison.

She seemed to think better of sharing her problems with me. Probably a smart move.

"I was just about to put out a bunch of books on the new book shelf." She indicated a book cart next to her. "Want to take a look?"

"I got to go," I said. "I got an appointment with my parole officer. I'll be back afterwards, though, and get a few books."

Her eyes opened wide. Had she forgotten that I'd used a prison ID to get my library card? If so, I was sorry that I'd reminded her.

"See you later." I waved and moved toward the door.

I arrived at the parole office a little early again. The dingy basement waiting room was empty. I signed in on the clipboard, sat down, and waited.

The lady who came to check the clipboard was someone I hadn't seen before. She was a large woman, her enormous bosom encased in a voluminous blue sweater with two snowmen who stood with the tops of their brooms pointed at snowflakes in the "sky" above them. The positioning was unfortunate; they were also pointing straight at the woman's nipples, which showed clearly through her sweater.

Rattled, I directed my gaze away from her chest.

She stood there holding a mostly eaten bagel spread with cream cheese. She took a large bite as she surveyed the room. A dab of cream cheese landed on her chin. My stomach grumbled. All I'd had before I came was a cup of instant coffee.

She crammed the rest of the bagel in her mouth, shut the door, and went back into the offices.

Fifteen minutes later, she came out again. She'd wiped the cream cheese from her chin. She had another bagel in her hand. Again, she surveyed the room, taking a huge bite as her eyes swept over me and the other benches. I was still the only one there.

The bagel looked really good. I swallowed. I wondered if I could afford a package of cream cheese and a few bagels. Maybe not the bakery kind—they were really expensive—but didn't they sell frozen ones?

Finally, without looking at me, she called out, "Jesse Damon" and opened the door that led to the offices.

I got up and followed her, trying not to stare at her rear end, which was of the same epic proportions as her bosom. She lifted the bagel toward her mouth.

A clean soap smell lingered in the air behind her, along with a whiff of cream cheese.

She seated herself at her desk. A half-empty box with donuts and more bagels stood open by her telephone. Next to it was a container of cream cheese with a little plastic knife. She typed away at her keyboard. When she'd stopped chewing, she said, "Mr. Ramirez is not in."

"Yes, ma'am."

She peered at the computer screen and frowned. "Forty dollars monitoring fee. You have to pay it even though you're not actively being monitored this week. Looks like that's it. No urinalysis or restitution that I see."

I took out two twenties and handed them to her. Her pudgy fingers smoothed them lovingly on her desk. She turned back to her keyboard and typed again. Sitting back, she reached a large hand toward the printer as my receipt came out and then gave it to me.

Glancing sideways at me, she reached for the phone. "Have a seat in the waiting room. Someone will be with you shortly."

I felt my throat begin to close. I managed to rasp out, "I thought Mr. Ramirez wasn't in."

"He isn't," the lady said. "But someone else will be with you. Just go have a seat in the waiting room."

I glanced back as I left the office. She was spreading cream cheese on another bagel. Then she picked up the receiver of her phone.

The heat in the waiting room seemed much worse than it had been before. A few other people were waiting now; they looked up listlessly as I came in and then returned to staring at nothing. I folded my jacket, careful to tuck the gloves and watch cap deeply into the pocket. Weak sunlight shimmered on the worn floor like a mirage. I fought down the temptation to leave; they'd just have me picked up, and then I'd be in worse trouble. I forced myself to sit down.

I didn't have long to wait. The door to the offices swung open, and two uniformed police officers stomped in. One looked bored, the other, annoyed.

They surveyed the now almost full waiting room. The bored one fixed his eyes on me. "Jesse Damon?" he asked.

"Yes, sir."

"Stand up and face the wall. Interlace your fingers behind your head. Spread your legs."

I could see panic and relief warring on the faces of the others who were waiting. Wasn't them being hauled off. They looked away, distancing themselves from what was happening to me.

My stomach in a knot, I complied with the orders. I knew the routine.

Maybe I should have just left. Gotten a few more minutes of freedom, anyhow.

One cop held his hand over mine on the back of my head while the other frisked me. He removed my wallet from my pocket.

"That your jacket?" he asked, nodding toward the bench where I'd been sitting.

"Yes, sir." I tried to keep all expression off my face and out of my voice.

He tossed the wallet on top of the jacket and ran his hands between my legs. He'd missed my keychain. I was glad I hadn't gotten any library books.

"Okay," he said, stepping back and picking up the jacket and wallet.

At least they weren't going to just leave them sit there. Wasn't really safe leaving stuff around a lot of the people who hang out in parole offices.

The other officer pulled my hands down behind me, one at a time, tightening cuffs on my wrists.

"Let's go." With a firm hand on each elbow, I was propelled through the door and down the hallway, to an elevator. We stopped to wait for it.

"Am I gonna be locked up?" I managed to ask.

One of the cops shrugged. "Not our call. We was just told to go down and get you. Somebody wants to talk to you. A detective. Up to him, or maybe your parole officer, whether you get locked up or not."

A detective. Belkins. Left word to hold me when I showed up for the parole appointment.

I ended up in the same interrogation room as before. I slumped in the same hard chair next to the same battered table, wishing they had gotten a waist chain and moved my hands in front of me. A lot more comfortable.

Someone—Belkins, I was sure—would be in when it suited him. Not a minute sooner.

I knew the room was being monitored. I couldn't lean back against the back of the chair without cutting off the circulation to my hands. I let my head fall forward on my chest and closed my eyes. Let them think I was calm enough to drift off for a nap. They wouldn't like that at all. Might hurry them up.

Sure enough. I heard the door open. I opened my eyes, but I didn't look toward it. I heard footsteps coming across the room, and a shadow fell across the table.

Neat pressed pants came into view. Impeccably shined shoes. The fresh scent of mint and aftershave. Montgomery. Not Belkins.

I wasn't sure whether I was relieved or not. Montgomery probably wasn't going to knock me around like Belkins might. But he was cold and calculated, a skilled interrogator. A more methodical, permanent threat to my freedom. Combined with Belkins' passion to see me locked up forever, that might make a deadly combination.

Montgomery didn't turn on the harsh light hanging over my head. He hitched one hip up on the table, resting part of his butt there, and folded his manicured hands. The polished stone in his ring winked up at me.

"I don't suppose there's much point in offering you a cup of coffee, is there?"

I shook my head.

"A couple of things I'd really like to know," he said smoothly. "Like what was going on between you and Tiffany Robinson."

I stared at the floor to the left of the table.

"You know what's interesting?" He crossed his legs and began swinging his left leg slightly, so that unless I moved my eyes, they would be in my field of vision. I continued to stare at the same place on the floor.

I shook my head.

"Tiffany Robinson says she doesn't even know you."

No surprise there. She didn't know me.

"Showed her pictures of you and everything. Said she'd never seen you before."

I shrugged.

"The kids, now." Light reflected off the polished surface of Montgomery's swinging shoe. "The kids say you came to the house. Drove their mom to the hospital. Fed them and did laundry and put them to bed. Even set up a Christmas tree for them. Strange, huh?" He waited for me to answer.

"I guess."

"I didn't know you had a driver's license."

He could check that easily. Probably already had. "I don't."

"So if you were driving, it would be a violation of your parole."

"Yes, sir."

He got up and paced behind me. "The brother, Carl, he's not quite so sure that the person he drove into town is that same as the person in the pictures I showed him. And he said he did all the driving. At least while he was around."

"Hasn't he got a license?"

Montgomery laughed. "Yes. And you're not going to get me off track so easily."

I hadn't really expected to. But it was worth a try.

"I suspect Carl's trying to shield you. Feels some misplaced sense of gratitude. You know the emergency room doctor said Tiffany probably would have died if she'd gotten to the hospital any later."

I couldn't keep myself from asking, "Is she gonna be all right?"

Behind me, Montgomery's footsteps stopped. "What's it to you?"

"Just wondered." I cursed my curiosity. Especially if he wasn't going to answer the question.

He resumed pacing. "She's out of the hospital. Taking some kind of heavy duty antibiotics. Her mother's staying at the house."

Encouraged, I asked, "How're the kids?" Wouldn't be revealing anything; he knew I had been minding the kids.

"They're fine. Thanks to whoever, they never even had to go into foster care. They had a good Christmas, as good as kids can have when their dad's dead and their mom's in the hospital."

"Their grandmother taking care of them?"

"That's the arrangement for the time being." Montgomery came back around and sat on the table again. "You know all this just makes you more attractive as a suspect, don't you?"

Here I sat, handcuffed, in a police interrogation room. Of course I knew I was still a suspect. The main suspect.

"And if he has to testify in court, I bet Carl Miller will change his story. Admit you are the person he found at his sister's house. Wouldn't want to risk perjury charges. Tiffany seems more certain she doesn't know you, but I bet eventually, we could get what we wanted to know out of her."

Probably. If pushed, Tiffany would get confused. She'd find herself agreeing to things she had no way of knowing. Or even to things she knew didn't happen. All she'd have to do was say it once, and they'd have her. And me. Whether what she admitted to was true or not wouldn't enter into it.

Montgomery stood up again. "Belkins asked the parole office to have you held when you showed up. That was back when he was mad because he couldn't find you. I guess he never cancelled it."

Thanks.

"I'm going to cut you loose. You're lucky Belkins isn't around this morning. He'd have wanted you locked up. But I figure we're better off with you out on the street. More chance you'll trip up."

I caught my breath. "Thank you, sir."

"I better be able to find you when I want you again." Montgomery examined his dark, lean hands.

"Yes, sir."

"Because I will want you again. I'm putting pieces together. When I have a clearer picture, I will definitely want to see you again." He stepped to the door and called a guard to come get me.

# CHAPTER 14

Midnight Monday, the beginning of a new shift. I welcomed reporting to work. Only a four-day work week, because of New Year's. The union guys would get a paid holiday; I would only be paid for the time I worked. Better than nothing.

Everyone looked groggy and out of sorts. More than a week on the same schedule with the rest of the world. Hard to make the adjustment back. I punched in and waited for my assignment. Plating room, I hoped.

I didn't see Kelly, but then, she didn't need to wait for her assignment. She'd be back in the shipping room, checking out the forklift that hadn't been used in days. Would she be happy to see me, or would she be embarrassed about how drunk she'd been when I last saw her? I wasn't sure how I felt about that, either.

John came in, clipboard in his hand. He looked around at us and frowned. Checking positions off with a stubby pencil, he called out assignments.

Plater number two went to someone called Steamboat, who picked up his things and went grumbling toward the plating room. The other three positions went to their usual operators.

I waited in uneasy silence as he read off the rest of the jobs.

"I got to talk to you, Jesse," he said, glancing at me. His bushy eyebrows crawled up his forehead. "Just hang tight." He disappeared through the door in the corner that led upstairs to the offices.

The whistle blew, signaling the start of the shift. The factory machinery groaned to life. I stood there.

If I wasn't on a job, I wasn't getting paid. Nervously, I shifted my weight, clutching my lunchbox with its tuna sandwiches. Shouldn't have indulged in that extravagance before I was sure I would be working. Peanut butter was good enough.

John came out of the offices. Sterling Radman tagged along behind him, having difficulty keeping up with John's long stride. John did not look happy.

"I still say we need to put it up for bid," John was saying. "Union'll be all over us."

"You let me deal with the union," Radman said, catching up with John as he stopped in front of me.

John looked mulish. "He hasn't finished his probationary employment; I don't think we should give him a job like that. That training's expensive; no guarantee we'll get it back."

Radman was impatient. "My problem, not yours. If he's not done with the probation, he's not in the union, right? Takes care of that problem."

John shrugged. He turned toward me.

"Jesse, Mr. Radman wants you to train to be forklift driver. Day shift wants their extra driver back ASAP. And Simon doesn't like midnights."

I stared at them. Certainly beat being fired, which was what I'd been afraid was happening. If I were successful in the training, it would give me a very marketable, transferrable skill.

I would be successful in the training. No reason not to be.

"Okay." Like I had a say in the decision. "When do I start?"

"Tonight," Radman said.

"We can't start him tonight." John looked up at the ceiling. "He needs to go on day shift to train. About a week, maybe a week and a half. Until he passes the test."

"I say tonight." Radman's face flushed. In his pristine business suit, he looked fussy and out of place out here on the production floor. "You've got two lift drivers on this shift; one of them can train him."

I wasn't at all sure I wanted Kelly to train me.

"Neither one of them is certified as a trainer," John said. "The only one we have works day shift. He'll have to train on day shift."

"And I say tonight." Mr. Radman's teeth were clenched. "He's not even in the union; I'll deal with them if there's a grievance."

"I'm not worried about the union." John shook his head in disgust. "State safety regs. Lift drivers have to train with a certified trainer. Five hours of classroom training. And they have to practice driving. Then they have to pass tests, paper and pencil and on the lift. Only day shift has anyone authorized to give the test. We'll have Occupational Safety inspectors up the wazoo if we don't follow the regs to the letter. Likely to end up with a big fine."

It was Radman's turn to look unhappy. "Then arrange for it tomorrow. Send him home now and have him come back at eight, when the day shift starts."

"Sir." I was back on my strict monitoring schedule. "I need to call my PO and get permission to switch work hours. I don't think he'll have a problem with it, but I can't really work another shift until I get his okay."

"Call now. From here." Radman was becoming increasingly annoyed.

"All I'll get would be an answering machine, sir," I said. "I could leave a message, but Mr. Ramirez doesn't start work until nine tomorrow. At the earliest."

"He can start Wednesday morning and still get the twenty hours of training in this week. Even take the test, if he's doing well enough," John pointed out. "And it'll give the day shift a chance to make arrangements to free up the trainer."

Mr. Radman scowled.

John pushed his advantage. "They don't just have a trainer sitting around, you know. And they like to train a few people at a time."

"If that's the best we can do. But I want it to happen. I don't want a bunch of lame excuses for why it won't work." He turned on the heel of his expensive tasseled loafer and stalked back to the door to the offices.

John watched him go. "Damn fool," he muttered under his breath.

"I didn't ask for the job as lift driver."

"I know you didn't," John said. "Nobody has. And he's got a real bee in his bonnet about who drives the lifts. Insisted on Mitch, even when he wasn't doing the job right. No good reason for it. But he's the boss. I guess it don't have to make sense to me."

"What about tonight?" Don't tell me to punch out and go home. I couldn't afford to miss a whole shift.

John shook his head. "Packing room, I guess," he said. "They're a man short tonight. Go report to Greg. He's the lead. He'll be glad not to have pull Kelly from the lift."

I gathered my things and started through the plating room toward shipping. Looked like I would be seeing Kelly tonight after all.

I nodded to Hank as I passed him. He was standing in front of plater two, watching Steamboat struggle with the small grids the plater was running. At least he wasn't starting with those big heavy pieces I'd had.

"Sorry to lose you," Hank shouted over the machinery as I passed him. "I'll try to get you back."

I smiled gratefully. But if Radman wanted me driving the lift, I had a feeling Hank could try all he wanted without any luck.

Pretty uncomfortable, Radman singling me out like that to learn to drive the lift. Wasn't doing me any favors, as far as I could see. He didn't even like me. Even seemed a little afraid of me. Kelly said he'd taken an unusual interest in Mitch. He might have been into drugs. Did he think, like Aaron, that I had access to them? He was going to be very disappointed if that were the case. I hoped that wouldn't cost me my job.

I reported to Greg in the packing room. He looked relieved as he stepped aside to let me take over pulling shallow wire trays off the line.

"Pack fifty to a row, three rows to a layer, four layers deep." The packing room was quieter than either the shop floor or the plating room, but he had to shout over the sound of a radio someone had set on a crate, tuned to blaring country music. He gestured at the container by his side. "Put paper between the layers. Watch your count. Lift driver'll keep an eye on it; she'll pull this one and put a new one in its place when you need it."

The lift driver. Kelly. I looked around.

She was maneuvering to pick up a load. She swung the lift around and disappeared through a big door onto the loading dock without so much as glancing in my direction.

I settled in to work. Compared to the plater, this was easy. Except for the need to keep count. When I filled a container, Kelly drove up with an empty. She pulled out the full one and replaced it with the empty. I tried to catch her eye, but she didn't acknowledge me. She dismounted, pulled out a tag for the full load, tied it on, got back on the lift, and then drove away. I missed her smile. This didn't look good.

Greg relieved me for lunch. Grabbing my lunchbox, I went back to the table where we ate. Someone was sitting there already, back to me.

Kelly.

I hesitated but saw no good reason not to go sit down with her. I walked around to the other side of the table, put my lunchbox down, and slid onto the bench.

"Hi," I said.

Kelly narrowed her eyes and stared at me. She said nothing.

"How was your Christmas?" I opened my lunch box.

Kelly glared at me and started shoveling the remains of her lunch into her lunchbox.

"Don't you speak to me," she hissed.

I wasn't sure what I expected, but this wasn't it. My mouth open, I stared at her.

"How do you think my Christmas was?" She swept her trash into the waste bin. "After what you did to us?"

I blinked a few times. This couldn't be over the sandwiches I'd taken, could it? There'd been plenty of other food in the house. "I'm not sure what you're talking about," I said.

"Right." She slammed the lid down on her lunchbox. "I guess I deserved whatever you did to me. I was really drunk and all. My fault. But I still didn't expect it of you. Stupid me; I didn't believe what everybody was saying about you."

"What's everybody saying?"

"That Mitch was right; that you're some kind of pervert."

I wasn't sure how to respond to that. I said, "I covered you up is all. It was cold. And I took the wrapped stuff down and put it under the tree for the kids."

"Yeah. And what did you do to me before you covered me up?"

I thought back. "Rolled you over so you wouldn't choke if you threw up. And straightened you out so your feet weren't hanging off the bed."

"And took off most of my clothes."

"That's the way I found you. I didn't take off any of your clothes."

"Oh, no. I usually get half-undressed and leave my bra unhooked. Not to mention leaving my panties pulled partway down. Or were you trying to get them back up, so I wouldn't realize what you'd been doing?"

I sat speechless. What could I say to convince her I hadn't messed with her? I couldn't think of anything.

"That was bad enough." She reached back and tightened her ponytail. "But what you did to Brianna was unforgiveable."

"Brianna? I just read her a story and took her up to bed." Poor choice of words, I realized too late.

"She told me. And kissed her all over." Tears were gathering in Kelly's eyes.

"It wasn't like that," I protested. "I only kissed her where she told me to."

"That's right. Typical child molester. Not only can't admit you did anything wrong, you try to make it out like it was her fault. What, for being a little girl? She's six years old. You're despicable."

I sat in stunned disbelief.

"Don't think I wasn't tempted to call the cops." Kelly got to her feet. "People like you should be locked up. Forever. But Fred's looking for any excuse to have me declared an unfit parent. If it weren't for that, I'd make sure you were locked up where you can't hurt any more little girls. As it is, if I ever catch you even looking at a child, I'll call your PO. I might anyhow. So stay away from me and my kids, and don't let me hear about you hanging around any schools or anything."

She grabbed her lunchbox. "If you get locked up again, you'd better hope you don't end up back where my daddy's doing his time. He'll make sure you pay for what you did to his granddaughter." She stomped off.

At the exit, she turned and cast one more hateful glance back at me. "I should say, when you get locked up again. Not if."

I sat and stared at my tuna sandwiches. A few minutes ago, I'd been looking forward to them. Now they looked like so much cardboard filled with slime. Smelly slime.

I wasn't too worried about getting beaten up in prison. I was confident I could hold my own if I ended up back there. Yeah, I might get knocked around some. Been there, done that. I'd probably survive it and give as good as I got. Make sure anybody would think twice about trying it again.

I thought I'd been prepared for facing the world with a murder conviction under my belt. A lot of people wouldn't want to have anything to do with me. What did I expect most people would think about me when they knew? Wasn't pretty.

But I had to admit I cared what some people thought about me. The Colemans. Hank. John. Maybe Mandy. Kelly. Especially Kelly.

Nothing had prepared me for the burning hole I had in my gut right now. Pervert. Child molester.

Couldn't waste the sandwiches. I choked them down and went back to work.

The shift couldn't end too soon. I concentrated on taking the wire pieces off the line, arranging them carefully in their rows and keeping the count correct. I felt my stomach knot up every time I heard the lift approach; I couldn't even look up at Kelly.

Finally, the whistle blew. Was I imagining the disgusted looks and sneers? Had Kelly told everyone? I hung back until everyone else had punched out and only then slid my timecard into the clock and left, alone.

Hunched into my jacket, looking down at the sidewalk, I quickened my pace and headed toward home.

I heard footsteps crunching on the salt and ice behind me. I moved closer to the wall of the building I was passing so it would be at my back if I had to turn to confront someone.

"Jesse." I didn't recognize the voice. For sure not Montgomery. Too nasal for Belkins. "Please stop. I really need to talk to you."

I edged against the wall and glanced behind me.

A skinny male was struggling to catch up with me. Aaron. The kid with acne who worked on the packing line.

Who hadn't been working last night. At least on the packing line. In fact, I'd probably taken his place. What did he want?

I stopped and turned to face him. He half-ran the last few steps and raised a hand toward my head.

I clenched my fists and ducked away from him, keeping the wall close behind my back. If a fight came to Mr. Ramirez's attention and I had gotten in the first blow, I could hardly claim self-defense. I waited to see what Aaron would do.

But he was just reaching out a hand to steady himself. He leaned an arm on the wall, gasping to catch his breath. He didn't seem to notice how close I had come to belting him one.

"What do you want?" I asked.

Aaron shook his head and kept gulping for air. How could a young man like him who earned his money doing physical work be so out of shape? "I got to talk to you," he managed to wheeze out.

"You said that."

"Can we go someplace to talk?" he whined. "Get a cup of coffee or something. It's cold out here."

I didn't want to go anywhere with him. I didn't want to waste the money on a cup of coffee. And I wasn't about to let him pay for me. The less I had to do with him, the better off I'd be. I shoved my hands deeper into my pockets. "Anything you got to say, you can say it here."

"Look, dude." Aaron's breath was coming a little easier now. "I'm getting desperate. I mean, I got the money, I can do whatever you want, but I need the contacts. You know what I mean?"

I had a pretty good idea, but I said, "What kind of contacts?"

"You know. I need to score. Bad."

I looked at his bloodshot eyes, his dripping nose. "Score what?"

"Oh, dude." He wiped his nose with his sleeve. "Don't do me like this. Ice. Or anything."

"Crystal meth?" I prodded.

"Yeah. I used up all I got from Mitch."

"And look what happened to Mitch."

Aaron shook his head. "Didn't have nothing to do with the meth."

I let that statement sink in. "So what did it have to do with?"

"Oh, man. I don't know." Aaron wiped his nose with his sleeve.

"What do you know about Mitch being killed?"

"How would I know? I just know he was doing good with the meth. Wouldn't none of us who was using would've offed him or nothing. I mean, look at the mess it got me into. I got no source now. You must have some somewhere. Or know where to get it."

"Don't have none of that. Or anything else. I don't use. And I don't deal."

Aaron drew a ragged breath. "Look, dude. I know you got no reason to trust me. But didn't Mitch tell you I did whatever he said? Slipped stuff into the shipments, passed it to the truckers, put the marks on the shipping tags. I never said nothing to nobody."

Except me. "Why are you telling me this?"

"You got to know where to get stuff. I mean, you got the connections, don't you? I never gave Mitch any money—just helped him out. But I got money. If that's what you need."

"I don't need no money," I said. At least not from Aaron. And certainly not for any controlled dangerous substances.

"I got to score, dude." Aaron's eyes were wild. "If I got to, I'll run down to Park Heights in Baltimore. But I don't know nobody down there who's selling."

"You don't know nobody here who's selling, either," I said.

"Dude. What do you want me to do?"

"Check into rehab. Or call Narcotics Anonymous. They'll help you out." Not likely he'd actually do it, but definitely his best bet.

"Oh, man. You got to be kidding. How about a quick hit? Just one. Then I can think straight and figure out what I got to do. I'm not so strung out I can't get it back together."

"What happened to you at work last night?" I asked. "Didn't see you there."

Aaron bowed his head. "No, dude. I been having trouble sleeping. I fell asleep, and it was real late when I woke up. I wasn't in shape to work anyhow."

I'd seen lots of guys like him. Probably not a bad kid. But until he got his habit under control, all he'd ever be was a druggie. Maybe I should report his requests to Montgomery. Getting locked up for a while might be the best thing that could happen to him. Get the drugs out of his system and let him make a decision about whether he wanted to stay clean or not. Probably not, but at least it would be a choice, not a drug-craving driven reaction.

I was sure that everyone on the shift had been questioned. Montgomery should know Aaron was a druggie and away from his job at the crucial time. Of course, if they took that seriously, they'd realize I couldn't've had anything to do with Mitch's death.

Since Aaron was so convinced that I was involved in the drug trade, he'd sound very sincere when he talked about it with Montgomery.

A marked patrol car cruised by on the street. It slowed up as it passed us and then turned the corner.

I had the uneasy thought that maybe I was being set up. Had Aaron been picked up on drug charges and was playing informant to cut his sentence?

Aaron grew impatient with my silence. "Well?" he said. "You gonna help me out here?"

"Nothing I can do." I turned to walk away.

"Dude. Can you at least tell me where I can go to find somebody who can do something?" Aaron grabbed at my sleeve.

"Let go of me. Call Narcotics Anonymous. I'm not kidding." I kept walking.

The patrol car passed us again. Must have circled the block. It pulled over to the curb ahead of us. The doors opened, and the cops got out, one leaning on each side of the car.

"Get out of here," I hissed at Aaron. "Unless you want to get both of us locked up. Then you'll get your chance to kick the habit. Cold turkey in a detox cell."

Aaron peeled away and headed off unsteadily in the opposite direction. I ducked my head and walked on. Kept my eyes straight ahead.

"Good morning, Damon," one of the cops said. He was tall and muscular, with a thin, blond mustache. His gloved right hand held handcuffs.

I glanced over at him. "Good morning, officer."

"Any problems here, Damon?" he asked.

"No, sir."

"Where are you headed?" He tapped the cuffs on the leather-clad palm of his left hand.

"Home, sir. Got to check in."

He nodded. "Sounds like a plan to me." He got back in the car.

It was just a few more blocks to my apartment. I didn't look back, but I was conscious of the patrol car creeping along behind me.

First thing I did when I got inside was call Mr. Ramirez. Of course it was too early. I got voice mail. I left a message about being switched to day shift and then lay down on the bed, trying to read and waiting for him to call me back.

After about an hour, the phone rang. Only one thing it could be. I'd never gotten a call here that wasn't related to parole.

I picked up the receiver. "Hello."

"Jesse Damon? This is Filipe Ramirez, your parole officer."

"Yes, sir."

"I'm returning your call."

"Yes, sir."

"And I've been looking at the entries that were made in your file while I was out. You've been busy."

I shifted uncomfortably. "Not really, sir."

"No? But you were picked up for questioning. What, twice?"

"Yes, sir." Apparently the conversation with Montgomery outside the hospital hadn't made the file. I wasn't about to volunteer that bit of information.

"I see you were released both times. Anything you want to tell me about what's going on?"

Definitely not.

Mr. Ramirez was waiting. I had to say something. "Just that there was a problem at work, sir. But I wasn't really involved."

"Yes. I would say one of your coworkers being murdered qualified as a little problem at work. Where were you when this happened?"

"I was working, sir. In the plating room." Thank goodness for Hank's meticulous record keeping. "Group leader and foreman could testify to that."

"So they have. Yet apparently Detective Belkins still considers you a suspect."

"Yes, sir."

"Would you care to comment on that?"

Not at all. "I was just working in the same building, sir. And since my conviction was for murder, I think he just figured it was likely to be me."

"I see. I haven't spoken to him yet," Mr. Ramirez said. "I imagine that if they thought they had enough to hold you, they would have done so."

"Yes, sir." I was relieved he was thinking that way.

"So you want to switch to day shift?" he asked, abruptly changing to the original subject.

"Not what I want, sir. What I'm being assigned to."

"I thought day shift was the preferred shift. You haven't been there long enough to get on the preferred shift."

"No, sir. I think this would just be temporary. They want to train me to drive a forklift."

"I find that very interesting." Mr. Ramirez paused.

I remained silent.

"Wasn't the man who was murdered a forklift driver?" he finally said.

"Yes, sir." An uncomfortable thought.

"And you'd be his replacement?"

Another uncomfortable thought. "Yes, sir."

"I suppose it's a little far-fetched to think that you might have killed someone so you could get their job as a forklift driver, isn't it?"

"Yes, sir. I didn't ask for the job, sir. The plant manager is assigning me to it."

"The plant manager? The plant manager decides who's going to be the lift driver? I'd have thought that would be up to the shift foreman."

"I don't know, sir." I rubbed my forehead nervously. "All I know is he wants me to report tomorrow morning at eight a.m. for training. Work days until the training's done."

"But you're supposed to report here at ten a.m. on Thursdays. Won't that interfere with your shift?"

"Yes, sir, I suppose it will. I don't know what I can do about that."

"You say this is a temporary assignment?"

"Yes, sir. Just until I qualify on the lift. Maybe a week or two."

"Do you even have a driver's license?"

"No, sir."

"Seems strange to me that they should want you to drive the forklift. You can't even drive a car."

"Yes, sir."

"I'll tell you what. You come in later this morning for this week's appointment. I have to be in court this morning, but you can report to the secretary if I'm not back yet. Then we can figure out what to do for next week. Okay?"

A relief. "Yes, sir. I'll come right now."

"I'll leave instructions to change the time you're monitored. Have you got the fee for this week?"

"Yes, sir."

"Good." The phone was silent for a minute. "Is there anything else I should know about?"

"Not that I can think of, sir."

"When you get here, just sign in. Since you don't have an appointment, you might have to wait until someone's free. Okay?"

"Yes, sir."

We hung up. I'd have to take a quick shower and change my clothes; my shirt was soaked with sweat.

Kelly apparently hadn't called in to accuse me of child molestation. At least so far. If she had, Mr. Ramirez wouldn't be so casual about my appointment. I hoped she didn't change her mind.

Unless, of course, they were playing the old "Why bother to look for him when we can tell him to just come in and report?" game.

No way for me to know that until I showed up. And no way to tell what kind of time restrictions I'd end up with after I met with Mr. Ramirez. Anticipating the worst, I looked at my dingy surroundings with a fond appreciation. Might be the last time I ever saw it.

I gathered up the library books I'd finished. If I dropped them off on my way to the parole office, they wouldn't get overdue, whatever happened. And if my new monitoring schedule would allow for visits to the library, I could stop on my way home to get some more.

# CHAPTER 15

More people were in the parole office waiting room late on a Tuesday morning than there were early on a Thursday. The heat and humidity were worse with so many people jammed together. The smell of unwashed bodies and clothes hit me as soon as I opened the door.

I signed in on the clipboard, took off my jacket, and looked for an empty space on one of the benches. There weren't many. I sat down next to a muscular black guy with a shaved head and tattoos on his neck. At least he seemed to have showered recently.

Name after name was called. Lunchtime approached, and finally, I was the last person sitting there. The overly curvaceous clerk who I'd seen last time looked at the clipboard, looked at me waiting there, and frowned. This time, she had the remains of a jelly donut in her hand. Powdered sugar covered her bosom.

"You got an appointment?" she asked.

"No, ma'am. But Mr. Ramirez told me to come in," I said.

"Really. Weren't you just in last Friday?"

"Yes, ma'am. Thursday, actually."

"I thought they locked you up on a violation," she said, narrowing her eyes and staring at me.

"Just had a couple of questions they wanted to ask me," I said.

She snorted. "A couple of questions? Looked a lot more serious than that."

"Yes, ma'am." No point arguing with her.

She spun around, her rubber-soled ankle boots squeaking on the hard damp floor. The door swung shut behind her.

She returned in a moment. "Mr. Ramirez will see you now. He's in his office." She swung the door wide.

Clutching my jacket, I followed her.

Mr. Ramirez was coming down the hall toward us.

"Here you go," she said. "I'm going to lunch now."

"Fine. Thank you." Mr. Ramirez's bottomless black eyes snapped through his thick glasses.

I stood a good six inches taller than Mr. Ramirez, but he probably outweighed me.

He escorted me back to his office. His desk chair groaned as he lowered his bulk into it. "Have a seat," he said to me.

I sat down. The temperature back here in the offices was much cooler than in the waiting room. The air smelled much better, too.

"Now," Mr. Ramirez said, tugging his shirt cuffs, "let's go over what's been happening in the last two weeks."

I had no idea how he expected me to respond. I just sat there, willing my hands to lie still in my lap.

Mr. Ramirez leaned back in the old wooden desk chair. Its wheels squealed as it moved under his weight. His gaze rested on my face.

I looked down at my hands. They were still a little raw from being out in the cold, but with the gloves I'd gotten from Mitch's house, they were getting better. The scar across my right palm itched.

"Got anything you want to tell me about the last few weeks?" he asked.

That one I could answer honestly. "No, sir."

Mr. Ramirez laughed. "Let me rephrase that," he said. "Anything I should know about happen in the last two weeks? Like this fellow at work who was killed. Any idea of what happened?"

How many times were we going to go over this? Probably until I tripped up and contradicted myself. Encouraging thought. "No, sir. Just they think somebody killed him."

"I see. And who do 'they' think killed him?"

I shook my head.

"Come on. You must know something."

"I'm not sure, sir. Detective Belkins, sir, he thinks maybe I had something to do with it."

"And did you?" Ramirez pushed his chair away from the desk, crossing his ankles in front of him and leaning farther back in the chair. He stared down at his hands clasped over his belly. They were square and heavy, just like the man.

"No, sir. I was working. The group leader can vouch for me."

"And did he? What's his name?"

"His name's Hank. He could see me pretty much the whole time."

"Has Hank got a last name?" He scratched his nose with a blunt finger.

"He must have. But I don't know it," I said.

"And you couldn't have just snuck away for a little while?"

"No, sir. Hank would have noticed."

"Why is that?"

I blinked. Hard to describe the plating room operation to someone who'd never seen it. "The plater I was operating would have been stopped, sir. Hank and the other three plater operators couldn't have missed that."

"Even if you'd just run to the men's room or to get a drink of water?" He was leaning even farther back in his chair. I wondered if he would flip over backwards in it. Probably hit his head on the file cabinet back there. Get a traumatic head injury. If that happened, of course I'd be charged with assault.

"Yes, sir. I'd have had to get Hank to take my place if I left it at all. He'd have known."

"I see. So why does Detective Belkins think you were involved?"

"I'm not sure, sir. Mitch and I had a few words before the shift started. And there's my record."

"Ah, yes. On parole for murder. That would make anyone investigating a murder take a second look at you if you were in the vicinity, wouldn't it? Especially if you'd, as you say, 'had words' with the victim that evening."

"Yes, sir."

"Mitch is the man who was murdered?" He was deliberately using the word murder repeatedly, undoubtedly hoping to unhinge me a bit. It was working.

"Yes, sir."

"And these 'words' you had with Mitch, what were they about?"

"He thought I was looking at his wife. But I wasn't." Now we were getting into very uncomfortable territory. What would I say if he asked me if I knew the wife?

"And what happened? Did it come to blows? Or near blows?"

"No, sir. John, the foreman, stepped in. He sent Mitch off to start work."

"I see. And what did you do?"

"John assigned me to the plating room, so I went there. Hank can vouch for me most of the rest of the night."

"Most?"

"I had my two breaks and lunch. But that was before Mitch was killed." I wished he would listen to Hank, not Belkins.

"You sure about that?"

"Pretty sure."

"What do you mean, 'pretty sure?'" His intense black eyes didn't blink.

"I don't have any way of knowing exactly when he was killed. And I don't remember if he came by after my last break."

"Were you brought in for questioning that night?"

"Yes, sir. It was more like morning by then."

"By Detective Belkins?" Mr. Ramirez shifted in the chair. It squealed alarmingly.

"Yes, sir."

"Anyone else?"

"You mean brought in for questioning? Not that I know of. But it's not something anybody'd be likely to tell me."

"No. Did anyone else question you?"

"Detective Montgomery was there, too."

"I see. Anything I need to know come out at the interrogation?"

I resisted the urge to bring my hand up to touch my cheek where it had been swollen and bruised. "Not that I can think of, sir."

"You weren't monitored for almost a week and a half. Anything happen I should know about then?"

Should I tell him about the time I spent at Tiffany's house? Montgomery knew something had gone on there. But he might be keeping his mouth shut about it. And, heaven help me, I didn't want anybody inquiring into what went on at Kelly's house. Or what Kelly thought went on. "I don't think so, sir."

Mr. Ramirez sat up and focused his eyes on me. The chair groaned. "Sure about that? I'd much rather hear things from you than from someone else."

I shrugged. He either knew everything Belkins and Montgomery knew, or he could find out easily enough. "I think you know everything, sir."

"Any additional sources of income besides the job?"

What was he getting at now? "No, sir."

"So the only place you got any money was from your paycheck."

"Yes, sir." I tried to think.

Tiffany's sixty dollars. I hadn't stolen that; Carl had given it to me. For babysitting. He didn't have to, but it wasn't like I hadn't earned it. Should I mention that? I didn't see how I could do that without going into the whole thing about being at her house with the kids. Wouldn't be doing me any good. Especially if Kelly got it into her head to call and talk to Mr. Ramirez. It'd sound like I'd set myself up to be with another bunch of kids. Unsupervised. Best keep my mouth shut.

He sat back in his chair. "Been using drugs?"

With that one, I could be completely honest. "No, sir."

"Or dealing any?"

"No, sir." I shifted uneasily. Returning to possible drug use. I supposed it was a fairly standard area of suspicion for parole officers. Probably Aaron's big mouth had spread rumors that had appeared on the police radar.

"You know I can order a piss test any time I think it's a good idea?" Mr. Ramirez shuffled some papers on his desk. He pulled out a multipart form.

"Yes, sir."

"Any objections to giving a sample?"

"Only the amount it would cost." They were expensive. "I don't have a lot of extra money by the time I pay my bills and buy food and stuff."

Mr. Ramirez's eyebrows shot up on his fleshy forehead. "What do you mean by 'stuff?'"

Now I'd done it. "You know, shaving cream and deodorant and laundry detergent. Stuff."

He didn't look convinced. "How about a test on your hair? Doesn't look to me like you've had a haircut since you've been released. Should cover the entire time since you hit the street. And the last few months of incarceration."

True.

"Well?"

"I got no problem with the test, except for if I have to pay for it." I reached up, plucked a strand of hair from the top of my head, and offered it to him.

Mr. Ramirez shook his head. "Not now. Maybe later."

I leaned over to toss the hair into the trash can. I wondered if he would fish it out when I was gone and send it for testing.

Shouldn't be a problem.

Someone knocked at the door.

"Come in," Mr. Ramirez called.

The door opened. The familiar scent of mint and aftershave wafted through the door. Montgomery followed it, looking grim.

"I just talked to Detective Montgomery." Mr. Ramirez leaned back in his chair again. At least if he fell over and cracked his head now, Montgomery would be a witness. "About the murder investigation and other things. He has a few questions."

I just bet he did.

Montgomery squeezed by the chair I was sitting in and leaned his trim rear against the desk. "Hello, Jesse." Jesse, not Damon. His voice was misleadingly friendly. His grim expression contradicted his soft tone.

"Good morning, sir."

"I think it's afternoon already, Jesse." He shot his wrist out of a starched cuff and checked a large gold watch. "Definitely afternoon."

"Good afternoon, sir."

"Accuracy is important, Jesse."

"Yes, sir."

"I wouldn't want to think you were less than accurate when you answered my questions, now, would I?"

"No, sir."

"There's more than a few things I'd really like to know." Montgomery stood up, but there was no room in the office for him to get behind me to pace. "But right now, I'll settle for this one. Where did you get those twenties that you used to pay the monitoring fee last week?"

I'm not sure what I'd expected him to ask, but it wasn't that. "I guess the bank," I said, "When I cashed my last paycheck."

"Not the bank." Montgomery's eyes bored into my face. "All the banks were on the lookout for them. Think about it."

My stomach knotted up. Were they counterfeit? I'd distributed them. Would anyone believe I didn't realize it? Probably not. And even if I didn't catch criminal charges for them, they'd be confiscated. Being out forty bucks would be a real problem for me.

I tried to think back. I didn't spend money that often; I didn't have much to spend. Certainly not where I might get twenties back in change. When I'd cashed my last check, I'd set aside enough to pay the monitoring fee. Folded the twenties and put them in the back section of my wallet so I wouldn't accidently spend them. Like I could really forget.

But I hadn't taken those bills out when I'd paid the fee. I had enough in the front section of my wallet. If they weren't from the bank, had I gotten them in change somewhere?

Of course not. Carl Miller gave them to me. They had to have come from Tiffany's purse. But I couldn't very well say that.

"Maybe from a guy at work," I said lamely, thinking madly. "I keep all of my money in my wallet; somebody wanted to change a fifty."

"If you changed a fifty for someone, you'd have the fifty and he'd have the twenties. And a ten."

Good point. I felt sweat form on my forehead. "Other way around. Somebody wanted a fifty for two twenties and a ten."

"And why would somebody want to do that?" Montgomery's icy gaze took in my discomfort. He knew very well I was lying.

I willed myself to not fidget. "Something about putting it in a Christmas card. A fifty lay flatter than two twenties and a ten."

"Strange." Montgomery leaned against the desk again. "What's this guy's name?"

"I don't know the names of a lot of the guys at work." That, at least, was true.

"It's not that big a shift; I'd think you'd know everybody. Or at least their names."

"Well, I don't." My hands were sweaty; the scar itched like crazy. I had to resist the urge to rub it.

"But you could point him out if I asked, couldn't you?" Montgomery examined his manicure.

If I picked out someone at random, I'd just make trouble for them. And of course they'd deny the whole thing. I shrugged. "Maybe."

"I find it hard to believe that someone at work, someone whose name you don't know and who you might not be able to point out among the very limited members of your shift, approached you and asked you to give him a fifty for two twenties and a ten."

Put like that, it sounded really stupid. "He just asked in general," I offered.

Montgomery raised his well-shaped eyebrows. "I would believe that you didn't know what you had there. If you'd known, you wouldn't have been stupid enough to hand them in to the parole office for your monitoring fee."

Right about that. If I'd noticed anything strange about them, I certainly would not have used them to pay the monitoring fee. "Are they counterfeit?" I asked.

Montgomery laughed. "No, Damon. They are not counterfeit."

Then what? I noticed he'd gone back to calling me Damon instead of Jesse. He was past pretending to be friendly. "I didn't see anything different about them," I said. My palms were really sweating now. The scar itched.

"I'm not surprised."

I tried to remember them. Crisp new bills. I didn't think they had any unusual markings on them. Bait money of some sort? Photocopied and the serial numbers recorded? Given to an informant to buy drugs? Didn't they usually arrest people right there and then, while they could trace the exchange of money for drugs? Maybe something had gone wrong with the buy.

That thought chilled me.

So the twenties had made their way to Mitch. Made a certain amount of sense. Tiffany had gotten them from Mitch. Again, made sense. And I'd ended up with them. Great.

Montgomery stood up. "Don't think I'm going to get much more out of him," he said to Mr. Ramirez. "He knows more than he's saying. But we're not going to hear about it."

Mr. Ramirez reached for his phone. "Want me to get someone in here and have him locked up? That might change his mind about telling you what he knows."

"No." Montgomery brushed imaginary lint off his pants leg. "That would just cost him his job. And then the state'd have to support him again. I think we'll learn a lot more by keeping an eye on him than by locking him up again."

I tried to keep my face expressionless.

"Whatever you say." Mr. Ramirez took his hand off the receiver.

Montgomery slipped past me and opened the door. I felt his gaze on my face. "Sooner or later, I'll figure this out, Damon. Don't you forget that. And if I find out you did kill Mitch, I'll make sure you never get parole again."

I didn't bother to answer. Or look toward him.

He left.

"Interesting," Mr. Ramirez said. "You got anything else to tell me?" He leaned back in his chair.

*Don't flip out now,* I thought. "No, sir."

Mr. Ramirez sat up straighter. I wiped my sweaty palms on my pants. "You sure?"

"Yes, sir." Getting much too complicated. Much easier if I could just stick to the truth. That, of course, was why lengthy repeated interrogations worked so well.

Mr. Ramirez shrugged. "Got your monitoring fee for this week?" he asked.

"Yes, sir." I pulled out my wallet and got out the bills I'd folded and tucked away before I'd gotten Tiffany's twenties. I knew these ones came straight from the bank.

Mr. Ramirez took the bills and studied them.

"What was the problem with the other twenties, sir?" I asked. "Detective Montgomery said they weren't counterfeit."

"That's right. They weren't." Mr. Ramirez was holding one of the twenties I'd just given him up to the light. Looking for the line in it, I guess, to make sure it wasn't counterfeit. "You're not stupid. I imagine you can figure out why the police might be interested in who has certain bills."

"Because they were used for a drug buy?" I speculated. "And the cops didn't make an arrest at the time. Either something went wrong, or they were trying to follow where the money went?"

He looked at me. "And where did the money end up?"

Would I ever learn to keep my mouth shut? "In my wallet."

"Yes. In the wallet of a paroled murderer. Interesting. Maybe we should be testing you for drugs."

"I don't have a record of drug use," I said. The cost of the urinalysis would be a real blow to my finances.

"I'm aware of that. And that is, in and of itself, also interesting. If I recall correctly, the person you killed was a drug dealer. And you were carrying a whole shitload of drugs, mostly heroin and rock cocaine, when you were arrested. How did you manage to get out of that without a conviction for possession with intent? Or a 'record of drug abuse?'"

I lowered my eyes. No point in saying anything about not having killed anyone. That conviction was a done deal. "Plea bargain," I said.

"You know the courts come down harder on people who deal to make money than on people who deal to support their own habit?" He crossed his legs at the ankles. He was wearing bright red socks with green Christmas trees on them. "About that drug test..." He opened his desk drawer. I had no doubt he had urine sample kits in there.

"Yes, sir." Hadn't we been through this? Of course he could order a drug test. He could order just about anything that he thought up and there wasn't much I could do about it. Except cooperate and probably pay for it. If he was going to order it, I wished he'd just go ahead and do it, not keep harping on it.

Mr. Ramirez let the silence settle around us. Then he said, "What's your new schedule look like?"

"Eight a.m. to four p.m.," I said.

He frowned. "And exactly how do you expect to come in for your appointments here?"

"It's just for a week or two, sir," I pointed out. "For training. Then I ought to be back on the midnight to eight. If I have to, I'll take time off to come in for an appointment." Quality Steel Fabrications might not like it, but it was the best I could do.

"I guess we can see how it works out." Mr. Ramirez reached for his calendar. "What kind of training was that again?"

"Forklift."

Mr. Ramirez flipped the pages on his calendar. "It's a little after one now," he said. "You'll be able to get home and check in by four thirty this afternoon?"

"Yes, sir." Over three hours from now. Of course I could get home by then.

"Then you'll be working eight to four. Seven a.m. give you enough time to get to work?"

"Yes, sir."

"How about a seven p.m. check in every day? Or would you rather check in at five most days and have a nine p.m. check in once a week? Give you more time for the Laundromat and such."

"Seven every day is fine, sir." Actually, it would give me a lot more time than the old schedule. I wondered if he realized it. He must. Maybe it was at Montgomery's request. I'm sure they were familiar with the expression "Give him enough rope to hang himself."

"Same thing weekends."

"Thank you, sir." Lots more time. Or more rope.

"We'll see when you get back on midnights. If you get back on midnights. Call me as soon as you're switched back, or at the end of next week. Whichever is sooner. You can skip the appointment next week. Got it?"

"Yes, sir."

"I'll hand this in." His pudgy hand held up the two twenties I'd given him. "That's this week. Don't forget you'll owe for next week, even if you don't have an appointment. You'll have to hand in eighty dollars the next week."

"Yes, sir."

"Hope I'm not going to find these serial numbers on any lists." He looked at me over his glasses.

"I hope not, sir."

He got to his feet. The chair sighed in relief. He opened the door and held it for me to leave. I slipped out. He followed me to the waiting room, which was beginning to fill up again.

"Stay out of trouble," he said.

"Yes, sir."

"And stay out of Detective Belkins' way."

"I'll try, sir." I didn't need to be told that twice.

# CHAPTER 16

I had plenty of time to stop by the library. I needed something I could immerse myself in without having to think. Nothing too heavy. Mandy was at the desk, but she was busy with other people. Gustavus leaned against the wall next to the magazine racks. I wondered how much time he spent at the library. Not really my concern. It was a public place, and it was warm.

I went into the stacks and found a few promising books. I didn't have to be as careful about the time or when they would be due; the new schedule would let me make it to the library almost whenever I felt like it. I could afford to start a book and decide I didn't want to finish it.

I brought my selections up to check out. Mandy smiled at me. I smiled back.

She took the books and glanced around behind her. Leaning over the counter and keeping her voice low, she said, "I want to talk to you. Is that okay?"

I was surprised. "Sure. What do you want to talk about?"

She shook her head. "Not now. I get out for lunch soon. Can you wait?"

"I guess."

"Meet me on the front steps in ten minutes." She put the books in a plastic bag and handed it to me. Then she turned to the paperwork on the desk.

Mystified, I went outside to wait for her.

A few minutes later, Mandy came down the front steps. She was wearing a long, stylish coat and warm boots. She had leather gloves and a big purse with some kind of abstract design on it. A scarf of something that looked like cashmere to my unschooled eyes was wrapped around her neck. She wasn't particularly pretty, but the expression "well turned out" sprang to mind.

Gustavus followed her out the door. He pulled a cell phone out of his pocket. I reflected that everybody but me had cell phones these days. Even homeless bums who had nothing better to do than hang out in the library.

As Mandy came up to me, she took my arm. In my work boots and hooded jacket, I was very conscious of the contrast in our appearances. If she noticed, she didn't mention it.

I caught a whiff of expensive perfume. I'd taken a shower, so maybe I smelled okay despite having worked up a nervous sweat during Montgomery's questioning.

"It's my lunch hour," Mandy said. "Let's get something to eat." She started off down the sidewalk in the opposite direction from McDonald's and the diner.

"Okay. But—" I started to say, halting.

"My treat."

We went to a trendy little café next to the courthouse. The menu was posted on a board out front. Without any prices. Through the window, I could see tiny round tables and ferns hanging from the ceiling. Mandy opened the door and threaded her way past vacant tables to the last in a row of booths along the wall in the back.

In my bulky jacket, I felt like I took up too much room. I followed her slim form to the booth and slid into the seat opposite her.

A waitress came up. She had spiky hair and long, purple fingernails.

"I don't know—" I started to say.

"We'll have two of the soup and sandwich specials," Mandy told her. "I'll have unsweetened iced tea. What would you like to drink?" She turned toward me.

"Coffee?" I said. I glanced around, wondering what the special would be. Another copy of the menu was written on a whiteboard on the wall. A choice of cream of squash or watercress soup. Cream of squash sounded bad enough. What the hell was watercress? With feta cheese and arugula on coarse-ground, seven grain bread. I had to assume that was something edible.

"Which soup would you like?" the waitress asked. "The cream of squash is especially filling in this weather."

"We'll take that."

Mandy was paying, she got to choose, I reminded myself. I was hungry. For sure I'd eaten far worse than whatever they were going to serve up here. "Filling in this weather" sounded promising, even if it was squash.

The waitress nodded and hurried away.

"I'd like your opinion on something." Mandy's gaunt hands fiddled with the large pendant hanging from a woven silver chain encircling her neck.

"My opinion?" I couldn't imagine what good she thought that would be.

She shifted uncomfortably. "You know who my husband is?" she asked.

"Sterling Radman. Plant manager at Quality Steel. My boss a couple of levels removed." My turn to be uncomfortable as reality sunk in. What in heaven's name was I doing sitting across from Sterling Radman's wife in a ritzy restaurant, right in the middle of the county building complex? A stone's throw from the police station and the parole office and the local lockup.

I was far more at home in those places than this fancy café.

Mandy nodded. "We've been married for three years now. We met shortly after he moved here to take over operations at Quality Steel."

I started to say he must have been a good catch but realized just in time how offensive that would sound.

She seemed to have read my mind anyhow.

"Yeah. I was getting a little old. Most of the girls around here marry their high school sweethearts. While I was away at college, mine moved to San Francisco and met the love of his life. Another man."

"Just as well," I said. "Would have made for a disastrous marriage." Why was she telling me this? None of my business.

"I suppose you're right. But it hurt." Mandy blinked rapidly.

"I imagine it did." *Don't cry on me,* I thought. *I'm no good at that.*

"My parents were killed in a traffic accident when I was twenty," she continued. "Brakes failed on an overloaded mine truck when they were coming back from my grandmother's funeral in West Virginia. I'm an only child. No family left. I'd driven separately so I could go right back to college. Sometimes I wish I'd been in the car with them."

I didn't know what to say.

Her eyes glistened. "I got a big settlement from the mining company. And of course I inherited the house and everything. So I came back and went to work in the library."

"At least you didn't have money problems," I said awkwardly.

She gave me a withering look. "That has been the least of my worries."

Never been the least of my worries. But I could see where I must have sounded heartless.

The waitress placed lunch on the table. "Two cream of squash soups with grilled panini."

I inhaled the steam rising off the soup. Wonderful aroma. I spooned some into my mouth. Smooth and rich and creamy. It might be squash, but I'd never tasted anything so good.

Mandy nibbled at her sandwich. "When Sterling arrived in town, he joined the country club. My family has always belonged, so of course I was a member."

Of course. I looked at the sandwich. Green, plant-looking stuff peeked out from under the flat grilled bread. I took a bite. Sure enough, some kind of tangy cheese. The green stuff must be arugula. It was actually quite tasty.

"I met him there. He was so nice. Swept me off my feet. We got married almost right away."

"Sounds like a fairy tale." I stirred my soup.

"Doesn't it?" Mandy wiped her mouth with the napkin. "Did you know that all the original fairy tales had bad endings? A few people told me I was being too hasty. They were right."

"Not a good marriage?" I asked.

"I don't think he loves me." A tear escaped and trickled down her cheek. "He's never home. Sometimes I think he might be using drugs. He never lets me in on how he spends money, even though most of it's mine. And lately, he's been being mean to me."

I remembered the bruises on her neck. "Does he hurt you?"

She nodded. Her hand strayed to her neck. "Sometimes."

"File for divorce."

"I've thought about it. But he had me sign over power of attorney."

I looked up at her in alarm. "You shouldn't have done that. You need to talk to a lawyer. Get that rescinded. Right away."

"He always knows what I'm doing. It's like he's psychic or something."

"How can that be if he's always off doing his own thing?"

Mandy looked around furtively. "I run into Gustavus all over. I think Sterling's paying him to spy on me."

"That's no way to live." Even I knew that. And Gustavus had seen us leave together.

"You're right." She sighed. "He's trying to get a mortgage on the house."

"On the house you inherited from your parents?"

Mandy nodded.

"I don't know that much about marriage law or real estate law, but you have to get a lawyer. Now."

She ignored that and went on. "I found some things. In the back of his closet."

"What kinds of things?" I envisioned drug paraphernalia. Or love letters from another woman. Or pornography.

"Cash. Lots of it."

"Lot of people keep their money in cash these days," I said. Not me, of course. "Hard to trust investments or anything right now."

She gave me a withering look. "But they put it in insured money market accounts. Or at least safe deposit boxes. Not bundles of cash in the closet."

Couldn't tell that by me. "Lot of people are worried about banks failing."

"I found other things, too."

"What else?" Cash—even a lot of cash—didn't seem to be something to really worry about.

She looked down at the table. "Passports. In other names. Drivers licenses. Birth certificates."

I thought about Reggie's new identification. "Did you know the people in the pictures?"

"Not in some of them. But some had Sterling's picture."

"With another name?"

"With two other names." She wiped her eyes with her napkin.

Worrisome. "What do you think he plans to do with them?"

"Take off and leave me. After he gets the mortgage on the house. And drains all the other accounts."

"You really do need to talk to a lawyer. Now. You got a cell phone? Make an appointment with the lawyer who handled your parents' will."

Tears were rolling down her cheeks in earnest now. "I'll think about it. But first, I wanted to ask you if you would do something for me."

My soup was gone. Mandy wasn't touching hers. What a waste. "Don't see what I can do to help you," I said.

Mandy lowered her head and looked at the table. "I want you to kill him for me."

I sat in shock. "Kill him?" I whispered.

"Yes." Her face went fierce. "If you don't want to do it yourself, find me someone who will. I can pay. I can pay a lot. A hundred thousand dollars. Is that enough?"

"Mandy, that's not something I can do." The coffee in my cup had cooled. "That's not something you should ask anybody to do."

She seemed to be pretty good at ignoring things she didn't want to know about. She didn't pay any attention whatsoever to what I said. "You're a murderer, aren't you? I'd think it'd get easier after the first time. And we could set it up so no one suspected you."

"They'll suspect me, all right." I stared at the tabletop. "But you know, I never really killed anybody. I'm not about to start now."

"You were convicted of murder, weren't you? There must have been something behind that." Her voice was fierce. "I can get more money if that's not enough."

"Mandy. There have to be other ways to deal with your problems. We'd both go to prison. For years. Maybe for the rest of our lives."

"It'd be worth taking the chance." Her voice was rising. Her hands were clenched white in front of her.

"No, it wouldn't be. I know what I'm talking about. And this is not the time or the place to be talking about this." I slid out of the booth and reached for my wallet. Had to get out of here fast, even if it took most of my money.

Mandy opened her purse and put a twenty-dollar bill on the table. She thought a second and added a ten to it. "Ought to take care of it. And the tip." She slid out of her seat.

Standing, she adjusted her well-tailored coat and fluffed her scarf around her neck.

I grabbed the plastic bag with the library books and shoved my wallet back into my pocket.

I glanced at the booth adjacent to the one we had occupied. It had been vacant when we'd sat down.

It wasn't vacant now. A slender black lady with an elegant upswept hairdo sat sipping a glass of iced tea.

I glanced across the table at her companion.

Montgomery.

My mind froze. How much had he overheard?

His eyes met mine. He winked and gave me a thumbs up. He mouthed something at me. It looked like "Gotcha."

I walked Mandy back to the library.

"Just think about my proposal," she said. "A hundred thousand dollars is a lot of money. Get back to me."

"There's not enough money in the world," I said.

"Everybody's got their price. Let me know what yours is."

I shook my head. She ignored that, too.

I watched her climb the stairs to the library. I turned back toward my apartment.

As I rounded a corner, the wind tore at the bag in my hand. I wrapped the plastic closely around the books. With an effort, I managed to stuff them into the voluminous pocket of my jacket. I flipped up my hood, slipped my hands into the warm gloves, and ducked into the wind.

As I passed the doorway of an abandoned store front, I felt a hand clasp my shoulder. I spun around in alarm, my fists raised.

Belkins.

"Go ahead." He took the unlit cigar out of his mouth and held it at his side. "Do me a favor. Hit me." He grinned.

I dropped my hands.

"Turn around and face away from me," he ordered.

I did so.

"Keep looking at that wall. Take everything out of your pockets and drop it."

I removed the plastic bag from the library and tossed it a little in front of me and to the side. My wallet, keychain, and gloves followed.

He yanked my hood down. "Now interlace your fingers behind your head and spread your feet apart."

I followed his orders.

"Anything else on you I should know about?" he asked.

"No, sir." I could feel his rancid breath on my neck as he leaned over me. His pudgy hands patted my pockets and felt between my legs. A car door slammed behind us. A siren screamed its approach.

A calm, smooth voice sounded behind us. "That's dangerous, Belkins." The scent of mint and aftershave reached me. Montgomery.

"What? I just apprehended a known felon. Of course he's dangerous." Belkins coughed.

"Grabbing him from behind. You should have ordered him to stop. Waited for backup. And asking him to empty his own pockets. If he'd had a gun, he could have shot you before you could do anything about it."

Belkins' laugh turned into another hack. "I was kind of hoping he'd give me a hard time. I would have had to use force. That would have felt good. And I could have pulled him in for resisting."

"You should have waited for backup," Montgomery said.

"I knew you wouldn't be long."

A patrol car skidded to a stop at the curb, the siren fading. I heard the driver climbed out. A dog barked excitedly. "What have we got here?" he asked. I didn't move; I could practically feel him looking me over from head to toe.

"Convicted felon in possession of CDS, I imagine," Belkins said.

Was he planning to plant something on me? Could he get away with that in front of Montgomery and the occupant of the patrol car? I wouldn't have thought Montgomery would go along with it, but what did I know?

"What's he got?" Montgomery sounded surprised.

I was surprised.

"An informant told me that he's made a pickup. Let's see what's in that bag that he's being so careful with." Belkins coughed again.

From where I stood, hands behind my head and feet spread, I could see the uniformed officer reach for the plastic bag.

"We both saw him throw that down," Belkins said. "Right, Montgomery?"

"That we did. Let me see what's in it." Out of the corner of my eye, I saw Montgomery's slender dark hand take the bag. I hoped that meant Belkins wouldn't have a chance to slip something into it.

"Are the wallet and stuff his, too?" Montgomery said. "You might want to pick them up."

The officer did so.

I heard the plastic bag crinkle in Montgomery's hands. "Library books," he said.

"What?" Belkins dissolved in a coughing fit.

"Library books," Montgomery repeated.

"What the hell's he going to do with library books?" Belkins demanded.

"I imagine he's planning to read them," Montgomery said.

"What would he be doing reading library books?"

"Improving his mind?" Montgomery suggested. "Passing the time he's supposed to be in on home detention? Legally?"

Belkins snorted. "He's up to something."

"He may very well be," Montgomery agreed. "But we haven't caught him at it yet."

"He's supposed to have crystal meth."

"Your informant must be wrong. Or he's already dropped it off." Montgomery folded the bag around books. "He's got nothing now. The dog would have alerted."

"You still need me?" the patrol officer asked.

"I think not," Montgomery said. "Damon, you can put your hands down now."

"So you're just going to let him go?" Belkins said.

"Possession of library books is hardly grounds for violating his parole," Montgomery said.

I put my hands at my sides, careful to keep them in full view. I heard the door of the patrol car slam shut and the car pull away.

Montgomery handed me back the plastic bag, my wallet, the key, and the gloves.

"Thank you, sir." I took them and stowed them in my pockets. I wondered if they'd been listening to Aaron.

Belkins threw down his cigar in disgust. "Remember. We're watching you. Sooner or later, we'll see you violate. And when you do something serious enough, we'll be there to bring you in."

Montgomery shook his head. "You can go home now, Damon. I'd suggest you do so."

I headed for home and stayed there. I didn't get much sleep, but I read through two of the books. I couldn't have told anyone what I'd read, though.

At seven in the morning, I left for work. A lot more people worked on day shift than on the midnight to eight. I knew that, but I still wasn't prepared for the throng crowding between the vending machines and the time clock.

I stood in line to punch in and leaned against the wall, waiting for Arnold, the day shift foreman, to get around to telling me what to do.

As Arnold barked off assignments in his high-pitched voice, making hurried notes on his clipboard, the workers drifted off, adjusting hardhats and pulling on gloves. When the whistle blew, I was the only one still without an assignment.

The overnight shift straggled by, clocking out. A few people nodded a greeting, but mostly, they ignored me.

Kelly whizzed by on her forklift, pulled it down the hallway, and parked it. She came back and punched out. I didn't turn to look at her, but I did watch her out of the corner of my eye. She didn't even glance in my direction.

Aaron didn't look much better, but at least he'd shown up for work. He started to say something to me, but he would have had to raise his voice to be heard over the machinery and Arnold was standing right there, looking at me and frowning. Aaron shrugged and walked off.

I straightened up and walked over to Arnold.

He looked from his clipboard to me and back again. "Who are you?" he asked.

"Jesse Damon," I said. "I was told to report to this shift for training on the forklift."

Arnold's frown deepened. "We're not giving forklift training today. Who the hell told you to do that?"

John emerged from the door to the offices. "Mr. Radman."

"Why did he tell someone to show up for training when we got none scheduled?" Arnold said. "And why is Radman deciding who gets trained?"

"Your guess is as good as mine," John said. "But Jesse's right; that's what Radman told him."

"So I'm supposed to call the instructor off work to train one person?"

"I guess." John scratched his beard under his chin. "I suppose you could have him train a few if you had some others you were thinking about."

"I do, but I got to check with the union to get the okay on them." Arnold shook his bald head. "How about this guy? The union okayed him for training?"

"Probationary employee," John said. "Don't need union okay."

"You want me to train a probationary employee?" Arnold said. "Suppose he don't make the grade? Total waste of money."

"I don't want you to do nothing." John didn't look any happier than Arnold. "It's Radman's idea. Go take it up with him."

"I will," Arnold said, slapping his clipboard against his thigh. "Meanwhile, what the hell am I supposed to do with this guy? Pay him? Under what job number?" He gestured toward me.

"Put him to work while you straighten this out," John suggested. "If you hurry, he'll only miss a tenth of an hour's work."

Arnold looked me up and down. "What can he do?"

I would have thought I'd have gotten used to people talking about me like I couldn't understand or speak for myself, but I still hated it. I didn't see that it would help to put in my two cents' worth.

"I had him working plater. Pretty good at it, too. Before that, root baskets."

"If he's a good plater operator, why did you let them pull him for forklift? Good plater operators aren't that easy to find."

"Tell me about it." John shook his head. "I don't want to lose him from the plater, either."

"I got enough plater operators right now," Arnold looked around. "Taylor," he hollered at a man walking by. He wore a leather apron and sported a heavy tool belt. A set-up man. "Take this guy over to the forty-inch root baskets and get him started on them."

Arnold turned to glare at me. "I hope you can make rate on them. Don't like people working my shift who can't keep up."

Root baskets were abbreviated, cone-shaped contraptions used by plant nurseries to hold the root ball of large trees for transport. They were made of crude unfinished wire and left to rust in place in the ground when the tree was planted.

"Do my best." I didn't anticipate a problem; I'd been able to make rate and then some on root baskets before I got put on the plater.

I trailed behind Taylor until he stopped at a free-standing spot welder in a dark corner of the shop floor. Next to it stood a rack with rings in three sizes. Another rack held steel loops three feet long that would be welded onto the rings.

"You ever run these things?" Taylor asked doubtfully.

"Yeah," I said.

"Show me." Taylor handed me a pair of heavy heat-resistant gloves, stepped back, and slipped his gnarled hands under the bib of his shop apron.

I slipped on the gloves. I positioned myself to the right of the welding machine, adjusting the racks to within easy reach.

With my left hand, I took a ring from each holder on the rack, being careful to keep them in order. My right hand griped a loop. I strung the rings into the horizontal slots of the welding rig, smallest to largest, slapped the loop into the vertical double slots on the rig, pulled my hands back, and stepped on the pedal of the welder. It slammed down, and in a burst of sparks, fused the wires where they crossed. As the welding head raised, I lifted the welded assembly slightly and jerked it to the next position on the rig. With my other hand, I reached for another wire loop.

Four loops around, and I had a completed root basket.

I swung the root basket onto the pallet next to the ring rack and scooped up another set of rings.

Taylor watched silently as I ran a few more, his eyes narrow. Finally, he nodded. "You got it, all right. Stacks of fifty, two stacks to a pallet. I'll let the lift driver know you're back here; he'll need to bring you more parts and pick up the pallet when it's full. And I'll see if I can't get those overhead lights turned on."

I nodded, continuing to work. The practiced motions came back easily. I'd make the required seventy-six an hour and half again as many.

Looking around at the unused machinery around me, I thanked whatever luck that had made John assign me to the plating room the night Mitch had been killed. If I'd been working this job in this deserted corner, no one would have been able to vouch for my movements. And a little checking on the number of pieces I could produce would verify that I could have left the job for a while and returned without falling behind. Long enough to have killed Mitch.

Through the grimy windows against the wall, I could see pale shafts of sunlight creep higher in the sky, piercing the threatening clouds. I tried to drain my mind and concentrate on the job, but this wasn't one I had to think about or even pay much attention to.

All I wanted was to keep out of prison and keep this job. Well, maybe not all, but those were the most important things. And I couldn't do anything else if I got locked up again. The prospect of endless days of trudging across the compound to the chow hall, of standing for head count, of seeing only the dreary prison compound out my window—assuming I was fortunate enough to have a cell with a window—made my gut churn.

Belkins just wanted to make sure I went back to prison without a chance to ever see the outside again. Montgomery didn't care about that, but he did want a conviction that would stand up even if I somehow managed an appeal.

The only one who cared what happened to me was me. A few days ago, I would have said Kelly cared, too. But probably now she'd be just as glad to have me gone, too.

# CHAPTER 17

When the whistle blew for lunch, I restocked the rack with rings and went to eat at the tables jammed between the vending machines and the time clock. Lunch was noon to twelve eighteen for everyone except those working on the lines that never shut down. Like plating and packing.

I sat at the end of one of the crowded tables. No one said anything to me, and I didn't start up any conversations.

Arnold, looking sour as ever, came around. He stopped beside me. At my eye level, he clutched his clipboard tightly in a bent and gnarled hand. The hand seemed to be only part of a hand; it had the stubs of two fingers and a thumb. Had he been injured in an industrial accident? I'd heard rumors of the old days, before most of the safety regulations, when injuries were commonplace and workers' comp hard to come by.

I finished up my bologna sandwich, courtesy of Tiffany's sixty dollars. Without that unexpected windfall, I most likely would have been out of even peanut butter and bread this long after my last paycheck.

"Jesse." He consulted the clipboard.

I turned to look up at him. "Yeah?"

"I hear you done good," he said. His mouth moved in a grimace that might have been his idea of a smile.

"Thank you," I said, brushing some crumbs from the table into onto the plastic wrap I'd used for my sandwich.

"I got the forklift crap set up. You and two guys from this shift are gonna take the classroom portion of the training this afternoon. Then tomorrow, you start driving."

"Okay." I looked up at him. "How long's it going to take?"

"Classroom training is mandatory. After that, you practice until you pass the driving test." He gave a quick grin. "Or until Mac, the trainer, gives up on you. And he don't give up easy."

After lunch, the three of us assembled at a scuffed table in the back of the shipping room, where the equipment noise was a dull roar instead of an ear-shattering din.

Mac, an older man with gray hair and a limp, arrived carrying what looked like elementary school workbooks. He handed them out and stood glaring at us.

"You two, I know," he said, nodding at my companions. "You, I don't. You gonna go back to midnights when you finish the training?"

"I think that's the plan," I said.

"You gonna take Mitch's place on that shift?"

"Somebody's got to," I said.

Mac rocked back on his heels and peered down his nose at me. "Ain't you the guy killed him?"

No good answer to that, but I said, "Wasn't me killed him."

"Ain't you a murderer?"

That kept coming up. "Do have a murder conviction," I said.

"Skin charges, too, I hear." Mac scratched his nose.

My gut tightened. I got a grip on my anger. I wished that rumor hadn't gotten started. "That's wrong. Never charged with sex offenses."

The other two men turned to look at me. One moved almost imperceptivity farther away from me.

Mac scowled. "And yer out on parole?"

"Yeah."

"And now yer gonna take Mitch's job?"

"Look." I sat up straight and squared my shoulders. "I didn't ask for this job. I'm doing what I been told to do. If you don't want to train me, just tell Arnold you don't think I'll ever make a lift driver, and they'll have to find someone else. I'm not going to argue about it. And I'm not going to beg you to include me in this class."

Actually, I might beg, if it meant my job. But not to this guy. If Radman wanted me to drive the forklift, for whatever reason, I had to learn to drive it. Life as an unemployed parolee looked pretty bleak. And short.

Mac shrugged. "Nothing to me. I just train whoever they send me." He dug in his pocket, brought out short stumps of pencils with no erasers, and handed them out.

The method of instruction consisted basically of Mac reading the workbook to us, letting us complete the exercises, and moving to hands-on training.

The workbook part came easy to me. All those hours spent reading. I had no trouble with the exercises. I finished and waited patiently for the others to catch up.

Driving the lift was another matter. At first, it seemed to have a mind of its own about where to go. I finally realized that because its steering wheels were in the back, not the front like a car, it could pivot on a dime.

I had to adjust my expectations of what the front end would do when I tried to steer it.

At least I wasn't the one who knocked over a whole stack of pallets. The rest of us jumped back away from the tumbling pallets and saw first-hand that the protective cage over the driver's seat was a pretty good idea.

When we got the results of the written test, I discovered I'd aced it. Mac read over the answers in my test booklet and nodded. He moved on to the next one. Glancing up at one of the other men, he said in disgust, "What's the first rule about driving a forklift?"

The guy shifted uncomfortably on his feet. "I dunno."

"What did you put down?"

Looking sheepish, he said, "Don't run down the foreman."

Mac frowned. "You think this is a joke?"

"No. I just didn't know the answer. So I put down the first thing that came to mind."

Mac turned to me. "What's the answer?"

I didn't like to show anybody up, but I answered, "Run with your forks down."

"Right. If you do hit somebody—and Lord knows you better not—you don't want to run a fork through their gut."

We spent the next three days loading trucks, moving parts, stacking containers in the warehouse. On Friday afternoon, all three of us passed the driving test. I felt like I needed more practice, but Mac seemed satisfied.

Had to pay more attention to what I was doing than most of the jobs, but it was a lot easier than running a plater.

Friday afternoon. People milling around the time clock. Everyone else got a paycheck; vacation pay for the holiday week off. I stuck my hands in the pockets of my jacket. I had the monitoring fee for next week and not a whole lot else. But I had two slices of bologna, a big jar of peanut butter and a loaf of bread. And some instant coffee. I'd make it.

"Congratulations." Arnold, the day shift foreman, handed me a manila envelope. "You passed all the tests. Yer certified on industrial trucks. I talked to John; yer to report on the midnight shift Sunday night."

"Thank you," I said to Arnold, taking the envelope. Great. That wouldn't give me time to get in touch with Mr. Ramirez to adjust the time by Sunday night. Maybe I could just call and leave a message. Tell him I would go ahead with the schedule change unless I heard back from him.

I was tired. I turned toward my apartment. Weak winter sun glittered on the dirty ice patches on the sidewalks.

"Jesse." A familiar woman's voice came from behind me.

I swung around.

Kelly stood there, dressed in a clean hoodie and jeans, next to her parked car.

I stopped and looked toward her. What did she want? I hadn't been near her or her kids. My stomach clenched in a knot. I tried to keep my voice calm. "Yeah?"

Kelly looked down at her boots. "I figured you'd be getting off now. I wanted to talk to you."

I kept my distance and nodded.

"Wanna go get something to eat?" she asked.

I tried to smile, but I don't think it worked. "I don't know what you're getting at, but I'd be totally crazy to go somewhere with you. And I'm not that crazy."

"What do you mean?"

"Look, I appreciate you not calling my PO about what you think I did to Brianna. Or to you. But I'm not gonna put myself in the position of being alone with you. I don't need no more rumors started." I shivered and pulled my jacket tighter around me.

"Yeah. That." Kelly pushed her hair back from her eyes. "That's what I wanted to talk to you about." She looked around uncomfortably. "This isn't a good place."

"It's the only place. Out in plain sight. Look, I'm sorry it happened. I didn't do what you think I did. But I can't blame you for thinking it. What else is there to say?"

"I owe you an apology."

My turn to ask, "What do you mean?"

"When I was talking to the kids about going with their Dad this weekend, Chris assured me he wouldn't say anything about me drinking and falling asleep before I got my nightgown on. I asked him what did he mean." Kelly looked down at her boots and shifted her weight.

"What did he say?"

"He said Christmas Eve, when he and Brianna got home from their grandmother's, they'd gone up to get ready for bed. Evidently I was asleep on my bed, mostly undressed. An empty bottle was on the floor. He said I hadn't managed to get my nightgown on."

"Yeah. You'd grabbed it, and you were holding on to it for dear life. But that was about as far as you got with it." I grinned at the memory, realized how that might look, and wiped the grin off my face.

Kelly smiled. "So I take it I must have been pretty drunk."

"Well, you weren't sober." No point mentioning the snoring if the kids hadn't.

"Chris said you went in my room after he and Brianna were in bed," she said. "He was worried, so he got up and watched. He's seen me and his daddy get into some real fights when we were both drunk. You didn't close the door. He said you straightened me out on the bed and covered me up. Otherwise, you didn't touch me."

"Well, I did roll you over, too. I didn't want you to choke if you puked." I was still cold, but I'd stopped shivering.

"Thank you," she said.

"Anytime." Stupid thing to say.

"Then I asked Brianna exactly where you kissed her when you 'kissed her all over.'" Kelly didn't meet my eyes.

"What'd she say?"

"She pointed to both cheeks and her forehead."

"Yeah. That's about right." Muscles in my shoulders and neck that I hadn't realized were tense relaxed.

"Just like her daddy used to do, she said." Kelly looked sheepish.

"Wouldn't know about that."

"She said she had to show you where to kiss her." Kelly rubbed her nose with her gloved hand.

I nodded.

"I guess it looks like I jumped to the wrong conclusion," Kelly said, raising her eyes to my face. "So I guess I owe you an apology."

"Don't worry about it. You were looking out for your kid. Right thing to do." I didn't point out that drinking that much and leaving the kids with someone she didn't know all that well was not exactly looking out for her kids. Maybe she'd learned something.

"It would have really hurt you if I'd called your PO." Kelly bit her lip.

"But you didn't. No real harm done." How much had she said to people at work? And to her father? That might cause real harm, but it couldn't be undone.

Kelly took a step toward me and planted her feet defiantly. "I really want to say I'm sorry."

"Apology accepted," I said. Didn't change the rumors, but it was probably the best she could do. And she didn't have to do that. I turned to go.

"I meant it about getting something to eat," she said.

"And I meant it about not being totally crazy. I'm not getting in your car right now."

"How about I meet you at the diner? Their suppers aren't as good as their breakfasts, but they're not bad. I usually get a hot roast beef sandwich and mashed potatoes."

That sounded good. But I had no money. I wasn't going to eat yet another restaurant meal paid for by a woman. "I got to get home. I'm back on the monitoring." I didn't add that I had a while before I had to check in.

Kelly nodded.

I wanted nothing more than to sit across the table from Kelly and feel her knee brush against mine. Time, though, to make a smart decision. Who knew what Kelly might say next time she was drinking? And who she might say it to? "Maybe another time."

Kelly looked like she might cry.

I felt like somebody had punched me in the stomach. But I turned and walked away.

I spent most of the weekend wishing I could have gone with her but glad I had enough guts not to.

\* \* \* \*

Sunday night—really, Monday morning—at work, I looked around for Kelly. What would I say if she talked to me? But she was nowhere to be seen.

John glanced up from his clipboard when I approached him. His face was expressionless. "So now you're certified as a driver, huh?" he said.

"Yeah. Do you want me to start tonight?"

"Might as well. Simon can work with you for tonight, show you what needs to be done. You'll have to pick it up quick. After tonight, you can ask Kelly if you need help." He put a mark on his papers on the clipboard.

"Do my best." I hoped it wouldn't be too different from days. I'd prefer not to have to ask Kelly for help if I could avoid it. And if Simon was with me, Radman probably wouldn't be asking me to do anything weird. Tonight, at least.

Simon was anxious to show me the ropes; he wanted to get back to day shift.

Turned out to be easier than driving days. Not nearly so many people; I didn't have to stop so often and wait for the aisles and passageways to be clear. On the other hand, it would be a lot easier to get careless and not pay enough attention to the people and things that did suddenly appear in front of me.

With Simon walking behind the lift, I picked up a pallet of unplated wire shelves from the production floor and moved it to the plating room. I dropped it, pulled out the empty pallet, and then put the filled one in place.

Hank stood back and watched. "How's it coming?" he shouted to me.

"Okay, I guess. Haven't run anybody down yet."

Hank grinned. "If you decide to do that, let me give you a list."

I grinned back. This easy kidding was a new experience for me. It felt good.

I glanced at plater two, with Steamboat, the new operator. It was running lightweight wire shelves. Might take a bit of getting used to, but shouldn't have been a real problem. As I watched, two sets of empty hooks swung down from the plater. The shelf on the third set hung crooked, secured by only one hook.

I swung the lift around to pick up the empty pallet.

The shift ended, and I still hadn't run anyone down. Simon ran through the check-out procedure so fast, I couldn't follow the steps. But there was a written checklist I could refer to. I punched out and left with everyone else.

Two patrol cars were parked on the street in front of the exit door. My stomach sank. I ducked my head and tried to walk past.

"Damon." A uniformed officer opened the door of one car and climbed out. "Hold up there."

The blond cop who'd made such a point of letting me know he was keeping an eye on me the other day. Why couldn't he pick on Aaron instead? He was the one looking for drugs.

I stopped and took my hands out of my pockets. This was getting old.

"You know you were supposed to be home last night? Until seven this morning."

"Yes, sir. My work schedule got changed. I'm back on midnight to eight."

"And did your PO approve this change?" He reached for the cuffs on his belt.

"I called and left a message, sir. He's been pretty supportive of the schedule changes." Since I hadn't known about this until after work on Friday, I hadn't been able to actually talk to him.

"You don't call and leave a message. He has to approve of the change."

I knew he was right. "Yes, sir."

"The monitor went off when you left early. We got orders to bring you in."

By now, the three other cops were out of the cars and standing around. Two of them had their holsters unsnapped and their hands on the butts of their guns.

Most of the shift who had streamed out of the plant with me had stopped to watch.

"Lean on the hood of the car," the blond cop said. "Spread your feet."

I leaned on the car and spread my feet.

He ran through the frisking procedure, removing gloves, wallet, and keychain from my pockets and tossing them on the roof of the car.

He pulled one of my hands behind me, tightening the handcuffs. The other hand followed.

I looked down at the ground. I really didn't want to see what my coworkers were making of this scene.

Maybe John's fear was right; maybe the lift training was going to be wasted.

"What's the problem, officer?" a voice said, near at hand. A female voice. Kelly.

"Please back up, ma'am," the blond cop said. "We're apprehending a convicted felon here. With a history of violence. Could get dangerous."

"I know he's a convicted felon. But he's on parole."

I took a risk and looked over at her. My co-workers stood around, watching. I said, "Just don't get involved, Kelly. I violated the monitoring. They're just doing their job."

She stood with her hands on her hips. "But you were at work. How is that a violation?"

"My PO hasn't approved the shift change. I was supposed to be home last night."

"Doesn't he want you to work?"

"Yeah. I think so." I didn't know what else to say.

"What are you doing with him?" she asked the cop.

"Taking him in on a parole violation." He tugged on my elbow, pulling me toward the open rear door of the car.

One of the other cops reached into the car for the radio. They had no way of knowing how this small crowd was going to react. I was sure they wanted to get me out of there as fast as possible. I wanted to get out of there as fast as possible.

"You mean you're locking him up again?"

"Yes, ma'am."

"Sending him back to prison?" her voice rose.

*Kelly, stop,* I thought. *Let it go. Don't need to make it any worse than it already is.*

"Holding him until his PO makes a decision," the cop said. He maneuvered me into the car, using his hand to shield my head from banging on the doorframe. "You can check with his PO if you have questions. Parole office opens at ten."

"Who's the PO?" Kelly demanded.

"I'm not sure. You could call—"

I raised my voice so she could hear me. "Mr. Ramirez. But Kelly, it's okay. They're just following orders."

The door slammed behind me, and the car started up quickly.

I hoped someone had gotten my stuff off of the roof.

I ended up in a holding cell, without my jacket, boots, or belt. Just in time for the cart to pull up with breakfast. An egg sandwich, made from instant eggs. Carton of milk. Banana. Cardboard cup of coffee. A nice break from the peanut butter sandwiches I was relying on until I got paid again.

I settled in for a long wait. This early, I had the cell to myself. I stretched out on the bench, trying to get a little sleep.

The door opened. A disheveled man, either a left-over drunk from last night or an early morning indulger, entered the cell unsteadily. He sat down at the end of the bench and promptly fell in a deep, snoring sleep. When two teens, bloodied from a fight and then bandaged, were brought in, I sat up, figuring I had to share the bench.

One of the teens restlessly paced the cell, complaining loudly that there had been no reason for the police to intervene; it had been a "personal" matter. The other sat glumly and eventually told his companion to shut up. I wondered if the fight was between them or if they were on the same side of the altercation.

Lunch was a bag with the standard bologna and cheese sandwich, an apple, and a carton of milk. Even when prodded awake, the drunk didn't want to eat his; I took care of that for him. I hoped that Mr. Ramirez was working today and that Belkins was not.

The young combatants were taken to see a magistrate; they didn't come back. Either released on their own recognizance or bailed out. I lay back down on the bench and slept.

"Damon."

I woke with a start and sat up.

Mr. Ramirez stood outside the cell, shaking his head and looking at me. "What happened this time?"

I scrambled to my feet. "I got switched back to midnight shift. I called and left you a message, but I didn't think you'd get it until after I was supposed to report to work."

"So what did you do?"

I shrugged. "Reported to work."

"And the phone monitor called in as soon as you were out of range." Mr. Ramirez's expressionless dark eyes peered into my face.

"Yes, sir."

"And you didn't know somebody'd come looking for you?"

I hung my head. "I guess I didn't think about it, sir. I mean, does everyone on home detention get picked up whenever they're not where they're supposed to be?"

"No. But then, not everyone on home detention is a paroled murderer under suspicion for another murder. High flight risk."

I hadn't thought of it like that. "I'm sorry, sir. I didn't want to miss work. I know I was supposed to get permission before I switched shifts. I didn't know how to go about doing that."

"So what do you think I should do?"

Shoot me? "I don't know, sir. I guess I did violate. Should've stayed home if I couldn't talk to you before I switched shifts."

"Think it would help to lock you up again? Finish out your sentence? Then we wouldn't have to worry about whether you were going to stick around until this investigation is complete."

I winced. "No, sir. I won't take off. If I get sent back to prison, I won't like it, but I'll go and finish up my bit."

"And suppose you're charged with another murder?"

Harder question. "Probably never get a chance to take off. They'll hold me until the trial. Can't imagine getting bail on another murder charge. Or posting bail if it was allowed."

Mr. Ramirez laughed. "At least you're realistic. I'll have them release you. I want you in here at ten o'clock on Thursday. We'll go over your new monitoring schedule then."

"What kind of schedule should I follow for now?"

"How'd you do the week or so you weren't monitored over the holidays?"

"Okay. I mean, I did get picked up a few times. Just for questioning. They let me go."

"Right. So let's just let it go until Thursday. No monitoring."

I could hardly believe it. Back to enough rope to hang myself?

"And there's a young lady waiting to give you a ride. She's anxious to get home before her kids get home from school. So you'd better get a move on."

Had to be Kelly. Why was she waiting for me?

# CHAPTER 18

I got my jacket, boots, and belt back. Much to my relief, they also returned my wallet, keychain, and gloves. Somebody had retrieved them.

The security grill by the property room swung open, and I stepped through, carrying my things. I fought down a temptation to just keep going out the main door and away from there. Made a lot more sense to stop and at least put my boots on.

Kelly stood just inside the entrance, pulling up her sleeve impatiently to glance at her watch. "Hurry up. I need get home by the time the kids get there."

I shoved my feet in the boots, did a half-ass job lacing them up, and followed her out to her car, juggling the other things. "What are you doing here?"

"Creating a polite stink." She pulled her coat closer around her shoulders. "So they realize that if they just let you sit forever, someone will be asking questions about why."

"But I'm on parole. They can let me sit forever. Or at least send me back to prison until my mandatory release date, which isn't until fifteen years from now. Don't need a reason. Nothing I can do about it."

She turned and glared up at me. "You're such a wuss. I know you're not gonna stand up for yourself. Just like my dad. That's where I have to come in. I'm a concerned member of the public. And a registered voter. I can ask questions, and they'll take them fairly seriously. They don't want me calling my state senator's office, or the newspaper, or even the head of the parole division."

I shook my head in disbelief. "Why should they care what you do?"

"Because they don't want to look like a bunch of negligent idiots. Or like they may be violating your civil rights. Touchy subjects. Much better not to get the Civil Liberties Union involved." Kelly unlocked the car.

"But I'm on parole," I repeated.

"Yeah. You are. So technically, they can leave you locked up. But they won't. Not if they know someone's watching. I learned that a long time ago with my dad. Let them know you don't mind making a big issue out of things, and they go by the book. They don't do anything they can't defend, and they have their explanations ready in case somebody asks. Get in the car."

I slid into the passenger seat.

"If you want me to drop you off at your place, I can do that," Kelly said. "I have to get home for the kids. And I'd like to try to get a few hours' sleep before we have to be at work."

"Were you waiting the whole time since I got picked up this morning?" I asked.

"Yeah. I asked to see Mr. Ramirez. Good thing you told me who your PO was; they weren't anxious to give me that information. Kept me waiting awhile, but when they realized I wasn't going away, he saw me. I told him I knew you'd been at work the whole time. And that he could check with the foreman if he didn't believe me."

I couldn't imagine talking like that to a parole officer. But then, Kelly wasn't on parole. "What did he say?"

"He said he'd get back to me. I said I'd wait. So he did, reasonably quickly."

"Probably when he came to see me in the holding cell."

"All I know is you came out a half hour or so later." Kelly checked her watch.

"You don't have to go by my place if you're short on time," I said. "I can walk."

"What time do you have to check in?"

"Mr. Ramirez told me I wouldn't be monitored until I have my next appointment. Thursday."

Kelly turned to look at me. "Really? That surprises me."

"I think they expect me to mess up. They think I'm up to something," I said glumly.

"And just what are you up to?"

"Not a whole lot. Work. Go home. Do my laundry. Take books out of the library."

"Do you want to come over to my place for supper?" she asked. "The kids have been asking about you."

I smiled. "They think you need a boyfriend."

She actually blushed. "Did they say that?"

"Chris did. He said his dad has a girlfriend. His dad told him that only losers don't have boyfriends or girlfriends."

Kelly snorted. "That sounds like Fred. What did you tell him?"

"That I must be a loser."

Kelly laughed. "So you want to come over?"

"Okay. I got some sleep in the holding cell. I can keep an eye on the kids if you want to take a nap."

Kelly didn't answer.

"If you think you can trust the situation," I added quickly. I couldn't bring myself to say "trust me." "I don't want you to be uncomfortable. Or to do anything you're afraid wouldn't be good for the kids."

She smiled. "I'm too suspicious, huh?"

"Can't be too careful where your kids are concerned."

"I checked with my dad," she said. "He says he asked around. A lot of people who know you would be very surprised if they found out you were some kind of pervert."

"Really?"

"Yeah. Said you were always kind of a prude. You didn't go for the skin mags like a lot of the guys do. And you didn't talk about hiring a hooker the minute you hit the streets. They said you never showed interest in any joining any of the stuff going on in the cellblocks, either way."

"Yeah. I always figured, don't matter whether you're pitching or catching, it's still playing ball. And I got no desire to play that kind of ball."

We pulled into Kelly's driveway just a few seconds before the school bus pulled up. The kids came tumbling out of the bus and up the porch steps. Kelly leaned down to be kissed and shooed them into the house.

I followed.

Kelly headed for the kitchen. The kids dumped their backpacks, and Chris went to turn on the TV.

I frowned, trying to remember what the routine had been in the Coleman household after school. "Aren't you guys supposed to change out of your school clothes?" I asked.

They looked at me as if I had asked if they were supposed to fly to the moon.

"We wear the same stuff all day," Chris said.

"Oh." They were wearing jeans and shirts, not "school clothes" the way I remembered. "How about homework?"

Chris looked at Brianna. "We do that after supper," he said.

"Actually," Brianna added, "we usually don't do it at all."

"How do you expect to get good grades if you don't do your homework?" Mrs. Coleman talking through me again, I realized.

The kids looked at each other again. "We don't."

I was surprised. "You don't? Do you want to get left back?"

"Brianna might," Chris said. "She's in Remedial Reading, and if she doesn't pass that, she has to be in first grade again."

Brianna looked like she might cry.

"Well, let's get out that homework and see what we can do with it," I said. Mrs. Coleman had always had me help the younger kids with their homework. How different could this be?

We emptied the backpacks on the dining room table. I sorted through the loose papers; there were several newsletters and forms that were dated from weeks ago. I smoothed them out as best I could and put them aside for Kelly to read.

Chris was supposed to draw a picture of the solar system. I was a little rusty on the planets and where they went. He dissolved into typical third-grade giggles over the name of Uranus. And what happened to Pluto? But I had to figure the textbook he'd brought home would be more accurate than my memory.

Brianna was working on matching upper case and lower case letters. Still learning her letters in first grade? I thought she should be way beyond that; no wonder she was in Remedial Reading. I wondered if she'd been tested for a learning disability or something.

Kelly called us into the kitchen. She'd made chili and cornbread. Delicious and filling. She looked exhausted.

"You go lie down," I told her after we ate. "On the couch in the living room if you want to be nearby. I'll do up the dishes and help the kids finish their homework."

She looked a bit doubtful.

No point worrying her. "Or I can take care of the dishes and go on home. You can get the kids to bed and grab at least a few hours' sleep."

She smiled and made up her mind. "Thanks," she said. "If you don't mind staying, I'll go catch some shut-eye." She kissed the kids and went upstairs.

A real show of faith. I washed the dishes, saw that the kids finished their homework, and asked them what they wanted to do next.

"Play a game?" Chris said.

"Read us a story?" Brianna said.

"What games do you have?" I asked.

Chris looked doubtful. "Candyland?"

It seemed a little juvenile for him, but I agreed readily. "How about a quick game, and then you can choose a book for me to read? Maybe for a bedtime story?"

They squabbled over which book, so I told them they could each choose one and I'd read both. "How does your mom decide which book to read?" I asked.

They looked at each other. "Mom doesn't read us stories," Brianna said.

"Daddy used to," Chris offered.

Didn't all "good" parents read bedtime stories to their kids? No wonder Brianna was having trouble reading.

I decided not to insist on baths. Missing one night wouldn't hurt, and for sure I didn't want to be in the position of telling Brianna to get undressed. I sent the kids up to put on their pajamas and brush their teeth. I made sure it was Chris's bed we sat on to read the books. Although I suppose if somebody was looking at it from the wrong angle, that might have looked worse. Then I tucked them into bed.

I told Brianna that I felt a cold coming on and shouldn't kiss her. Or even her teddy.

I went back downstairs and fell asleep on the couch. Compared to the lumpy bed in my furnished apartment, it was comfortable. And that lumpy bed was a big step up from thin, fire-retardant prison mattresses.

Just after eleven o'clock, Kelly woke me up and handed me a cup of coffee. "The babysitter'll be here any minute. I made us lunches for work."

She handed me a bag that looked like it would measure up to her usual abundant standards. "I have to move the car out of the driveway so the babysitter can park there."

"You want me to wait in the car?" I asked her.

Kelly gave me a puzzled look. "Why would I want you to do that?"

"In case your ex's lawyer starts asking the babysitter whether you have men stay overnight."

"This isn't exactly overnight," Kelly pointed out. "And Louise already knows about you."

"True." Not my place to worry about that.

She shrugged. I followed her out and climbed in the car. She parked it on the street and went back inside. A few minutes later, another car pulled into the driveway and the driver hurried into the house.

Kelly came out, and we headed for the plant.

My first shift as lift driver without close supervision. I tried hard to keep track of what I should be doing, getting new parts in place before the machine operators needed them. I was less sure about where to put all the finished products; John told me to just line them up in the front of the warehouse and the day shift could sort them out.

The whistle blew for shift change. I parked the forklift in its place in the warehouse and swung off the seat. I wasn't used to sitting so much, and my back was stiff.

Mac came to pick up the lift. He stood and watched me go over the checklist. "How'd it go?" he asked.

"Okay, I hope."

He nodded. "John said you're doing good. Says you don't need to be told what to do next, keep an eye on it yourself. Once you got the driving skills down, that's the most important part of the job."

I hadn't thought of it like that. I was pretty sure John wasn't going tell me I was doing a good job. Not his style. "Thanks," I said.

Mac grunted in reply and climbed into the driver's seat.

Radman had been nowhere in sight all shift.

I was a little late clocking out. Everyone else had left by the time I punched out.

The weather wasn't bad. I didn't have to go straight home. I decided to take a little walk to work the stiffness out of my back before I went home and went to bed. I would sleep well. Benches in holding cells aren't known for their comfort as beds.

I probably should stop by the library and make it clear to Mandy that I had no intention of getting involved in her crazy ideas. I could see the headlines now: "Paroled Murderer Kills Again." And I'm sure it would be hard to convince people it was all Mandy's idea. Not that it would make much difference when they sentenced me.

Maybe I could get her to see how stupid it was to even think about getting rid of her husband by having him killed. That's what divorce courts are for.

As I passed McDonald's, I noticed a sign saying all sizes of coffee were a dollar. I had a few coins in my pocket. Maybe it was an outrageous luxury, but I went inside, got an extra-large with plenty of cream and sugar, and sat down to nurse it until the library opened.

Mandy was busy checking out books to someone else. I stood looking at a display of paperbacks. Some of them looked pretty interesting. I hadn't really intended to get anything out—I still had two unread books at home—but I picked up two anyhow.

When Mandy was alone at the counter, I went up and gave her my books. "Things any better?" I asked her.

Her face expressionless, she shook her head. "Not really. But I've thought some more about what you said. You're right. Killing Sterling would be stupid. Even if he deserves it."

I nodded in relief. One problem solved.

"So I called the lawyer who handled my parents' will. I made an appointment for lunch time. And I told everybody I might have to take the afternoon off."

"That's the way to go. Get out of the house if you're worried about your safety."

"I have no place to go."

"Go to a woman's shelter."

"I don't know where one is."

"You work in a library, for cripes' sake. Ask the reference librarian. You don't have to say it's for you. Or look it up on the internet. Shouldn't be hard to find."

"But it's my house. Why should I be the one to leave?" Her mouth was set in a stubborn line.

"Because you want to be safe." What was the matter with her? "That's more important than who stays in the house. Besides, it was yours before you got married. I bet the lawyer will make sure you get it back."

Tears glittered in her eyes. "All my old friends think Sterling's such a great catch. They think I'm stuck up now. They never invite me anyplace anymore. How can I tell them I'm getting a divorce?"

"They'll get over it. So will you. I don't think you'll be sorry you went the divorce route."

"Look." Mandy's fist clenched. "You won't say anything about, you know…what I was talking about at the restaurant, will you?"

"Nope. I'd get in as much trouble as you. Probably more."

I had no way of knowing how much Montgomery had overheard. Even now, an investigation might be underway. Might already be in a lot of trouble over it. Not much I could do about that.

"Thank you. I just must have gone a little crazy, you know." She leaned over the counter and lowered her voice. "Look, there is something I want you to do for me."

Uh oh. "What is it?" I asked.

"Come look at some of Sterling's stuff that I found. I'm not sure what to make of it."

"I'm not sure that's a good idea."

A tear brimmed over her eyelid. "I don't know what to do," she said. "I'm so scared. But suppose the lawyer just thinks I'm a hysterical female? I want to be able to tell him what I found. And I don't really know what it is."

"Why don't you just bring some of it in to show the lawyer when you go to see him?" The further I was away from all this, the better.

Mandy blinked rapidly. "I don't want Sterling to know I found it. Suppose he came home and some of it was missing? I don't know what he'd do."

"Not much, I'd think. Not if he thought you'd taken it to a lawyer."

"Oh, I'm not telling him about the lawyer. Not until I know where I stand. He'd kill me."

"Make sure you get to a safe place," I said.

"I'll try," Mandy agreed reluctantly. She looked up at me. "If something happens to me, I want someone to know what was there."

"You think anyone'd take my word over Sterling Radman's?"

"They don't have to believe you," she said.

*Gee, thanks,* I thought.

"You just have to give them enough information to start investigating. He can't hide everything. Especially after I talk to the lawyer."

She didn't need me. What could I do?

"So will you meet me at my house?"

"No point in it. Just tell the lawyer."

"Please? If he finds me looking at his stuff, I don't want to be alone."

I knew this wasn't a smart thing to do. And if Mandy was right that Gustavus was spying on her, everything she did was likely to get back to Radman anyhow. But I looked at the tears in her eyes and said, "I guess."

"Good." She scribbled down an address. "I'll run in and see how soon they can get someone to cover the desk here. Be over as soon as I can get away."

I stuffed the paperback books in my oversized jacket pocket and looked at the address. It was a few blocks away. I could get there, look at whatever she wanted me to look at, and then get home in time to get a good day's sleep.

Mandy's house was a well-kept older Victorian house with lots of gingerbread. The house she'd inherited from her parents.

I stopped in front of the house and looked around uneasily. Why had I agreed to come there? Kelly was right; I had to stop letting other people make decisions for me. I should have said no.

I had no way of knowing how long I would have to wait until Mandy came. The houses here were set on large lots, with landscaping and fencing surrounding them. They all looked genteel and well-to-do. Looked like the kind of place where, if someone called 9-1-1 to report a prowler, the cops would respond quickly. Not a good place for me to be hanging around.

I heard a car door slam and an engine start up. I turned up the walk to the house. The expansive front porch was partially hidden from the street by bushes.

The porch contained no furniture. Probably put away for the winter. I sat down on the floor in a corner, out of the wind and out of sight from the street.

I had just about decided I had waited long enough when I heard footsteps coming up the walk. Mandy, in her fashionable long coat and warm boots, climbed the stairs and started to open the front door.

I got up and walked over to her.

"There you are." she said. "I was afraid you'd changed your mind."

I probably should have. But I said, "No, I been waiting for you."

"Well, come on in. It's cold out here."

It wasn't much warmer in the house. I followed her into a stone-floored entryway. Closed pocket doors flanked either side of the hall and an ornate staircase led to the second floor.

Mandy led the way through a door at the end of the entryway. We stood in a huge vintage kitchen, with white tile on the floors and the walls. Mandy took off her coat and hat, laying them with her bag on the worn surface of a big wooden table.

"Sterling hid some of the stuff in the pantry," she said. "He probably figured I wouldn't be looking in there; I don't cook much. But I decided to fix dinner for Christmas." She snorted. "Bad idea."

She opened a door toward the back of the kitchen. Reaching around, she grabbed a pull chain that turned on a bare light bulb hanging from the ceiling.

Bending down to a bottom shelf, she pulled out a box neatly labeled "First Aid Supplies and Emergency Candles" and set it on the counter that ran the length of the pantry.

"I decided to look for candles for the dining room table for Christmas dinner." She pulled out several boxes of squat white candles. "And I found these."

She plucked a manila envelope from the bottom of the box and emptied the contents onto the counter.

Several passports. A California driver's license similar to the one Reggie had picked up from Mitch's hidey hole in the fireplace. Several New Jersey drivers licenses, one with Radman's picture on it. And the name "Quinton Barton."

I didn't want to leave my fingerprints on anything. I covered my hand with the sleeve of my shirt and shifted the pile around. A couple of credit cards, two with the name "Quinton Barton."

Mandy took out another, smaller manila envelope. That one contained a few birth certificates. One of those also read "Quinton Barton."

"And look at this." She opened yet another envelope. It contained money. A big stack of hundred-dollar bills. "Do you think Sterling's planning to run off? And take the money with him?"

"Could be," I said.

"What should I do?"

She asking me? "Don't you have an appointment with the lawyer? Take it all with you and show him."

Mandy looked stricken. "Suppose Sterling comes home and looks for it?"

"How likely is that? Isn't he at work?"

"I guess. But he'd be furious if he knew I'd found all this."

"That's why you're seeing a lawyer. So you can find out how to protect yourself."

"Suppose the lawyer tells me not to go home?" Mandy chewed the side of her lip.

Was she dense? Or just really upset? "Then you don't go home. If you take that money, you'll be able to stay in a motel or something and buy anything you need for a few days. If you're not safe here, you shouldn't stay here."

Mandy started to get teary again. "My mother's things are here. All her tableware and her lace and her jewelry. Suppose he does something to all that?"

"He probably won't. But if he does, it's just stuff." I tried to be patient. "I don't think your mother would have wanted you to get yourself hurt because you were trying to keep her stuff from getting broken."

"You're probably right," she said, carefully returning the envelopes to the bottom of the box and covering them with the candles. She put the box back. ""There are other things in the garage. I don't even know what they are. Maybe you can tell me." She slipped her coat on and led me out the back door.

We entered the garage through an unlocked side door. Mandy switched on a light. She went to some shelves stocked with garden tools and flower pots.

"The staff at the library always has a Christmas grab bag." She reached up and took down a clay pot. "I got an amaryllis bulb. I came out here to find a flower pot for it. Look."

I peered into the pot. A few tiny baggies. Covering my hands with my sleeves again, I emptied them onto the counter. Little white chunks in some and white powder in others. "Looks like crack cocaine. And crystal meth. Hard to tell in this light."

"How about this?" She took down another flower pot.

It held a glass pipe and a bit of steel wool. "Crack pipe. The steel wool's like a filter. Keeps you from inhaling the burning rock."

"So he's using drugs?" She looked perplexed.

I shrugged. "Maybe. He don't look to me like he's got a bad habit. Good color and healthy." I thought of some of his irrational statements at work. "But he might be a recreational user."

"How about dealing?"

"I suppose he could be. There's not enough here to make it worthwhile. Looks like a personal stash. But you got to be real careful. If the cops find this on the premises, they can ask the court to make you forfeit the property."

"But it's my house. And Sterling's drugs."

I shook my head. "Can't speak to that. Talk to the lawyer. But you have to do something. I'd flush the drugs. And toss the pipe."

She had that scared and stubborn look on her face. "I'll think about it." She put everything back in the flower pots and flower pots back on the shelf.

As we left the garage, a movement caught my eye. The kitchen door we had come out of not ten minutes ago opened. I grabbed Mandy's arm and pulled her back.

Gustavus stepped out onto the back porch. He turned and locked it behind himself with a key. He held a manila envelope.

I tried to pull Mandy back into the garage, but she pulled away from me.

"What do you think you're doing?" she asked Gustavus. "And where did you get a key?"

Gustavus smirked. He didn't look the least bit surprised or upset to see us there. I didn't remember seeing him at the library. Had he followed Mandy here?

"Mr. Radman, he sent me to pick up something for him. He done gave me the key. A long time ago."

"He had no right to do that. You just give me that key right back. Now." Mandy held out her hand.

One of these days, Mandy's tendency to expect us lesser beings to do her bidding was going to get her in trouble. If it hadn't already.

Gustavus grinned and shook his head. "Mr. Radman, he wouldn't like that." He pocketed the key. "Ain't you s'posed to be at work?"

Through her thick coat, I could feel Mandy tense up. "Come on," I told her. "You got an appointment. Let's get you there." I tugged at her arm.

"My purse is in there." She took a step toward the house.

Gustavus stood his ground, blocking the door.

"Forget the purse," I said. "Let's get going."

Finally, Mandy let me steer her around the garage and into the alley. "Where's this lawyer's office?" I asked.

"Down by the courthouse," she said. "But now I can't pay him or anything. I ought to go back and get my purse. My checkbook's in there. And my credit cards. He'll take them."

"The lawyer can bill you." I continued to propel her down the alley toward the street. "If Gustavus has had the key for a while, why would he start stealing things now? Especially something like your checkbook."

She shook my hand off her elbow. "I can walk by myself."

I let go but continued to walk with her. "I'm gonna walk you to the lawyer's office," I said. "I want to see you get there."

Mandy cast a baleful look toward me, but she let me accompany her the few blocks to an old brick office building past the municipal building. A shingle hanging in front listed the names of several lawyers.

I stood on the sidewalk as she went in. Through the glass in the front door, I saw her talk to the receptionist. She was escorted through an inner door.

I turned and headed toward home. I hoped Mandy came to her senses and told the lawyer everything. And then listened to what he told her to do. She had to start making some smart choices about how to take care of herself.

I shoved my hands in my pockets. The thought occurred to me that that she wasn't the only one who needed to start doing that.

# CHAPTER 19

Another shift out of the way. Another day closer to getting a paycheck. Where would I have been without Tiffany's extra sixty dollars?

Maybe stirring up less suspicion for dealing drugs.

Since I was new at this, I took a little extra time with the end of shift checklist to make sure I'd finished everything up and the lift was charging for later in this shift.

Mac stood back, watching approvingly. I didn't get paid beyond my eight hours, but I didn't want some stupid oversight to cost me this job.

The day shift was in full swing when I clocked out and gathered my jacket and lunch box. The weak winter sun glinted off piles of dirty slush by the sidewalks. I headed toward home.

A group of elementary school students huddled at a bus stop in front of a vacant storefront. A little girl shivered in a short jacket, her legs bare between her socks and skirt. One boy huddled into his hoodie, his hands jammed into the pouch pocket. They probably all lived in the rundown apartments over the stores. A bedraggled looking mother, wrapped in a threadbare coat, supervised listlessly, a cigarette dangling from her reddened fingers.

An old car hugged the cracked curb, engine idling. The driver slouched in studied nonchalance behind the wheel, his eyes hidden behind wraparound mirror shades.

Was he scoping out the kids? None of my business, really, but I kind of wished more adults were out there keeping an eye on the kids. I glanced at the car's license plate. It was covered in mud, and I couldn't read it. Cold as it'd been, I wondered if the mud had been deliberately smeared on the plate.

Where were the police when they could serve a real purpose? I didn't have a cell phone. I could call in and report a suspicious character lurking around the bus stop when I got home. If Belkins found out about it, he would probably think I was mocking him. Maybe I'd better forget about it. Unless I could find a pay phone. Not too many of them left in this part of the world.

Instead of crossing the street to avoid the throng on the sidewalk like I usually would, I continued on a course that would take me right next to the car.

I tried to see what the driver was doing without being obvious about it. I didn't have the advantage of mirror shades.

I saw the man's head move slightly. He was looking in the rearview mirror. The kids were up ahead. What could he be watching?

Me.

I felt his eyes on me as I walked by. I tried to keep my back straight, but I felt myself hunch into my jacket. I stepped into an alleyway next to a closed liquor store. Striding quickly, I circled back around the store, coming out a walkway down the block and behind the car.

The driver was leaning forward, peering intently toward the alleyway where I'd disappeared. He glanced around. As soon as he caught sight of me in his mirror, he slouched down again behind the wheel.

I'd had enough time to see the top part of the yellow lettering on the back of his vest. POLICE.

Probably meant the kids were safe. Was he assigned specifically to watch out for me? To see if I tried to accost one of the little girls? Panic began to rise in my throat.

*Be sensible,* I told myself. I was later than usual. No kids here most days when I walked by. So even if he was here to keep an eye on me, no way could he have been sent specifically to see if I interacted with any of the kids at the bus stop.

I cut in front of the surveillance vehicle to the other side of the street. He couldn't miss seeing me. No point getting near the kids and giving him anything additional to report.

The school bus lumbered up. I stopped to look at a dispirited display in the window of one of the remaining stores, waiting to see if the car stayed after it left.

The bus pulled off. I turned to see the car ease out of its place by the curb and head down the street. The lone parent backed into a sheltered entryway to an abandoned store and pulled out her cell phone.

Maybe the surveillance had nothing to do with me. Maybe someone had reported something around the school bus stop, so an undercover cop had been dispatched to keep an eye on it. Drug sales? Seemed unlikely with kids that young.

Or maybe they just made it their business to keep an eye on kids waiting for the bus.

I heard footsteps approaching from behind. I moved over close to the window I'd been looking in, moving so the wall would be at my back if I turned around.

"Jesse."

I turned to face Gustavus.

He stopped in front of me, a smirk on his face.

Interesting that he knew my name. Hard to tell if that should worry me or not. I remembered the old saying about being paranoid. Once people know you're paranoid, they can do pretty much anything and figure you'll put any suspicions down to your own paranoia.

I didn't say anything. If he wanted something, he'd start talking.

"I got to talk to you, man."

This was getting old. I took my hands out of my pockets. "So talk."

He jerked his head toward an alley entrance. "Not here. Over there."

I wasn't about to go hide in an alley with him. "Here or nowhere."

He shrugged. "Suit yourself."

I waited. The silence grew uncomfortable. He was trying to make me say something first. That would give him a better sense of control. Wasn't going to happen.

The smirk faded from his face. He shifted from one foot to the other. It was cold, and he wasn't as warmly dressed as I was.

Finally, he shook his head. "I got a proposition for you."

"Oh?"

"Yeah. I can help you out." He wiped his nose with the back of his hand. He wasn't wearing gloves.

I flexed my fingers inside my gloves. Mitch's gloves, really. "I doubt it."

"Let me tell you what I can do for you."

Might as well hear him out. "I'm listening."

Gustavus glanced around.

I wondered if Gustavus had seen the surveillance car. Or if they were somehow connected. Why couldn't everybody just leave me alone?

Gustavus evidently decided it was safe to talk. "I got some information you'd be willing to pay for."

I laughed. "You're talking to the wrong man. I got no money to pay you."

"You will have."

"Don't see how."

He licked his lips. "Look. I know a lot of what goes on around here. More than you think. I sell information to the highest bidder."

"So not only do I have to pay you to find anything out, but as soon as anybody else can outbid me, you'll tell them about it."

Gustavus shrugged.

"Let me guess. Sterling Radman can outbid me for sure. So can the cops. Especially Detective Belkins."

A look of confusion came onto Gustavus' face. Followed by a mulish expression.

"Am I on the right track, here? Radman pays you to find out stuff for him."

"He keeps me on payroll. Then he gives me a bonus when I do something extra."

I thought about Mitch. "Like killing someone?"

Gustavus looked stubborn. "Wouldn't do that. Not unless it was an accident. Or paid really well."

I raised my eyebrows. Mandy didn't know how close she was to someone who might carry out her murderous plans for her. Hopefully the now-abandoned murderous plans.

He shivered and shifted from one foot to the other. He wore an old pair of dress shoes; the thin soles wouldn't keep out the cold for long. "And Detective Belkins pays whether you tell him the truth or not. He even gave me a cell phone so I could call him anytime."

"So you tell him what he wants to hear."

"Yeah."

"Some of it about me?" I could just imagine.

"Well, yeah. But nothing that could get you in trouble."

I narrowed my eyes into a prison-yard stare.

He looked away from me and shifted on his feet.

"You don't want to hear about nothing?" he asked.

"How could I know if you was telling me the truth? Or making everything up?"

Gustavus got a crafty look in his eyes. "I'll tell you some stuff, and you decide whether it's worth paying me for."

"I got no money."

"You can use what I tell you to get some money."

"You don't think I'm going to do anything that could get me locked up, do you? I like not sleeping locked in a cell."

He appeared to think about that for a minute. "You could get rich."

"Rich don't do me much good if I'm locked up."

Gustavus blinked, trying to digest that. "Mitch was dealing crystal meth," he said.

"Tell me something I don't know." This was getting tiresome.

"He was handling shipments for Radman."

"Drug shipments?"

"Not so much. That was more Mitch's sideline. More like fake IDs. And credit cards got with stolen IDs."

"Like I say, tell me something I don't know."

"Radman is cashing out what he can. He's going to change his name and leave. With a lot of cash."

"Why is he sticking around at all?"

"He made some commitments to some big-time types. With the fake IDs. He got to finish up that."

"Why? Why can't he just take off?"

"These people. MS 13 or whatever gang he's gotten mixed up with. They'll track him down if he don't finish what he told them he'd do."

I hadn't heard of MS 13 dealing in fake IDs, but what did I know? They had a lot of immigrant connections, so I could see where it might be an attractive sideline. "What's to keep them from tracking him down anyhow? I wouldn't think they'd want to leave any loose ends."

Gustavus looked thoughtful.

"You been working with Radman. And the cops. Why are you telling me this?"

"I thought we could team up. Get some of that cash. Radman's got lots of cash stashed all over."

"Like the envelope of hundreds hidden in the pantry at his place?"

Gustavus's eyes opened wide. "You know about that?"

"What you think I was doing at his place with his wife? Screwing her?"

"Well, yeah."

I looked at him in disgust. "You don't need me. You're gonna rob the man who's been paying you all this time, you can do it yourself."

"I need somebody to help me. I can distract him while you kill him."

One of the disadvantages of having a murder conviction was that people tended to get the idea that I might be willing to kill someone.

I clenched my fists and turned away from him. "Don't want to get involved. I got no money. Even if I was to give some thought to doing something that might get me locked up again—and I'm not, mind you—it wouldn't be with someone who'd sell me out to anybody willing to pay a little more than I could. Even the cops."

Gustavus looked at me from under lowered eyelids. "You calling me a snitch?"

"A snitch who does it for money. Worst kind of snitch."

Wouldn't do me any good to let my anger get out of hand. I ducked my head into the wind and walked away from him, forcing myself not to look back.

I got a half block away when I heard footsteps running behind me. I stopped and started to turn.

Just in time to feel a fist smash into my shoulder.

I staggered forward, but quickly regained my footing. I spun around, raising my fists.

"What the hell, man?" I faced my opponent, dropping into a crouch.

Gustavus. His eyes were wild.

"I told you all that stuff. You owe me." He took another swing at my face.

Amateurish. I avoided his fist just by leaning back. I let loose with one of my own, hitting him in the gut and knocking him over backwards.

"You'd better lay off the meth, or whatever you been taking," I said. "Your mind isn't working straight."

Gustavus lay on the icy sidewalk for a minute, his chest heaving.

"You done?" I asked.

He had trouble catching his breath. "Yeah."

"I don't want no trouble. I don't want to do business with you. Or with Radman. Or with Belkins. Understand?"

Still on lying on the sidewalk, Gustavus scowled. He wiped his nose. "Yeah."

I held my hand down to help him up. He grabbed it and struggled to his feet.

"Okay. Now exactly what did you want to tell me? But I ain't paying."

Gustavus shook his head. He rubbed his nose with the side of his hand. "I'm gonna tell Belkins you been seeing Mandy Radman. Stalking her. Everybody knows she ain't wrapped real tight." Then he made a fist and slammed it toward my face.

Damn Mandy and her lunch. I got my arm up in time to deflect Gustavus's ineffective blow, but he followed it with a left, which landed on the side of my jaw. "That other detective saw you at the restaurant with Mandy. They'll believe anything I tell them," he said between clenched teeth.

I countered with another punch to his gut, this one with some momentum behind it, and he went down again. Some people never learn.

I resisted the urge to kick him.

Sirens. I looked around. The lady with the cell phone watched, open-mouthed. She'd probably called 9-1-1. Backup for the bus stop surveillance wouldn't be far away.

Not good. I doubted I could get far. Besides, Gustavus knew who I was.

I straightened up and stepped back from Gustavus's writhing form.

A patrol car angled in at the curb. The first cop out of the car stood behind the open door, his gun trained on me. His partner circled around behind me and hustled me to the hood of their car, slamming me face first into it. He grabbed my hands and cuffed my wrists behind my back.

I closed my eyes and bit my lip, willing myself not to start cussing. I felt his hands search me. Wallet, key, and gloves thumped as they were tossed on the roof of the car.

Strong hands pulled me erect and spun me around, pushing my back against the car. I looked past the cops, out into the dirty wet street. I reminded myself they were just doing their job.

Two other cars pulled up, one marked, one not. Montgomery was driving the unmarked one. He and Belkins got out and came over.

"What's he done now?" Belkins demanded.

The cop shrugged his shoulders. "When we pulled up, he was standing over this other guy." He indicated Gustavus, still lying on the sidewalk. His partner had holstered his gun and was leaning over Gustavus.

I noticed bitterly that no one was shoving Gustavus onto the hood of a car and cuffing him.

Belkins grinned around the soggy cigar. "Assault."

"Maybe more of a fight," Montgomery suggested, looking at my rapidly swelling jaw.

"Assault, fight. Who cares? Ramirez'll have to violate him for either." Belkins leaned close enough that I could smell his sour breath. I thought I detected alcohol.

Montgomery stepped between us and took me by the elbow. He shoved me toward a neglected store entryway and nodded toward the front step. "Sit down, Damon."

I looked down at the dirty, wet, cement step. I tried to flex my wrists in the cuffs. Tight enough to hurt. If I managed to stay out of prison, was this what the rest of my life was going to be like? Couldn't even walk home from work without ending up in custody. Maybe I should stop fighting this and tell Mr. Ramirez to send me back to prison. At least I'd know where I stood.

Montgomery squeezed my elbow gently and leaned in close to my ear. "Don't be stupid. Sit," he said.

I sat.

"Stretch your legs out in front of you and cross your feet at the ankles."

I stretched out my legs and crossed my ankles.

With assistance, Gustavus had struggled to his feet. Montgomery took him aside to talk to him. Belkins came over and stood over me. "So what happened?"

The angle I had to hold my arms was uncomfortable. The cold damp was seeping into the fabric of my jeans. I stared at the sidewalk beside my legs. I thought about ignoring him. But I said, "I dunno. We was talking, and then I went to leave. He hit me."

"Just like that?"

"Yes."

"For no reason."

"Ask him." I nodded toward Gustavus.

Belkins threw the cigar down. "I'm asking you." He grabbed my hair and yanked my head up. "And you look at me when I'm talking to you."

I tried to keep from grimacing. I gazed straight ahead.

"What were you talking about?"

"He had a few things going, and he wanted to know if I was interested."

"Like what kinds of things?"

This line of questioning could lead to no good. "We didn't really get into it. I just told him I was on parole. I can't afford to get mixed up in anything."

"Damn straight. I want to know what was going on here."

"I told you what I know."

"I'm going to find out. And then I'm going to see you get charged with whatever I can figure out." He jerked my head down again and let go of my hair.

I felt my stomach knot tighter. I clamped my teeth together to keep from saying anything.

Montgomery signaled one of the uniformed cops to come over and stand by Gustavus. He still wasn't in handcuffs; pretty obvious who would be picking up charges, if any were filed.

Montgomery pulled his cell phone from his pocket and talked into it. He glanced at Gustavus and then came over to where Belkins still stood menacingly over me.

"No charges," he said quietly, but loud enough for me to hear.

"What the hell do you mean, no charges?" Belkins spun to face him.

"Gustavus was the one who stopped Damon. They talked for a few minutes, and then Damon started to walk away. Gustavus followed him and threw a sucker punch."

"Like I really believe that." Belkins snorted.

"Yeah, well, it was a surveillance officer who just told me that. He moved up a block, but he was still watching Damon. He saw the whole thing."

Never thought I'd be glad I was under such close surveillance.

"Drug deal gone bad?" Belkins looked hopeful.

"I don't think either one of them has been searched yet. We'll see if they have anything." Montgomery addressed me. "Got anything I should know about, Damon?"

"No, sir." I spit out the "sir."

Belkins threw me disgusted look and moved away.

"You know this guy?" Montgomery asked.

"Not really. Name's Gustavus. He works for Radman. All I know."

"Radman, huh? At the steel plant?"

He knew more than he was letting on. He always knew more than he was letting on. Just trying to see if I'd lie. "At the house."

"And you would know this because…?" Montgomery rocked back on his heels.

"I was at the house."

"Really." It wasn't a question. Of course he knew.

Glad I hadn't tried to deny it. "Once."

"Ah, yes. With the wife, right?"

Montgomery had seen me at the restaurant with Mandy. What did he think I was going to say? "Yeah."

"Interesting how much time you seem to spend with other people's wives."

I didn't answer that.

"And what were you doing at Radman's with his wife?"

I was tempted to say, "Screwing her." But that wouldn't help me or Mandy. "She just wanted to show me some stuff."

"What kind of stuff?"

"She thought Radman might be into drugs. Or something."

"Was he?"

"I don't know. But she did show me a crack pipe and some rocks. And some powder."

"What did you do with them?"

"Didn't touch 'em. Told her to get rid of them."

"Did you know," Montgomery said, leaning down so I could smell the mint and aftershave, "that no one has seen Mrs. Radman since she was seen with you?"

I looked up in surprise. "She hasn't been to work?"

"No. Someone—a man—called in and said she would be out for a while. Few weeks at least."

"Really?"

"Yep. I'm wondering if you were the man who called."

"Nope."

"Then do you have any idea where she is?"

I shrugged. "I walked her to her lawyer's office. Last I saw her."

"Why would she be going to see a lawyer?"

"She had an appointment with a family lawyer about getting a divorce. She was scared of Radman. I saw her go in and talk to a lady at a desk inside. Maybe they know where she is."

Montgomery's thoughtful eyes bored into me. "What was the name of this lawyer?"

"I don't know," I said. "But I know the building where his office is. That red brick one down by the courthouse where a couple of lawyers have their offices."

Montgomery straightened up. "Stay here," he said.

Like I was really going to get up and stroll away with all those cops around and my hands cuffed behind my back.

He sat in the car with the door open and pulled out his cell phone again. He made a few calls. Then he got out of the car and went up to Belkins. They talked. Finally, he came back over to me.

"Okay. The lawyer knows where Mrs. Radman is. He told her to stay out of sight for her own safety."

They wouldn't be charging me in her disappearance. One less worry.

"What I'd like to know," Montgomery said, "is how did you come to know so much about Radman's marriage?"

I shook my head.

"And how much do you know about Radman's trade?"

Once again, I shook my head. I should control what I said, but I was getting fed up.

"I think you're in this up to your ass. What do you think?"

"You can think whatever the hell you want to think. Don't make it true."

"Might send you back to prison."

"Still don't make it true."

Montgomery's handsome dark face broke into a grin. "I'm trying to figure out how you and Radman are connected."

"He's my boss. Several times removed."

"And he was Mitch Robinson's boss. But he wasn't around when Mitch was killed. Neither was Gustavus."

Of course he had talked to the people at the plant. He knew Radman had been there. He was trying to get me confused. "Radman was there. Don't know about Gustavus. Maybe he came with Radman."

"Did you see either one of them?" Montgomery asked.

"No. But Radman was definitely in the plant that night. Foreman ought to be able to tell you that." I wasn't going to mention Kelly seeing his car parked by the fence.

"Are you sure?"

I glanced up at him. Instead of sporting his usual poker face, he looked puzzled.

"We looked at the security tapes pretty thoroughly. They cover all the entrances. Last we see is him leaving about seven in the evening."

"I bet they don't have a security camera on the side entrance to the warehouse," I said.

He looked thoughtful. "No. But you have to go through the shipping yard to get there. And the cameras cover the whole shipping yard."

"Not if you go in the gate on the road behind the plant."

"What gate?"

"Side, by the gravel road."

"Locked. Big old padlock. And the gate's rusted shut."

"Maybe." I took a deep breath. I'd already said a lot. No point keeping my mouth shut now. "But the whole section of fence swings out on hinges. Gate and all. So it don't look like an entrance."

Montgomery peered at me. "And how would you know that?" he asked.

I still didn't think I was telling him anything he didn't know. "Common knowledge?" I suggested.

Montgomery snorted. "I don't think so. But that's the second piece of useful information you've given me today. Looks like we may be getting somewhere." He walked away and pulled out his cell phone again.

Maybe he hadn't known about the gate? How the hell could I ever explain knowing about it? Had to get a grip on my anger; I was starting to say dumb things.

In a few minutes, Montgomery returned. He grabbed me by the arm and helped me to my feet.

"We're going to cut you loose," he said. "Again. I'm getting a little tired of this."

He was getting tired of it?

He waved over one of the uniformed officers, who unlocked the handcuffs.

I wiped my hands on the damp seat of my pants.

Belkins looked over and snorted. "Wet yourself?" he asked.

I ignored him.

I glanced over to where Gustavus was sitting out of the wind in the back seat of one of the patrol cars, the door open and his hands uncuffed.

Montgomery followed my line of vision. "You got a problem with us cutting him loose, too?"

"Why would I?"

"According to the surveillance officer, he attacked you. You could file charges."

My laugh was bitter. "Against a police informant? You think I'm totally crazy?"

Montgomery raised his well-shaped eyebrows. "And what else do you know?"

# CHAPTER 20

When I got to work that night, I punched in and went to report to John.

He was standing talking to a man in a suit. I stopped short and stepped over against the wall, out of the way.

The man in the suit was Sterling Radman.

So far, Radman hadn't approached me about doing anything "extra" for him, but I couldn't believe he didn't have something in mind when he'd insisted I become lift driver on this shift. What I'd learned from Mandy and Gustavus did nothing to dispel that notion.

Radman walked away without looking in my direction.

Maybe things were getting too hot for him and he would just clear out without bothering me. I could hope.

John came up, shaking his head. "Jesse," he said. "There's been some kind of a mix-up. Radman just gave me a bill of lading that the dispatcher didn't get out. The truck's due at seven tomorrow morning. Do you think you could try to help Kelly get the pallets out of the warehouse?"

"Sure."

"You're both gonna need to keep up with your regular tasks, too."

"Do the best I can."

He thought for a few seconds. "I'll keep an eye on what needs to be moved out on the floor and tell you, so you can skip your usual rounds."

"Sounds like a plan to me. Just tell me what I need to do."

"Kelly knows. Just do what she tells you to."

If I'd thought working with Kelly would be a pleasant experience, I found out differently. She was even more rushed than I was and barked orders, growing impatient if I didn't understand right away. Her lift was bigger and faster than mine, so sometimes she had to wait for me to catch up.

By the six a.m. break, we pretty much had the shipment assembled out by the dock.

Kelly parked her lift by the passageway to the warehouse, climbed off, and came over to me.

I leaned down to hear what she had to say to me.

"Look," she said. "I got a truck due in at six I got to unload. You think you can get the last few pallets?"

"Yeah. What do I need to get?"

"Three loads of root baskets." She gave me the bill of lading. "Then put this in the basket on the wall by the dispatcher's office door."

She glanced around quickly behind her. Then she grabbed my shoulder, pulling me toward her. "Look," she said. "I know I've been a bitch about this. Sorry about that. It's my ass if the shipments aren't ready." She stood on her tiptoes and gave me a kiss on the cheek. "When we get a chance, I'll make it up to you."

She climbed back onto her lift and swung it back out toward the shipping docks.

My cheek burned where her lips had touched. I was afraid to speculate on what she meant. Or when we'd "get a chance."

I figured I could just skip my last break. If I stopped work, I might have trouble getting started again. The last two days in a row, I'd spent a good hunk of my time in handcuffs or in a holding cell. Not exactly conducive to peace of mind. I hadn't slept well, even after I got home.

I still had to make sure all the machines were well stocked with parts for the day shift.

I decided that after I got off work, I was going to go straight home and get some decent sleep. Let a surveillance car follow me home. Just don't stop me.

I drove into the warehouse, found the row of the right-sized root baskets, and pulled three out, one at a time, setting them in the aisle. I took one out to the loading dock and set it with the rest of the shipment.

When I returned to the warehouse, I climbed off to check the tag on the next pallet.

Radman appeared out of nowhere. Actually, I guess it was from back in the gloom of the warehouse.

He hefted a small wooden box. "This goes in that shipment." He pointed to the stack of root baskets. "Nestled way down inside the bottom stack of baskets. You have to undo the load, put it in, and then fasten the load down again."

"And then?"

"And then you mark the tag with a green check." He pulled a green magic marker out of his pocket. "And take the pallet up to the shipping room. It'll be loaded on a truck this morning and shipped out."

"What would be in the box?" I asked.

Radman narrowed his eyes. "I don't see that's any of your affair. Just pack it up and send it. You'll be reimbursed for your trouble."

"It's my affair if I'm taking risks to pack it," I said.

"I'm not asking you to do this." Radman stood in front of the lift. "I'm telling you to do it."

"It might be illegal," I said. "You know I'm on parole; if I get caught with drugs or something, I'm gonna go back to prison. Probably for the rest of my life."

Radman laughed. "Drugs. I wouldn't get involved in shipping drugs. That's high risk, with limited reward. All it would take is a drug dog to sniff it out. Drugs were Mitch's idea. And a stupid idea at that. Look at what it did to him."

"What did it do to him?"

"Whatever he was taking—methamphetamine, I think—made him paranoid. He got to the point where he thought everybody was out to get him."

"Somebody was out to get him. Somebody killed him." I leaned forward on the steering wheel.

"You do have a point." Radman turned and set the box on the pallet next to the stack of root baskets. "But it never would have happened if he'd stuck to my business. We'd still be making money hand over fist. Now you can do that."

"I don't want to make money hand over fist. I just want my freedom. And my life."

Mr. Radman stepped back from the lift. "Do you call that living? You make what, a few hundred a week? You don't even have a car. Believe me, I've had someone look into what it takes to make you tick. And it's not much."

I just sat there.

"I was going to cut you in on this deal. Make you a lot of money. If you won't cooperate, I'll see that you lose this job."

A grim thought. "I can go back to running the plater," I said with more confidence than I felt.

"No, you won't. If you're not driving this lift, you're not working here. You think I can't arrange for you to be fired?"

My stomach was knotting up. Of course he could. "I'll get another job."

"In this economy? With your record and the reference from here I'll make sure you get? I seriously doubt you'll be able to get a job as a street sweeper."

I didn't see what was so bad about street sweeping, but I didn't think it would help to point that out.

Radman continued, "If you won't cooperate, you leave me no choice."

I felt my palms start to sweat. "No choice as to what?"

Radman's eyes narrowed. "I let you come back to work when they thought you'd killed Mitch. Everybody else said you ought to get fired."

"You knew I didn't kill Mitch."

He smirked. "That may be true. But no one else knows that. I arranged for you to be the lift driver. You ought to be grateful, or at least do what I tell you to. Without arguing. You'll be well paid."

"The cops are keeping a pretty close eye on me. I don't think I could get away with spitting on the sidewalk." I sat motionless.

"This has worked well for months. Over a year. It'll work until I get this finished up. Then, if you want a new ID, I'll get it for you. You can start out somewhere else, fresh. You'll have money in your pocket. No one will know about your criminal record. Or that you're supposed to be on parole."

"And you?"

"That's what I'm planning to do. Take the money, change my name, and leave."

"How about your wife?"

He snorted. "She seems to have already left me. She hasn't been home in days. I'm supposed return a call to her lawyer. She hasn't been going to work."

"Mandy don't deserve what you been doing to her."

"What's it to you?" Radman sneered at me. "I have it from the best of sources that you've been seeing her. Have you? I also heard you're some kind of a sex pervert. What does she like? I haven't bothered to find out."

I didn't rise to that bait.

Radman said, "I don't care. Do whatever you want with the stuck-up bitch. It was a mistake to stick around so long. I should have cleared out her accounts and left. In this economy, I'm not likely to be able to get much of a mortgage on that house of hers, anyhow."

"I'm not going back to prison over stupid stuff like this," I said.

"You worry too much. You'll be long gone before anyone figures anything out."

"So what happens if I just report all this to my parole officer?" I asked. Like I'd really do that.

Radman laughed. "You think anyone would believe you? Especially anyone in law enforcement? I've talked to that Detective Belkins. I told him I thought you were up to something. That's why you wanted the forklift job. Begged me for it. Pick up where Mitch left off."

That sounded too believable for comfort. But I said, "I didn't ask for this job. Everyone knows that."

He raised his eyebrows. "That's not exactly true. Everyone knows you *said* you didn't want this job. If it comes down to your word against mine, who will everyone think is lying? Not me. Did you ever hear the expression, he protests too much? That's what people will say is happening."

"Never heard of that." The lady doth protest too much, methinks. *Hamlet.* Act Three, I thought. Funny where the mind turned in tense moments.

"You can still change your mind," he said.

"What are you gonna do if I don't?" There was no doubt in my mind now that Radman had killed Mitch. But would I ever be able to convince anyone else of that? Maybe they'd believe it after he killed me, which I was sure he was willing to do, but that would be a little late for me. "You gonna beat me to death like you did Mitch?" Despite the chilly air in the warehouse, sweat was beginning to soak my shirt.

His laugh sounded bitter. "Mitch lost any sense he had. He'd become a real liability. Still, I didn't mean for it to happen like that."

"And how about Gustavus? How are you going to deal with him?"

Radman shook his head. "Gustavus is an idiot. He'll do anything as long as the pay is good enough."

He had a pretty good handle on Gustavus, I thought. "And if someone else offers him more than you do?"

"Who could do that?" he asked.

"Well, maybe not more, but do you really think he's above collecting two payments for the same information?"

Radman looked a little less certain. "And who else would be interested in buying what he had to sell?"

"He thought I might be," I said. "And I'm sure the cops can come up with some kind of payment."

"He'd just be implicating himself."

"He tailors his information to the buyer. I bet he's not even above making stuff up."

"Gustavus isn't smart enough to do that."

I was pretty sure Radman was underestimating Gustavus. People like him and Mandy knew they were smarter than most people. They might be, but that didn't mean they could discount what people like Gustavus might say or do. Or me.

"How did Mitch mess up?" I asked, trying to buy time. Maybe John or Kelly would come looking to see what was holding me up.

Radman grimaced. "I had a shipment to go out. He got it mixed up with one of crystal meth he was sending somewhere. Can you imagine how my customers reacted to getting a shipment of crystal meth instead of documents?"

I smiled at the thought. "Probably not happy."

He nodded. "For one thing, they thought they had a handle on the crystal meth production and distribution in the area."

"Nobody can keep that under control. Too easy to make it."

"I know that now. And I also realize I should have stepped in when I first realized Mitch was piggy-backing on my methods and sending his merchandise to purchasers in the middle of what looked like legitimate shipments of root baskets."

I took a deep breath. "So you killed him."

"I had to. I came in to talk some sense into him. It was pretty obvious his thought process was too far gone for that to do any good. I heard about what he'd said to you before the shift began."

"And you thought I'd end up taking the rap."

Radman frowned. "I was hoping. In fact, I still think you may take the blame ultimately. Especially if you're not around."

"Why would I not be around?"

"Because you'd come to your senses and took the ID I'll give you. And disappeared."

I shook my head. "They'll catch up with me eventually. I'm sure I'd have a fugitive warrant on me."

Radman looked at me in disgust. "They'd have to find you before they could serve it."

"They would, sooner or later. Nobody lives so they're never picked up for anything."

Radman laughed. "I do. I've never been picked up for anything in my life."

"Not even a traffic violation?"

"With the kind of money I'm talking about, I'll hire a chauffeur."

"Well, I don't know nobody else who's never been stopped for something. And I bet I can't live like that. So why would I do anything to help you?"

Radman looked crafty. "You could move away. Live somewhere like New York City, where you wouldn't need a car."

Even if he didn't drive, I wondered if Radman had given any thought to what it would be like to live the rest of his life looking over his shoulder and worried that they'd run his ID for something. It looked like he planned to spend his life like that. Of course, he might not have his fingerprints on record the way I did. Maybe he could get away with it.

"And if I won't do it?" I asked.

Radman reached his hand into his breast pocket. "Then I guess I'll have to take care of you, too."

"I won't go so easy as Mitch did." I shifted uncomfortably in the seat. "For one thing, I'm not high, so I can think straight. For another, it's too late to sneak up on me."

"Very true." He drew a small black automatic pistol from his pocket and pointed it at me. "If they didn't lock you up for Mitch's murder, I was probably going to have to have you killed, anyhow. But far away from here."

I took a guess. "I don't think Gustavus has got the guts."

Radman's eyes narrowed. "You may be right. So I'll just plan to take care of this myself. They say the first killing's the hardest. You ought to know. I'll find out."

He flicked the safety off the gun. "I'd hoped you'd cooperate. But of course I didn't want to be unprepared if you didn't." He pointed it at my face.

I felt my gut freeze. Wasn't the first time I'd ever had a gun pointed at me. But it was the kind of thing that doesn't get less scary with repetition. I tried to keep my voice steady. "And you don't expect anyone to come see what's going on when you fire a shot?"

"Pretty loud out on the shop floor and in the plating room. I don't think anyone will hear."

"This time, nobody can think it was me. You don't think they're going to look at you?"

Radman smiled. "They think I left just after the shift started. Gustavus is waiting out in my car. I'll make sure he shows up on the security tapes."

"Why should he go along with that?" I was still stalling for time. I didn't want to die. Maybe I could think of something.

Right. My mind was frozen. Only my mouth seemed to work, almost on automatic pilot. "Gustavus'll roll over on you."

"I'll pay him. Then I'll give him the gun and tell him to get rid of it. But I know him. He'll think he can sell it. So he'll probably still have it when they start really looking at him."

"Gustavus'll tell them he got it from you."

He raised the pistol a few more inches. "Why should they believe him?"

"He tells Belkins what he wants to hear. Belkins thinks he's a reliable snitch." I wasn't so sure about that, but how would Radman know?

"Double-crossing bastard." Radman straightened his arm and supported his elbow with his other hand. He knew how to shoot.

Forklifts pivot on a dime. I wondered wildly if I could swing it around and knock him off his feet before he got a shot off. Doubtful, but I moved my hand toward the gear shift, hoping he was concentrating on his aim so much that he wouldn't notice.

"So you just gonna shoot me?" I said. "You don't think you'll go down for that?"

"I don't think so. Even if they discover I did it."

Seemed to me his thinking was getting more and more muddled, too. Stress does that. "I thought you were gonna blame it on Gustavus."

"I will if I can. But even if they figure out it was me who shot you, they have to catch me before I leave town. You're a convicted murderer—one I gave a break to, no less—who tried to run me down with the forklift. I was armed—I do have a concealed weapons permit—and I shot you. Unfortunate, but what other recourse did I have? Completely unnerved me. I went into a panic. Didn't have enough sense tell anybody at the time. Went straight to my lawyer."

"Yeah? Then how you gonna explain shooting me in the back?" I swung myself around as far as I could without leaving the seat. My back was toward him. I kept my head turned away from him. I closed my eyes and waited for the shot.

"Damn it. Face me," he said.

"Or what are you gonna do? Shoot me?"

# CHAPTER 21

I heard a scuffle behind me. "Drop the gun." A clang of metal on concrete.

I turned around to look.

Montgomery, dressed in pressed jeans, a dapper plaid shirt, and un-scuffed work boots, held Radman with his arms pinned behind his back. He leaned into a radio on his shoulder and said something.

"Detective," Radman said. "Am I glad to see you. This man was about to kill me."

"Oh, yeah?" Montgomery asked, reaching for handcuffs on his belt.

Radman's face was flushed. "Yes. Just like he did Mitch Robinson."

"Looked to me like it was you with the gun."

He drew himself up and tried to free his hands. "Lucky I had it, or I'd be dead by now."

"Really." Montgomery snapped the cuffs on Radman's wrists.

"Yes. And I'm lucky you came tonight. Gustavus was supposed to tell you to come tomorrow night. That you'd find all the evidence you needed to put this murderer away for the rest of his life." Radman winced as Montgomery pulled him across the concrete floor, away from where the gun lay.

"Tomorrow night, huh?"

"Definitely. I was making sure the evidence was still here. I guess Gustavus told you the wrong night. He's not all that bright, you know."

"No. Gustavus told me tomorrow night."

So Radman had been going to turn me in tomorrow night. Probably planning to plant drugs. I wouldn't have stood a chance to deny anything.

Radman's face twisted in anger. "Then why are you here tonight?"

"Just checking things out." Montgomery started to run through the Miranda rights.

"You don't have to tell me," Radman protested. "It's Damon over there you should be worried about."

"Oh, I think Damon'll just stay where he is until I tell him to move. And he knows his Miranda rights pretty well. Am I correct about that?" Montgomery stared at me meaningfully.

I nodded. I wanted to wipe the sweat off my face, but I was afraid to move.

"But I do think it'd be a good idea, Damon, if you turned off the forklift and tossed the key on the floor."

I did so.

"Aren't you going to arrest him?" Radman demanded.

Montgomery kept a tight hold on Radman's arms. "You have the right to remain silent. I suggest you use it," he said.

I wondered how much Montgomery had overheard. Enough, I hoped.

Bootsteps echoed from the passageway and into the warehouse. The bright overhead lights flickered on. Several uniformed police officers rounded the corner, escorted by John.

"Search this one," Montgomery said, relinquishing his hold on Mr. Radman. "And search and cuff that one." He nodded toward me. "Damon, get down."

I climbed off the forklift, careful to keep my hands where they could be seen.

John frowned. "So Jesse was in on the whole thing?" he asked.

"I don't know yet about that," Montgomery said. "But I do know that I have a paroled convict who I need to take in for questioning. We won't be transporting him unrestrained."

So much for making it home today without being cuffed and detained.

"But is that really necessary—" John started to say.

"He's right." I looked at John. "They got guidelines for transporting convicted felons they got to follow."

I spread my feet apart and interlaced my fingers behind my head.

Montgomery laughed. "You do know how these things work, don't you, Damon?"

This time, at least they took us out the side door into the truck yard, rather than parading us through the whole plant. I would have been grateful for that, if Kelly didn't happen by on her forklift, just in time to see two burly cops hustle me toward the door, each with a firm hurry-along grip on one of my elbows.

I glanced up at her and gave her a sad smile. She looked at me like I had cussed her out or something.

At the police station, I ended up alone in a holding cell instead of an interrogation room. I lay down on the bench, my head on my hands, staring up at the ceiling. Seemed pretty clear that Radman had been running some kind of a business with the fake IDs. The pressure from Mitch's death had been enough that he decided he needed to shut down the operation, but he was too greedy—or had made too many commitments to people who didn't take kindly to broken commitments—and he wanted to finish up the deals he had in the works. He thought that since I was a criminal type anyhow, he could convince me to join the scheme. He could always hold the parole over my head.

The important question was, would it all seem so clear to Montgomery? I didn't expect Belkins to consider the whole thing with a mind open enough to figure it all out. But Montgomery had been savvy enough to come in when Radman didn't expect him. I hoped he'd been a position to overhear some very incriminating stuff. I also hoped he interpreted it the way I did. And believed that I wasn't involved.

I got breakfast. A paper bag with a hardboiled egg, a carton of orange juice, a bagel, and a cup of coffee. My stomach rebelled, but I ate it anyhow. No telling when food would be coming my way again.

I was putting the trash back into the now empty paper bag when the door to the cell block opened. Belkins strode in. Alone. The door shut behind him. I was glad I was inside the cell and he was outside. I backed up out of reach.

He looked rough. He was never exactly well groomed, but now he looked positively disheveled. His clothes were wrinkled, and his tie askew. As he approached, I could smell alcohol on his breath. His hair needed combing, and his eyes were bloodshot.

"So, Damon," he said, grabbing onto the bars of the holding cell. "Looks like we got you where you belong. C'mere and answer a few questions." He gestured for me to approach the front of the cell.

"I can answer questions just as well from back here," I said, pressing my back up against the rear wall of the cell.

"No. Come up here. I want to look you in the eye." He swayed a bit and shifted his grip on the bars.

I wasn't about to get within arm's reach if I could help it.

"Think you can get away with it, don't you?" he said, slurring his words. "But this is my investigation. I say how it goes. Not Montgomery. And I say I need to take you somewhere, make you talk."

I hoped someone was listening. The deputies guarding the cells weren't going to confront him, but maybe they would find a supervisor. Or something. I really didn't need to be left alone with him in either a cell or an interrogation room.

"What's it to you, anyhow?" I felt like shouting, but I tried to keep my voice calm and reasonable. "I never did nothing to you. I done my time. I'm just trying to make it out on the street, keep a job, and pay my taxes."

He laughed. "You're a murderer. And a pervert. Don't deserve another chance."

"I got a murder conviction. But no skin charges."

He leaned his head up against the bars. "Plea bargain, huh? Dropped the other charges?"

"They were drug charges. And weapons. No sex offenses." But I don't think he was listening.

"Creeps like you don't deserve another chance. They should execute you. Or at least keep you locked up for the rest of your life. You know what pervert murderers do when they get out on the street?"

I didn't answer. I didn't need to. Belkins answered his own question.

"They target innocent people, that's what they do. My daughter..." Tears filled his eyes.

The door opened again. Montgomery came hurrying to join Belkins. He grabbed him by the arm.

"Go home," he hissed. "I'll get someone to drive you. You're drunk on duty. You'll get yourself fired."

Belkins turned to face him. "You gonna report me?"

"Not if you if contact the employee assistance program on your own," he said. "You're slipping out of control, Belkins. You're jeopardizing this investigation. Not to mention your job. You need to do something."

Belkins turned and gestured toward me. "And Damon there, the pervert killer? What's gonna happen to him? He gonna go free?"

"Depends on what the investigation turns up," Montgomery said. "Right now, we don't know if he was even really involved."

"Sure as hell shows up in the middle of things a little too often," Belkins said. His nose was beginning to run.

"I tend to agree with that assessment," Montgomery said, grabbing Belkins by the arm. "And I'm going to get to the bottom of it. But right now, you need to go home."

Reluctantly, Belkins let Montgomery guide him through the door.

An hour or so later—hard to keep track of time—a guard came in, keys in hand. I stood up and walked to the cell door. At least I probably wouldn't be facing Belkins. The guard wasn't carrying a waist chain, so I turned around and put my hands behind my back for the cuffs.

"No restraints. My orders are to release you," he said. "But Montgomery does want to have a few words with you before you leave. Said for you to pick up your things from the property room and wait out front."

Didn't have to tell me twice. He stepped back and let me precede him through a few doors, to the property room window, and then into the waiting area in front of the desk officer. "Have a seat."

Nobody'd ever asked me to take a seat here before.

I sat on a bench along the wall and put on my boots. I glanced around the room. It was early morning; the sun probably wasn't even up yet.

Where did all these people come from? One lady, dressed in a ragged coat and mismatched boots, was standing at the front desk, haranguing the desk sergeant. She kept insisting that someone be sent immediately to apprehend the devils who were sticking pitchforks into her when she tried to sleep under the railroad bridge. A sad woman, eyes closed, sat on a bench across from me, her swollen face wrapped in a dirty scarf. Two young men in a corner seemed to be engaged in a lovers' quarrel. One reached out and slapped the other. The sound was lost in the sobbing of an elderly man who kept trying to remove his coat but was having trouble with the buttons. Just as well, since I saw no evidence that he was wearing any trousers beneath it.

A defeated-looking woman came from the back of the station, carrying a black garbage bag. I pegged her as the social worker on call. Sure enough, two children dragged after her. Poor kids. Been there, done that. No good solutions here for anyone.

I closed my eyes and leaned back.

"Jesse." One of the kids ran up to me and climbed on the bench next to me.

I opened my eyes. Brianna, Kelly's daughter. She was carrying a teddy bear. Christopher stood uncertainly across the room, next to the social worker. He also clutched a teddy bear.

Part of the cops being friendly to kids program. Give them teddy bears to hold while they watch their world fall apart.

"Brianna," I said, reaching to catch her as she scrambled onto the bench and almost tumbled off. "Where's your mom? Or your dad?"

"Mom's back there talking to somebody," Brianna said. "Daddy's gone in the ambulance."

Hesitantly, Chris approached us. The social worker with them just looked tired.

"Ambulance?" I asked, raising my eyebrows. "What happened to him?"

"We were in an accident," Chris said. "Going back to Grandma's house from the bar. Daddy got hurt."

"Coming back from the bar?" I said. "You weren't in a bar with your daddy, were you?"

"No. He left us in the car. He said we had to get some sleep so we could go to school today. But the lady says we don't have to go to school for today."

I tried not to let my dismay show. "How come you couldn't stay with your grandma?" I asked. "Isn't that where Daddy usually leaves you when he goes out?"

"Sometimes," Chris agreed. "But he said we were going on an adventure last night, camping out in the car. It was supposed to be our secret."

"I see."

"But it wasn't much fun," Brianna said. "We had blankets and pillows, but it was cold. And all we got for supper was potato chips and root beer."

"Then what happened?" I asked.

"Then Dad came out. Then we got in the accident," Chris said. "And the police came."

"We got to ride in a police car," Brianna said. "Did you ever get to ride in a police car?"

"A few times."

"They wouldn't use the siren, though. You ever get to ride with the siren going?"

"Yep." Although it wasn't anything I'd particularly want to tell the kids about.

"They gave us teddy bears. Did they ever give you a teddy bear?" Brianna said.

"Can't say as they ever did," I said.

"I'm too big for a teddy bear," Chris said bravely. He set it on an empty chair and stepped back. "I have a stuffed tiger at home."

I looked at the stuffed toy. "No one is ever too big for a teddy bear," I told him. "Sometimes people say they are, but it's not really true."

"Really?"

"Really," I said.

Chris looked thoughtful and patted the bear's head.

"He'll get lonesome." Brianna set her bear on the same seat.

The tired social worker finally spoke up. "The children's mother is here," she told me. "The children will be released to her. I couldn't release them to you, anyhow. You're not a parent. Or a guardian."

I was surprised she'd even consider that. But I supposed social workers were in the business of viewing all adults with any connection to a child, no matter how tenuous, as a potential caretaker. Or abuser.

"No, ma'am. They should go with their mother."

I saw Montgomery across the room, looking at me. I hadn't noticed his entrance.

"Excuse me," I said to the kids. "I got to go talk to this man here." I got up and crossed the room to him.

"More children?" he asked, stroking the side of his dark face with his meticulously manicured fingers. "Those aren't some of the Robinson kids, are they?"

"No, sir. I work with their mother."

"And the kids know you?"

"I been over their house."

"I thought you were on home detention."

"Yeah. But Mr. Ramirez has given me some time off, too. Long as I make my curfew."

"I left a message for Mr. Ramirez," Montgomery said. "Hard to explain all this in a voice mail. I imagine you'll be hearing from him."

"Yes, sir." I didn't have much to add. I wondered if I should be thanking him for heading off Belkins. Or just pretending that hadn't happened.

"Tell me straight. Are you someone I ought to be worried about with kids?" he asked.

"No, sir."

"Or women?"

"No, sir."

"Because there are still some things going on here I haven't figured out yet. And I'll tell you right now, Damon. If I find out Belkins is right and anybody, especially kids or women, gets hurt because of you, I won't rest until your ass is locked up for the rest of your life. At least."

I wondered how my ass could be locked up for longer than the rest of my life. But I probably didn't want to know.

"Be sure you're where we can find you if we want to talk to you." Montgomery turned and went through a door into the back of the station.

"Jesse!" Brianna launched herself across the room and jumped up against me, clutching at my shirt.

With a grin, I lifted her into my arms. "What, sweetheart?" I asked.

"You gonna come home with us when Mommy gets done talking to the people?" she asked.

"I don't know about that," I said, giving her a hug and looking toward Chris, who hung back.

"Damon."

A commanding voice came from behind me. I turned to look. A uniformed deputy, looking stern. His hand rested on the butt of his gun, which was still in the holster. The holster was unsnapped. Seconds away from being leveled at my chest. Why couldn't they leave me alone?

Mr. Ramirez lumbered behind him.

Oh, jeez. Not with the kids here.

I put Brianna down. "Go wait by the lady." I pointed at the social worker.

"I wanna stay with you," she said, clinging to my leg.

"I need you and Chris to go wait by the lady," I said urgently. "Do it. Now."

Looking up at me uncertainly, she didn't move.

The social worker seemed to wake up to the fact that her charges might be in a precarious position. She hurried over and grabbed Brianna by the arm.

I stepped away from the kids toward the deputy. "I'll come quietly," I said. "You don't need to make a fuss in here." And please don't cuff me in front of the kids, I thought.

"Thank you, officer," Mr. Ramirez said, stepping in front of him. "I appreciate you finding him for me. I can handle it from here."

"Thanks," I said to Mr. Ramirez, careful to keep my hands in sight. "I don't want to scare the kids." But it was really more that I didn't want them to see me shackled down. Selfish, I guess.

"I certainly wouldn't want to do that," Mr. Ramirez said, glancing past me toward the kids. "Is that their mother?"

I looked over my shoulder. Kelly was lifting Brianna in her arms and hugging Chris to her side. She was still in jeans, work boots, and a sweatshirt. Her work clothes.

"Yeah. That's their mother." She would take care of them now. Social services don't want to be bothered with any kids if they can find a suitable relative to take care of them.

To my horror, she started toward us. "If you're gonna lock me up, do it quick," I said. "Don't traumatize the kids."

"Don't want to be embarrassed in front of them? Or your girlfriend?" Mr. Ramirez had an amused grin on his face. He had a good read on the situation.

"She's not really my girlfriend, but yeah, you get the picture."

"And why would I be locking you up?" he asked.

I shrugged. "Parole violation?"

"Something I'm not aware of that I should be?" He rubbed the side of his beefy face with his hand.

"Not that I know of," I said, trying to hedge. I had no idea what he knew and what he didn't.

"Tell you what," he said, his eyes narrowing as he looked at me. "When you come in for your next appointment—Thursday, is it?—we can discuss this. Meanwhile, I'll take you off home detention. Assuming I don't hear of any more problems from Detective Montgomery or anybody else that leads me to change my mind. We can remove the ankle monitor when you come in. That'll save you the monitoring fee. How does that sound?"

Was this some kind of a joke? "Why are you gonna do that?" I blurted out. I wondered if my ears were playing tricks on me.

He raised his eyebrows. "Some reason why I shouldn't?"

"No, sir. I just didn't expect that. Not with all the times I've been pulled in lately."

"And I think you pretty much cooperated every time, didn't you?"

I wondered if he'd discussed that with Montgomery or Belkins. But I wasn't going to argue. "I tried to, sir," I said.

"And now I understand that they've arrested someone else for Mitch Robinson's murder. Right?"

"I think so." I hoped so.

"Seems to me that, if you were going to take off, you would have done so a while ago. But you've reported every time you were supposed to, you're working a steady job, you're making friends—" he nodded at Kelly, who had come up to stand a few feet away "—so I think you're a pretty good risk. And if you did decide to abscond, I wouldn't expect electronic monitoring to stop you. What do you think?"

"I think you're right, sir," I said, licking my suddenly dry lips. "I'll report whenever you tell me to."

Brianna, in Kelly's arms, reached over and grabbed me around the neck. "Hold me," she said.

I shifted her weight to my arms. Kelly put her arm around Chris and pulled him closer to her side.

"Next Thursday. Regular appointment," Mr. Ramirez said.

"Thank you, sir," I said.

He nodded and walked back toward the offices.

Brianna hugged my neck.

"They called me at work," Kelly said. "Fred got in an accident. DUI. At four in the morning. With the kids in the car."

I nodded.

"They could have been killed. I'm hoping this will be the end of unsupervised visitation for him."

"Could be," I agreed. "You gonna push that?"

"Yep. I'll call the lawyer as soon as we get home."

"Sounds like a plan." I started to shift Brianna back over to her mother's arms, but the child clung tight to my neck.

"Do you wanna come home with us?" Kelly said. "If I understood what he was saying right, you're off monitoring."

"True, that."

"And these kids need to get some sleep. I'm gonna get them home to bed." She took me by the arm and started toward the front door.

"They do look tired." I brushed Brianna's hair back from her forehead and put her back on the floor. "You two aren't gonna leave the teddy bears sitting here by themselves, are you?"

She and Chris scampered across the room to get them.

Kelly gave me a meaningful look. "Then maybe we ought to do the same. Get to bed."

Familiar dread rose in my chest.

"Kelly…" How could I say this? "I just thought you should know, I don't know how…I mean, I got locked up when I was pretty young. I've never, you know…"

"Been with a woman?" she finished for me. "Then isn't it about time you learned?" She stood on her tiptoes and kissed my cheek.

The kids raced back, teddy bears safely in their arms.

I felt a foolish grin spread across my face. "Now that sounds like a plan to me," I said.

# ABOUT THE AUTHOR

KM Rockwood has a diverse background including working as a laborer in a steel fabrication plant, operating glass melters and related equipment in a fiberglass manufacturing facility, and supervising an inmate work crew in a large medium security state prison. These jobs, as well as work as a special education teacher in an alternative high school and a GED teacher in county detention facilities, provide most of the basis for novels and short stories.

www.kmrockwood.com

# PREVIEW THE NEXT BOOK IN THE SERIES

**FOSTERING DEATH, by KM Rockwood**

## Chapter 1

"She didn't have to die." Mr. Coleman, aged considerably in the twenty years since I'd last seen him, lifted a crisp handkerchief to dab his eyes. Blue veins snaked over the back of his trembling hand. "Especially like that." His voice was thin.

A plump lady in a big hat took his other hand and patted it gently. "Your wife will get her reward in heaven. She believed in the Lord. And she helped so many unfortunate children!"

Trying to be as invisible as possible, I eased myself back among the flower arrangements on easels, choking on the cloying scent of chrysan-themums. I rubbed my freshly shaved face with my rough hand. Maybe I shouldn't have come here.

"The mortician did a good job," the lady said. "She could be asleep. Quite natural."

Mr. Coleman glanced into the coffin, then quickly looked away.

Straight at me.

His already pale face went paler.

"What are you doing here?" he asked, his reedy voice rising.

Other conversations ceased as all eyes turned toward me.

I'd been right. I shouldn't have come.

He looked me over, head to foot. "And you couldn't even dress properly."

Inwardly, I winced. I clutched my jacket to my chest, folded so its worn black lining showed instead of the garish red plaid. I'd worn my darkest flannel shirt and clean jeans. The work boots were the only footwear I owned.

"When you wrote that letter to her from prison, didn't I write back to tell you she never wanted to hear from you again?"

"Yes, sir. I never tried to write her again."

"What made you think you'd be welcome here?"

I had been among the dozens of foster children who'd passed through the Colemans' house over the years. Mrs. Coleman was the closest thing to a mother I'd ever known. I said, "I'm sorry, sir. I didn't mean no disrespect. She meant a lot to me."

His quavering voice grew even louder. "I find that hard to believe. You were a huge disappointment to her. She looked on you almost as her own, keeping you for all those years. She thought she *saw* something in you. But she was wrong, wasn't she?"

I had no answer for that. I inched toward the door.

"She cried after she read about you in the newspaper. Did you know that?"

"No, sir," I said. "I'm sorry."

"Sorry doesn't quite cut it, does it?" Fury blazed in his pale eyes. "Since when do they let killers out of prison, anyhow?"

Everyone was staring at me. I didn't think this was a good time to start explaining about parole.

Two burly men in somber suits were bearing down on me. I turned and strode out of the viewing room to the entry hall.

As I skirted a stand by the door, the lady standing next to it chirped, "Don't forget to sign the visitor's book!" and tried to hand me a slim gold pen.

I ignored her and kept on going, out the front door and down the granite steps, which were getting slippery from the falling sleet.

Angry at myself, I swiped my face with my sleeve. For the first time in years, I couldn't will away the tears that stung my eyes.

I stumbled at the bottom of the steps and turned into the alley next to the funeral home, anxious to get away from everyone. A few feet down, I stopped and took a shuddering breath. After the overheated air in the funeral home, the fresh air felt good as I gulped it into my lungs. Maybe it would help clear my head.

How could I have been stupid enough to have come here? What did I think was going to happen? That I'd find a connection with my past, and we'd all link arms and sing "Kumbaya" together? All I'd managed to do was upset Mr. Coleman when he could least afford more grief. And make myself feel crummy in the process.

I shivered and shifted the jacket in my hands, trying to unfold it.

"Well, look who's here, Detective Montgomery. Jesse Damon," a voice said behind me.

"Interesting indeed, Detective Belkins. I have to admit I hadn't expected to see him here," came the answer.

"Didn't sound like he was particularly welcome."

Detectives from the local police force. Of course they'd recognized me. Since my release from prison, Belkins especially had taken it upon himself to make sure I knew I was being watched.

With the cuff of my shirt, I swiped at my eyes again. I wasn't going to let them know I'd been crying.

Belkins tapped me on the shoulder. Hard. "You know the routine, Damon. Drop the jacket and assume the position."

I tossed my jacket onto the damp asphalt, trying to avoid the slushy puddles. I spread my feet and leaned on the rough brick wall of the funeral home, bracing on my hands.

"Anything on you we should know about?" Montgomery asked as he stepped up behind me. "Weapons, drugs—anything you want to tell us about?"

"No, sir." I had more sense than to have anything I shouldn't be carrying. I wasn't about to violate parole over something stupid like that.

Quick professional hands frisked me, removing the wallet and key ring with its single key from my jeans pocket, skimming over my clothes, under my arms, and between my legs.

Montgomery's strong dark hand reached up and grabbed my wrist, pulling my hand behind my back and turning the palm out. I felt the familiar cold bite of handcuffs. He repeated the motion with my other hand, tightening them enough to hurt. I knew Belkins would have put them on even tighter.

"Turn around. Slowly," Montgomery said.

I turned around, trying to shake the dark curly hair out of my eyes.

Montgomery was pulling fur-lined leather gloves over his manicured hands. My wallet and keychain lay on the pavement next to my jacket.

Both of the detectives were dressed warmly. Belkins wore a squashed fedora on his head, melting sleet dripping from the brim. His teeth clenched an unlit cigar.

Montgomery stood a head above him, his mahogany face handsome above his spotless tan trench coat, a jaunty hat perched on his shaven head. I wondered how he managed to look unrumpled and dry standing out in this sleet.

"Damon knows his place, doesn't he? Knows there's no point objecting." Belkins chomped on the cigar. His watery blue eyes squinted to mere slits above his bulbous red nose.

Montgomery frowned at him and turned back to me. "You're still on parole, aren't you, Jesse?" he said, his voice deceptively friendly.

"Yes, sir." They knew the answer to that. They also knew that if I was on parole they didn't need a warrant to detain me or bring me in for questioning. Not even reasonable cause for suspicion.

Belkins reached over and jerked up the leg of my jeans. "No black box?" he asked. "When'd you get off home detention?"

"Little while ago, sir."

He shook his head. "Don't know what your PO was thinking."

I saw no point in trying to answer that.

"What are you doing here?" Montgomery asked.

"Mrs. Coleman was my foster mother. Just wanted to pay my last respects."

"Don't think that was a particularly good idea." Montgomery adjusted the scarlet muffler a bit tighter around his neck.

Shivering as melting sleet dripped off my hair and down the back of my shirt, I shook my head.

"How did you know where the viewing was being held?" he asked.

"I saw a funeral notice," I said. "In the newspaper. At the library."

Belkins raised his bushy eyebrows. "The library. Did you know he could read, Montgomery?"

"Oh, Jesse's nobody's dummy." Montgomery rocked back on his well-shod heels. "Does some stupid things, sometimes, but he's smart enough."

"Not smart enough to mind his own business." Belkins took the cigar out of his mouth and peered at me. "Do you know how she died?"

I hadn't thought much about it. She wasn't young, and all the years I'd known her, she'd never really been in good health. All I'd read in the paper was when the viewing and funeral would be. "Not really," I said.

Montgomery just stared at me, his dark eyes giving me no hint to what was going on in his mind.

I forced myself not to fidget. It had to have been a natural death. Or maybe an accident.

Who would want to kill Mrs. Coleman?

Belkins looked like he thought he knew someone who would. Me.

"Somebody kill her?" I blurted out. Instantly, I regretted saying anything. I made a mental note to get to the library and check out the newspapers for the past few days, see if I could find anything out.

Assuming, of course, I didn't get locked up right away.

"You tell me," Montgomery said, his eyes boring into my face. I looked down at my boots.

"Refresh my memory, Damon," Belkins said, staring at the unlit end of the cigar. "How long were you in prison?"

"Just under twenty years."

"And what was the conviction?"

He knew all this. He just wanted to make me say it. "Murder. Conspiracy. Possession of a handgun during commission of a felony."

"And you pled guilty?"

"An Alford plea." That plea—not admitting guilt but conceding that the state had enough evidence for a conviction—had been a problem from the start. Parole boards and counselors like to hear convicts express remorse. Hard to do when not admitting guilt.

"That's right. Wouldn't take responsibility, eh?" Belkins stuck the cigar back in his mouth. "Then or now."

Montgomery changed the subject. "Still working night shift at Quality Steel Fabrications, Jesse?"

"Yes, sir."

"Still driving a forklift?" Montgomery tugged his collar a bit more snugly around his neck.

"Yes, sir."

"When I check with them, will they tell me you've been missing a lot of work?"

"No, sir. I been there every night." As if I could afford to take a night off. Between paying for the rent on my little basement apartment and the monitoring expenses for parole, I didn't have much money to spare.

Belkins adjusted his hat, shielding his face better from the sleet. "I say we haul him downtown and see what we can find out. No sense standing out in the cold here."

"I want to see who else comes to the viewing," Montgomery said.

"We can get someone to take him in and hold him until we're done here."

Montgomery eyed me. His gloved fingers stroked the cleft in his chiseled chin.

Out of the corner of my eye, I saw people leaving the funeral home and turning down the alley. They stopped when they saw us and retreated. I felt the drip of melting sleet running from my wet hair down the neck of my shirt become a rivulet. The shirt was already drenched, so I guess it didn't really matter.

"It's my anniversary," Montgomery said. "Cecile and I have reservations for dinner. She won't be happy if I tell her I'm working late."

A mean smile played on Belkins' lips. "I got no plans for tonight. I can see what I can get out of him."

My gut tightened. Belkins wouldn't be particular about the methods he used for interrogation. I didn't really want to face him alone. Montgomery was young and hungry. He wouldn't want anything on his record that might stand between him and a promotion. Much better for me if he were present.

But there wasn't a damn thing I could do if they decided to run me in.

"We know where he lives and where he works," Montgomery said. "We can always pick him up. Or ask his PO to hold him when he reports in. He's not going anywhere."

"True." Belkins continued to grin at me. "He knows he'll be locked up for the rest of his life if he takes off. Which is where he belongs."

"Besides, you know he's not likely to tell us much anyhow." Montgomery checked his watch.

"I bet I could get him to tell me something." Belkins' grin turned into a leer.

Montgomery glanced over at him. "Does us no good to get information we can't use in court."

Belkins shrugged.

Montgomery grabbed me by the elbow and spun me around. He unlocked the handcuffs.

It took an effort, but I didn't rub my numb wrists. I knew better than to move until they told me to. I stood, looking at my wallet and keychain as they lay where the brick wall met the cracked asphalt of the alley. The slush puddle was swallowing them rapidly.

Montgomery finally said, "You can go. For now."

Another group of people stepped out of the funeral home and straggled across the entry to the alley.

I leaned down, scooping up my wallet and keychain. Then I picked my jacket up from the wet pavement and turned down the alley, away from everyone. I took a tentative step, expecting Belkins to change his mind and tell me to stop.

"And don't even think of going to the church funeral service," Montgomery called after me. "That poor old man's been through enough."

He was right about that. I kept my gaze straight ahead and kept going. I didn't know where the alley went. With my luck it would dead-end at the garage. I'd climb a fence to avoid walking back past them if it came to that. Or hide behind a dumpster until the alley was clear again.

What did they throw in dumpsters out behind funeral homes, anyhow?

I turned at the corner of the building and saw an opening between the garage and another building. I walked toward it, hoping it was a through walkway. It was. I didn't let myself glance back until I was halfway down it.

No one was in sight. The detectives weren't following me. I unfolded my jacket and put it on. It was damp, but at least it blocked the needles of sleet that were driving into my shirt. I pulled the watch cap out of the pocket and pulled it over my head. Wool holds body heat even when it's wet, although I wasn't sure my body was producing any heat to speak of.

I emerged on the street behind the funeral home and saw a patrol car idling by the corner. The driver eyed me as I turned in the opposite direction and walked away.

After a few blocks, I thought I heard the sound of a car close to the curb following me, but between the wind and the sound of the sleet hitting the sidewalk, it might be just my overactive imagination hearing things. The area between my shoulder blades, the place where "INMATE" would be stenciled in white letters on an orange prison jumpsuit, itched. Word was it was positioned so the tower guards would have a target to aim for in an escape attempt.

I wished I'd taken the opportunity back in the alley to check to see if anything I didn't know about was in my pants pockets. I didn't doubt Belkins might slip me some crystal meth or something if he thought he could get away with it, but it had been Montgomery who had frisked me, and he'd be too professional for that kind of nonsense. I hoped.

Shoving my hands into the jacket pockets, I ducked my head into the wind. I wasn't about to give anybody watching the satisfaction of seeing me check my pants pocket. Or even look back to see it somebody really was following me. One good thing about the sleet—my face was so wet it hid any tears.

When I turned the corner to head toward the aging building where I rented a basement apartment, the patrol car was sitting in the alley. They must have swung around the block. Or maybe it was another car.

Had a car been following me? Entirely my imagination? Without breaking my stride, I glanced back.

A battered, blue pickup truck was creeping along by the curb, lights out. What was that all about? I couldn't see a cop, undercover or otherwise, being caught dead in a pickup in that bad shape.

I looked back at the patrol car. It was pulled up in the dead-end alley that the single window of my basement window looked out on. Its nose hung over the sidewalk. I'd have to pass it to get to the stairs that led down from the sidewalk to my front door. As I approached, the cop in the passenger seat, a woman with her hair pulled back in a severe bun, rolled down the window. She stared at me.

I didn't stop or make eye contact, but I did take my hands out of my pockets and let them hang by my sides. No point giving anyone an excuse to go for a Taser. I'd never been tased myself, but I'd seen it done, and it didn't look pleasant. I had no desire to experience it firsthand.

Resisting an urge to wipe my eyes again, I concentrated on keeping my breathing regular. I'd keep walking if they didn't say anything to me.

If Montgomery had slipped something into my pocket and told them to search me, they'd stop me.

Unless they were waiting for me to go in so they could search the apartment. Not that they'd need reasonable suspicion for that, either. The parole papers I'd signed gave permission for warrantless searches any time.

Biting my lip, I reminded myself that parole was well worth all the restrictions that came with it. My apartment might be a dingy single room with the kitchenette in one corner and a tiny bathroom off another, but as long as I paid the rent, it was mine. And the key that opened the door was in my own pocket, not hung on some correctional officer's belt.

The cop made no move to open the car door. Another advantage to the weather. She wasn't going to get out of the warm, dry car unless she had to.

As I approached the top of the stairs, I listened for someone to shout, "Stop!" But no one did.

I slipped my hands back into my pockets and hunched down into my jacket. The sleet looked like it might be changing to snow. I didn't look back. That would only make me look nervous. And guilty.

The cops were going to keep a close eye on me. It went with the territory. Cops don't like parolees. They would be sure I was up to something. They were waiting for—what? Something I said or did that they thought tied me to Mrs. Coleman's death. And anything else they could incidentally pin on me.

That meant the detectives investigating her death would probably put a lot of their efforts into trying to show that I'd killed her. Unfortunately, that meant they might not investigate what had actually happened.

Montgomery might be my best bet. If I could find out anything useful, he would listen. And look into it. Solving a homicide would be a big deal. And a detective bucking for a promotion didn't want to be part of a team that made an arrest that ended in an acquittal. Or worse, in a conviction that was reversed on appeal.

I did have one advantage over any official investigation. I *knew* I hadn't killed Mrs. Coleman.

Salt crunched underfoot as I approached the outdoor stairs down to my apartment. The janitor had spread it to keep ice from forming.

I heard the heavy *thunk* of a vehicle's door slamming.

# Chapter 2

"JESSE!"

I froze. That whiny voice didn't sound like it was coming from a cop. Resting my hand on the railing of the stairs down to my front door, I glanced over my shoulder.

The blue pickup stood at the curb, engine running and lights out.

"Jesse. You got to help me score."

Aaron. A kid from the packing line at work. A kid who was going to get fired from a good job because he kept missing work. A kid who was into crystal meth and whatever else he could get his hands on. A kid who might well have turned police informant to save his own ass. That might explain why he hadn't been fired yet for all the absences from work. Also why it didn't bother him to be stopping me to ask about drugs in front of the cops sitting in an alley a few hundred yards away.

I turned to face him. "I don't 'got' to do nothing." I reached for my key, ready to continue down the stairs and into my apartment.

"You're right, you're right." Aaron's bloodshot eyes watched my hand reach into my pocket, and he flinched. Then he grinned and sniffed, pulling out a small packet of tissues and wiping his nose. He stuffed the tissues, including the one he'd just used, back into the pocket of his jacket.

I looked at the jacket with a tinge of envy. It was an expensive jacket, down-filled and undoubtedly very warm. I shivered in my damp wool hunting jacket from Goodwill.

"I was just hoping you would," he said. "I got to score. Bad."

"You know better than that."

Aaron's eyes were filled with the genuine anguish of a jonesing addict. "What am I gonna do?"

"I told you before. Call Narcotics Anonymous. They'll help you."

"They'd tell me I got to stop using."

"They'd be right."

Aaron rubbed his arm. "It's freezing out here. Let's go into your place so we can talk."

"Let's not. We got nothing to talk about."

Aaron nodded. "You're not gonna say anything that's gonna get you in trouble. I get that. You're smart."

"If I was smart, I wouldn't be standing here talking to you at all," I said.

"I'm getting desperate."

"You told me you could run down to Park Heights in Baltimore and pick up anything you wanted."

Aaron's face fell. "I tried that. Cost me a whole tank of gas. They sold me a little crystal meth and said that was all they had. So I got a couple of rocks that they said was crack. But it was just little white pebbles."

In spite of myself, I laughed. "Real rocks, huh?"

Aaron shook his head. "Expensive ones, too. I got to do something." He reached into his jacket pocket.

What did he have? I tensed and half-raised my fist.

He pulled out a wad of bills and shoved them toward me. "You don't have to handle nothing. Just tell your contacts they can trust me. I can pay. Plenty more where that came from."

Which, I suspected, was seed money from the vice squad.

I stepped back and put my hands behind me. Last thing I needed was for the cops to see me take money from Aaron. Especially if the serial numbers had been photocopied.

"Don't you see that patrol car right there?" I nodded toward it.

Aaron glanced toward the alley. He seemed surprised. "Where the hell'd that come from?"

I just shook my head.

"You should let me into your apartment," he said. "Then nobody could see what we're doing."

"Nothing for anybody to see. And I bet you got something on you that could get me in real trouble."

"Nope." Aaron scratched the three-day stubble on his chin. "If I had anything, I would've used it."

"How about all that money? Where'd that come from? You could buy anything you wanted. Who told you to come to me?"

Anger flared in Aaron's eyes. "Are you calling me a snitch?"

"You said it; I didn't."

Aaron's voice started to rise to a shout. "You think you're tough, don't you? You think you can treat me like dirt and get away with it."

I turned away. I wasn't going to dignify that stupidity with an answer.

He pulled the tissue out of his pocket, wiped his nose again and grabbed my jacket with his other hand, still clutching the money.

Mindful of the patrol car, I forced my hands to remain motionless. At this distance, the cops in the patrol car probably couldn't hear what we were saying. Unless Aaron was wired. But they could see. I didn't want to look like I was threatening him. If I made a move to push him away, would they come to his rescue? Or just write a report to be resurrected later when they could use it?

The interior light in the cab of the pickup by the curb came on. I glanced over; the door was open a crack. What kind of backup had he brought along?

"Aaron!" a plaintive young voice called.

He loosened his grip on my jacket. "What?"

"You told Mom you'd pick me up, and we'd come straight home. That was hours ago."

I backed up a step. "You brought a *kid* with you when you're trying to score?"

Aaron shrugged. "My mom'll only give me gas money if I do stuff for her, like pick up my kid brother if she's at work."

Disgusted, I said again, "And you brought him along when you're trying to score?"

"Hey, I left him in the truck. He's too little to know what's going on. He'll be fine."

"You got no idea what you're playing with, do you?" I shook my head. "Did you take him down to Park Heights with you, too?" I didn't want to think about what could happen to a little kid if he got in the way of a deal that went down wrong.

No cop would knowingly send an informant out to make a buy with a kid in the truck. So maybe this really wasn't a set-up. Or the cops didn't realize that he'd be idiot enough to bring the kid along.

Aaron pulled another wad of bills out of his pants pocket and added it to those in his hand. "Come on," he said. "I know you got something. Either sell me some or tell me where to go to get some."

"You really gonna give me some of that money just for telling you where to go?"

Aaron sniffed. "I trust you, Jesse."

My eyes narrowed, I stared at him. Kid in the truck or no kid, this *had* to be a setup. If I took any money, even if I didn't supply anything, I'd be up against an intent to distribute conspiracy charge. "Only one person you can even begin to trust," I said.

"Who?"

"You're standing right there in his boots."

"Me?"

"I'm not sure even that's a good idea. But for sure you can't trust nobody else. Including me."

Aaron stood up a bit straighter and stared down the steps to my apartment. "I know how much you make. You live in a crummy basement room. You got to pay all those parole fees and court costs. Extra money would come in handy. You gonna help me or not?" He held up the bills again and waved them in front of me.

"Not." I took a step back.

Aaron's face twisted in anger. "You know, I could make your life pretty miserable. Get you fired from the job."

He probably could—I didn't think it would be that hard. But I just said, "Try it. I don't think you've got much credibility with anybody at work anymore."

"I could tell that girlfriend of yours some things."

Ouch. This was a sensitive area. I took a deep breath. "I don't have a girlfriend."

"Sure you do. Kelly? From work? You know she's been putting out in the warehouse to anybody who'll pay her. I been with her myself."

My chest tightened. Kelly wasn't my girlfriend, but I'd certainly like her to be. She treated me just like a regular person, not like a paroled murderer.

She was just divorced, with two kids to think about, so she spent most of her non-work time with them. I realized neither one of us was in a position to make any kind of commitment, and I think she did, too.

A couple of times she'd invited me over to her house for supper. I'd help out with the cooking and cleaning up, then sit down with the kids and their homework. Or just watch TV with them. Give Kelly a little time to herself and hope she didn't open a bottle. It almost felt like I was part of a family, and I was achingly aware that I could become overly dependent on the warm feeling it gave me.

After the kids were asleep, sometimes we went to bed ourselves. If she hadn't drunk too much. I didn't drink. I wasn't about to take a chance on violating my parole over something as stupid as drinking alcohol.

Kelly had introduced me to sex, and no matter what she did or what anybody else said about her, I would be eternally grateful to her for that.

But if she reached the point where she might be looking for a steady boyfriend, if she ever did, what could I offer her? A future of uncertainty, stepping carefully and never sure I wasn't about to be picked up and sent back to prison to serve out my backup time? That was no way for a woman to live. Especially a woman with children. She deserved better than that.

Aaron was standing there, swaying slightly and still holding out the money. I knew he was lying about her putting out in the warehouse. Her job almost never took her back there, and I was in and out all shift long. She could be seeing other men, but it wasn't during work hours. I'd never asked her about other men.

Really none of my business. I shouldn't care.

So why was that sour taste rising in my throat? I felt like I might vomit.

Without me paying much attention, Aaron was babbling on. Since he hadn't gotten a rise out of me with the job or Kelly, he'd changed topics.

"You can't tell me you're not using," he said, giving my arm a shove.

"Don't touch me," I warned.

"Your nose is running, and your eyes are red. You've been snorting something, haven't you?"

I stirred myself to answer. "Maybe I just got a cold." I wasn't about to tell him I'd been crying.

"Riiiight." He stuffed the money back in his jacket pocket. "I know you could turn me on to a few contacts. Wouldn't do you no harm."

I just stood there, trying to keep an eye on the cops as well as Aaron. The sleet was changing to snow, which didn't make any noise as it hit the ground. I wished he'd lower his voice. Although if he was wired, they were listening to every word we said anyhow.

"You're gonna be sorry," he said, turning toward the patrol car and away from his brother in the truck. "I could tell them things about you. Get you locked up again."

My muscles tightened, and my mind started to go blank. Raising my clenched fists, I took a short step toward him.

Aaron flinched back.

A light in the patrol car winked on. I stopped, took a deep breath, and made myself drop my arms to my sides and back up a step toward the stairwell. This wasn't prison. The consequence for giving Aaron a little of what he deserved wouldn't be a month in disciplinary segregation, it would be street charges for assault. Possibly on a police informant, and in front of two officers. Not smart.

Aaron wiped his nose one last time, threw the tissue on the sidewalk, and scuttled over to his truck, climbing in and slamming the door. It lurched forward. I watched the taillights until it turned the corner. The patrol car just sat there.

I shivered and started toward the stairs. If the cops were going to burst in and search my place, there wasn't a damn thing I could do about it.

Beyond the stairwell, a sign above the entry to the first floor store front hung by one corner, banging in the wind. The sign was pretty new. Just recently, the abandoned pizza parlor had been rented out to a store-front church. Seemed more like a cult, really. They'd made a big deal about dedicating their new hand-lettered sign. It read, "All-Seeing Tabernacle of Inaccurate Conception." Underneath, in smaller letters, it said, "Seek Impotent Wisdom—A Pure Mind in a Pure Body."

That seemed pretty strange to me, but then the church members were pretty strange themselves. From what I could see, they were all male, and

I figured they must have embraced celibacy in their quest for enlightenment. Or whatever they were seeking. They must have been pretty proud of it, and pretty weird, to announce it to the world like that.

As I watched, a gust of wind caught the sign and sent it tumbling to the pavement. I picked it up—it was surprisingly heavy for its size—and propped it against the brick wall in the sheltered entryway. It might be a weird sign, but they'd gone to the trouble of painting it and hanging it, and it'd be a shame to have it ruined, lying face down on the wet sidewalk.

I glanced back at the patrol car. The interior light was still on. The cop in the passenger seat brought the radio transmitter to her mouth.

They would sit there for as long as they wanted to. Nothing I could do.

The wind picked up, and snow blew harder as I finally started down the steps to my apartment. My feet crunched on the salt. I pulled out my key.

I didn't think I'd ever get over the sense of satisfaction that came with holding the key in my own hand and unlocking the door myself.

A movement in the dim corner of the landing at the bottom of the stairs caught my eye. Half-frozen slush was beginning to pool around the drain in the cracked concrete. I peered more closely.

A small figure was huddled in the corner, somewhat out of the sleet. A cat. I eased my hand toward it. The cat cringed back further, but didn't hiss, and it didn't try to get past me. I scooped it up and looked at it.

It was wet and bedraggled, but it wore a red collar heavy with gaudy rhinestones and gems, and it wasn't starving. If anything, it was fat. Had to be somebody's cat. I carried it up the stairs to put it on the sidewalk. Going up on the salt couldn't be good for its paws.

The patrol car ripped out of the alley, its light bar flashing. As it careened down the street, the siren rose into a scream.

They had something better to do than tear my place apart. At least for tonight.

The cat clung to my jacket. I let it snuggle against me until the lights and siren had faded. Then I put it on the sidewalk, giving it a little shove. "Go home," I told it. "This is no weather to be out in."

The cat stood in the dim light from the entrance to the temple. Its fur was a mixture of blacks, reds, and tans. It stood on the sidewalk, now getting even more thoroughly soaked and stared back at me with startling amber eyes. Its fur flattened against its body, ears and tail drooping.

"Go home," I repeated. Like it could understand me.

The cat just stood there.

I went back down the stairs, into my apartment and shut the door firmly behind me. My clothes were soaked, and I was freezing. I took my boots off, loosening the laces and pulling out the tongues. I set them under the radiator to dry. I had to wear them to work tonight. At least I had dry socks I could put on. Maybe turning the jacket inside out and putting it on the back of a chair in front of the radiator would dry it out some by the time I had to leave. Stripping off the wet flannel and T-shirt, I replaced them with dry ones.

A cup of instant coffee sounded good, but I was due at work at midnight, and I needed to get any sleep I could. With my stomach still tied in a knot and all the thoughts racing around in my head, it was going to be hard enough to doze off as it was without putting any caffeine into my system.

My jeans were more than damp. I tossed them onto the seat of the chair with the jacket. I did have a dry pair for work. Then I sat on the edge of the bed to change into dry socks.

The bed that came with the furnished apartment might be lumpy but it sure beat the thin foam mattress with a slippery fire proof cover I had in prison. And instead of one skimpy blanket, I had a pile of bedding I could snuggle down into. When I got covered up and warm, I could relax and maybe fall asleep.

I thought of the cat, staring at me reproachfully as it huddled in the snow. And here I was, settling down comfortably.

Surely it would go home. The owners would be glad it came back and let it right in.

Unless it was lost. And if it wasn't lost, what was it doing there outside my door in the first place?

It was just a cat.

But all I would be able to think of was the cat, out in the cold, and I'd never get to sleep. Not if there was something I could do about it.

Cursing my own stupidity, I switched on the outdoor light in the stairwell and opened the door.

The damn cat was back in the same corner, now wetter and more miserable-appearing than before. It looked at me and opened its mouth in a pathetic meow.

With a sigh, I stepped out into the cold and reached for the cat. Again, it didn't hiss or try to move away. My foot landed in the slush. The new sock was now completely soaked. Sleet stung my naked legs.

I brought the cat inside and shut the door. It looked up at me and meowed again. It might be chubby, but when had it eaten last?

I was planning to make tuna sandwiches to take for lunch at work tonight. I supposed I could spare a bit for a cat. I put the cat down and grabbed the can opener and the can of tuna. I put a little of it in a bowl and put it in front of the cat.

It gobbled the tuna down and looked up hopefully.

I put some more tuna in the bowl.

The cat downed it and looked up again.

Oh, well. I could make peanut butter sandwiches for lunch. I emptied the rest of the can into the bowl. The cat ate it.

I looked around. I didn't have anything faintly resembling a litter pan or cat litter. But I couldn't put the damn thing out again until the weather got better. I'd bought a newspaper so I could cut Mrs. Coleman's obituary out of it. I retrieved the rest of it from the trash and tore it into little pieces, putting it in a box that I lined with a trash bag. I lifted the cat into it and moved its paw in a digging motion. It got the idea right away and peed, then covered the spot with shredded newspaper. That didn't mask the smell all that well. Great.

And of course it would need somewhere to sleep. I'd gone to the Laundromat that morning, wanting to be sure my jeans and shirt were clean to wear to the funeral home. I hadn't put the clothes away yet, so I opened a drawer in my decrepit dresser and dumped the clean clothes in there. Then I put a soft towel in the bottom of the laundry basket and shoved the whole arrangement out of the way so I wouldn't step on it, half under the foot of the bed, near the radiator. When I lifted the cat into the basket, it settled right down, purring.

At least it appreciated my efforts.

Changing to yet another pair of dry socks, I checked the alarm and climbed into bed.

\* \* \* \*

When the alarm shrilled, I was heavily asleep. I reached over and slammed it off. A warm lump was nestled up against my neck and shoulder.

The cat.

Reaching over, I stroked it. It nuzzled my hand.

In bed, I was warm and comfortable. The air in the apartment was cold—the heat went off around nine p.m. I could feel the chill on my arm.

I knew better than to lie there after I'd turned off the alarm. I struggled up, trying not to disturb the cat too much. It didn't have to go work a midnight to eight shift at a factory. It sat up on the bed anyhow, watching me.

My boots weren't quite dry, but that couldn't be helped. I pulled on another pair of socks, these ones wool, over the ones already on my feet.

I finished dressing and packed my lunch—peanut butter sandwiches and a Thermos of instant coffee. Not the best lunch in the world, but come four a.m., I'd be glad I had it.

The cat was still sitting on the bed, now scratching at its ridiculous collar. I unbuckled it and hefted it in my hand. It was heavy. Who would put it on a poor cat? I tossed it onto the dresser and gave the cat a scratch on its chin.

"Sorry. I got no more tuna. Or cat food. I'll see what I can get on my way home from work." Like it could understand me and I could really afford to spend money on cat food and litter.

Stupid. The last thing I needed was a pet. What would happen to it if I got locked up again? Besides, it obviously had a home. Look at that collar. Someone would be searching for it. I should keep an eye out for posters for a lost cat.

As I tugged on my jacket and watch cap, the cat wound around my feet and followed me toward the door. I held the door open in case it had had enough of me and my apartment and wanted to go home. But it got one look at the chilly night and jumped back up on the bed, sitting and staring at me.

"Well, I got to go," I told it, feeling foolish for talking to a cat.

"Meow," the cat answered.

In spite of myself, I grinned and gave it a final ruffle behind the ears before I left.

As I passed the alley, a flicker of light caught my eye.

A door to the Tabernacle was propped open and one of the members, dressed in the characteristic saffron robes which could offer little protection against the chill night air, sat on a cinderblock next to the dumpster. Next to him sat a kid, maybe about nine or ten years old. The kid was wearing regular clothes. The light flickered again, and the man lit a cigarette. Or a joint. The security light shone down on him, shadowing his features.

I knew the cult had some pretty strict guidelines, and I doubted smoking anything was acceptable.

And what was a kid doing there?

None of my business, really.

The man lifted his head and looked in my direction, but didn't say anything.

I shrugged mentally and hurried on to work.